Literary Dreams

Novel Deaths

A Marc Kincaid Mystery

by

Donald Owen Crowe

Other Books by

Donald Owen Crowe

Trinkets in Love's Lost and Found

The Gryphon and the Greeting Card Writer

The Innocent

Whispers on Woodsmoke

Published by W and B Publishers

For Information:
W and B Publishers
An Imprint of Argus Books
9001 Ridge Hill Street
Kernersville, NC
USA
27284
www.a-argusbooks.com

Author's note: This book is a work of fiction. Names, characters, places and incidents are either the product of the author's imagination or are used fictitiously, and any resemblances to actual persons, living or dead, events, or locales, is entirely coincidental. Please note that no animals were used, or injured in any way, in the writing of this book.

ISBN: 97816355482110

Book Cover designed by Melissa Carrigee

Printed in the United States of America

Acknowledgements

Rarely is a book penned by a single person.

I would like to thank Bill Connor and his staff at W and B Publishing for their support and guidance in bringing this book to fruition. As usual, their time has proved quite valuable.

Kudos go out to Shirley, my first reader, for her constructive criticism, and for her ability to ensure I stay on track – or at least on the rails she insists I follow.

The novel would not have been completed without the direction of Brent, my personal computer wizard who tried to make the keyboard a friend and not an enemy, and I thank him for that.

I'd also like to acknowledge my family and friends who always make sure I stay focused and keep working.

And most of all, I'd like to thank Rena Michaels for her patience, assistance, calming support, perseverance, and all the time she spent working directly with me to finish this book. Borrowing from the master Camus, she doesn't walk behind me, nor in front: she walks beside me, as the love of my life.

Dedication

In the foreword to *Skylight,* José Saramago's brilliant posthumous novel, (Mariner Books, 2015) Pilar del Rio, the president of the José Saramago Foundation, recounts a fascinating insight into the Nobel Prize (1998) winners experience with rejection. Mr. del Rio describes the young artist's descent into the literature and personal abyss when he failed to receive a reply to his submission of *Skylight* in the 1940's. Saramago knew this story about a rooming house in Lisbon and the characters who lived inside was a great novel that would one day generate many wonderful books, and he couldn't believe that he didn't receive a reply from the publisher. In actuality, however, the typewritten pages he'd submitted were lost in some forgotten drawer, only to be found decades later when the publishing company moved. Saramago's rejection was really a rejection by omission. It pushed the sensitive writer to the brink of nothingness, changing both the author, and the man, for decades. Rejected and numbed, the future Nobel Laureate didn't write anything for twenty years.

Therefore, *one* rejection – just *one* – may have cost the literary world some of the greatest novels ever written.

*

In light of José Saramago's intense feelings about rejection, *Literary Dreams, Novel Deaths* is dedicated to writers everywhere who have suffered the pain and angst of having their work – and themselves – torn apart by a thoughtless letter that destroyed their aspirations and their needs. It is also dedicated to the people who've sent those terrible letters, who have never stopped to think about the damage their dismissals might have fostered.

And the feelings of revenge they may have provoked.

Literary Dreams

Novel Deaths

A Marc Kincaid Mystery

by

Donald Owen Crowe

Tonight

He sensed death coming.

The darkness descends, stealing color from the night. Pain and blood, a swollen face, a taste he didn't recognize that numbed his throat.

Covered in shadows, he was hanging from a thick branch of a huge maple tree. The rope taut, his neck cracked at a grotesque angle, his spine arched, his broken body ratcheted straight out. He dangled a dozen inches from the ground.

A foot to freedom. The wind teased him back and forth like chimes, the gnarled limb moaned beneath his weight. He could almost see the grass below, almost touch it. But each time he reached down the rope tightened again, the coarse knots biting deeper into his flesh. Tried to breathe. Couldn't.

The cuts stung. Vomit burned against his raw, skinless neck. Blood streamed down his chest and legs, dripping into widening pools at the base of the tree.

Something rustled in the branches above his head.

An animal, waiting?

The last thing he saw was a hint of moonlight through his tears.

Three Months Earlier

Devlin Turner, Literary Agent
In Association with Meredith House Publishing
112 Fallingdale Drive Toronto, Ontario   M4Z 3X8

March 14th, 2022

Lawrence Johnnson
8 Waterhill Road apt. # 1110
Philadelphia, PA   24654

Dear Writer:

What is it you fail to comprehend? As I indicated in response to your query and follow-up missives, *"Shooting The Messenger"* reminds me of those disgusting little blind, hairless moles that spend their existence moving backwards underground. Neither those wretched, featureless creatures nor your pathetic excuse for a "novel" will ever see the light of day.

I certainly don't mean to be mordant – well yes I do – but the closest you'll ever get to a contract is for a janitorial one: your script could be used to clean the bathrooms. You have single-handedly elevated solecism to a unique art form, and have brazenly made the idea of writing a novel a prosaic exercise in pedantry that grinds the reader into a level of banality that defies comprehension.

Allow me to reiterate. Even your opening sentence remains pretentiously puerile. It reads, *Crouching down in the thick reeds and bulrushes, Quincy's patience was stretched as thin as the last breaths of a drowning man.*

Your rather feeble attempt to correct the verb confusion is woefully misplaced. It is evident you do not understand the fundamental tenets of grammar or syntax. Seek out the "spelling/grammar" key on your computer. My fear is that this procedure will only highlight your persistent mistakes, and will not mitigate the flaws in your writing, plot, characterization, or shameful misuse of language.

Let me reiterate in words you might understand – *you are not a writer.* If you desperately need to see your name in print, then pay a Vanity Press to produce your 'novel,' or upload it to an internet publisher that feeds off the dopamine-fueled egos of people with your lack of talent. With the explosion of self-publishing, anyone – even you- can be an author in the most lugubrious and profligate sense of the word.

For some reason you believe I empathize with the fact "you're on the edge of an abyss" and that your writing life is "dangling by a thread." I don't care in the least. If I were Fate I would take scissors to that string.

I implore you – and I cannot emphasize this enough – never send me anything in your vast repertoire again. It will not be read. You are dead to me. Do not seek any form of polemic. My lips are forever sealed.

Aghast,

Mr. Devlin Turner

Devlin Turner, Literary Agent
112 Fallingdale Drive, Toronto, Ont. M4Z 3X8

April 6th, 2022

Mr. Turner;

Pretentiously puerile? Why send back something so hateful? Why make it so personal? You could've sent a form letter with "no thanks" scribbled across the top. Or, "We're not accepting manuscripts right now." Some people write simply because they have to. It's in their heart, their soul, in everything they think about each day. All of us aren't born with the gift, but I know there are lots of people out there who have two jobs and still try to put in a few hours every day to get better, to improve their skills, to try and become better writers. This book might be my first, but it's not my last. Your letter devastated me. Why destroy everything someone's struggled with for so long, that's given their life some meaning?

You may be one of the best literary agents in the country, but that doesn't give you the right to ruin someone's life with a rejection. But do you know what? You never know where that last dismissal is going, do you? To a stable person, who looks at your snide rejection and just throws it away, or to an insecure writer, hopeless and sad and angry who feels his heart torn apart? It might be a writer's second rejection– or another person's hundred and second – their last one, the one that shreds all their hopes and dreams. But what do you care?

Ohh, but you should. You'll send one to someone who knows that the pen is indeed mightier than the sword. He's going to stalk you. Watch where you eat, drink, work, park. Haunt you. Get close. Then one day, a day like all the others, he's going to be in your house, waiting for you, and he's going to take one of your precious little pens and stab it so hard through your fucking eye it's going to tear your brain apart, and then he's going to grab another one and stab it through your God-damn chest, and then the next one's going to tear through your mother-fucking . . .

You're the one that's going to be rejected.

You're fucking dead, you bastard.

See you soon.

Tonight

So this is what it's like to die.

Punctured. Can't cry for help. Choking on gurgling blood you can't swallow. Unbelievable pain. *God, how his mouth hurt.*

The more he bled the harder it was to untangle the few scattered images still knotted together. Coherency faded with the color of his face. He struggled to think about something, *anything*, but there was nothing left to unweave.

Nothing to think about . . . *nothing to thi . . .*

Sprawled face down, his head jammed awkwardly into the crook of his elbow so he could see the letter opener impaling his hand to the desk, Devlin Turner watched his forearm hairs shiver with his last, raspy breaths. Even as he slipped from the precipice of light and plummeted backwards into eternal darkness, he realized the transition between worlds would have been far less horrific if he hadn't been forced to endure the excruciating pain of each slow, jagged stitch as his lips had been sewn together.

He still felt the first stitch.

Gloved hands cracked his mouth open painfully wide. The needle tore through the fleshy part of his bottom lip, and then a quick push rammed it through until it scratched his teeth. The needle wriggled up, drawing a pinprick of blood from the roof of his mouth. It poked through the back of his upper lip and was yanked out the front. The coarse thread drawn just tight enough to hold the skin together but not enough to let it tear. The next stitch began.

Poke it through the bottom lip, draw it up inside, wedge a new space open with your fingers, stab the needle through the back into the top lip, wriggle it out the front. Tug it tighter. Poke it through the bottom lip . . . stab it through the top one . . .

A cadence born in Hell.

An hour earlier

Devlin Turner stumbled home as he often did, rubber-legged but not quite inebriated, his balance and mood confounded by the belated effects of the double martinis he'd compulsively downed at *The Bamboo Garden*. Swaying beneath the meager porch light and shooing moths away, he fumbled with his keys. He tried three before the deadbolt finally clicked open.

Muttering incoherently, he teetered into the vestibule, kicked the door closed, and slumped against the wall. The alarm pad blinked. *Shit.* The police hated drunken false alarms. Devlin rubbed his eyes, tried to focus. He leaned forward, aimed his finger, and with an alcoholic's unconscious precision, jammed in the code. The lights stopped blinking. Devlin smirked.

Except for the incessant hum of the furnace and the officious cadence of his wife's Grandfather clock, the house was deathly still. No whining, no paw nails *click click clicking* over the tiles, so Shakespeare, his faithful blue Collie, must be out in the back yard.

Devlin Turner weaved down the hallway, shedding his overcoat and jacket, then kicked off his shoes and tossed his clothes into a heap on the stairs. The metallic *tick* of the clock was more annoyingly shrill. *Like Dorthea.* Devlin promised himself it would be the next thing to go. That, and her precious collection of Royal Doulton figurines, that useless gallery of dust-gatherers that sucked his wallet dry and cluttered up the dining room. Just like *her*.

His foot found the first stair, but he banged his knee on a wooden spindle. *Fuck me.* He slipped twice, but managed to grab the handrail. He looked up: the stairs were swaying. They'd have to wait. He staggered across the foyer toward his study. *She* wasn't allowed in, but he knew the shapeless bitch snuck in when he wasn't home. Devlin teetered inside. He felt his way around his desk, collapsed into his chair, and clicked on the lamp. He yanked open a drawer, and rummaged through a mess of files until his fingers closed around a half-finished *I-still-can't-get-the-bitch-out-of-my-mind* bottle.

Time to toast her. Literally. Like a Viking funeral, where they'd drape her in white sheets and he'd arc a quiver full of flaming arrows into her boat as she sailed away to Valhalla. He'd wrap her up nice and tight but make sure she was still alive *before* they cast her adrift.

Devlin downed a double, wincing. It tasted . . . *odd*. Forcing his eyes open, he shuffled through the mail Mrs. Dempsey, his housekeeper, had left neatly piled on his desk before she'd left. Manuscripts on the bottom, book chapters he'd requested, queries, bills, regular shit, and on top, his personal mail. He leafed through the envelopes, sending them sailing to the floor until he found the one he'd been dreading, the one he'd bemoaned all night at *The Bamboo Garden. Dorthea and her fucking lawyer.* Devlin pounded back another shot and grabbed his letter opener from the desk caddy. He mangled the envelope open and clumsily unfolded the letter.

Shit the scotch was strong. Why the fuck was it so hard to see?

Blah blah blah Devlin Turner, blah blah blah his poor wife and devoted companion Dorthea Turner, blah blah blah . . . Whoa. What? *Half the fucking house?* No way. *And* the condo in Boca? *And the beach house in North Carolina?* He'd fucking kill her first.

Fighting a stiffening stupor, he heard a noise from out back. Maybe there was a fight in the alley that separated his yard from his neighbors. Why wasn't the dog barking his bloody head off?

Devlin staggered around his desk and stumbled down the hall. He weaved into the kitchen and grabbed a knife from the counter. The back door was closed. No smashed windows. He flicked on the porch light and stepped outside, the knife shaking, whispering for his dog.

He scanned the darkness, trying to adjust to the shadows. It was a second before he saw him. Shakespeare. His neck broken, his long body stretched out and hanging from the maple tree. Moonlight silhouetted the dog's body as it swayed in the breeze. The branch groaned. Blood everywhere. He'd been – God, he'd been s*kinned.*

Devlin walked slowly toward the tree, dazed, his mind on fire, bile in his throat. He slashed the rope four or five times before the knife cut through. Shakespeare crumpled to the ground in a thick pool of black blood. Turner spewed his last drinks into the night. His eyes filled with tears as he scrambled back inside.

Covered in sweat, he staggered back to his office and crumpled down into his chair. *Where the fuck was his cell?* He grabbed the landline and dialed 911. Nothing. He punched in the numbers again. No dial tone. *What the fuck was going on?*

By the time he sensed he wasn't alone, it was too late: the shadow was already moving. Hands sheathed in surgical gloves covered his mouth and nose, cutting off his breath and choking his scream into silence. Devlin thrashed wildly from side to side, feebly trying to pry the hand from his face, but the grip was too strong. His head was snapped back and pinned against the chair. Suffocating, he weakened in seconds.

Ten. Twenty. The hand let him go. He gasped for breath. He felt his arm being yanked across his desk and caught a glint of metal out of the corner of his eye. The letter opener came down with savage fury, skewering the back of his hand and impaling it to the desk. Blood seeped across the lawyer's letter. Before he screamed, the hand was covering his face again, fingers digging into his flesh. His caddy was knocked over, pens and pencils rolling everywhere. Fingers curled around a sleek silver pen engraved with his initials. It was jabbed back in a blur, piercing the little hollow at the base of his throat and burying itself into his larynx. The unmistakable sound of splintering bone. Blood sprayed in a sputtering arc.

The hand grabbed another pen and stabbed it into Devlin's chest. It caught on a rib, cracking the bone. His assailant breathed a curse and wrenched it free. He rammed it back again, harder this time and more precise, puncturing his lung.

The stabbings came in a frenzy. A sharpened pencil slammed into Devlin's shoulder. Another speared his neck. One lanced his back, scraping his spine. His attacker circled it around, widening the wound, shredding the skin. Bones cracked, tissue tore. Each stab, each thrust, was exhilarating, cathartic, soul-freeing, and each one sank in deeper than the last. The smell of blood seeping down Devlin's chest was sickening sweet and intoxicating at the same time.

Then, a thick fountain pen. The attacker palmed it for a moment, testing its weight, and then with one fluid stroke, buried it halfway into Devlin's stomach. Blood bubbled from his mouth. The hand reached out tentatively, choosing. An old-fashioned quill with ink-stained feathers. A quick shot buried it through Devlin's left eye, deeper, deeper, into the flesh of his brain.

Drowning in blood, Devlin heard the chimes of the Grandfather clock. He wheezed, tried to breathe. Couldn't. Air and blood gurgled from his punctured lung, and a dark, hazy film slowly began to glue his eyes shut. He was pulled back into the chair, gently this time, the pen that had been rammed through the back of his neck neatly propping him up. The letter opener was pushed down hard, flattening Devlin's hand against the desk. Something was placed carefully in front of him: small and round, a glinting stick balanced on top. Blinking the blood and tears from his eye, Devlin tried to bring the thing into focus.

A needle and spool of thread.

Somewhere, he felt himself scream.

Turner heard paper being torn. Fingers stuffed shredded pieces down his throat until he gagged. They pried his teeth apart and pressed his lower lip back in a roll. The needle pierced his skin.

Poke it through the bottom lip until it hits teeth, draw it up through the back of the top lip and yank it out again. Pull it tight. Poke it through the bottom . . .

Swift and precise, the stitches were rendered with an embalmer's eye for poetry in death. The needlework started on the right side of his mouth and ended with a flourish tied-off on the left.

The killer grabbed a fistful of Devlin's hair, yanked his head back, checked the stitches. Turner's skin was already turning a nicely mottled blue. A quick push and Devlin collapsed across his desk. He heard his visitor's chair being dragged closer. Then words, words that came in a low, patient voice that droned on and on like the clock in the hall, going on forever. Devlin barely understood a sound. Then, silence . . . only deeper.

He peered at the quivering letter opener. Light steps quietly padded from the room. The *beep beep beep* of the alarm system being turned on. The front door opened and closed. Then, nothing. The blood pooling in his lap overflowed and dripped down into widening puddles under his chair. Devlin's swollen tongue felt thick and heavy against the stitches. His pierced eye couldn't close, but darkness still descended. The wispy hairs that speckled his forearm swayed with his final breath, then were still.

Chapter One

Two Weeks Later

By special arrangement, the doctor's office opened early. Detective Marc Kincaid was the first patient of the day. A sleepy-eyed receptionist let him in a side door, then discreetly disappeared to hunt down more coffee. There was *early* and there was *this*. God, it wasn't even morning yet!

Alone in the sterile waiting room, Kincaid flipped through his dog-eared copy of *The Gryphon,* but couldn't concentrate. Unsettled, he changed chairs: twice. Everyone who saw Dr. Chadpur harbored an innate degree of anxiety, and despite over twelve years as a homicide detective, Marc Kincaid was no exception. He'd disarmed murderers, been stabbed, shot, and had literally stared straight down the barrel of a sawed-off shotgun, but this was different. Dr. Chadpur didn't dispense opinions: he confirmed, or mollified, your deepest fears about mortality.

Slipping the book into his coat pocket, Kincaid stood up the moment the physician's door opened. Tall and lean, with caramel colored skin and black, expressive eyes, Dr. Chadpur had an engaging smile and gregarious disposition. He was immaculately yet modestly dressed in a dark blue suit and brightly polished shoes. His crisp white turban accentuated the softness of his features, and highlighted the first few streaks of gray in his tightly woven beard. With a slight bow and delighted grin, Dr. Chadpur ushered Kincaid through a labyrinth of corridors to one of the smaller examining rooms.

Kincaid had always liked the man. It didn't matter they were both in their early forties, had gone to the same university, and loved sports and old movies; from the moment they met, Kincaid found him one of the easiest people in the world to talk to. To *really* talk to. Dr. Chadpur always encouraged an open, empathetic relationship with people, especially the ones he respected and cared for so deeply.

Perhaps that was it: Dr. Chadpur didn't deal with *patients,* he dealt with *people* and the challenges they couldn't fathom . . . the ones they dreaded most. Life wasn't a close-up in a *film noire* scene, where Bogart barks over a dangling cigarette *"Give it to me straight, Doc. How much time have I got?"* then stoically takes the news with a grin and a gin. Dr. Chadpur answered the questions that tore at your heart and kept you up all night, the ones that festered like malarial sores, or bit at your subconscious like a shark on a seal. Dr. Chadpur and Kincaid were brothers in despair: they had to tell you the things you didn't want to hear, things that had the power to change your life forever, the ones that ultimately defined your existence.

Dr. Chadpur clasped a hand to Kincaid's shoulder and offered his other. He spoke the Queen's English in one breath, his words tightly clipped, and there was a light, almost singsong cadence to his voice, like the soft trill of a baby sparrow. He waved toward the table.

"Yes, please sit. It's good to see you again Kincaid." He watched his friend closely.

"Thanks for seeing me so early."

"That's quite all right, Detective. It's good to change routines. I rarely get to see the sunrise, and it was beautiful." He gestured to Kincaid's pocket. "What are you reading now?"

"The Gryphon and the Greeting Card Writer."

"Ah, the modern-day dilemma of Cyrano de Bergerac. Conrad risks everything to help the little girl who is so lost and afraid. And the woman who changes all the faces."

"And saves himself in the process."

"Sad and heroic, like life, my friend. So tell me. How are things?"

"Fine."

Dr. Chadpur tolerated the stock answer and acquiesced with a smile. "No, really."

"My leg still feels numb, occasionally. My arm, too."

Dr. Chadpur jotted down a note. "Have there been any other significant changes since your hospitalization?"

Kincaid weighed his words defensively. "My appetite is still off. I eat when I have to."

"Ah, you're missing out on one of life's greatest pleasures."

Kincaid had lost more weight: he was probably down to about one hundred and eighty. At six foot three and normally quite fit, he looked a little lean. But his color was good, his blue-green eyes bright and clear. He'd lost the irritating little tic that had plagued the corner of his mouth.

"How is your sleep?"

"I get a few hours, usually in the middle of the night."

Dr. Chadpur's pen continued its illegible scrawl. "When you wake can you get back to sleep?"

"Sometimes."

The doctor frowned. "And today is the day you'd like to go back to work."

"Yes. Light duties."

"Have you explained the severity of your situation –?"

"No." He'd been quick and sharp. "Sorry."

Dr. Chadpur waved the apology away. "We've already discussed this. I still believe it is important you share your concerns with your colleagues. It will help them, and it will most certainly assist your own well-being. We all need support, my friend. Allow others in."

"I understand. But I'd like to keep things as private as possible. I've only talked to the people who absolutely have to know."

"I respect your position, but you don't work alone. If your problems are exacerbated, other peoples' lives might be at risk, as well as your own."

"You know I wouldn't put anyone in jeopardy."

"*Not knowingly*. There's no one I'd want with me in a crisis more than you. But *knowingly*. That's the key."

Dr. Chadpur started Kincaid's physical.

"I'll take it as easy as I can," Kincaid offered reassuringly. "But we're stretched to the limit, just like the hospitals. The refugee re-settlement program has been a disaster. And with the chance a new strain of COVID-19 might have infected some migrants, we might be in even more trouble."

Dr. Chadpur knew Kincaid was right. The SARS outbreak in 2002 and the second mutation in 2005, were the first two China refused to acknowledge and had teetered on the edge of becoming a pandemic. COVID-19 had been a worldwide awakening, but we still hadn't learned the fundamental lessons battling SARS. So far, the new strain of COVID was just a haunting threat, but several Border Control officers had been quarantined. *What if it got worse like the outbreak in 2020?* He stroked his beard, offered a simple nod, but made no commitment . . . yet. He went through the litany of symptoms that had troubled Kincaid during his recent two week hospitalization.

"Vision?"

"Clear."

"Hearing?"

"What?"

"Hearing?"

Nothing. Dr. Chadpur looked up anxiously, smiled, then lowered his voice. "Bodily functions?"

"No problems."

"Memory? Intermediate and long-term?"

"Nothing I've noticed."

"Dizziness?"

"Not since I was in the hospital."

"But still there? *At all?*"

"Only if I'm really tired."

The doctor watched Kincaid's eyes. "The headaches?"

"Not as bad."

Dr. Chadpur paused. But not any *better*. He checked Kincaid's eyes, ears, mouth, hands, feet, fingertips, and nails. "No episodes like the last one?"

'No.' *An episode?* That seemed pejorative. What would a full-blown *attack* be like? The new medication had helped immensely – for now.

"I can alter the dosage, and we can see –"

Kincaid shook his head. "No, I'm good." He felt lethargic and muddled enough in the morning as it was.

Dr. Chadpur checked Kincaid's reflexes. When the hammer hit his right knee, Kincaid's leg shot out like it was spring-loaded. When he tapped the left one it barely moved.

"What about the level of your pain?"

"I can handle it."

"I have no doubt about that," Dr. Chadpur said softly. Rarely had he seen anyone with Kincaid's tolerance threshold. Mentally or physically. "But it is not what I asked."

"It's bearable."

He frowned. *Was the answer being sincere or evasive*?

Dr. Chadpur reached around his patients' back and gently walked his fingers down his spine. The lower he got the tenser the muscles felt. Kincaid grimaced, then jerked forward.

"Has anything else felt different over the past fortnight?"

Fortnight? When was the last time someone said that? "No."

While Kincaid dressed, Dr. Chadpur scanned his recent file entries. "The results from your blood work and the other tests have come back and everything seems quite normal."

Then why the pain in my neck and back? And why does my head feel like it's going to implode? But he knew why. Partly, anyway. Some kind of neuropathy. Nerve damage from the shrapnel all those years ago. And the menacing tumor. He realized he was rubbing his temples, and stopped. The betraying compulsion was an easy *tell.*

"I spoke with Dr. Torvay, the neurosurgeon. The prior CT scan was almost eight weeks ago, so he wants it repeated. He wishes to make sure there haven't been any significant changes. He would also like me to schedule you for another MRI and EKG."

"They did those in the hospital."

"He wants them repeated. As do I."

Case closed. So was Kincaid's file. You didn't argue with Dr. Chadpur. "I believe when we have the latest test results we will know the best course of action to follow."

Kincaid stopped buttoning his shirt and raised a questioning eyebrow. There was a deep scar above it.

"Whether or not you need surgery, my friend. If it can be done, and when."

Kincaid frowned. The other part of the equation had been intentionally ignored. If surgery wasn't possible, what were the other viable options? Kincaid was fully aware of the ramifications. He asked if Tuesday was fine for the MRI.

"It should be sooner if possible."

"If I'm starting back today, Tuesday's the earliest I can manage. *If I* am.*"*

His friend leaned against the examination table, crinkling the paper cover. "I know you, Kincaid. And I understand what the psychological effect would be if your action, or worse still, your inaction, was the causative factor in a colleague being injured."

"I live with that scenario every day."

"This is different. This . . . problem . . . is not something you or I can completely control yet."

"So what happens in the interim? You don't have a complete diagnosis. You can't keep holding me back on tests you're still waiting for."

Noticeably uneasy, Dr. Chadpur was carefully weighing the consequences of his decision. His gut feeling was to keep Kincaid off work for at least another week, so the tests and scans could be completed. Yet he knew how much the man's job meant to him, emotionally and psychologically. And how much he was needed.

"You've spoken to your Lieutenant?"

"Yes."

"Are you sure you won't discuss your situation with your colleagues."

"I'm sure. I appreciate your concern, but this is the way it has to be."

Another thoughtful silence. "Okay, my friend. A compromise? We'll let you go back, see how things feel. But you must keep me informed of any problems you're experiencing. Especially anything new or more intense." He poked Kincaid in the chest with his finger.

"And I mean *anything.*"

Kincaid smiled like a schoolboy being released from detention.

The doctor's face was placid. "If something feels different – no matter how small or seeming inconsequential, you'll contact me immediately." It wasn't a question.

"I'll call in every couple of days if you want. Keep a journal. Whatever you need. And you can pull me out if you think it's necessary."

Dr. Chadpur stared back. It wasn't often he came in contact with such stoic reserve when people were trying to come to terms with what his friend was facing. He offered his hand as Kincaid stood up. He didn't let go. "Please be optimistic. Regardless of whether we need – or can – operate, I am certain that everything will be fine. God willing. This doesn't have to be the end – it can be a new beginning. Never forget that."

Kincaid felt the man's grip tighten, and a surge of empathy rippled through his senses. Their vocations and responsibilities weren't that much different. He realized he felt sorry for the man.

What was Donne' famous eulogy?

Each man's death diminishes me, for I am involved in mankind.
Therefore, send not to know for whom the bell tolls
It tolls for thee.

Was *the bell* ready to toll for him?

Chapter Two

Kincaid wheeled into the precinct underground garage and stopped in the area designated for senior detectives. He stayed in his car, ruminating about his conversation with Dr. Chadpur. Was he taking an undue risk being here? Could he be endangering the lives of his friends and colleagues? Perhaps the Lieutenant was right: maybe he should work with someone else and see how things progressed. He took a few moments to collect his thoughts before going inside. He went up the back stairs so he didn't have to confront the myriad first floor personnel.

As he reached for the door he heard the *click click click* of high heeled shoes coming down the stairs: Vice and Robbery.

"Hey, big boy," the woman purred in a throaty, sultry voice reminiscent of Lauren Bacall in *'To Have and Have Not.'* "Can I buy you a drink?"

She put the tall mugs she was carrying on an adjacent ledge and hugged Kincaid hard. He leaned around her and reached for the coffee. Pouting, the woman feigned a sense of wounded pride that he'd want his caramel latte more than her. But there was only one woman Kincaid might have wanted more. A name crept into his senses like wizard's fog over a battlefield: *Stephanie.*

But Amy MacKenzie was special too, very special, and they had history. She was delicately pretty in an unassuming way. The kind of woman who never wears make-up but always looks fresh and invigorating, like the ones in television ads who roll out of bed completely made up before they've even stretched awake. Petite, yet hard bodied through a regimen of strenuous exercise. Short brown hair that curled softly under her chin, eyes that made you stop and think, an infectious grin, and a tiny little mole on her throat Kincaid found immensely appealing. They'd been out to dinner several times, and once he'd found himself staring so hard he forgot what they'd been talking about. A detective for just under two years, she was the second best marksman in the precinct. But the most important target she'd missed was Kincaid. So far. And not by much.

Amy loved the way Kincaid looked. If it hadn't been for the jagged scar that zigzagged above his eyebrow and the lines of worry the tragedies of life had etched into his face, he'd be on the billboards that advertised mens' cologne. The scar was a reminder of a carjacker from days long past that you never let your guard down. His chin square and angular, he had strong facial lines and deep-set, blue- green eyes. There was a small cleft in his chin, and beside it, another mottled, ridged scar from a shrapnel wound. His curly brown hair was showing the first streaks of grey.

For Amy MacKenzie, it all came down to the subtle sense of vulnerability in his eyes, and the fact he had no idea of the affect he had on women. Young, middle-aged, or mature: when he smiled, his eyes incited feelings of arousal, of the hopes and expectations that many women never experience. He made them wonder *if only . . .*

There'd been a spark between them from the moment she'd walked into the squad room. The flicker had simmered and flamed, but had never ignited and engulfed them into the passion Amy wanted. They were close and intimate, but not in the way she needed. They'd come close to breaking the barrier between friends and lovers – oh, so close – but it was still a wiggling line in the sand they hadn't crossed.

"I'm glad you're back." Questions dangled, but she settled for a mock reprimand. "You should have called more. I could have helped with whatever you needed."

Kincaid raised an eyebrow.

She blushed. "You know what I mean." A whisper. "How'd everything go?"

Other than his superior, Amy was the only person that held Kincaid's confidence. "They need to do more tests. I should know something in a couple of weeks."

"Why don't we take our coffee to the cafeteria where we can have a little privacy?"

Except for a handful of kitchen workers in hairnets who were arranging things on the counters, the cafeteria was practically deserted. They sat at a little table near the exit. Kincaid licked a dollop of whip cream from his cup.

"I hear congratulations are in order. You did a great job nailing down the ShoeCam operation."

Amy reddened a little. "We're still unraveling the interconnected web sites because of that perv. We found thousands of pictures on sticks, and there's dozens of boxes we haven't even opened yet. We're still scratching the surface."

"What was he using?"

"State of the art digital and pinhole cameras, automatic zooms, fiber optic lens, pocket recorders. One camera came up through an eyelet on his shoe."

"Where did you start?"

"In the subway. Belanger and Taylor were with me, with Dufresne on point. I couldn't have done it without them."

Kincaid smiled. Amy was quick to dole out the credit – too quick. She'd have to tighten up her political play if she was going to rise through the ranks. But it wasn't her style.

She held her thumb and forefinger half an inch apart. "It was this close to being a sting, so we ran everything by the D.A. first to make sure it wasn't entrapment."

Amy brushed some foam from Kincaid's lips. The latte reminded him just how atrocious the hospital coffee had been.

"So, tell me."

"You know the story – undercover work isn't as glamorous as it is in the movies. Especially vice, and particularly for a woman."

Kincaid nodded.

"The subway was too awkward to stake out cleanly, but we made a few collars. When the women were going up the escalator or standing on the platform, a guy would come up behind them, inch his foot forward, and snap away. They kept their equipment in a gym bag, a backpack – wherever they could hide it."

"I heard you wore stilettos, a garter, the whole nine yards."

Amy sneered. "No, that was all Taylor. He was our plant – he wouldn't have been able to hold the camera steady if I had. The idiot likes spreading rumors. Sometimes I wonder who the real pervs are."

Kincaid knew some of the jokes circulating the House would be a little raunchy. "Don't let it get to you, Amy. You're the newbie. They're just making sure you can take it like everybody else."

She looked uncomfortable.

"Has Taylor been giving you grief?"

"Nothing I can't handle."

Kincaid guessed what was going on. Taylor was the squad's asshole. Figuratively and literally. A transfer in from God knows where because he was related to a few blue bloods downtown.

Amy could take a joke. Whatever happened must have crossed the line: that bothered him. "Forget Taylor."

She sipped her coffee. "I had regular exercise briefs on under a short skirt. Lettered."

Another blush.

"What?"

"*Busted.*"

Kincaid laughed for the first time in weeks. The pain didn't seem so bad. Amy's spontaneous grin set her face off like a bright light. He thought about Stephanie: he'd been thinking a lot about both women while he was hospitalized. Mortality will do that to you.

"Anyway, we nailed a bunch of bottom feeders. A real loyal bunch. A bit of pressure and they rolled over on each other like newborn puppies in a window cage. We found hundreds of flash drives at their apartments. They posted their stuff to the ShoeCam guy to sell across the Web. The field guys got a kickback."

"Did any of the women realize . . . "

"They were being photographed? No. You wouldn't believe how many smartly dressed women don't even wear little G-strings. Just – *nothing.*"

Kincaid leered over the rim of his cup.

"Down boy. And yes, I always do."

Kincaid's tone deepened. "Children?"

"No. But there were tons of shots of young girls in school uniforms, teens who don't think about how they're sitting or standing. Or how much they've jerked up their little dresses."

"LT told me about the creep who staked out the cubicles in the unisex stores."

Amy sighed. "You go shopping for a pair of jeans and the next day your "up shots" are plastered all over cyberspace. He'd slide a gym bag against the wall and click away. The second I started changing the bag moved closer. I let him peek, but kept my back against the opposite wall."

Kincaid took her arm and gently rolled up the edge of her sleeve. A scraggly line of ten stitches were still healing. "You should've waited for back-up."

"Like you would have?"

Caught.

"It was a lucky slice. He pulled the blade as soon as I kicked in the door. Eight seconds and he was down. Two elbows to the face and a knee to his package."

"Ouch."

"I had a good teacher."

"So they led you to ShoeCam?"

Amy watched a cafeteria worker pile fresh dishes where the check-out line started. Earphones on and oblivious to the world. "Luck and those rollovers. We were going through the photos and something caught my eye."

"What?"

"A logo that appeared again and again. The edge of a few letters, possibly a sign. The tech guys blew it up as much as they could. I wracked my brain over the thing for days."

"A company name?"

"Close. Two sets of letters right over each other. CY. The 'C' had a little curlicue after it."

"So?"

"Two of the best womens' shoe stores are on the second floor of the Eaton Centre. They frame a restaurant. The one to the right's called '*Tracy's Fancy's*'. The letters were in the upper right corner, so the perv had to be taking them when the women went up the escalator."

"So LT authorized a sweep?"

"We had them the first day. ShoeCam worked a team. They'd wait at the bottom, watching for the easiest ones to shoot. Heels and short dresses. They'd go in turns, following them up the escalator."

The main doors opened and the first few civilians came in for their break, vanquishing the silence.

"How did you play it?"

"Belanger pretended to be freelancing. Carried a pro kit. He started riding the escalator up and down. After about ten minutes, our guy comes over and stands beside him. Tells Belanger he knows he's taking *upskirts*. They compare notes, talk about techniques, equipment. The perp's talking so much we almost ran out of tape. What an ego. He tells Belanger his timing's off, so he's going to show him how a real pro does it. That was my cue. He follows me up the escalator, and then shows Belanger his shots."

"Unbelievable."

"Dufresne had a couple of uniforms waiting. Turns out he's one of ShoeCam's main ops. He ran the pay-for-view sites."

Amy licked the last bit of whipped cream from the corner of her lips. Kincaid didn't know which was more enticing – that subtle movement, or the delicate little mole.

"The usual threats and lures and he rolled over like a fish out of water. They raided his place that night. He had thousands of pictures: women on escalators, stairs, bending over at a fountain to wash a child's face. Unisex change areas and public washrooms."

Kincaid saw the "but" in Amy's eyes.

"He lawyered up. There are some legal problems. The assistant D.A. thinks it'll be a tough case to prosecute. A real acid test about privacy issues. The laws don't cover much, and what they do is pretty vague. So's the Charter of Rights. And most women I've contacted don't want to testify."

"What's the other problem?"

Amy leaned closer, her eyes sad. "A personal one, with a victim. Heavy residual damage. I've got a woman who's basically become a hermit because of these guys. Her boyfriend was one of the ops. We're not talking about a couple of pics in a bikini bottom. This was a full scale attack."

"Her *boyfriend*?"

"She'd been seeing him for about a year. When she posted his bail she found out everything. I had to tell her – and show her – he's been plastering her photos over voyeur sites everywhere. K, she almost died."

K. Only the people closest to him ever called him that.

"The little shit had cameras all over the house. *Everywhere.* 24/7. He even rigged her desk at work so he could take pictures when she wore a dress. When she was sleeping, in the shower –" Amy paused and looked down at her cup "– even using the bathroom."

Kincaid's hands clenched into fists.

Someone dropped a tray in the kitchen – metal rain followed by a slew of curses. The cafeteria was filling up quickly. Several people waved when they saw Kincaid. Amy leaned closer.

"The boyfriend says it was a consensual sex game." Amy's lips quivered. "She's lost all sense of privacy. A few months ago she was a bank manager – now she's agoraphobic. A complete recluse. She can't go out, and she's terrified of anyone seeing her. She walks around her house all day completely wrapped up in blankets. She wears a cover like some Middle Eastern women do."

"The *burqa*." Kincaid often saw women completely covered from head to toe. He'd volunteered three times on behalf of the police detachment to go into hot zones to do training exercises with law enforcement recruits. He'd taught dozens of rookies the fundamental principles of policing in Bosnia, Iraq, and Syria.

"She doesn't even get undressed to go to the bathroom, and she bathes by doing one small body part at a time. She imagines cameras everywhere. When I go over, I have to call from her driveway and then from the hallway outside her apartment before she'll speak to me through the door. It's like rape without the physicality."

Amy picked at the rim of her cup. The cacophony of conversations erupting around the cafeteria suddenly seemed immensely annoying.

Kincaid looked into her eyes. "It sounds like she's not even close to talking to a man yet, so there's nothing I can do. I know a great psych over in 52 Division. Jayne Gee. Specializes in rape and stalking cases. If anyone can help, it'll be Jayne."

He pulled a card from his pocket and jotted down a name and number.

Amy choked back a dry gulp. The healing process for the young woman would be painfully tortuous. Could she – would she – ever heal? Or would trust be a dream only other people had?

"Thanks." Amy reached out and took his hands between hers. "And for listening." She watched his eyes, leaned closer, and lowered her voice.

"Speaking of help, don't shut me out. I want to know how you're doing. What I can do. And don't think I don't know when you're in pain. Your forehead looks like a washboard and you can't sit still."

Kincaid didn't want to let her hands go. Amy MacKenzie was a wonderful woman. In any other situation, things would have been different. But not now, not with the sentence he was expecting from Dr. Chadpur. And what about Stephanie? He'd walked away from the person he'd loved more deeply than he'd ever dreamed possible. Did he really want the same thing to happen all over again? A shotgun blast can heal: the bullet love uses leaves a gaping wound that might never stop bleeding. The question wasn't whether or not he could love Amy, because he knew he could. It was whether he could risk loving anyone at all.

Chapter Three

Kincaid had a healthy relationship with practically everyone in the precinct, yet the squad room seemed imposing. The coffee had helped – so had Amy – but Kincaid didn't want to be betrayed by a tremor or forced smile. These people made their living, and stayed alive, by noticing the slightest nuance in any situation. He hoped his colleagues would bury their concerns and let everything go on as it was. So he wasn't prepared for the palpable sense of unease when he walked inside. Fingers paused over keyboards, pens scratched to a sudden stop, and the bustling throb of frenetic activity quieted with an anxious hush. Somewhere, a telephone rang, unanswered. Probing eyes watched him carefully.

Kincaid smiled as he weaved his way through the rows of desks toward his office, nodding warmly at everyone who met his gaze. Heads turned as he passed, and he had the rather discomfiting perception he was running a gauntlet – a prisoner shuffling past the silent horde as he's led to the gallows. It had only been three weeks, for Heaven's sake. He wondered what kind of rumors had been circulating in his absence. People often expect the worst. Surely he didn't look *that* much different. Yet he knew nothing made people more distressed and apprehensive than the unknown. The threat of what *might* be.

The ice finally broke. Someone stood and took his hand. Another Detective did too, then whispered something that made both men laugh. The room came alive with well-wishes. Smiles. Pencils tapping desks. A few 'nice holiday?' made everything seem right again. Jibes and jabs. But Kincaid sensed some of the things that *weren't* being said, too.

Rising and smiling, a young woman intercepted him just before he reached his door. She touched him lightly on the shoulder.

"I know I speak for everyone, Sir, when I say how happy I am you're back."

Shelley Vargas, one of the civilian clerks. Tall and slender with a cyclist's calves, she wore a tight, knee-length blue skirt with a matching jacket and cream-colored blouse. Low heels, and her nails perfectly manicured. She'd only worked Homicide for five months, but was fitting into the rotation quite nicely. She handed him a large bouquet of freshly cut carnations. Red, white, and a soft, blended pink. The entire room erupted with '*ooos*' and *aaah's*, catcalls and whistles. Kincaid was as red as the flowers.

"A secret admirer?" someone teased.

Another voice chimed in. "You must have done *something* good."

Blushing, Kincaid asked Shelley if she'd scrounge up a vase and give them some water.

"Of course, sir. And if you need anything –"

"Thanks, Shelley. I will."

She gestured toward an adjacent hallway. "He said he wanted to see you right away."

Kincaid walked down the narrow corridor to the Lieutenant's office. Interview rooms, complete with adjacent viewing areas and one-way mirrors, lined the hall. Heavy glass doors muffled sporadic yells and curses. There was a special holding cell halfway down the hall, Room 3, with a secured metal door and watch-window. A man sat on the floor, talking to himself in a variety of different voices and banging on the walls.

The reception desk was empty: Maisy Orton was on an errand. Kincaid sighed. Despite Dr. Chadpur's support, this is where his fate would be decided. It was the old-fashioned litmus test – the Lieutenant's eyes. He'd be sent home or allowed to work. He had to look calm, controlled, painless. He knocked, heard a garbled reply, and walked in.

Perched behind a desk laden with teetering mounds of files, Lieutenant Davis was rifling through a thick folder. His "in" tray was crammed full. Kincaid couldn't stop a burgeoning smile as he took a seat.

"You look like a hamster stashing food for the winter."

"Piss off."

An intimidating presence, Reg Davis was almost as tall as Kincaid, but much heavier. He had the thick neck of a football player and the large, weathered hands of someone accustomed to physical labor. But his features were fine, his eyes bright and inquisitive, the deep blackness of his skin smooth and practically flawless, except for a small ridge that ran along the edge of his hairline. The trail of a bullet that had almost cost him his life. But today his cheeks were so swollen his entire face was distorted. Davis looked like an angry blowfish.

"I guess I shouldn't ask how it went."

"How it went? How the hell does it look like it went?" Wincing, he forced his words through partly clenched teeth.

"Bloody dentists. If he wasn't Shawnna's fiancé, I would have strangled the prick. Had one on the right side pulled, and this one" – he gingerly touched his jaw – "was an infected root canal. I swear he dug it out from one side of my face to the other. It throbs like fuck."

"No, I mean other than that."

"Bite me."

"Maybe he was just nervous working on his future father-in-law."

"They're sure as shit not getting any presents now." Davis closed the folder. Enough of his own pain. His eyes brightened a little. "It's good to see you."

"It's nice to be back." *Not too subtle.*

"How'd everything go?"

"We've already talked about that, Reg," Kincaid replied evasively.

"I want to hear it again so I can watch your eyes."

Kincaid stared back. They'd been friends for a long time, and he knew Davis would gladly have switched places with him if he could. When the symptoms re-surfaced after being dormant for so long, Kincaid knew this was something he'd have to face on his own.

"I won't know anything for a few more weeks."

"You're having the tests done again? The CT and all that?"

He'd obviously heard from Dr. Chadpur. Kincaid nodded.

"And there's still no indication if – "

They can operate?– sliced the air between them like a knife.

"No."

"Is there anything –"

"Thanks, but no."

Kincaid was one of the LT's closest friends. His best Detective, too, and Davis didn't want to rush him back or push him too hard. Nothing that might exacerbate the situation down the line. Better to ease him into it, or not at all. That's what Dr. Chadpur had said earlier this morning. But getting Kincaid to do anything at half-speed was like telling a snowboarder to miss every mogul on the run.

Speaking obviously hurt, but Davis could still stare. "If you need more time . . . "

"I said I'd keep you up to date. When I know something, you'll know. But I need to work, Reg. I can't sit at home and think about it."

Davis knew Kincaid wouldn't do anything to jeopardize his colleagues. Like Dr. Chadpur, however, his concern was Kincaid might not realize he was having a problem until it was too late. That's what happened before his hospitalization: he hadn't been aware of how much pain he'd been in.

Kincaid nodded toward the squad room. "You're running on empty."

He was right. Davis needed the manpower. Three officers were quarantined at St. Mike's. Four or five others were doing their best on half power after suffering virus-like symptoms. COVID wasn't the culprit, but even the possibility of its resurgence had been enough to paralyze the city. The problem hadn't stopped there. Abetted by the government's lack of screening programs, the latest strain of Asian flu, as well as a small number of TB cases, had seeped in undetected with the recent group of refugees Immigration was trying to re-settle. The CDC in Atlanta had quickly countered with vaccines and staved off an epidemic, but front line forces had been decimated. Again, rich Arab nations were still refusing to accept the predominately Muslim refugees, so the process was overwhelming, and the crisis grew worse.

Davis poured himself some water, downed a couple of painkillers, and picked up a manila folder. He tossed it across his desk: the Devlin Turner murder investigation.

"This one's yours. It's pretty ugly." He winced, cradling his jaw with his palm.

The case would probably have been his to begin with, but the symptoms Kincaid had been trying to hide re-surfaced the night Turner and his faithful collie had been torn apart. Kincaid had been hospitalized the following morning. He flipped through the pages while Davis gave him an update through parted lips.

"As shit goes, Gerbec was about five days into it before his appendix burst. Right in an unmarked with Michaels on the radio. They almost lost him."

"How is he?"

"Better. But an infection will lay the poor bastard up for a month."

"And Heather?"

"Still working. She spends as much time at the hospital as she can. Gerbec's team managed to do some preliminary work, so the crime scene has already been completely sanitized. And compromised."

"Pictures?"

"Some. Farther in."

"I know you're hurting, but will I have any help?"

Davis nodded, wincing. "Your doctor didn't really want you on your own anyway. I can loan you Richardson when he's not on call. I don't know how much or for how long."

"Is he still deep in the DiMatteo thing? The last time we spoke he said his CI was ready to roll over on the whole crew. Blow the turf war between The Rock and Hell's Angels out of the water. They both want to control human trafficking across the border."

"DiMatteo caught the ice and went to ground. It might not even go down."

"Damn."

Davis tenderly massaged his jaw. "He'll give you a hand until he's on."

"I heard Sergeant MacKenzie did extremely well on the ShoeCam op. Maybe it's time for her to step up."

How the Hell did he know about that? "My thoughts exactly. But I've seen the way she looks at you, Kincaid. You heard the story about the lamb and the lion?"

"I'm not sure who'd be the lion if we were caged together."

"That's what I'm afraid of."

"I'll take the risk."

"I thought you would. But this will be her first major case, so keep her on a tight leash."

"I get the feeling you've already talked to her, and told her the same thing about me."

"Protocol. And your doctor's orders. She'll be watching you, alright. To learn, but to assess, too. She'll be reporting to me, and she can pull you out. Know it."

"Understood." Kincaid glanced at the folder, pausing when he saw the first few photographs of the murdered man.

"Fucking gruesome, right? Something you'd expect in a teenage slasher movie."

Kincaid couldn't remember the last time he'd seen so much blood in such a confined area. Pools of arterial spray. Thick red-black veins streaming down the walls. Clumps of –something – all over the desk. "The short version?"

"With this mouth that's all you get." Davis sipped some water through a straw. "Devlin Turner. Fifty-four. Owned one of the largest and most prestigious literary agencies in the city. Represented some of the best writers here and abroad."

Kincaid turned over another page. "Holy Jesus."

"Great income, bordering on high end. A real power player with the city elite. Drank too much, liked cigars, loved his dog, hated his wife. Going through a messy divorce."

"Is Mrs. Turner in the frame?"

"Gerbec didn't think so. Neither do I. And she's got a stone cold sober alibi – fucking her lawyer at the time."

"Literally or metaphorically?"

"Both."

The next picture made Kincaid wince. Davis rubbed his jaw. "Mutilated in his study. First floor, right off the main hall."

Kincaid tried counting the pens. *The letter opener through his hand. The fountain pen neatly imbedded into his eye. Two in the neck. Cheek. Throat. At least four in the chest.* This was overkill, and very, very personal. He glanced at the next photo and mumbled *Oh my God.* He asked if there were any detailed blow-ups.

Davis knew which picture caught his eye. "Of that one? It's in there somewhere. But it's what it looks like. Poor asshole had his lips sewn together."

"Post mortem?"

"Nope. His mouth was crammed with pieces of paper. Most of it bore his letterhead."

A bolt of pain seared down Kincaid's back, and he shifted around. There was a distance shot from the doorway – one of the visitors chairs had been pushed up against the desk. *Had they been talking first? During?* Kincaid thought about the fountain pen. *Was that why he'd been propped up?*

"How many times was he stabbed?"

"Pathologist says at least twenty."

"They can't tell for sure?"

"Several punctures came in a frenzy, hitting the same hole more than once and making it wider or deeper. Even the ones twisted around weren't deep enough to kill him. Initial COD is he bled out."

Kincaid frowned. *Who'd want to murder – no, torture – an elite literary agent to death. And why the poor dog? Just to gain access? Or was it something much more personal?*

"How far did Gerbec get?"

"Notes are on his desk or in there. He did the crime scene, bagged and tagged, initiated a house to house, and sent everything he had to forensics. He'd just started checking out Turner's itinerary when his appendix burst. How do you want to handle it?"

Kincaid held up the file. "I'll start with this."

"You'll have to track down what's missing."

"Richardson and MacKenzie are in for some leg work."

A memory popped up, making Davis frown. "Hey, what about Ryan? Aren't you taking your little buddy to the game tonight?"

"No. Wednesday."

"Oh, right. He knows?"

Kincaid smiled. "I couldn't keep it a secret if I tried."

"I bet he's excited."

"Excited isn't the word."

Davis watched his friend's eyes. Kincaid had worked with the *Children's Wish Foundation* for as long as he could remember. He took kids camping, canoeing, on sightseeing tours and day trips, but most of his time was devoted to fundraising. Golf tournaments, local police versus old-timers hockey, wine tasting evenings: anything to keep the money flowing. Kincaid had been involved with a number of children over the years, and had always struggled to maintain an emotional distance, for his sake and theirs, especially with the ones that tugged relentlessly at his heartstrings. It made the pain a little easier to bear. But Ryan was special: like a probing root, he'd seeped through a crack in Kincaid's concrete defenses and slowly wriggled his way into his heart. Davis knew how deep a nerve the boy had struck in his friend.

"How's he doing?"

"He's hanging in there, Reg."

Kincaid closed his eyes and pictured the child again: the curtained off cubicle, the boy tucked in beneath the starched white hospital sheets, the IV's and dangling tubes, the incessant blue lines that *blipped* across the monitors, the tray stacked with pills, the oxygen mask always *hissing*.

"It's a shame he couldn't make it to Disney World."

"They couldn't risk it. He was really weak from the chemo."

"Maybe next time."

Silence. There probably wouldn't be a "next time" for Ryan. Kincaid shuffled the pages back together. Witness statements, forensics, house to house results, the coroner's preliminary notes, and more pictures than he wanted to see. He slipped the file into a manila envelope, stood up, and walked to the door. He turned back when Davis mumbled something.

"Make fucking sure you keep me up to speed."

"Yes, sir."

"Damn sure. We've talked. MacKenzie's your protégé *and* your shadow. She won't hesitate to pull you out."

"Don't worry."

"It's my bloody job to worry." *And part of our friendship.*

"Reg?"

He was already opening up another file. "What?"

"Can I call you *Chippy?*"

"Piss off, Kincaid."

"*Harry the Hoarder?*"

Davis struggled to bark through the balloons in his cheeks. "Leave while you've still got legs, asshole."

The threat hung impotently in the air: his door had already swung closed.

Chapter Four

Lieutenant Davis buzzed his secretary. "Maisy?"

She came in immediately. Forty-three, a tad on the 'matronly' side, and an industrious woman who left the job on her desk so it never affected her family. Thoughtful and reliable, she always had a smile for everyone.

"Amy MacKenzie?"

"I believe she's downstairs in the evidence room, sorting through the pictures from the ShoeCam operation."

Davis rubbed his swollen jaw. "I need to see her again. And have someone tell that shithead in holding to shut up or I'm going to play basketball with his head."

"Right away, sir."

*

Amy was upstairs in five minutes. Walking down the corridor to the Lieutenant's office, she noticed the guy in number three was taking a breather and being quiet.

"You wanted to see me, Sir?"

Looking through another thick folder, Davis gestured to a chair with an impatient wave.

"You're going through the ShoeCam files?"

"Yes sir." She tried to stay relaxed. They'd spoken about the situation with Kincaid twice. *Had he made a decision? Was this her chance?*

"Let them wait. I'll have a civy do it. Kincaid's taking over the Devlin Turner investigation. It's getting cold already. You know the window – forty eight hours and we start to lose witnesses, and their memories. He'll need help." He paused. "He asked for you. I agreed. Can you handle it?"

Amy sat up even straighter. *Homicide. And he asked for me.*

"Yes, sir."

"There's no better time to get your feet wet. And no better Detective than Kincaid. So –"

"Listen and learn."

"Exactly." A frown.

Amy waited. She knew where this was going from their earlier meeting and still wasn't sure she liked it.

Davis knew what he was asking went against the grain for everyone, but there wasn't any other choice. "You know what I want you to do, Sergeant."

A nod. A small one.

"Priority one. You've got to make *me* sure he's okay."

"No offense, sir. But as I said this morning, I'm not I.A."

Davis almost smiled. His demeanor softened. "I'm not asking you to be. But you've got some history, and he trusts you. We're the only people he's talked to about – his situation."

Amy waited, statue still.

"He needs someone to watch out for him. I know how he'd feel if he made a mistake and the perp skates on some minor technicality when the thing goes to trial."

"I'm sure Kincaid would say something if he wasn't up to par, Lieutenant."

"Normally, sure. But I know the man. With the pressure he's under – he might not be able to judge things as well as he usually would."

Another nod.

"He needs someone to have his back." Davis watched her closely. Assessing, always assessing. "You're not a spy, Amy. Or a rat. And you're sure as shit not babysitting him. You're taking a step up, but you're going to have another responsibility, too. To be a safety valve."

Amy kept staring.

"I know what I'm asking. You're in a tough place. If I thought it would be an easy stretch I would have picked someone else. Whatever you tell me will be vital in any decision I make. But I have to know I can count on you for an honest appraisal. If things go south –"

"Yes, sir. You can."

Actually, it was the position she wanted to be in. She'd be close and have his back. And she'd be the one next to him if things felt wrong. *Could she be objective when push came to shove?*

"Have you –"

Davis raised a hand. The pain was getting worse and he was starting to slur his words.

"Of course he knows. Reverse things: wouldn't he do the same for you?"

"Well, yes. I hope so."

"Damn bloody straight." More water and pills. "I don't want anything to jeopardize the investigation. *Or* Kincaid. Keep me informed. *Well* informed, for everyone's sake. I'd rather pull him out – and believe me, MacKenzie – *he'd* rather I'd pull him out – if a wrong decision cost us everything. I don't want to be left hanging because someone's afraid to make a judgment. So if you're not up for this –"

Amy stood. "I am, sir."

"Good." Davis seemed satisfied. "He's in his office going over Gerbec's notes. And Sergeant?"

"Lieutenant?"

"Is everything perfectly clear?"

"As a bell, sir."

"Keep me posted." He returned her stare. "Don't disappoint me. And don't fucking let me down."

*

Kincaid sifted through the information Davis had given him on Devlin Turner's murder. Unfortunately, LT was right: numerous pieces from interrelated departments were missing, leaving huge gaps in the material he needed. In a bureaucracy synonymous with red tape, it wasn't difficult to lose a file when it had to be transferred, regardless of the physical distance it actually moved. The trick was to keep it intact: regrettably, there weren't many magicians who could perform the task. Paper or disc: it didn't seem to matter. When an investigation changed hands, or another department became involved, information entered the Bermuda triangle of paperwork and disappeared, only to miraculously reappear days later. Kincaid hoped Amy MacKenzie and Richardson would be able to gather up the rest of the information floating ethereally around the precinct.

*

A soft knock on his door: Amy poked her head around the corner. Kincaid was on the phone and motioned for her to sit down.

"Richardson," he said, hanging up. "I left him another message."

MacKenzie smiled nervously. "Thanks."

"Don't patronize me. I know it's your first homicide, but you're ready for this. You've earned the right. Besides, you're the one helping me. By the look of it, I'm going to need all the hands I can get."

Anxiousness tinged her eyes. She tried to sit still. There was something he wanted to say, something he needed to get off his chest.

"Homicide is different than vice, Amy. Or robbery. Time's an issue. You have to be confident you can work with me. Running a crime scene isn't like going out to dinner. You're assigned to work under me. Our friendship stops when you walk through that door. You okay with that?"

"No problem. Sir."

"Good. Richardson's floating and has to stay close to the House, so I'll be counting on you. Ever met him?"

"No."

"You're in for a treat. Do what I tell you, and don't follow up on anything unless you run it by me first. Take some initiative, but don't overstep yourself. Or me. The one thing I don't want is to have to keep telling you what to do or where to go."

"You just want me to read your mind and be one step ahead of you all the time."

Kincaid smiled. "Exactly."

"LT said a lot of the paperwork wasn't in the file." Amy gestured to the one spread across Kincaid's desk. "Why don't I go on a scavenger hunt and see what I can find?"

"See, you're reading my mind already. Questions?"

"No."

An uneasy silence. Kincaid sighed. "I talked to Davis. I know he wants you to cut your teeth on this one, but he also wants to make sure you have my back and that I'm doing alright."

"Kincaid –"

"And it's the right call. You're the one that has to be okay with it. You probably made some smart-ass comment about not being in I.A. That isn't what this is about."

Silence.

Kincaid checked his watch. "I'll see you back here in an hour."

She left without a sound. Kincaid turned back to the file. Judging by what he'd pieced together from Gerbec's notes, he figured the best place to start would be interviewing the dead man's colleagues. The first person was Gail Meredith, the owner of the publishing house Turners' agency dealt with almost exclusively. The second was Cynthia Baxter, Turner's partner at the literary agency, *Creative Author's Creations.* He also wanted to talk to the staff at *The Bamboo Garden* – someone there was probably the last person who'd seen Devlin Turner alive.

Before he'd been punctured and had his lips sewn together.

When Kincaid called Turners' agency, he was advised Ms. Baxter was out of town at a conference and wouldn't be back for two days. So, after a stop at *The Bamboo Garden*, he'd start at the top with Gail Meredith.

*

Other than painkillers, Dr. Chadpur had Kincaid on a cocktail of five different medications throughout the day. With an office glassed in on two sides, Kincaid often felt like a fish in an aquarium, so he went to the men's room to take his pills. He filled the sink with cold water, and bathed his neck and forehead with moistened paper towels. It was only when he was drying off that he noticed the myriad pictures dotting the walls.

He was appalled. Disgusted. Shamed. His cheeks flushed. Fun's fun, and everybody should be able to take a joke or two or they wouldn't be able to survive on the job. But this was different. This was belittling, repulsive, hurtful. He felt sorry for Amy.

Most pictures were upskirt shots, copied from whatever was confiscated at the ShoeCam guy's apartment during the team's initial search. But there were a lot of explicit ones, too. Teens in change rooms, trying on thongs. Women in G-strings, doing up shoes. A skirt billowing out as a subway car came whistling into a station, the woman naked underneath. About a dozen had been photo-shopped with Amy's face superimposed on the images. Kincaid felt his teeth grinding together. *Taylor.*

The door swung open, and who of all people swaggered in? The man himself.

"Hey, heard you were back, Kincaid. How they hanging?"

All class. Taylor was a big man, with broad shoulders, thick forearms, and a wrestler's neck. His unkempt hair was far too long for his age, and two or three days growth invariably lined his jaw. Supposedly ex-infantry, ex-narc, with stints undercover, although no-one could ever find any actual proof of assignments or deployments. The waters of his murky past stayed muddied. But he had the family's blue bloodline; there was no doubt about that. An ancestry of *who's who* in almost every department. 'Brass' was always there to protect him.

He smiled at the walls as he unzipped himself. "Like our collage? A real piece of art, eh?"

"Take them down, Taylor. All of them. And whatever's in the locker room."

"Whoa, hold on there, cowboy. I was just having some fun. You can't tell jack shit from these photos. Everybody knows it's not *what's her name."*

"Amy. To you, Sergeant MacKenzie."

"Fucking right. *Amy.* Well, except for a couple." He nodded and laughed.

"That makes it worse. How'd you feel if there were a few upshots of your daughter? What's she now, sixteen?" Kincaid pulled a graphic close-up off the nearest cubicle. "Let's put her face on this one. Still funny?"

"Come on, Kincaid. Nobody can fucking tell who's who. They're just crotch shots off the Net."

"She's a fellow officer, for Christ's sake, Taylor, who'd put herself on the line for you in a second. You can learn something from that. One of the pervs cut her for ten deep."

Taylor zipped up but didn't bother washing. He'd only seen Kincaid angry on a few occasions: despite his size, he didn't like the feeling of being on the receiving end. But he didn't want to back down, either.

"Pussy's pussy. You think I can't take a hundred up-shots like that little fucker did, show them around, and everybody's going to pick out who's who? Half the guys wouldn't even recognize what they've been screwing for ten years. Beav's beav, right? So what's the big fucking deal?"

Kincaid was breathing hard. "I wonder how many guys could pick out your wife."

"You fuck . . . "

Taylor turned, swinging at the same time. Kincaid deflected the oncoming right and let it glide past with its own momentum. Taylor couldn't stop his half spin. Kincaid's thick arm was around the man's throat before he could catch his balance. The outside door opened. Two officers walked in, took one look, and did a 180°. Pushing his head awkwardly against his arm, Kincaid squeezed Taylor's windpipe until the man's face reddened and his eyes started to bulge. He shook him back and forth for a second, then let go just long enough to grab Taylor behind the neck. His fingertips pressed hard on the man's carotid artery. Taylor trembled, his legs weakened, unconsciousness creeping in. Kincaid jerked him forward, leaned him over the sink, and pushed Taylor's face into the icy water.

"A man can drown in an inch of water, Taylor. I wonder if the depth's the same for an asshole?"

Kincaid yanked the guy's head back. Taylor gasped for air, his shirt and jacket soaked. Another bit of pressure on the artery, just so Kincaid didn't have to struggle to hold him. There was no use working up a sweat over this: Dr. Chadpur told him he was supposed to stay as calm as possible. Just one more dunk.

He spoke slowly and clearly. "You know, you're the only guy in the squad room I wouldn't want behind me. If too many people think like that, you'll be out on your ass, no matter what kind of brass you're related to downtown. So smarten up, get rid of that mickey of rye you keep in your third drawer, use the lotion if you don't wash your hands after you've played with your prick, and try to pretend you're a real cop."

Kincaid released the pressure. Taylor collapsed against the sink, gasping and sputtering for breath, his face a mottled red.

"Get them down. And make sure MacKenzie knows they're down."

Taylor nodded, the blood still pounding through his neck and temples as he stumbled back from the sink.

Kincaid turned to go, but stopped. He tore a picture down: an upshot of a woman's long legs. High heels, nylons, and black bikini panties pulled up tightly into her sex. She was bending over, fixing an ankle strap, her long red hair falling over her shoulders. ShoeCam had caught her perfectly, looking right back at the camera. Too perfectly: this was a model in a staged shot. Professional pictures mixed in with the amateur ones never hurt on the Web's pay sites. But when you looked closer, it was pretty obvious there was a penis tucked into the bikini. Kincaid folded the picture into his jacket pocket.

*

Back in his office, Kincaid read the reports from the first officers on the scene at Turner's house. He wished he could have been there. A quick knock at his door: Amy came in with an armload of files.

"Find Richardson on your travels?"

"Yes. A bit on the weird side, sir."

"I think you have to be a little off the wall to do what Richardson does."

"We scrounged up what we could. He says he'll have more by tomorrow. Forensic information is still floating through the computers."

"Good work. Don't worry, things will keep coming in." He glanced at the files: it was more than he expected. He tossed MacKenzie his car keys. "Know where I park?"

A nod. And a seductive smile. "You mean you've forgotten me already?"

He almost told her he couldn't get the steam off his windows for a week, but frowned instead.

"Is that supposed to be funny, *Sergeant?*"

"Sir. No. It won't happen again." Amy's face was crimson. "Sorry."

The parameters were set. Kincaid waved the apology away. This was going to be a little difficult for him, too. Perhaps more than a little.

"Meet me out in front in ten minutes. I have to stop at processing."

*

Down on the first floor, processing was a beehive of activity. Bookings, discharges, potential cell mates talking it up already. Boundaries being established, and officers and civilians moving in a blur. Everyone outside the cages seemed to have a moment for a friendly word with Kincaid. Handshakes, backslaps, a few concerned smiles. He found who he was looking for in fingerprinting. The man was trying to get an ink spot off the cuff of a brand new shirt.

Kincaid grinned. "Stella's going to kill you."

"She bought me this freaking shirt for my Goddamn birthday."

Leonard Jones smiled, a large, beaming smile that seemed to take up all of his face. He stopped fussing with his shirt and took his friend's hand. Six five, strong shoulders, huge hands, two-time state wrestling champion, and one of the best left guards State had ever seen. But his right knee was cursed: it cost him two careers. An accident in his junior year – a torn ACL – ended his chance at professional football, so he joined the police force. He would easily have been a detective by now, but in the middle of a street takedown when he was still in uniform three Teflon rounds ricocheted off an ETF officer's shield and shattered the knee again. Kincaid had pulled him to safety behind a nearby van and took out the perp. But his friend's limp was awkward and severe.

On the plus side, Jones' size, strength, and demeanor made him a perfect fit for processing, a frenetic place where all Hell could explode in a second.

"Rinse it really well with cold water, then use a bleach pen and she won't even notice."

Jones grinned. "So how you feeling, bud?"

"I'm good, Len, I'm good."

"You're working the Turner case?"

Kincaid nodded. "Amy MacKenzie's helping me."

"Now you just keep focused on the job. I've seen the way you look at each other. I haven't seen you look at anyone like that since . . ."

Leonard had talked himself into a corner. "Well, you know. Stephanie."

The sparkle dissipated from Kincaid's eyes. The surrounding noises suddenly seemed terribly grating.

"Look Kincaid, I'm – "

"Don't worry about it." He pulled the envelope from his jacket pocket. "Do me a favor?"

"Done."

He showed Leonard the picture from the washroom.

"Whoa, nice legs. And those nylons. Hey wait. *She*'s got a penis."

"Really? Get a file photo of Taylor and do the best facial imaging you've ever done. Then copy enough to circulate through the departments. Don't worry – he'll never know it was you."

"Like I care what that little weasel knows?" Leonard snorted and squeezed Kincaid's hand. "Now I remember why I like to stay on your good side." There was an awkward silence, and then the confabulation of sounds burst alive.

"Keep me in the loop, K. And whatever you need . . . "

"I will." Kincaid glanced at the envelope. "And thanks. Taylor's going to want to have one framed."

Chapter Five

The Bamboo Garden

The sign on the front door said 'Closed until 11:30.' Kincaid and Sergeant MacKenzie's trespass was announced by a large set of chimes hanging above the entranceway that click-clacked together and resonated like a sweet chorus of pan flutes. Kincaid had called ahead, and the owner, Estavelle Cruz, quickly gathered her staff together in the small office at the rear of the restaurant. People sat wherever they could find an empty place. They weren't pleased with the interruption and murmured half-heard grievances. It clearly put a dent in their preparations for the approaching lunch hour rush.

Kincaid and Amy leaned against the owner's desk. "I'd like to thank everyone for your patience and co-operation," Amy smiled, trying to put them at ease. She explained they were there about Devlin Turner's murder.

Someone in the back said, "We've already talked to someone about that."

"Yes, I know."

"Then what's the problem now?" The impatient speaker stayed hidden.

Without going into specific details, Kincaid quickly explained Gerbec's hospitalization, and told them they were taking over the investigation. The staff wasn't appeased.

"We need to double-check some information to make sure we haven't missed anything. There's a good chance someone here was the last person to see Devlin Turner alive."

The detectives went through a litany of questions paraphrased from Gerbec's notes, but all of their queries were reluctantly countered with one or two word replies. He'd hoped for more. But it was obvious after just a few minutes that no-one was deeply affected by the man's demise. Anything pertinent was difficult to extract. The initial stream of questions and answers quickly slowed to a dribble. Basically, no one saw or heard anything they thought might be helpful. Devlin Turner was alone, as usual. He was rude, demanding, fussy and condescending, which was all pretty normal. His complaints were constant. He drank until he was rubber-kneed, talking and arguing with himself until he was distracting too many of the other customers. He left his dinner half-eaten. It took three waiters to help him to the door. *No,* he didn't try to hurt anyone. *No,* he wasn't hurt, and nothing was broken – this time. And *yes,* he refused to take the cab they'd called.

Mrs. Cruz asked if Kincaid was finished, politely reminding him they had to prepare for the impatient patrons that would besiege the little restaurant for lunch.

"One more question. Who served Devlin Turner that night?"

Some people shifted uneasily. Mrs. Cruz exhaled a slow breath. "My son."

"Then perhaps we can have a few minutes of his time. Everyone else is free to leave." Amy thanked everyone for their time and patience.

Martin Cruz, Estavelle's eldest son, reluctantly remained. The young man was pale and slender, with almost no muscle tone in his small body. He had the long, thin fingers of a pianist. An oval face, with a smooth, clear complexion. He was training with the chefs and wore a white apron, but had taken off his hairnet. Long brown curls hung down over his shoulders. He was nineteen, but easily might have passed for three years younger. He was having trouble standing still and fidgeted anxiously with his hairnet.

Kincaid smiled. "We just need to clarify a few things, Martin. Are you okay with that?"

The boy nodded.

"So you served Devlin Turner that evening?"

"Yes." He pointed toward an imaginary table for four in the far corner of the adjacent room. "He sat in my section. Mom asked him to move to a smaller table but he refused."

"How much did he drink?"

"He shrugged. "He was belting back martinis pretty fast. Five, six maybe?"

"Was that usual?"

"Sometimes more, sometimes less."

"Did anyone join him?"

"No, sir."

MacKenzie kept jotting down notes. "Was he alone all night?"

"Yes ma'am."

"Was he on the phone very much?"

"Not really. He was talking to himself most of the time."

"About?"

"His wife and everything. They're getting divorced."

"And?"

"He got pretty loud and obnoxious. He wouldn't settle down. He got a couple of warnings, and then we asked him to leave. He wouldn't so Mom had him walked out. Three waiters helped."

Amy asked, "What time was that, Martin?"

"About 10:30. Maybe a quarter to eleven. Mom called a cab but he wouldn't take it. He kept swearing at everybody about his keys, but Mom wasn't going to let him drive, so he must've walked home. It's only about twenty minutes from here."

"Did you see him after that?" Amy held his gaze, her pen poised above her notebook.

"No ma'am."

Kincaid stared at the boy. "Did anyone else leave at the same time?"

"Not that I remember."

"Did any cars pull up when he left?"

"No, sir."

"What about the cabbie?"

"He came in and got a coffee."

"Did you notice if anyone might have started walking in the same direction?"

Martin closed his eyes. "No."

"What did you do after work, Martin?"

He looked down and shrugged. Kincaid caught the subtle change in his eyes.

"I had to clean up. Then I went home."

"You live with your mother?"

A nod.

"Was she with you?"

"No. She stayed to do the receipts and things."

"She's just off Queen Street, right? So it couldn't have taken you more than say, fifteen to twenty minutes to drive home."

The hairnet was scrunched up in the boy's hands.

"You must have read about all the problems the traffic police have been having, Martin. People running reds. Drivers texting or on the phone."

Martin bit his lower lip. "Yes. They – they've put cameras at some of the intersections. A friend of mine got a ticket for not stopping at a red. No one pulled him over or anything. It was all on tape."

"And that's where we have a problem, Martin," Amy said.

Kincaid kept watching the boy. "Turner lived in the upper Beaches, in the opposite direction from where your Mom lives. A surveillance camera photographed your car making a right just off Woodbine. That's only two streets over from Turner's place on Fallingdale. The time stamp on the picture is just after 2 a.m."

Any last vestige of color drained from the young man's face. His finger tore a hole through his hairnet.

"That's a lot of unaccounted time, Martin." Kincaid lowered his voice. "What happened?"

"I must have stayed cleaning later than I thought." He gulped. "Or maybe that was the night I had to come back because Mom's car wouldn't start."

"Martin . . ."

The boy didn't believe the lie himself. He shifted from side to side. Anxious seconds passed. Neither Kincaid nor Amy moved a muscle.

The boy's voice was soft and fragile. "Please, do you have to tell my mother?"

"It depends on what you tell us. But we don't usually bother with anything personal unless it directly affects our case. Understand?"

"Yeah." He looked through the office window. His mother was checking receipts at the front cash, but he could tell her antennae were up.

"I left when I said, but – but I didn't go straight home."

Kincaid waited patiently.

"I went to see someone."

Amy pocketed her notebook. "Someone from the restaurant?"

A quick glance, then a whisper. "Miguel. The new bartender. We went to his house."

Kincaid was fairly certain he knew the answer to his next question, but asked it anyway.

"You didn't go clubbing, did you, Martin? You stayed at Miguel's."

The boy nodded, half relieved and half ashamed the truth was out.

"Please," he begged. "Don't say anything to my mom. She doesn't need to know. I'm going to tell her, but I don't know how yet." He tried to straighten up. "It's hard, you know. But I am who I am, and I'm proud of that. And Miguel is helping me understand everything. But I swear on the Virgin's life that's where I was." He looked back and forth at the detectives. "We were at his house until about two, then I drove home."

"If I walked out right now and asked Miguel, would he confirm what you've just said?"

"Yes, he would. Only my mother. . . "

Kincaid stopped him with a raised hand. "Your mother won't hear anything from us, Martin. And it's none of our business. But maybe you should think about talking to your mother. It's better your story comes from your own heart and lips than it does from someone else's. What if she hears a rumor from one of the other waiters? I can see you're close. Talk to her."

He nodded, his body sighing with relief. He wiped a small tear from his cheek. "I will. Thanks."

Miguel waited in the office until Kincaid and Amy left, finally breathing when he heard the clacking call of the wooden chimes. When he looked up, his mother was staring into his heart.

Chapter Six

After comparing notes over lattes at one of the iconic yet insufferably banal coffee shops that infested the city, Kincaid decided to take Amy to the morgue before they went to Turner's house. It was something she'd have to get used to if she wanted to work homicide. Since they'd missed seeing Turner's crime scene, with his body *in situ*, this was the next best thing in understanding a killers violence, rage, and psychopathology – and coming to terms with your own psychological reaction to it.

"We're going *where*?" Amy asked as Kincaid handed her his keys.

"No one likes the morgue, Sergeant, but pictures aren't enough. Without seeing the real thing we don't have anything to compare it to. There's always information you can acquire from the body you simply can't obtain anywhere else. It's a vital perspective in any investigation, and it will give you insight a two dimensional photograph can't. It gives you a personal feeling for the victim as well."

"Like the crime scene, even if it's weeks later."

"Exactly. A hands-on experience that rarely fails to stimulate ideas and second thoughts."

Amy sighed. She'd attended the requisite training courses that took rookies into the bowels of the hospital. Like half her class, she hadn't been able to keep her breakfast down when the first incisions were made, the sternum was sawed open and the ribs were winched apart. She had to do better this time.

*

The morgue was discreetly housed in the bottom two levels of the hospital on Grenville Street, next to the Police Museum. No matter how many times he'd descended into these subterranean halls, Kincaid never got used to the abrupt, jolting stop at the bottom, or the loud clanging sound as the heavy doors cracked open. From the moment you walked in, everything – the walls, doors, floor and ceiling – was gray. The smell of disinfectant and formaldehyde immediately permeated your skin. It was cold and sterile, the silence unnerving. You couldn't help imagining . . .

The three physicians responsible for the post mortems were either out or working on new cases. Kincaid peeked into a handful of rooms until he found a lab technician. The kid looked like she was barely out of college: tall and lean in her white coat, fashionable glasses, the tiniest bit of makeup, a tattoo on her wrist, and the remnants of a fresh bout of acne. She led the detectives to a bank of vaults that stretched along two sides of the room. She double-checked their paperwork with the tag, then slid the body out on a long, gray gurney.

Kincaid pulled the sheet back. Amy gasped, her hand instinctively covering her mouth. She tried to keep her breath slow and light, but it was almost a minute before the color returned to her face. She'd studied the original photographs with Kincaid, but seeing the actual wounds to the dead man's too-white body was something else. More pervasive, more unnerving. The "y" incision was lumpy and jagged and been hurriedly stitched closed, but Amy couldn't help thinking the corpse could bolt forward at any moment. She looked at Turner's body for a couple of minutes before she needed fresh air, and stepped out into the hallway. When she came back, her face was red and there was a small bead of perspiration on her brow and upper lip.

"Sorry."

"No need to be." Kincaid put his hand lightly on her shoulder. "All right?"

She managed a nod.

Kincaid continued examining the wounds, carefully comparing them to the pictures. The deep cuts and holes on Turner's face and upper chest proved he'd died in terrible pain. And slowly, very slowly. *It was almost as if he'd been ritualistically bled to death.* The thread that had sewn his lips together had been cut away and tagged as evidence. He'd check back later with one of the coroners, but he didn't hold out much hope of finding very much that wasn't in the preliminary report. One thing he was particularly interested in was Turner's stomach contents, but he'd have to wait for toxicology for confirmation. *Had he been drugged?*

He pointed at Turner's chest. "Look at these wounds. They were done with a variety of pens and pencils. There are traces of lead and ink at each puncture site."

"But they're so wide."

"So?"

"He was stabbed repeatedly in the same spot."

"Or?"

"The punctures were deliberately enlarged." Amy envisioned the pens being wriggled back and forth, the holes dug deeper, wider.

"What about the stitches?"

Amy took a breath and leaned closer. "Slow and careful. Neat, I guess. He – or she – wasn't in a hurry."

"You're right. They're practiced and precise. And look at his hand."

She stared at the crater where the letter opener had pinned Turner's hand to his desk, and shook her head.

"Closer."

"Oh. It looks like the original wound was widened, too."

"Or it was slowly rammed down farther and farther, up to the hilt."

"So he couldn't move it."

Kincaid nodded. Something troubled him about Turner's lips. *How had they been sewn together? From behind, or was his assailant in front?* The position would make a big difference. He pulled the sheet up over Turner's head and slid the gurney into the wall. The door clanged closed, sealing the room into silence.

"I'll take the report back to the tech. You go on."

Amy was waiting for him by the elevators. Her cheeks had returned to their normal color.

"Okay, Sergeant?"

She nodded.

"It never gets any easier," Kincaid sighed. "And you don't want it to."

*

Amy rolled their unmarked car to a quiet stop in front of Devlin Turner's house. Strafed with a thick band of dark clouds that stretched across the horizon, the sky was backlit with rays of luminescent sunshine. Last night's downpour still soaked the grass. The leaves were still. Well off the main thoroughfare, Turner's side street was almost too quiet. It had been almost two weeks since the murder: the police vehicles were gone, the reporters' cars were parked in front of some other tragedy, and the shameless gaggles of onlookers were staring at another place of horror, blitzing their phones with photos some poor relative of the dead might see in cyberspace. But the pall of death still haunted the street like a threat. Amy thought about the morgue. And Turner. Holes everywhere. *Everywhere.* His eye. And so deep. . .

Kincaid was right; she didn't want to get used to that. As they got out of the car, Kincaid caught the flicker of light in several windows as curtains were parted across the street.

"Feel like you're being watched?"

"Sure do. Sir –"

"What?" He hadn't meant to sound antagonistic. "Sorry." He leaned against the car.

"You looked a little off-balance for a moment. You okay?"

"It's nothing. Just some pain. It depends on how I move."

"Is there –"

He raised a hand. "I don't mind you having my back, but I don't want to feel like I'm under surveillance. Are you alright with that?"

"Of course."

"Beautiful old neighborhood, isn't it?"

Amy nodded and smiled. She looked like Audrey Hepburn. More curtains parted. It wouldn't be long before someone called the police. People here liked their little enclave of security. Turner's death must have been quite a blow. Kincaid waved at someone standing behind half-opened shutters. They closed in a second.

Kincaid had Turner's keys. Following his lead, Amy ducked under the yellow police tape that crisscrossed the portico. Ignoring the prickly sensation in his neck, he paused before pushing the door open. This was another thing he'd always found difficult: seeing the things he didn't really want to see. You had to abandon a part of your humanity, your *being*. When that was lost, you didn't get it back. The momentary panic, the threat of bile rising in the back of his throat, the tremor in the knees. They all reminded Kincaid no matter what he faced, he was still human. Crime scenes remained stoic testaments to the horror people are capable of. And more often than not, normal people. *The ones you see every day.*

The detectives snapped on surgical gloves, then pulled some floppy paper slippers over their shoes. The house was cold: the cold a thermostat wouldn't help. The Grandfather clock gonged with the hour. The kitchen area seemed undisturbed, but Turner's office and the main hall were cordoned off. The sense of death lingered everywhere. The detectives ducked under more yellow tape. Without stepping in any farther, they looked carefully around the room from the doorway.

It was still in shambles. Tiny flags poked up beside various items scattered across the floor, and numbered tags marked smaller pieces of evidence on the walls, desk, ceiling, even the lights. The room had been sprayed after Turner's body had been taken away, but the essence of death insinuated itself into everything left behind.

Kincaid quietly compared what he was seeing to the photographs and what he'd seen in the morgue. Amy had an armful of her own copies. Cautiously side-stepping the papers, pencil shafts, pieces of ripped paper and blood splatters, Kincaid walked to one side of the room. Stoically still, he stared at everything in his line of sight, equating what he saw to the pictures. Several minutes passed, and then he moved over and performed the same ritual from another spot.

"Why the perspectives, Sir?" Amy waited until each spot was vacated, then filled the place where he'd stood herself, trying to see what he saw. She jotted down questions and notes.

"I need to see everything from a different angle, to watch the scene I imagine unfolding from disparate eyes. You don't want to limit yourself to a preconceived notion or perspective. You walk around a sculpture, right? It's the same thing. Seeing what you might have missed from one side by looking at it from a number of others."

Kincaid checked his own notes against Gerbec's records, and question-marked points he found distressing. He returned to the photographs again and again: something didn't feel right.

When they were finished examining the room from various angles, Kincaid and Amy carefully moved in closer to Turner's desk, methodically scrutinizing every broken pen, every shattered pencil, used in the stabbings. No, they weren't all stabbings: there were pricks, punctures, gouges and jabs that had barely broken the skin. The pathologist's notes confirmed what Kincaid saw: on their own, none of the wounds could have killed him. Numerous punctures were bunched together like stars through a telescope, yet they didn't have the power to take his life. Some were deeper and wider than the others, but they'd all missed the major arteries. Luck, or exacting precision, like the needle marks in his lips?

This was a meticulously rendered *bleeding.* Slow and tortuous. An execution carried out over an extended period of time. Turner's life had seeped away with his blood, and someone had controlled the rate as his veins and arteries emptied. Faint chalk marks showed how the victim had been found, sprawled across the desk and his hand impaled with the letter opener. Turner's blotter caught a great deal of the blood that had dripped from the stitches in his mouth.

His nerves on fire, Kincaid leaned from side to side, flexing the muscles in his lower back, but the pain persisted. He crouched down behind Turner's chair and scanned the room. What had he been thinking in those final minutes as each pulse of his heart pushed a little more blood away and he slipped into the darkness of unconsciousness?

Amy tried to breathe normally, but she was struggling not to be sick. She'd never seen this much blood. "I can't image what he thought when he saw the needle and thread."

"Do me a favor and sit here for a minute." Kincaid turned Turner's chair towards her. She shivered and lowered herself down. "Hand out?"

"Please."

Amy stretched her arm across the desk. Trying not to touch anything, she leaned over the way Turner was positioned in the photos.

Kincaid stood behind her and to one side, precisely where he assumed the murderer must have stood when the first few stabs were delivered. He pantomimed a series of movements meant to simulate the attack. Everything looked right, but he was still troubled by the position of the visitor's chair. If the murderer had stayed behind Turner, then why was the chair so close in front? Did his attacker talk to him after Turner was *already dead*?

"Stay still, okay?"

Amy nodded, but the dried blood splattered all over the desk was making her nauseous. Kincaid moved around to the other side of the desk and reviewed Gerbec's photographs of Turner's blood-soaked body. The man's head had been turned at an awkward angle, so his chin was tucked into the crook of his elbow. Kincaid told Amy to adjust the position of her head so it matched the photos. Kincaid assumed that when Turner was released and collapsed forward, his head would have lolled over to one side or the other.

"Pretend you're passing out. Let your head fall forward."

The moment she did, her head turned slightly and rolled into the crook of her arm, the arm with the hand impaled to the desk.

Kincaid inched closer, then propped her head up so she was looking across the room at the door. He squatted down in front of the desk, pretending he was sitting in the visitor's chair. Seconds passed: he told Amy to let go. She was quick to oblige.

"His head would've lolled to the side," Kincaid explained. "The murderer had to physically move Turners head. The perp positioned him so he could sit across the desk and look right into his eyes. Gored and pierced, he would have undoubtedly bled to death sometime during the night anyway. He probably would have choked on the paper that was forced down his throat before that. The autopsy report shows there were wads of it in his stomach. So why the lips? Why the overkill? Rage? Unimaginable hatred? If it was done for a reason, what was the message?"

Amy frowned. "Maybe it was a warning? Perhaps Turner had talked about something he shouldn't have, so his mouth was shut forever? He might have said something he wasn't supposed to. Leaked information?" She looked around again. "Or maybe – maybe he'd literally been forced to eat his own words?"

"If you're right, who'd want him to do that?"

Amy thought for a moment. "One of his writers? Someone he criticized? Rejected?"

Kincaid nodded. "Sounds like a good place to start." He stared at the visitor's chair again. "I think that at some point, Sergeant, as the blood seeped away from the wounds, Turner's killer talked to him as he was dying. He leaned forward, face to face."

Amy shuddered. "He *talked* to him?"

"Scolded? Sermonized? He had a captive audience, after all. Sprawled forward, impaled, his lips sewn together. His killer told him something as Turner choked and bled to death."

Silence. The Grandfather clock suddenly gonged. Amy jumped.

Kincaid smiled. "So, Sergeant. All you have to do now is to find out what that one-way conversation was about. You'll have your motive, and probably your killer."

"Then I should have everything wrapped up around noon." She flipped her notebook closed. "Now what?"

"Now you get a chance to refill that monstrosity you call a coffee mug. Then we make one more stop before heading back to the station. I think –"

The front door opened. A woman of about sixty-five walked boldly into the foyer. Scowling.

"How did you get in? And just what do you think you're doing? More reporters? My goodness! Get out right now or I'll call the police."

Kincaid smiled, and the detectives proffered their badges. "You must be Mrs. Dempsey. I heard she was around fifty and quite good looking."

The woman blushed a bright red. Grey hair, perfect dentures, a rather non-descript dress, and a pair of comfortable loafers. She looked at the yellow tape stretched back across the den's doorway and shivered.

"Why are you here?"

"The Detective handling Mr. Turner's case fell ill and –"

"Oh my, he wasn't shot, was he?"

"Thankfully, no. Appendicitis. We've taken over the investigation. Why are *you* here?"

"*Mrs. Turner* "– she practically spat out the name – "called me a couple of days after – *after what happened* – and said she wanted me to stay part-time for a bit. She wants to be sure the house looks spic and span when she sells it." She nodded at the den. "I'm not to go in there, though, and I don't."

"Perhaps you could help us, Mrs. Dempsey?" Amy asked.

"Sure. Let me put on a kettle and we'll have tea in the kitchen, won't we?"

Donning a brightly colored apron, Mrs. Dempsey hummed as she worked and made small talk. Still the host and housekeeper, she put out a plate of cookies then poured the tea.

Kincaid leaned forward. "Do you recall if there were any unusual deliveries for Mr. Turner that week, Mrs. Dempsey? Something personal you had to sign for?"

She hesitated. "All of Mr. Turner's bulky deliveries, which were usually manuscripts, came by a courier. I knew most of them." She offered the cookies around. "I'm pretty sure there wasn't anything different that week. No. I jot them down in a little book so I don't forget." She tapped the side of her head. "It isn't quite as sharp as it used to be."

"Could we see that book," Kincaid prompted.

"Oh yes. Right away."

It was in the top drawer of the commode in the front hall. She was reading when she walked back into the kitchen. "I was right. There weren't any special deliveries that week at all. Unless I didn't write it down, but I'm pretty particular about things like that, you know." She smiled at Kincaid, a smile that might have meant something else twenty years ago.

"Pick-ups?" Amy asked, sipping her tea. "Things Mr. Turner might have been returning?"

"Not that I recall." A note caught her eye. "There was one odd thing. I saw a van parked across the street a couple of times, in front of 92, the Jefferies. But they're on vacation, like they often are."

"What color was it?"

"Dark blue, I think. Almost black. I never checked for a license number or anything."

Kincaid declined another cookie and asked the woman if she followed a particular routine.

"Certainly. I do washing on Mondays and pick up the laundry on Fridays. Wednesday's my morning for grocery shopping. Tuesday I go out in the afternoon if Mr. Turner – when Mr. Turner – needed anything. Other than cleaning and cooking."

Kincaid glanced at Amy. "So other than the van, nothing unusual happened?"

Mrs. Dempsey rechecked her date book. "Well yes, one thing, actually." She moved her finger across the page. "There was a service call a couple of days before Mr. Turner – *died*."

"About what?"

"The satellite dish. The service man came up the driveway just as I was coming in with the groceries. He held the door for me while I turned off the alarm."

Kincaid glanced at Amy. "Had you called him?"

"No."

"What did he look like?"

Frowning, Mrs. Dempsey pictured the man behind closed eyes. "Medium height and weight, I think, and long brown hair. Early thirties. He had one of those funny looking beards, a moustache and little goatee. I think he was wearing a blue shirt and pants. Oh, and his name was Lloyd, or something like that. There was a little logo on his shirt and his name was under it."

"What did the logo look like?"

"A satellite dish pointed up. Nicely colored hand stitched. Quite bright."

Amy asked what was wrong with the dish.

"Nothing."

"Then why was he here?"

"To fix it."

"But if it wasn't broken —"

"No, I mean I didn't know there was anything wrong until he showed up. That's when I tried it. He was right, there wasn't a picture. Mr. Turner wouldn't like it if he came home and the dish was out. He watched things in bed so he could fall asleep."

"Was he able to fix it?" Kincaid asked, certain of the answer. The guy probably just disconnected the main cable leading into the house. After a good look around, he simply re-connected it to bring the service back on.

"Yes. He had to check each television, so I showed him around."

And he watched her punch in the alarm code, too, Kincaid thought. He probably met Shakespeare as well. A bit of drugged steak, the key pad number, and the times the house would be empty. He had it all.

Kincaid glanced at Amy. "One other thing, Mrs. Dempsey. Did you see Mr. Turner – that night?"

The tears finally came. Shaking, she dabbed her eyes with a tissue. "Not that morning, either. He was gone before I got here. He left a note saying he'd be late. I put a casserole for him in the fridge."

Kincaid smiled graciously. "I think that just about covers it. Thanks for your time, Mrs. Dempsey. And the tea and cookies. They were delicious. Home baked, right?"

She blushed.

"We'll let ourselves out." Kincaid stopped. "What is it, Mrs. Dempsey?"

She was wringing her hands together. "I know Mr. Turner wasn't very pleasant to everyone, but for sixteen years he was always fair and honest with me, and that's all I could have asked for. So if there's anything else you might need –"

Kincaid nodded.

"I want the person caught who – who –"

He put an arm around her shoulders and gave her a warm hug.

"We will." He meant it with every bone in his body.

He pulled the front door closed behind Amy, sealing the presence of death away like a tomb. He knew Mrs. Dempsey wouldn't go near the den: the yellow tape would be a daunting "x" that would haunt her throughout the day.

A reminder. A headstone.

He'd call later, just to make sure she was okay.

*

Kincaid had Amy stop for an iced coffee at a cafe off Yonge Street that specialized in exotic blends. Despite the cool breeze that whisked between the office towers, a couple of patrons sat outside, huddled under awnings and focused on their laptops, caught in a dopamine haze. The detectives sat on bistro chairs facing the street, watching the people hurry by with their hands glued to their phones.

"You're right," Kincaid continued, picking up their conversation from the car. "The planning was intricate and well thought out. Premeditated. Methodical."

Amy pictured the grotesque blood splatters that plastered Turner's office. They'd haunt her for a long time.

"Do you think Mrs. Dempsey is a credible witness?"

"I do. Forget the dark van for now. Check out the Satellite companies. See if they've had any uniforms stolen recently."

Amy licked some chocolate pieces from the foam. "He steals some shirts to get access to the house. He walks up, goes in, and checks everything out? Awfully bold, isn't it?"

"Why not? He's dressed for the part. He has all the tools, and he's probably carrying a clipboard with Turner's name and address on some fake work sheet. Mrs. Dempsey wouldn't suspect a thing. And remember, the satellite's just a few rungs up on the old antennae. I have no idea why it's never been taken down. All he had to do was undo the main cable, and the service would be off."

"So after Mrs. Dempsey finds out there isn't a signal, she'd think he was Prince Charming."

"Exactly. She'd want to make sure the television was fixed before Turner got home. Regardless of what she said, I doubt he was a very sympathetic employer."

Two women jogged past the window. "And he caught her just as she was coming home with the groceries. They didn't talk outside."

"That's right," Amy recalled. "He helped her in."

"I'm guessing he had a phone with his tools in case he couldn't see her use the keypad. Either way, he caught the access code for the alarm system."

Amy took a long sip of coffee. She fought the urge to get some more chocolate sprinkles. Perhaps a small croissant . . .

"It gave him time for everything he needed. The alarm information, the best hiding spots, even a few minutes to let Shakespeare get to know him. He gives the dog some treats and scratches his belly. All he had to do was make sure he could spike at least one of Turner's drinks back at *The Bamboo Garden.* And if it was a busy night, that shouldn't have been too difficult. Turner goes to the bathroom and *bam!* Before he downed the amnesiacs, his killer was already heading for his house."

"And the dog?"

"A bark, maybe two, but he probably recognized our killer and his tail was a tuning fork before the back gate was open. A nice piece of GBH laced meat and poor Shakespeare pawed his last sonnet."

Amy frowned. "But why kill the dog? Why not just drug him and leave him alone?"

"Perhaps he wasn't sure if he calculated the dose correctly. He – or she – didn't want the dog coming around when his master needed him the most. And the killer wouldn't have known when Turner would get home. Or how long the bleeding would take."

There was a more likely thought hanging in the air. Amy didn't have to ask.

He probably just wanted the dog to suffer. Slowly. Painfully.

Chapter Seven

Meredith House, one of the city's oldest and most prestigious publishers, dominated a cluster of office complexes at the bottom of Bay Street, the key avenue in the financial district on the edge of Lake Ontario. Rising up in successive layers of steel and opaque glass, the looming tower rippled reflections of the nearby buildings. Its foreboding size made everything seem congested and closed in – a claustrophobic's nightmare. Kincaid had Amy double-park in front. A cabby zoomed by, the driver swearing in a middle-eastern dialect.

Huge tinted glass doors swung open automatically. The detectives stopped by a security guard seated at a mammoth onyx console in the center of the cavernous foyer. The man signed a courier's delivery sheet, answered a phone, started to jot down a note, then reached for a binder. Kincaid grabbed his wrist, bent it back toward his forearm, and held up his badge again. Wincing, the guard apologized. He asked Amy politely if she'd sign in, then directed her to a bank of elevators across the hall.

"And is that your car?" the guard asked, pointing. It had *unmarked* written all over it.

"It is."

"Well it can't stay there. It's a 'no parking zone."

Kincaid laid his hand heavily on the guard's shoulder and checked his lapel badge. "I'm pretty confident you'll make sure nothing happens to it, Wayne."

Wayne nodded.

Snaking through a bustling tide of impatient, well-dressed men and women, the detectives weaved their way across the foyer: Kincaid felt like a spawning salmon trying to swim upstream. Huge pine trees grew in clusters in each corner of the foyer. They were manicured, tailored, sculpted, and constantly weeded out: just like the people rushing past.

It was a brisk ascent to the twenty fifth floor. An armed security guard met them as they stepped out, proffering *another* clipboard. He escorted them to a central reception area, identified them to one of the perfectly coifed women behind the counter, then mechanically returned to his post. Offering a perfunctory smile, the woman made a quick call, then led the detectives through a labyrinth of small offices and cubicles to the farthest corner of the floor. She stopped in front of a massive wooden door that was intricately carved like an antique bookcase, knocked lightly, then ushered them in. She extended a cursory introduction and softly closed the door behind her.

Spacious and well appointed, the office was accentuated by a large, solid oak desk and matching credenza. There was a black leather couch against the far wall, a glass coffee table with a sculpted marble base, and two luxurious high-backed matching leather chairs. Floor to ceiling bookcases on the opposite wall were crammed with countless volumes. One shelf had weakened with the perpetual stress and bowed slightly in the middle. The window behind the desk stretched from one side of the room to the other, offering a panoramic view of the lake and Island Airport. Pleasure craft crisscrossed the waves.

The woman behind the desk didn't look up. Scribbling furiously, she motioned to the chairs with a hurried wave. She signed the page with a flourish, shuffled a scattered array of papers together, then conspicuously turned them over. She purposefully glanced at her watch before looking at Kincaid.

"How can I help you, Detective –"

"Kincaid."

"Yes. So you're MacKenzie."

"*Sergeant* MacKenzie." Amy opened her notebook.

The woman offered a bored sigh. Gail Meredith was probably in her late forties, although she obviously took great pains to keep time's vitriolic violations at bay in an effort to appear a decade younger. She'd succeeded – so had her surgeon's scalpel. Accentuated with piercing blue eyes, a small nose, thin lips, and perfect teeth, her oval face was framed by short black hair that was cut once a week. Thin and defined, she had the body shape and tone of an aerobics disciple. She didn't diet, just ate right, and was undoubtedly aware of all the things detrimental to her optimal state of health. This was a woman you'd be wary to misjudge. A classic Type A, thriving on stress.

Ms. Meredith wore a long sleeveless dress that was cut becomingly low, and more bracelets than Kincaid could count dangled from her wrists. She bought her clothes for the label, but practically anything she wore would have been flattering. Efficient and calculating, she chose her closest friends for who they were and what they could do for her.

Gail Meredith leaned back and almost disappeared into the deep leather folds of her chair. She patiently unwrapped a slender cigar.

"A *triangulo.* Hand rolled in Greece," she explained, lighting her own. "Sun cured and perfectly fermented."

She offered one to Kincaid: his denial seemed to displease her. She'd assumed he would have shared her peccadillo for fine cigars. He was handsome, well-built, and from what she'd heard, athletic and intelligent. *What else would they share, then?* An old ferry left a dock far below for a trip to the little islands. Its melancholy foghorn drifted between the buildings like a ghost's mournful lament.

"I assume you're here about Devlin Turner?"

"We are."

"Horrible business, really." She blew a breathful of smoke toward the ceiling. "But I've already spoken to someone, haven't I? A smaller man. And not nearly as attractive."

"You did," Kincaid acknowledged. "Unfortunately, Detective Gerbec's been hospitalized, so we need to go over a few things with you."

Meredith shook her head impudently. "Well, if the police took a more strenuous role in ridding the streets of illegal firearms, things like this wouldn't happen."

Kincaid's confusion only lasted a moment. "Our colleague was felled by appendicitis, not a bullet."

"Oh." *Was she relieved or not?* Another time check. She made sure Kincaid knew this was an unwanted intrusion.

"Well, I told him everything I could. I didn't know Turner on a personal basis. He was a literary agent, a business associate."

Amy noted the denial. "What was he like?"

It was the first time Meredith looked at Amy. "A pompous ass. Vulgar and decidedly opinionated for someone with his shortcomings. However –"

"Yes?"

"He had a special knack for sluicing through the sludge and finding nuggets worth keeping."

Kincaid asked, "Then in your estimation, he was a good literary agent?"

"No. He was one of the best. Turner had a penchant for hitting great manuscripts after they'd been rejected numerous times. He possessed a skill most agents don't: he had an eye for *potential*. What could *be*. With the right editor, agent and ghost writer."

"And that's odd?"

Meredith shrugged and tapped some ash into a glass tray, her bracelets jangling. "Sometimes you get lucky. A gut feeling about a book or author. A few minor changes here and there, perhaps a larger one that makes the whole thing more palatable, some professional editing, and voila! It's a hit. Or, no matter what you do, it flops. Turner definitely had more than his share of phoenixes that rose from the ashes. That's why I bought what he sold. He was willing to take a chance on a book other agents wouldn't touch, and more often than not he was very successful. Sometimes a pick was wrong and got blown out of the water, but those were so rare they didn't matter in the grand scheme of things."

Smoke circled upward. Meredith smiled: Amy obviously didn't like the scent. Or *her*. Perhaps she could play with Kincaid for a while. Good shape, nice hands . . .

"Everything is cyclical, Detective. Writers flocked to him because of his track record. And the more they did, the more he sniffed out those future bestsellers other agents had rejected."

"Such as?"

Several lights twinkled on her console. Another look at her watch. "Brian McGuinty's *The Last Violent Storm,* Shiela Pooroo's *A Wife From Mumbai.* And his most recent find was *Diary of a Stalker.*"

Kincaid frowned.

"The release date isn't until May. It's going to scare the proverbial shit out of people."

"Who's the author?"

"Charles K. Tomlinson. Another newbie. He'd been rejected so many times I'm surprised he kept sending it out. We're ready to start a second printing before it's even hit the stores. He signed a two book deal, with an option for a third. It needed a great deal of work. When Turner's gang of editors and writers were finished, you'd never recognize it. Rather like "To Kill a Mockingbird." That's Turner to a "T." He saw the book's potential, and ended up with another blockbuster. He's pathologically prophetic. Well, *was*."

Kincaid imagined invisible little cash registers floating above the publisher's head. *Ca-ching. Ca-ching.* If only some of the mega-dollars that came with those contracts went to reading programs for the children he worked with, like Ryan . . .   But money never seemed to trickle down to the places it was desperately needed. Special reading assistants in schools, or audio books for the blind.

"So the majority of Turner's successes came from books previously rejected?"

"Definitely. When he sent us something, we accepted it, even if it was from an unknown author. If we vacillated, Turner didn't have any qualms about taking his work elsewhere."

Amy checked her notes. "Turner brought most of his work to you, but he represented writers who worked for other publishers, right?"

Meredith exhaled a long plume of smoke. "Like I said, Turner was a sports agent, saddled with a stable full of established mega-players and an up-and-coming corral of stars. He always brought his biggest clients to us first. Like Ian Nuraki. We invariably had first right of refusal, since Ian only dealt with one book at a time."

"Nuraki?"

"Really, Detective," Meredith scoffed. "I can't believe you've never heard of one of the most prolific and commercially successful writers of our time. And *yes*, it's a pseudonym, and *no* I don't know who he is. Turner owned him."

Kincaid shrugged. In fact, he had. He'd read one of Nuraki's books several years earlier and found it wanting. Not one to judge too hastily, he'd read two more. The books weren't the type to leave an indelible impression on the soul: mainstream historical romances, a couple of morbid vampire books, standard dramas and coming-of-age stories, and a smattering of celebrity confessionals. The man obviously had a very unique perspective and a provocative way with words, and he could pen just about any genre. He was certainly quite a cut above what was normally stacked with the other prosaic bestsellers who churned out cardboard copies of their other books twice a year. You could see it beneath his lines: he could write with an evolved and distinctive literary style. The potential was there to be one of the few true artists, but Nuraki chose to walk a different path. He stayed a commercial writer who wrote successful mass market fiction. Money makers made into movies.

"I understand you had an appointment with Turner the day he died."

A pause. "Yes, you're right. We'd scheduled lunch, but he didn't show."

"You didn't follow up with him?"

"Hardly. I assumed something had come up and he forgot to text me."

Kincaid didn't think Gail Meredith was someone used to being rejected. "Where were your lunch reservations?"

"Really, I don't think —" She watched his eyes. "The Four Seasons."

Kincaid jotted something down. "Did you have any special contractual agreement with Turner?"

"Why?"

Kincaid was growing weary with her defensiveness. The nerves in his spine cried out for another painkiller. He switched gears. "We've been told you receive a hefty amount of hate mail."

The question caught her off-balance. "Occupational hazard."

"We're going to need a list of the people who've threatened you over the last two years."

"You're joking! That's absurd." One look confirmed he wasn't. "You mean hate mail, dead flowers, midnight calls, that type of thing?"

"Everything."

"I can understand why you might want to look into Turner's files, but what difference does it make who *my* enemies are?"

"Because Turner worked with many writers you publish. And for every one you did, there's probably hundreds you rejected, right?"

She nodded irritably. "You're assuming Turner was murdered by someone he had business dealings with?"

Amy said, "If someone hated Turner enough to kill him, they could easily have harbored a great deal of resentment to you as well. If we can compare your records with Turner's, we might find a link."

Meredith's bracelets jangled. She made a little peaked chapel with her fingers. "Do you have any idea what you're asking?"

Kincaid spoke slowly and evenly. "You maintain a security company on a retainer. You've got dressed security in the foyer and at the desk in the hallway. I saw two hire-a-cop plainclothes guys in the lobby. You also have an internal security camera system second to none. We signed in twice, you've got fiber optic cameras outside your door" – he glanced at the bookcases – "and in the corners of your office. That sounds a bit obsessive for someone who doesn't harbor any safety concerns."

Meredith glared at the detectives, then stabbed her cigar out in the ashtray.

"The volume of hate mail isn't the issue: it gets worse all the time. We might get a hundred letters, we might get a thousand: that's not the point. We could get just one. There are a lot of disturbed people in the world. Lone wolves." She pretended her hand was a gun and pointed it at Amy. "All it takes is one asshole and one shot."

A valid point.

"I don't like to take chances. We protect ourselves because in this day and age, we have to. Turner found that out, didn't he?"

Kincaid watched her eyes. "We need a list of all the people who've sent you and your agency threatening communications over the past twenty four months. It might be inconvenient, but don't make this any more difficult than it has to be."

"You won't get a file – it will be a book."

She turned toward her credenza and poured herself a fresh brewed expresso. She didn't offer one to her guests.

"Are you familiar with the publishing industry at all, Detective?"

"Enlighten me," he answered quietly.

The publisher watched the steam curl into the air. "No, I can't. I have a business to run. And the longer I spend with you the less work my company produces. 'Time being money' is particularly evident in my industry. Did you get all that Ms.-"

"*Sergeant* MacKenzie. I did."

Meredith reached across her desk for a pen in her caddy. Kincaid envisioned an image of Turner impaled to his desk. *Had it been meant to show some form of crucifixion?* Meredith scribbled a name on the back of a business card and slipped it across the desk.

"Leeanne Davidivitch. We have a department that deals with unanswered queries, unsolicited proposals, and rejections. Ms. Davidivitch runs it. If anyone can help, she can."

"Does she keep records?"

"Not many and not for long," she admitted coldly. Meredith glanced deliberately at her watch and started packing up the files scattered across her desk.

Kincaid waited. "There's a 'but' in there."

Meredith was fixated on something on her desk. "But, she keeps the *real* hate mail. Not just someone blowing off steam because they're sad or disappointed. The threatening ones. From the people who contact us again and again. The ones who write threatening letters after they're rejected. Some are pretty hostile and aggressive. Vindictive. Personal. Ms. Davidivitch keeps those."

"Why?"

"So we don't read what they send the next time. *Return to Sender.* Eventually, they give up. If not, we keep what's sent for our legal department. So far, we haven't had a problem with anyone following through on their threats. But I don't want to be the first one who does."

"The second," Kincaid said softly, staring into her eyes.

"Yes, the second. *If* you're right and *if* it was a rejected author who killed Turner. Those are two big *ifs*, Detective."

"How long will it take to put the information together?"

"I'll call her right now. Perhaps she can have something in a couple of days."

"We need it sooner."

Meredith smiled a syrupy smile that had *pushy bastard* written all over it. She knew there was no use in prolonging the debate.

"How about we try for some time midmorning or early afternoon? Will *that* help?" Her eyes told him she didn't care if it did.

"Yes, thank you. Tell me something, though."

She raised her eyebrows like an insolent child.

"Turner seems to have had a penchant for writing personal rejections back to authors." He paused. "You look surprised."

"I am. That would take a great deal of extra time, which Turner didn't have much of."

"So, why make it personal? Why not use a form letter?"

She finished her coffee. "Maybe something caught his eye and he didn't want to burn the proverbial bridges. Perhaps he sensed the effort that had been put into the proposal and was being kind. Although I can't see Turner being kind." Bracelets jangled.

"But then he'd write something positive. He wouldn't write an aggressive rejection back."

"No. It would be like rubbing salt in a wound . . . you'd be asking for trouble. Why? What aren't you telling me?"

"From what we've seen, many of Devlin Turner's rejections were not only critical, but caustic and hostile as well. Hateful, and filled with hubris."

Meredith stiffened slightly.

"Our colleague found a folder in Turner's files that contained copies of personal rejections. He kept most of the hate mail he received as well."

Meredith stood up. Amy kept her notebook open and didn't move.

"I appreciate your cooperation," Kincaid said. "And your time. There's just one other thing."

"Yes?" she replied peevishly, crossing her arms over her chest.

"Did you have a personal relationship with Mr. Turner?"

"That's none of your business, Detective," she answered coldly.

"Actually, it is."

Smiling placatingly, she returned his stare. "No, I didn't. We worked together. That's all."

The moment Kincaid and MacKenzie rose to leave, she flipped her notes back over and started punching a series of numbers into her phone. Her secretary let the officers pass, then hurried into the office. Gail Meredith was already barking out instructions before they'd stepped into the hall. Her eyes burned a hole in their backs.

Chapter Eight

The stress of the first day back had been more than Kincaid expected. Sifting through the files, the morgue, the cat and mouse game at *Meredith House*, the downtown traffic, the interviews: his whole body hurt and he needed to rest. He'd arranged to meet Amy in the morning. He knew she'd report to Davis and he should have gone straight home, but he decided to make one more stop he knew would assuage the pain and make him feel better.

Veering off the Parkway, Kincaid wound his way deeper into a cluttered labyrinth of tree-lined streets that fanned out from Yonge and Eglinton. The viral plague of cars and buses gradually became a memory. He glanced up admiringly at the beautiful old houses. Had it really been almost half a year since he'd driven here? The modest homes were pleasantly appointed and nicely kept but certainly not ostentatious, with narrow rectangles of front lawns, stone planters thick with foliage, and cobbled driveways beaten beige by the sun.

Driving beneath a canopy of branches, Kincaid wistfully wondered what it would have been like to live here. *With Stephanie.* The place they'd looked at was just two streets over. To share a family, a life, their dreams and love? To suffer the pangs and beauty of *belonging* and *being?* But even then – *after what happened* – she didn't want to live – couldn't live – with the thought of him leaving in the morning and never coming back. When he was honest with himself, he knew that wasn't the only reason they hadn't stayed together. Times noose tightened another notch. One small rupture, one little coagulated clot that broke free from an artery. It wasn't just a metaphor: it was his reality. Dr. Chadpur's sharp warning hung in the air like a guillotine blade. *We'll know better in a week.* A promise and a hope. And a sentence, too.

The street narrowed with parked cars. A left and a short right brought him to the end of a cul-de-sac and a thin, two-story house that backed onto a ravine. Nothing had changed, which made him smile. The wood shutters, open just a slit; the screened in side porch; the firewood neatly stacked drying for the winter; not a twig or an errant pine cone disrupting the perfect symmetry of the lawn. The driveway was framed with impatiens of alternating shades of red and pink. Two large urns edged the stairs, leaking broad leafed ferns down the steps.

Kincaid had known Rebecca Potterdam for over half his life. Originally from Cardiff, her family immigrated to Canada shortly after the War. Settling in Ottawa, Rebecca's father, Arthur, a pressman, quickly found work with a small daily newspaper. But when a larger challenge beckoned, Arthur moved his family here to this brick two-story in a quaint residential district in Toronto's core.

Kincaid reached for the doorbell and wondered if the neighbors knew who lived behind the row of cedars that edged the front curb. Probably not. Rebecca Potterdam was one of the writers who, once discovered, are best known for their obscurity. She'd published eight novels to date, three non-fiction books, a host of magazine articles, and an anthology of inspirational poetry back in a time when people read those types of things, instead of suffocating themselves on anything digital. Despite her artistic success, Rebecca never made a name for herself in the world of mainstream fiction. She never wanted to: she was a literary writer, not a commercial one. She refused to write for the mass market, foregoing money and fame for the integrity of her art.

He rang the bell, smiling through the narrow side window as a shape drifted down the hall. Even through cut glass he could see the years continued to be kind to Rebecca. Sixty-six, she'd just started wearing glasses and had the hearing of a fox. She kept her gray hair short and simple because she couldn't be bothered playing with trendy styles. Slight and compact, she was on her way to becoming matronly. Her face was round and lightly wrinkled, which made her smile that much more radiant. Over the last few years she'd grown accustomed to denim, and rarely wore anything other than faded jeans and an oversized shirt with the sleeves casually rolled up.

She looked a touch listless when she opened the door, but her eyes brightened when they settled on Kincaid. He wrapped her warmly in his arms, and for just a moment, all the pain, all the fear and worry, were gone. Their embrace deepened as they traded excited whispers. Neither wanted to let the other go, but Rebecca, sniffling back contented tears, finally pulled away. She studied her old friend with the appraising eyes of a partisan grandmother. She put a hand to his chest.

"It's been so long, K."

"Way too long."

"You don't look as bad as I imagined." She wagged a gnarled finger. "Considering."

"You look absolutely wonderful."

"How's little Ryan doing?"

There was a sparkle of sadness in Kincaid's eyes. "He's brave. You'd be proud of him."

"He's always in my prayers."

Her smile fought a frown and she pushed the tears away. She squeezed his arm and ushered him into her study, quickly clearing a stack of papers from a Queen Anne's chair. Kincaid was overwhelmed with a soothing feeling of reassuring consistency. He felt more relaxed than he had in ages. The study had the slightly musty smell of too many old books crammed too tightly together that weren't dusted often enough. Her desk was so cluttered Kincaid couldn't tell the color of the grain. A laptop rose up from the confusion, teetering on the brink of a mountain of files and papers like lava on the edge of a simmering volcano. A white-veined vine crept along the top shelf of the bookcases, and a pair of clocks that framed thick tomes on the next shelf showed two completely different times.

Rebecca had apparently just turned off the computer, and Adolphus, her sleek, tan tabby, was curled up on the printer, savoring its warmth. She shooed him away. He purred indignantly. After a back-arching stretch and an unhurried paw-lick, Adolphus finally moved.

"I've just put the kettle on. You'll have tea, won't you?"

"Please." *And some homemade biscuits or cookies?*

"And some homemade biscuits or cookies?"

"Wonderful."

Rebecca rolled back a sleeve that wouldn't stay put. She scurried back into the study a few moments later while the water boiled, her face beaming. *A Godmother's love.*

"So. Is Stephanie back in your life? Is that why you called earlier? I *knew* you two couldn't stay apart. I've never seen —"

Kincaid shook his head. His eyes had the look of the very last puppy who'd spend the weekend alone at the pound.

Damn, Rebecca whispered. The wagging finger was back. "You're not getting any younger, K. One day you're going to wake up and the only thing you'll see in your mirror is your own face. Have you heard from her lately?"

"No."

"It's been awhile, then."

Not long enough for anything to heal.

"I saw her picture on the news about a month ago," Rebecca recalled. "She was talking about the Commonwealth Games. Evidently she's taking a hiatus from coaching. Has her own firm, you know. I thought you might have –"

"We haven't." An uncomfortable silence, like sitting through a drunken toastmaster's speech. "She was helping some kids on the junior team prepare for the nationals. She's such an inspirational leader."

"You follow her career but don't keep in touch. I see."

Rebecca promised Stephanie she wouldn't tell Kincaid when she called. And she did – often. It was a frustrating burden. She disappeared into the kitchen, checked the kettle, rumbled around for some cups, then settled in a chair beside him. A wistful smile. She wanted him to stay a week so they could catch up on everything that had happened during the whirlwind that was the last few months, but he'd come on business and time was short. *Time was short* – God, that sounded horrible. She blinked away a tear.

"If it's not love, then how can an old woman help the city's top detective? You said it was work related, about being a writer. We've talked about my career for ages. Inspiration, the muse, research, writer's block. All those things."

"I spoke to someone in the publishing industry today. I'd like to verify the accuracy of their information."

"The veracity?"

"Okay."

"Go on."

"I'm working on a murder investigation involving a literary agent."

Rebecca's hand went to her throat. "Oh my dear. Devlin Turner?"

Kincaid nodded.

"Lord. I heard it was quite gruesome. Apparently he wasn't just killed – he – was tortured."

"So much for keeping secrets internal. Did you know him?"

"I knew *of* him, since he was such a well-known face in the industry. I saw him at a few writers' conferences. Not many more successful agents, I can tell you that. But we never met personally. He does – well *did* – a lot of work with Gail, the publisher over at Meredith House. Two peas in a pod."

"That's who I spoke with."

Rebecca seemed surprised. "No scratches? A hard woman, that one. Not one of your more social beings. I'm glad I've never worked with her directly."

"Why?"

"Too much pressure. The bottom line is all that matters for her. She's highly opinionated, aggressive, and pedantic. Never genuine."

Kincaid nodded. The kettle rolled to a boil, whistling. When Rebecca returned with their tea and cookies she was still frowning. She slapped his hand away from the plate. "Wait until I put it down. You think one of Turner's clients might be involved, don't you?"

Erudite, intelligent, intuitive – Rebecca had it all.

"It's possible. I was hoping for a crash course so I can tailor my questions better. And where to ask them. I need to know why someone would want to kill a literary agent."

Rebecca's frown melted and the lines of her face blurred into a featureless mask. She poured their tea, filling the tiny room with the sweet scent of chamomile. "What are your usual motives for murder?"

"Jealousy. Greed. Revenge. Hatred. Retribution. And always, love."

"Most authors would add *ego* to that list." She glanced at the rows of spines on her shelves. Kincaid caught her before she drifted off.

"What?"

"They never know, do they?" she said quietly, sipping her tea. "Editors. Agents. Publishers. The power they wield, unconsciously or not. They never know where their responses to queries go once they fire them off to the slush pile in the mail room. They have no idea who's on the receiving end of their reply. Someone trying their damnedest to break into the industry? Or – "

"Or?"

"Someone with just a teeny bit of hope left, someone on the brink, ready to slip into the abyss of a complete emotional breakdown. One writer might not care. But to the next one, that rejection could be the proverbial straw that broke the camel's back. The one that crushes whatever hope he or she had left, whatever sense of meaning they tried so desperately to maintain. The ultimate denial."

She stopped staring at the books and gestured toward Kincaid's notepad with an arthritic finger. "Yes. Put ego down. And desperation. Meaninglessness. You've been rejected and life's over. Could a rejection kill? Could betrayal push someone to murder?"

"Indubitably."

Kincaid nibbled and smiled.

"Yes, a touch of cinnamon, just for you."

Rebecca never forgot a thing. She chewed over a thought and cookie. "How many people at Meredith House go home never knowing who they sent that last rejection to? Was it someone's first, or their fifty-first? Do they ever think of how meaningless – *or murderous* – it may be? How it might suffocate all of a writer's hopes and dreams?" She watched Adolphus lick a paw.

Kincaid thought about the pieces of paper jammed into Turner's mouth. "How does it feel to write for a living?"

"Most writers don't actually make a living," his godmother said sadly.

Rebecca tore a loose thread from the bottom of her sleeve. She seemed older when she wasn't smiling. Had this been a good idea? Kincaid wondered. Perhaps he was helping her dredge up memories she'd rather have left buried.

"I've just finished my very first book. What happens now?"

"You put it in a box, stuff it under your bed, and forget about it."

"Seriously?"

"Seriously." She corrected herself. "Well, that's what most people should do."

Kincaid raised a questioning eyebrow.

"Yes. And it's still there." She nibbled a cookie. "Let's pretend you honestly believe this is the one; a strong, stylistically written, timely drama perfectly edited you're certain should be published."

"Okay."

"First you write a query letter, which basically outlines the plot, characters, and a brief synopsis of your work. It's a glorified sales pitch, which tells the editor, publisher or agent whether or not you can string a couple of sentences together, let alone a novel."

"How do I know who to send it to?"

"There are standard references, like the Literary Market Place, that lists publishers and the types of books they represent. Basic requirements, needs, and so forth. There are cross-referenced sources on the Internet as well, but it takes some research. Cookie?"

"No thanks."

"Right. You're thin as a rake. Eat. I've already packed you a doggy bag."

"Okay. One more."

"Two."

"Does everyone do that?"

She grinned. "Oh my, not nearly enough. Most writers just pick a few publishers they've heard of and pop off a proposal. K? K, are you all right?"

"Just tired. It's been a long first day back."

"Then go home. Or better yet, stay in the guest room. We'll finish this after you rest."

"Thanks, but –"

"But you don't have time. I know." She shook her head *and* her finger.

"What happens then?"

"Their query sits on the bottom of an ever expanding slush pile, until a first reader – or a low-level editor, depending on the size of the House – finally takes a quick look. It's eventually returned or thrown out. Publishers hate it when writers don't follow submission guidelines. It's irritating and time-consuming to wade through a few hundred queries about poetry collections when all you deal with are coffee table editions of art books."

Kincaid carefully put down his cup to hide the tremor.

And then everything went black.

Chapter Nine

Seattle

High on blood, he was pacing again, like a lion after a fresh kill. Wanting more. Smelling more. *Needing* more.

Dieter Vollger. The man you saw everywhere but never remembered, the man you passed by all the time but never noticed. Oh, but *he* remembered *you*.

A living mug shot. Scruffy, like he always slept rough, legs pockmarked by bed sores or lice. If he worked it was something menial that never lasted. He'd fight or come in on meth or fuck a co-worker's wife or daughter. He was tall and rakishly thin, so he walked slightly stooped. Pursed lips, and eyes eerily colorless. His hair was too long, unkempt and dirty, and a scraggly, home-stitched scar joined his thick eyebrows together. He'd always been ashamed of the large, deep-red birthmark that rippled down the side of his neck to his shoulder like a pinched artery. It was a blemish that defined him and he hated it. *Goddamn birthmark.*

He stopped pacing and stared out the window of the squalid boardinghouse room, watching the morning light peel the lingering darkness from the buildings across the road. There was a pawnbroker's shop, an all-night check cashing outlet, a pizza place that laundered money, and another tenement apartment just like his, its neon sign pulsing behind last night's rain. The stores were covered with graffiti, thick steel bars and aluminum shutters.

Reeking of a thousand transient lives, his room defined sordid emptiness, just like all the others, two jail cells wide and barely as long, right over the dumpster. Shadeless lamps on each of the mismatched end tables, but only one worked. A chair, a table with folded cardboard tucked under two of its legs so it wouldn't tip over, a bare light fixture in the ceiling. A washbasin and toilet were separated from the rest of the room by a threadbare curtain. A cracked mirror made it hard to shave. There was a large binder on the bed, filled with partially written stories, plots, queries and proposals. And his manuscript. Newspapers were scattered across pillows most people would be afraid to touch. He flipped through the binder until he found the page he wanted, then walked back to the sink.

Dieter reeked of gasoline, ash, burnt flesh, blood. But it was a *nice* stench, a cologne he'd worn before. Anxious and manic, Dieter Vollger knew the only bad thing was that the night had ended too quickly, like when he came in his pants as a tired stripper gave him a lap dance. So much planning: stalking, learning the man's routine, memorizing the route he always took home, thinking he was safe. Never knowing he was being watched. None of them did.

He splashed cold water on his face. Blood swirled around the drain. The knots on the piano wire had cut his hands pretty deeply. He wiped his face and neck, then dried the rest of the blood from his pants. Bedside, Dieter smoothed out the letter. It was from Roland Steinberg, associate editor at *The Pacific Publishing House.* A taxi ride away from Dieter's tenement slum but another world entirely, a haunting, beautiful place where you could see the waves break against the massive stone pillars that guarded the driftwood-strewn beach, or watch the sunlight glint off the towering Space Needle that dominated the horizon.

But not for Roland Steinberg. Not anymore.

Dear Writer;

Thank you for your recent submission, but it's not for us. Frankly, it's probably not for any major house. You might try having an experienced proofreader go over the manuscript with you. Your local library can point you in the right direction. I'm afraid this book, as it stands, isn't a commercially viable product. I wish I had better news. Good luck elsewhere.

> *Sincerely,*
> *Roland Steinberg*

Dear Writer. Not even his fucking name. Turning, the crack in the mirror broke his face in half. *Sincerely.* The word tore into Dieter's brain like a pick axe. *Your book isn't a commercially viable product.* Neither are you, Dieter grimaced. He slammed the mirror with his fist. The glass splintered in spider veins, turning his image into a jagged kaleidoscope. *God-damn fucking birthmark.* At least Roland would never write another rejection.

Dieter Vollger closed his eyes and let the last few hours rip through his mind, feeling their edges cut through his thoughts once more.

*

Roland Steinberg lived in a small town an hour and a half northeast of Seattle's principal business district. It wasn't so much a town as a collection of commuter homes clustered around stores and artist's shops. The drive was long, but Roland didn't mind, especially now, just before the trees started to change, when it wasn't too cold and it wasn't too hot and a mellow breeze blew off the Pacific. And especially since he'd bought a friend's customized one hundredth anniversary limited edition Harley. Except for Roland, everything on the bike was polished chrome.

The wind gently puffed out his leather jacket and the setting sun dappled off his visor. Once he reached the city limits the main freeway turned north toward the Canadian border. Roland veered east and picked up a smaller, less traveled county highway. Whoever designed it had motorcycles in mind. The road twisted and turned through a tapestry of softly rolling hills, slowly weaving its way through a mosaic of farms, open fields, and trees that canopied over the road. It was a beautiful drive that let him clear his mind and leave his work behind. After about twenty minutes the road forked, branching off to the left and right. Although he could go either way, Roland leaned right and followed the road down a slow, curving decline that led him into his little hamlet's center.

Dieter knew Roland always turned right: he'd watched him do it enough times. About a hundred and fifty yards before the first bend was a speed limit sign that warned unprepared drivers to slow down. Fifty yards farther at the first major curve was one of those yellow signs embossed with a squiggly line that warned of constant twists and turns ahead. Just off the shoulder on the opposite side of the road stood a tall, majestic ash.

Dieter had lashed the piano wire around the tree, stretched it out, and tied its end tightly around the sign's metal pole. He went back to the ash tree and yanked the wire until it bit into the bark. The cut was deep enough Dieter could feel it in the dark if Roland was late and the sun had already dipped below the tree branches.

He'd double-checked the wire's height in the middle of the road, ensuring it was within an inch of his painstaking calculations. He let the wire fall to the ground and let out some slack, just in case another driver came around the bend first. A watch check. *What the shit was . . .*

And then Dieter heard the unmistakable sound of the Harley echo through the woods. The bike roared toward the fork in the road. Feeling the groove, Dieter yanked the wire up into place and quickly wound it around the tree's thick trunk. He crunched down in the tall weeds that covered the road's edge, and waited. Smiling. *Dear writer . . .*

Leaning hard into the corner, Roland came out of the first turn, the Harley rumbling, his jacket ballooning with the breeze. He never saw the sunlight glinting off the wire, never even felt it touch his skin before it sliced through his neck. It was the strangest feeling, the oddest perception he'd ever had. One minute he was *here*, and in the next he was *here and there*, watching himself tumble down the road in a haze of sparks and ripping leather and flying chrome. Minutes lengthened into hours, yet at the same time, everything was compressed into micro seconds.

Dieter watched it all in slow motion. The bike drove on for several yards, then toppled onto its side, pinning Roland's leg to the road. The bike skidded along, twisting and turning in a shower of glowing embers before it ground to a halt in the stones on the far shoulder. The air smelled of burnt leather and scorched metal. The back wheel kept spinning. Roland's helmet, the visor still down, rolled after the bike like a forgotten afterthought, finally coming to rest when it knocked against the handlebars. Dripping gas ignited and the bike exploded into a burning ball of flesh and metal. Flames shot everywhere. Smoke curled up into the trees.

Dieter coiled the wire up as fast as he could. There was a patch of blood in the middle where it had neatly severed Roland's head. He walked over to the Harley's bonfire, careful not to get too close in case there was another explosion. He kicked the helmet away from the handlebars, carefully picked it up, then pushed the visor open and looked inside. The man's eyes were still open. Dieter had waited so long for his moment. He stared into the helmet, wondering if Mr. Roland Steinberg knew what had hit him. Had he felt the wire slice through his neck? Had he any sensation at all of his head leaving his body? Dieter hoped so. With all his heart.

And then he saw what he'd been waiting to see. He was sure Steinberg's eyes moved for the briefest of seconds. Did he realize it was his own body that was making the flames dance? The stench of smoke and burning flesh was everywhere, thickening and wrapping itself around the trees. Smiling, Dieter made sure the visor was still up, then tossed the helmet into the roaring fire.

Was that a scream? He wasn't sure. But he'd read your brain could still process things several minutes after your heart stopped.

Was *that one* a scream?

All he could do was hope.

*

Sifting through the articles strewn across the bed, Dieter re-read one he'd printed off the Web. He'd learned about the Internet the last time he was inside. Blogs, twitter, Facebook, chatrooms – they were all superb barometers of people's feelings and agendas, their secrets and fears. And the best thing about it was that no matter how demented you were, you could always find a twin in cyberspace just as abnormal and dysfunctional. Dieter Vollger was no exception.

Numerous sites were devoted to disgruntled writers, literary wannabees who'd been rejected again and again, only to see lesser works by mainstream names published month after month. People who'd endured the waiting time, the sense of failure, the debilitating lack of funds they sacrificed in pursuit of their dreams, the mailboxes stuffed with rejection letters and returned manuscripts. The writers who didn't fit into the 'diverse' or 'special categories' the industry needed to see. All with an axe to grind – a very sharp axe many of them wanted to bury in a publisher or agent's face.

Today wasn't any different. The world of desperate 'authors' needing to see their name in print, by any means – like using self-publishers, vanity presses, online sites, or even simply paying to 'publish' their book on their own – was still whirling with the latest news about the grisly murder in Toronto. The tortured agent and the mutilated dog. Although the police tried to be uncommunicative about the investigation, the buzz on the Web confirmed the victim was indeed Devlin Turner, a high priced and celebrated agent for the largest publishing house in the city. Dieter searched through his notes, beamed, then sneered. He flicked his knife open and sliced one of the more graphic and morbid articles about the murder from a copy of the *Star*.

Devlin Turner, one of Toronto's most influential literary agents, was brutally murdered in his home last night. Apparently nothing was missing, so the police have ruled out burglary as a motive. Unconfirmed reports indicate Mr. Turner suffered an extremely violent death. What was left of the agent's bloodied and punctured body was found Thursday morning by his housekeeper . . .

Dieter was impressed. He skipped to a related article. *Inside sources say Devlin Turner's lips had been sewn together. His faithful Collie, Shakespeare, was left hanging from a tree.*

What a nice touch, Dieter thought, shivering and hardening in his pants. He tossed the articles aside, then scanned through his binder until he found the letter he was looking for. A rejection he'd memorized. It was neatly folded and taped on its own page. The words of contempt froze in his mind, still stinging like a scorpion on his eye after all this time. The signature was personal and refined. He forgot what they called old fancy writing. Something '*graphe*'. *Handgraphie?*

Dear Mr. Vulgar;

The writing in your query letter is so utterly pathetic I couldn't possibly stomach reading so much as a line of your manuscript. Give up your aspirations for a writing career and do something you might be capable of, perhaps a shit sifter, like they used in London sewers during the1850's. Do they have a Zoo in Seattle? A circus? Try those first, and use the pages of your book as scoops. I'm glad to see your American tax dollars are just as useless as ours tend to be during your incarceration and rehabilitation. Perhaps we should simply buy more rope for the inmates.

Quite impatiently,
Devlin Turner

Dieter smiled. He closed his eyes and watched Roland Steinberg's motorcycle helmet roll down the hill. Someone else, someone obviously very special, hated agents and publishers and fucking editors almost as much as he did. Devlin Turner had rejected them both. Where was this guy? Toronto. In a city that size there had to be a number of literary agents who needed to understand how painful a rejection could be. Two down – and many, many more to go.

Pages in another newspaper flipped by. Dieter found an article about Donovan, an associate editor at *Wolf's Head Publishing* in Minneapolis. *Another keeper.* Well, not yet, not completely. But it was going to be in the next few days. Shirley Donovan had sent him a rejection just like Steinberg and that puke Turner. Not as hateful, but it was still a rejection, of him and his manuscript.

Devlin Turner! Dieter took a long pull at a bottle of JD he'd jacked from the liquor store around the corner and toasted whoever had taken the fucker out – the guy who'd taken the time to sew the guys lips together. Dieter pictured the dog, the tree branch bending and creaking, the wind making him twist and turn.

Dieter Vollger sliced the article out with his knife and taped it to a fresh page in his scrapbook, next to his own rejection from Devlin Turner. A few more sentences that would curl around the pyre of his rejection and fan the flames of his hatred. He couldn't wait to meet the guy who'd shown Turner what it meant to be rejected. But he had things to do, people to see, souls to release. He'd work his way across the country, stopping for a few little side trips along the way. With Roland gone, Shirley Donovan would have the pleasure, and the horror, of being next. He couldn't wait to meet his brother in arms.

He knew he wouldn't reject *him.*

Oh, the fucking things they could do together.

He stroked the God-damn birthmark. Somewhere, some poor asshole was anxiously opening his mail, only to find another numbing rejection letter that broke his heart and stole his literary dreams.

And in some non-descript little office, without so much as a thought about where it was going and what it could do, some prick was writing another rejection. And another. And . . .

Dieter Vollger wondered who found Roland's charred head. He prayed it was someone from the asshole's publishing house.

Had his eyes still been open, blinking? Was he crying, or looking around?

Chapter Ten

Thirty seconds. A slice of eternity.

Kincaid's eyes flickered open. Closed. Was he alone? No. Adolphus purred from far away. *A tunnel?* He tried to move, but was stopped by Rebecca's firm hand. She whispered "lean back," then pressed a cold cloth over his forehead. He sighed as beads of water trickled down his cheek. Kincaid struggled to hear his friend's voice.

"Better?"

He nodded. The nerves behind his eyes burned. His head was splitting. Nausea clung to his senses, but it wasn't long before the feelings subsided. He tried to take the cloth away but Rebecca held it firmly.

"It's only been a couple of minutes. Leave it on a little longer. Can you keep your eyes open?"

He tried. Slowly. His dilated pupils were almost back to normal. Rebecca checked his pulse. His color was slowly coming back so she gently took the cloth away. He was still a little warm.

"Have some water. The crushed ice will take the dryness away." She dabbed his face with the cloth. "How often has this happened?"

Kincaid didn't want to lie. "Once or twice over the last month." *More before that.*

"What causes it?"

Kincaid remembered the concern in Dr. Chadpur's eyes. "They're not sure."

"You mean they're not *exactly* sure, *yet.*"

Kincaid nodded.

"It has something to do with that damn tumor in your spine, doesn't it, K? It's growing again, isn't it? Or that piece of shrapnel –"

Nailed. "Probably."

Rebecca drifted back through the years, tying the knot of memories together when her Godson had suffered a severe wound training security officers fighting poachers in The Democratic Republic of the Congo. He'd been flown home as soon as he was stabilized in Germany. The night was still a blur: Lt. Davis pacing, and dozens of cops quietly coagulating in the hall. The smell of the first gurney left behind, forgotten, against a closed partition.

The operating room doors that kept swinging open and closed. Nurses rushing by, their gowns laced with blood. The encompassing sense of hatred, the immediate need for revenge clinging to the walls. The minister's hands smoothing her vestments. Stephanie leaning against Rebecca's shoulder, crying. When they found the shrapnel still lodged in his brain the Spinal Tap showed something else, too – a tumor in his lumbar spine. He'd had it since before he was born—the third trimester. A month earlier and he would have been afflicted with Spina Bifida. Instead, it morphed into a Tarlov Tumor: the largest one the neuro-specialists had ever seen –and had grown exponentially *inside* his spine throughout his life. Depending on its position, it insidiously affected various parts of his muscular and nervous systems. It was deemed inoperable.

"More water? Another compress?"

"I'm good. It stops as quickly as it starts. It feels better already."

"Right. You can't fool me." She nodded toward her front door. "You came here on your own. What if it happens while you're driving?"

"The back pain is usually a warning, but there wasn't any this time. Someone's been assigned to be with me, Rebecca. Just not to and from home."

"Well, you better think about having someone pick you up, no matter how far it is. Maybe they could stay over until you're feeling better."

Amy? Overnight? That didn't sound bad at all. "I'll check with Davis tomorrow."

Rebecca squinted skeptically. "You might not be the only one who gets hurt remember."

She was right. This was the first time there hadn't been an aura, a sense that something was wrong. Until now, he'd always had time to react. There was an awkward moment of silence, and then he sat up straight, flexed his shoulders, and gently moved his neck from side to side. If it happened again. . .

"Do you remember what we were talking about?" Rebecca asked.

He did. His mind was clear, his recollection pure. No gaps. No residual pain. *That was a good sign, wasn't it?*

"You were talking about queries, and how terribly hurtful rejections can be for a writer."

Rebecca watched his eyes. "Good. So we'll stop there. I'll make up the guest room." Kincaid took her hand before she stood up. "I'm fine, Rebecca. I won't need the guest room. Just help me with a few more things."

Frowning, she went back to the kitchen and made a fresh pot of tea: an herbal mixture that would help Kincaid relax. She wanted to call Lieutenant Davis, but she knew that wasn't her place. When she returned, he was flipping through his notes.

"Gail Meredith said they get about two thousand queries a month. Does that sound right?"

"One hundred a day? Yes, I'd believe that."

"What do they do with them?"

"Shred them."

Kincaid's eyebrows rose.

"They'd probably like to. Most of them would be sent back with a form letter. Things like, 'thanks, but we're not accepting unsolicited work at this time; our list is currently full; we're already committed for another two years; we don't publish that genre'; etc." She slipped another cookie from the plate.

"So they're not rejected just because of the writing?"

"You're sure you want to keep going?"

"I need to."

"Fair enough. No, not just because of the writing. The first cut eliminates queries and proposals that don't conform to their mandate. Sometimes publishers are only looking for agent-represented submissions. Others might want medical mysteries. A lot of people who send out queries and proposals don't bother checking to see what a publisher wants or needs. Most houses get a number of interesting and well-written queries about books they don't print because they only deal with specific genres."

Kincaid sipped his tea. It was a delicious blend of mint and honey.

"Every book has to have a suitable niche for the House to make a profit. Indubitably, they turn down manuscripts that sound wonderful but simply aren't marketable."

"And the remainder?"

"The vast majority are rejected because of the quality of writing." Adolphus purred and stretched.

"How many would survive?"

"Out of two thousand? Perhaps fifty." Rebecca's eyes twinkled. "Surprised?"

"Naturally." *That's an awful lot of hurt feelings,* he thought. *A morass of pent up latent anger and resentment.*

Rebecca's lips curled into a sad smile. "The writer's life isn't for the faint-hearted, K; everyone wants to tell the world their life story. Unfortunately, their story isn't particularly remarkable, and in most cases, their writing skills are even less noteworthy. There's more to writing than wanting to see your name in print."

"So, after the first cut –"

"The ones that might have some potential are sent to the editorial department. Let's say that's ten for this month. Everything else is returned. The editors reassess whatever was forwarded. If they're interested, they contact the writers for a sample of their work – normally two or three chapters. Sometimes they ask for the entire manuscript. An editor screens it, then decides whether or not to refer it to a panel of senior editors. In small houses, it may go right to the publisher."

Kincaid looked at the cookies. So did Rebecca. Three left. They each took one. "How many would they look at?"

"Out of the surviving ten? They might seriously take the time to critically assess one or two. And even then there's no guarantee they'll take anything to publication. The numbers are staggering against a new author."

"That's *it*? Is there any way to improve my odds?"

"Sure. Write well, then try to match your book with a publisher or agent who deals primarily with your genre."

"So I find fifty places interested in my 'thriller.' Do I contact them one at a time?"

Rebecca giggled. "In theory."

She pushed the cookie plate toward Kincaid. Her hands were covered in little brown liver spots. *Life's connect-the-dots.* She was pleased with Kincaid's color, the clarity of his eyes.

"You've got to put some weight on, my love. I'm going to warm up the tea. Eat that cookie." Another finger-wag.

She was back in a minute with fresh cups. "Now, where was I? Oh yes. Publishers and agents expect to be notified if you're sending out simultaneous submissions. They don't want to consider something twenty-five other agents are already looking at. But it's not realistic – the process is simply too long. You can wait three months for a reply – which is usually a rejection. Neophytes throw caution to the wind and send out queries in batches."

"So I send out a collection of queries –"

"And the torture begins. You wait. *And* you wait. *And* you wait. That's one of the most dreadful parts of the process. You're always waiting."

"Email or snail mail?"

"Depends on the publisher. But the pressure increases as each day passes. It's like being incarcerated: the highlight of your day is when the mail cart click-clacks down the hall. The frustration usually comes moments later. First one query comes back, then two, three, then the rest, trickling in over several weeks or months. The constant rejections are bad enough, but each time you rip open an envelope and find another one, the pinch of the hope you've been holding onto disappears in a heartbeat. Your sense of hopelessness and despair rises exponentially."

Rebecca paused reflectively. "There aren't many professions I can compare it to." She sipped her tea and scanned the battered spines lining her shelves.

"You've poured everything you could into that manuscript. You've probably written it at least four or five times, and then you've rewritten it again after friends or colleagues give it a critical appraisal. Then you go over everything *again*, chapter by chapter, page by page, line by line, before you do a final edit and draft. You have that critiqued as well."

A dejected smile. "I've agonized over a certain passage, say an important transitional paragraph, for months. I'm not exaggerating. You spend so much time with the script it becomes brutally important to you." Frowning, she searched for the right words. "You *become* the book. If someone else reads it, their opinion is Damocles' sword: a word of praise can send you into a world of excited delirium, while criticism, no matter how kind, can throw you into a spiraling pit of depression or despair. They're not criticizing the book – they're criticizing *you* – *who and what you are* – and everything you've done."

Kincaid sipped his tea. "So you're constantly dealing with a regimen of rejection."

"And that's particularly hard to do when you're still working to perfect it." Rebecca lowered her voice for some esoteric reason. "It's the nature of the beast, Kincaid. It's a heartless heathen you have to learn to control or it will destroy you. Literally. Now it's not the same for everyone. Some people can send out a hundred proposals or queries and have them all rejected. So they start something new and leave the other book on the back burner for a while. That way, there's always fresh hope. For others, rejections can be life destroying. Look at Saramago."

"The Nobel prize winner. *He* was rejected?"

"Pilar del Rio, the president of the José Saramago Foundation, wrote about it in his forward to *Skylight.* Rejection that defined anguish."

"The novel published after he died."

"Yes. Saramago believed publishers had a responsibility to reply to writers, who were, as he says, "waiting impatiently and even anxiously day after day, month after month" to get some kind of a response back."

"Different than today, then."

"No comparison. He said "every book doesn't just carry words inside, it carries a real human being, with all of his or her intelligence and sensibility."

Rebecca pushed Adolphus off her desk. "Remember what I said about personalizing rejections. Something as simple as "sorry, we're not accepting submissions now" with his name at the top meant everything. That rejection was excruciatingly hard. Del Rio says that when he didn't hear anything, it evidently plunged Saramago into a 'painful, indelible silence' that lasted decades."

Kincaid was stunned. After seeing the letters returned, this seemed surreal. A Nobel Laureate who'd written some of the most wonderful lines put together – rejected without a word.

"How could a literary genius like Saramago have been rejected in the first place?"

"He wasn't. He submitted a type-written edition in the 1940's, when he was just 31. The publisher lost the manuscript. They only found it with some files because they moved. He waited almost 36 years for a reply. When the publisher realized what they had, they literally begged him to publish it. Of course he rejected them immediately," Rebecca snickered. "Saramago persevered, worked through his feelings about the rejection, and used his silence and solitude to write some of the best novels ever penned. But it shows you —"

"The power a rejection carries."

Kincaid reflected on the fervent hatred that effused every detail in the crime scene photographs of Turner's office: the blood, the stitches crisscrossing his lips, the gaping wounds the pens had made in the man's chest and neck and face. Turner and poor Shakespeare hadn't been murdered: they'd been slowly mutilated.

Rebecca smoothed a straggling hair back from her forehead. "If you're going to survive, rejection has to become a cool breeze on a hot summer day. I can't tell you how many personal and financial sacrifices you've made to finish your book. And the longer you've spent on it the more intimate the experience has become. That manuscript is part of you, an integral component that defines who and what you are."

"And it's rejected over and over."

Rebecca nodded sadly. One of the desk clocks struck the hour. Adolphus stirred, stretched, then slowly began the laborious process of cleaning himself.

"Each rejection represents another stab of failure, another closed door. Lost hope. That's why it's sad when publishers use form letters, and direct them to "Dear Writer." The person on the other end of that letter spent three years writing the book and then another couple of months refining a query, and they don't even use the person's name."

"What are the chances of getting a novel published?"

Rebecca's face crinkled up like an apple doll. "There are too many variables involved. But if I had to guess, I'd say around one percent for a first time author."

What had Gail Meredith said? *The odds are quite indomitable.*

"But it's that one sliver of hope that fuels so many writers' dreams. They'll risk everything in homage to those odds."

"But if I write extremely well, I'll have a better chance, won't I?"

"Perhaps. But success depends on factors you can't control."

"Such as?"

"Plain luck." Rebecca called Adolphus with a few sharp clicks of her tongue. He curled into her side and she caressed his back with gentle strokes.

"It's hit and miss. The literary world is full of infamous stories about best-sellers that were originally rejected thirty or forty times before someone picked them up. I've read some interesting articles where excerpts or chapters from famous authors were sent out under pseudonyms and they were rejected over and over again."

The cat's tail curled into a question mark. "Some houses might have half a dozen first readers. You can often get some type of agreement on style, characters, plot – that sort of thing – recommendations for fiction, are hugely subjective. One reader might think your manuscript has potential and fire it off to the editorial department for further review. The other five, however, may see the work as completely uninteresting. If your query reached those five, you wouldn't get any further."

"Quick cuts based on personal tastes?"

"Certainly. A manuscript can divide editors and publishers as well. Everyone has an opinion. The luck comes in when you hit the right reader or editor who likes your work. The person next door might have tossed it onto the 'return' pile before he's finished the first page." She glanced outside. Night was drawing closer, and the streetlights twinkled on. Grey clouds wandered across the sky. "That's what makes an agent like Turner quite valuable."

"Why?"

"He knows the industry. The houses, the readers and editors who work for them. A good agent targets a particular book to a specific editor he knows will be more amenable than someone else. He doesn't just send out things willy-nilly. He does his research. Then there's timing."

"Timing?" Kincaid looked away – he was getting tired watching the cat being rhythmically rubbed to sleep.

"The industry may be inundated with the latest batch of vampire books. *Your* vampire book might be the one the publisher can really sink his teeth into – Rebecca winced mischievously – but an editor won't even take the time to review it if she already has three or four they're working on. She's probably aware of other houses' agendas and upcoming lists, too."

"The books due out?"

"Yes. Lists can be filled up a year or two in advance. There's no point in saturating a market niche, because there's simply too much competition."

Kincaid reached for his cup but remembered he'd already finished his tea. He waved Rebecca back down into her seat and said he was fine. "But then why –"

"Are there so many books out there that aren't very good?"

A nod.

"It's like anything else. Politics, nepotism, and money. For the publisher, each new author is a risk. What if the book doesn't sell? What if it can't even be remaindered out? A great deal of money, time and effort is wasted if a novel doesn't sell enough to compensate for its publishing."

"Politics?"

"Isn't that what makes the world go 'round? Often *who* you *know* is more important than *what* you've written. A big named author can write a piece of trash, and publishers know people will still buy it, just because of the name, especially when you're dealing with mass market fiction. If you write a wonderful book about one man's attempt to overcome personal tragedy, for instance, you'll probably have less of a chance of seeing that book in print than you would have if you'd written a sex and violence-laced political thriller that sounded like a dozen others. A beautifully imaginative novel about love triumphing pain and suffering in a long term relationship won't be picked up as quickly as the latest celebrity tattle-tale about some perverse exploitation or divorce scandal."

Rebecca shook her head. "Now that the industry is overwhelmed with self-publishing companies, vanity presses, and things like MBI, it's even more difficult for good writers to get a contract with a trade publisher."

"MBI?"

"*MyBooksInternational.* It's a glorified Internet self-publisher. A writer is rejected fifty times. MBI, like vanity presses, offers to publish the work – but the author pays for it. Like other self-publishers, they offer a whole range of different programs, but you pay to have your book in print. For a thousand dollars, let's say, they'll publish your book, give you a black and white cover, and offer you five copies to go out and sell. Then you keep buying books from them – they get a percentage, and so do you. Now, for the two thousand dollar program, they'll do everything in color, design a back flap, and give you ten copies. On and on. With each package they offer you more 'help' –"

"But charge you a lot more, too."

"Exactly. You can't find a publisher, so you pay MBI to put your book all over the Internet. Suddenly, everyone that can put two words together is a 'writer.' They're not good enough to get a 'real' publisher, but they can pay MBI to stuff catalogues and bookstores with novels that would never be in print, especially without the Internet. Unfortunately, it all works to dumb down the industry, and really hurts small independent publishers trying to produce quality literature. Just like the education process that says teachers can't fail someone anymore."

Kincaid listened to the dueling pulse of the clocks. The process was longer and far more demanding than he'd thought. He was beginning to see how one cruel refusal could easily push someone over the abyss. Especially if they were already close to the edge. Had Devlin Turner battered one too many writers to the brink of the precipice once too often?

"One other thing."

"Go on."

"You mentioned form letters. Are rejections ever personalized?"

"No. Not with the volume agents and publishers have to sift through. You reject at least ninety percent outright. It would take too much time to write personal rejections. So they use forms letters. A spot for the author's name, then *"no thanks"* or something equally innocuous scrawled across the page. Larger companies, with a lot of readers, may write something like *"we enjoyed your book but unfortunately, we're already committed to many of our own authors at this point."* Or, *"your novel sounds interesting, Lisa, but our agenda's full. Best of luck elsewhere."* Those kinds of rejections give the writer a ray of hope and don't unduly criticize his work – even if it hasn't been read."

"Why would you use one?"

"I guess if the agent really liked the author's work but didn't have the time or money to pursue the book right now, he'd want the author to know they were impressed, and would be interested if another book became available. *'Don't burn your bridges* type of thing.'"

"Then the replies would be positive, not critical or provoking?"

"Of course."

"Turner had a penchant for sending back personal replies."

"You mean negative ones, don't you?"

"Scathing. Rejections that were humiliating, degrading, and sarcastic. *Taunting.* Why would he do something like that?"

Rebecca frowned. "I have no idea, K. It doesn't make any sense. Especially from someone as successful and time-constrained as Devlin Turner."

Kincaid handed Rebecca copies of some of Turner's rejections. She scanned them, and gulped.

"Dear me," she whispered, her face wrinkled with confusion. "I've never heard of someone sending a rejection like this. Or *this!* It's spiteful and cruel. Sinister, almost. My God. It's as if he was deliberately trying to provoke the poor man. I don't understand this at all."

That's what I thought. But why?

Shaking her head as she handed them back, Rebecca asked if Turner sent out many like these.

"Files full."

"No wonder he'd have so much hate mail. He wasn't just goading them, he was asking for trouble. Like he wanted them to suffer."

"Gerbec, put –"

"Gerbec? The detective with appendicitis?"

"Yes. He put a couple of partial lists together for us – "

"Us? Who's '*us*'?" Rebecca leaned forward, her face lit up, and her eyes and mouth puckered with the beauty of age. "The person who's driving you around?"

"I have a partner. Amy MacKenzie. A new sergeant from Vice and Robbery."

"Is she pretty?"

Kincaid blushed like a schoolboy. "Rebecca –"

"Well is she?"

He wasn't going to get out of this no matter how he played it. "Yes, she's quite attractive. Petite, intelligent, thoughtful, dedicated." God, he felt guilty. He hadn't mentioned her to Rebecca in almost a year. There was no time for this kind of distance and separation. Priorities had to change.

"Single?"

"Uh-huh."

"Have you been out together?"

"Rebecca, – "

"You sly old dog. You have! Bring her around for dinner. Anytime."

Kincaid smiled. "Thanks. So anyway, Gerbec started a couple of files. One names the people who persistently inundated Turner with hate mail. Another lists the writers who sent threatening letters to his publisher."

"Gail Meredith?"

"Right. Some resulted in restraining orders, others were charged with harassment. We'll cross-reference both lists. "

"That should be intriguing reading. So you think Turner's penchant for sending out degrading and caustic rejections might have been the thing that motivated someone to murder?"

"Like you said, ego is a powerful motivator. The book *and* the writer were rejected."

Rebecca sighed and finished her tea. "Enough of this morbidity. Are you going to stay in the guest room? Or have dinner, at least. You could tell me everything there is to know about pretty, single Amy." *And I can tease you a bit about Stephanie. Stir up the pot a bit.*

Kincaid glanced at both clocks before checking his watch. "I'd love to, but I can't."

"Then I insist you take a rain check. One you'll *use* this time."

"I will."

"Promise?"

"Promise."

"Perhaps you could bring Amy, and we could –"

"One step at a time, little matchmaker." Kincaid stood up carefully.

Rebecca rose with a heavy sigh, gingerly scooping Adolphus from her lap and curling him back on her chair. She didn't like this. The minutes had passed by far too quickly, and they hadn't talked about anything personal at all. She was concerned about how he was feeling, and tested the waters again as they walked to the door.

"I know you don't want to talk about it, K, and I respect that. But make sure you let me know when you hear about your results. Don't leave me worrying. That's not fair. Or loving."

"You know I will, Rebecca." They hugged. Kincaid leaned down and kissed her warmly on each cheek.

"Ryan, too. Keep me up to date on how the little guy's doing. And not by phone. That's so pathetically tiresome. And raw."

Suddenly, Kincaid felt rather weak. Disenfranchised, almost, the way you feel mingling with unknown mourners at a wake.

"And if you need anything, don't hesitate, right?"

"I won't."

"I'll make some calls, see what I can unearth that might help."

"Thanks, Rebecca."

"Oh, your cookies." She toddled off to the kitchen and came back with a tin filled to the brim. The top wouldn't even close. She picked up a package on the credenza. "And here's a little something for you, too." Two books were wrapped up. "The one on the top with the handmade bow is for you. The other one is for Eliza, your Lieutenants wife."

"*Watching Love Die?*" he smiled.

"With a little note."

"They'll love it. How did you know? She's one of your – "

Rebecca waved the accolade away. "Take care of yourself, my love. You've got to eat better and get some proper sleep. Don't push yourself too hard, and rest when you need to. Especially if you're in pain or anything. You – you really scared me back there."

"Rebecca –"

"I won't apologize. Once a godmother, always a godmother." She tried to smile, but when she looked up, her eyes were tinged with a worried, haunting sadness. "Remember Beatrice?"

"The godmother in *Trinkets in Love's Lost and Found?* How could I forget?"

"She's obviously more than just a godmother. But she never let's go or stops loving."

Kincaid leaned down, kissed her again, then gave her a long, lingering hug. He didn't mind the way Rebecca fussed over him like an overprotective mother – he wouldn't have wanted it any other way. He'd never had the chance to know his own mother, and it was a deep wound in his heart that had never healed.

Rebecca pulled on a denim jacket and followed him out to his car. Kincaid crunched down the gravel driveway. A wave, a honk, and he disappeared past the thick curtain of evergreens that blocked out the road.

Rebecca's hand went to her throat – safely out of sight, she could let the first few heavy tears come. She'd almost gasped when she'd first seen him. God, how gaunt he seemed. But what more could she have expected? He'd been through so much – tests and more tests. Countless nights in the hospital. And the pain, the incessant pain. In some ways he looked better than she hoped. She'd have him around for dinner, or at least lunch. She hadn't donned her robes in quite a long time, so her matchmaker role was weak and uninspired: that had to change, and fast. This new woman, Amy, might just be the thing he needed right now.

But she'd seen it in his eyes. What he really wanted was Stephanie.

Even if he couldn't say it yet.

Chapter Eleven

Morning sunlight drizzled through the glass encasing Meredith House, streaking the marble floor with a rainbow of vibrant colors. Despite the hour, people rushed around like lemmings – well-dressed lemmings. Straining to maintain his authority, the guard manning the lobby didn't bother asking Amy to move her car, but hesitantly asked Kincaid to sign in again.

Mingling with the throng, the detectives made their way to the bank of double elevators.

"Look around and see what you come up with, Sergeant," Kincaid said. "Talk to as many people as you can. See if you can unravel some of the threads weaving their way through the office rumor mill. I'm going to see" – he checked the card again – "Ms. Davidivitch. Call if you need anything. We'll meet back here in say, an hour."

*

At forty-seven, Leeanne Davidivitch could easily have been one of the 'mature' models consumer magazines and agencies were exploiting as the population gradually aged: the *mid-to-late-forty-something* look – and the "*natural beauty of the early fifties*" – poised, stylishly sure of herself, secure, confident, and still in great shape. A classic beauty in the timeless sense, she'd appeal to almost any man – and most women – of any age or position. She'd look perfectly suited on the arm of a multinational's CEO as she would trailing the latest young movie sensation in her wake. A woman who'd never fail to bring out a competitor's jealousy and weaknesses. A pussy cat and cougar all in one, but far too much of a woman to be either.

Her father was Ukrainian, her mother from Belgrade, right on the edge of Kalemegdan Park, and together they'd bequeathed proud, unmistakably Slavic features to their daughter. High cheekbones and a long, oval face highlighted with dark, brooding eyes and a provocative chin. Big boned and alluringly breasted, she still kept her thick black hair long and straight. Leeanne took great pride in her appearance and always wore a dress to work, no matter what her younger female colleagues whispered. This morning she was clothed in a pastel blue skirt and jacket, sensible heels, and a creamy white silk blouse that subtlety accentuated her strength.

Small and sterile, Leeanne's office was perfect for the ancient female cleaners who talked all night in dialects that made their children cringe, the ones who could move the dust from place to another without disturbing anything. The little room was overwhelmed by a desk, copier, shredder and coat stand. Matching silk plants framed broad, floor-to-ceiling bookcases. The only personal items in the office were random collages of old sepia photographs. They looked like they'd been thrown into the wind and scattered across the walls. One was of a beautiful Ukrainian castle tucked away in the steep hills of some verdant, magical forest. Another, slightly smaller, was difficult to make out, but looked like people digging on a slopped hillside. Bosnia/Herzegovina, '95, was scratched across the bottom. A large picture in a battered wooden frame that was probably eighty or ninety years old, showed ancient wheat fields being tamed by stooped peasants under a punishing sun. *1932.* There were numerous small prints, too: an overloaded wagon caught in the mud, a ship crammed full of greatcoats topped with unrecognizable faces, a pyre of a burning triangle.

The office was the only one without a window. Leeanne's work area didn't generate warmth or invite passersby to stop for a chat, which suited her just fine. Serious and conscientious, she detested most interruptions like the plague. But not all.

Leeanne leaned back in her chair and read the excerpt again, her smile broadening. What a gem: she had to see James right away. Victory was in her grasp . . . he'd be buying the drinks this week. Again.

*

Having just reached what he deemed "the ripe old age of twenty-six," James Lamberton was in the best shape of his life. His lunch hours were spent at the health club next door, and, weather permitting, jogged three or four times a week, as long as it wasn't raining or the midwinter cold made his chest ache. He left hair shirts to the medieval monks of old.

Clean-shaven, James kept his hair short and neatly trimmed. He had a small mouth, a dimpled chin, and wide, expressive eyes. At perhaps an inch and a half above six feet, he was slim and well-toned. The only odd thing about his appearance was his Adam's apple: most people agreed it was inappropriately large for his throat. No matter how much time they spent together, Leeanne's eyes were indubitably drawn to the bobbing bulge, especially when he spoke quickly.

Partially hidden by a wall of padded postal envelopes, James was bent over his desk, diligently trying to appear overwhelmed with work when the sound of knuckles drumming against his door rippled through his office. It was a comforting sound he knew well, like lake waves slapping against the side of a dock. His door swung open.

"Just me," Leeanne said cheerfully. "So stop pretending you're working."

James rose up from his burrow like a vigilant meerkat and beckoned her in. People in the outer office were still staring when Leeanne closed the door, softening the annoying *huumm* from the maze of cubicles behind her. *Let them talk.* Single by choice, she'd always had a soft spot for James. And he adored her. Although the pyres of scandal engulfed them in flames, nothing romantic ever kindled between them. That never doused the incessant chatter that burned through the cafeteria whenever they were together.

Leeanne smugly brandished a piece of paper threateningly in the air as she took a seat, her face breaking into an unrestrained smile.

"You're buying again Thursday, James. What's this now? Four straight?"

Each week, the two best readers at Meredith House sarcastically picked their *"favorite passage of literary merit"* from the numerous queries, proposals, and chapter submissions they received from prospective authors. *No*, it wasn't kind, and *yes*, it was a caustic and belittling thing to do. Cruel? Perhaps. Ridiculing someone's best attempts at breaking into the literary world certainly wasn't noble. But like Gail Meredith always said, the industry wasn't for the faint-hearted. It didn't seem all that terrible if they were the only two people privy to the submissions. And it certainly took the edge off some difficult days when they needed a laugh or two. No-one ever saw the excerpts, and they always took time to write a nice, encouraging little note on the bottom of the rejection letter to bolster the sender's confidence.

Whoever came up with the "winner"– the best of the worst – drank free at the *Dragon's Nest*, an intimate English-style pub on University Avenue that drew a lot of people from the publishing industry. James dropped in on Thursdays for a pair of martinis before sharing a cab partway home with Leeanne.

Yes, he'd lost four straight. But when James sank back down, his eyes twinkled with the thrill of a counterattack. "Don't count on it, Leeanne."

"Aww, a challenge. You first."

James swiveled from side to side, elbows against the armrests, his fingers peaked together in a triangle. "You brought yours to me. *You* go first."

Leeanne acquiesced with a nod. She cleared her throat with a dramatic cough.

" . . . The sky was a deep, dull, lackluster metallic black with no stars you could see, although they were still there, just far away, somewhere in the distance behind the clouds. Somewhere in the deepest, darkest depths of the blackened forest an owl turned his head around in a full circle and hooted. *No mice out yet tonight,* he thought. But a branch suddenly snapped, making the agent's heart flutter. Special Agent QT Quincy spun quickly around, pivoting swiftly on his rear foot, and deftly whipped out his weapon."

James guffawed. "Which weapon? Was his penis loaded?"

"You know the rules. No interruptions."

"Didn't it hurt the owl to turn his head right around?"

"James!"

"All right. I just can't stand the suspense."

Leeanne re-read the last line. Then,

" . . . QT Quincy methodically assessed the darkness, but nothing he couldn't see moved. He held his gun tightly. Dark black like a piano key, it was a lightweight 9 mm, semi-automatic Glock Special with an infrared sight. He flexed his index finger carefully around the trigger and anxiously tightened his firm grip on the metal gun handle until his hand hurt. In a few long minutes it would all be over, one way or another.

Either he'd be dead or someone else would be. He hoped it was someone else."

"Not bad," James admitted, still swiveling. "Male?"

"Lawrence Johnnson. *Murdering the Messenger*. It came from a little place west of Philly. That's from the second page of the first chapter – which is sixty pages long!"

Crossing her legs, Leeanne smiled confidently, and confronted her colleague with a stare. "Can you beat that or do my martinis keep flowing?"

James hid behind his best poker face. "Mine's an excerpt from a synopsis," he said. He too gave a throat-clearing cough, his Adam's apple bobbing, then added a few *ahems* before starting to read.

". . . had been on a virtual reality roller coaster of emotions all day. Up and down, up and down, up and down, rather like a yoyo goes. What had gone wrong? And why now, rather than at some other time that possibly might not have seemed so bad under disparate circumstances. Wasn't it true he could still be mistaken about the man? Chechenko tried to mentally picture the man again. Tall, too tall really, so tall it made his drab greatcoat look small. The man had wide, broad shoulders, a handlebar mustache, a scar on his cheek, thick and unruly eyebrows sporadically tinted with gray, and a Pinocchio-like nose broken at least once but probably more than that and had seen better days."

"Oh, that's absolutely wonderful," Leeanne admitted, dutifully applauding. "Well done! It appears we have a tie."

James bowed gracefully and accepted the stalemate with aplomb. "We'll share a drink, then?"

"Of course."

"And these two? Copied, hidden, and kept for posterity, I should –"

There was a light knock at his door. A receptionist cracked it open just enough to speak.

"Sorry, Mr. Lamberton."

"Quite alright, Julie."

"There's a man waiting to see you, Ms. Davidivitch." The young girl whispered nervously. "From the police."

"Did you show him to my office?"

"Yes."

"Tell him I'll be right there."

James perched forward. "Now what have you done?"

"I can't say." She gestured to the office with a nod. "But let them think about it for a while. Until Thursday."

Standing, she straightened the lines of her skirt and brushed an imaginary piece of lint from her sleeve. James scurried around the mountainous pile of folders on his desk and opened his door.

The police?

Her smile was forced, her face stern. He watched her walk toward the elevators, unabashedly admiring the thigh high skirt and sensing the softness of the nylon with his eyes.

Chapter Twelve

Standing by the bookcase, Kincaid was thumbing through the volumes when Leeanne Davidivitch walked briskly into her office.

"Caught in the act. And there's never a cop around when you need one."

He turned and smiled, discernably impressed. By the books as well. "I couldn't help noticing how many of these are personalized. The authors obviously respected your input and guidance."

"What's the old maxim? A gnome can see a little farther when he's standing on a giant's shoulders? I just help writers grasp some of the things they might have overlooked, since critiquing your own work is extremely difficult. I have the luxury of objectivity. And speaking of being overlooked, you were here yesterday, but we didn't have the opportunity to meet." She smiled warmly, accepting his hand. "Detective –?"

"Kincaid."

Well-manicured hands, but a strong grip. She let go reluctantly, her gaze lingering on his face, her senses teased by the trace of his after shave. Leeanne had been deceived by her own expectations. Kincaid certainly wasn't a stereotypical character or cardboard cut-out from the latest CSI knock-off. She hadn't anticipated he'd be dressed so nicely, or that he'd have such boyish charm. His suit was perfectly tailored and he wore it well. He'd wear anything well. Like nakedness. A crisp shirt, cuff links and a university tie pin – quaint, old fashioned values. Attractive in a humble sort of way. He'd hold your chair or send you a hand-written letter or bring you a flower because he wanted to.

She nodded at the volumes. "I don't see you as a mainstream fiction reader, Detective."

"I read as much as my profession allows. Anything well-written and evocative. Biographies, history, philosophy. From Shakespeare to Dickens, from Marquez to Camus. Fuentes, Lorca.

"Ah, so some Perez-Reverte, then?"

"Doctorow, and Jim Crace, too."

"And do a few LeCarre novels dot your shelves at home, Detective?"

"If there's something good out there, I try to find it. You'd be surprised at the treasures you can unearth in the remaindered bins." He smiled. "Well, I guess you wouldn't. So many books . . "

". . . and so little time."

Something caught Kincaid's eye. He reached down to an over-stocked shelf that sagged in the middle. He pulled out a slender volume, handling it gingerly as if it were made of eggshell.

"This is a first edition of *The Bridge of San Luis Rey*! It's not even in a dust jacket."

Leeanne smiled. "Naturally, I didn't help Mr. Wilder on that. He never would have required my assistance."

"A Nobel Laureate and he's still virtually an unknown hero in North America."

"Yes, it's a shame, really. A literary masterpiece rarely read. Please, take it."

Kincaid's eyes went wide, and he almost stuttered. "Oh, thank you. But I couldn't."

"I have another one at home. A signed proof copy. And it's protected by something more than a dust jacket. Please."

"I can't." Kincaid gently slipped the book back into the exact location he'd found it.

"Then feel free to borrow anything you'd like."

What a nice change from most of the men she met, Leeanne thought. Educated, and of all things, erudite, and an eclectic bibliophile. A nice, attractive companion to share a book and glass of wine with in front of a late-night fire. She looked down with a quick, appraising glance, confirming the absence of a wedding ring.

"The picture on the upper shelf, the one overlooking the terraced fields – "

"Yes?"

"Isn't that outside Pochayiv? The Cathedral of the Dormition of Theotokos?" He took it down carefully.

Leeanne was impressed he recognized the location. It certainly wasn't one of the more prominent tourist pilgrimages.

"How –"

Kincaid shook his head. "I've seen so many like this one," Kincaid said softly, studying the battered sepia print. His gaze wandered over the collage. "There's something so unnaturally familiar about the old photographs. The old men beaten down by a grueling sun. The grey sky, the stacks of wheat, the weathered women bent over their scythes, their kerchiefs blowing in the wind, damp with the strain, the endless fields in shadows beneath the distant cathedral walls. What they remember."

Leeanne was more than impressed: she was deeply touched. She took the picture back and carefully brushed it clean. "I doubt if any of the fields are there now," she said despondently.

"The Holodomor must have been terrifying, especially in the early 1930's."

Leeanne's lips tightened. "Yes, it was." Delicately, she put the picture back in the exact same spot. Suddenly, there was a sense of – nothingness – in her eyes. But this man – he wasn't Eastern European. *What did he know of that tragedy?* She was fascinated.

"*Davidivitch*," Kincaid offered quietly.

A moment later her smile came back. Almost. "My great grandparents were part of the scourge. The forced starvation. The genocide. Stalin's *work until you die*, philosophy."

"I'm sorry."

"The country was almost lost. So many hard working people died. So many relatives and friends. The Russians basically starved them to death. Whatever food we had they took. My great grandparents farmed themselves until they were nothing more than skeletons, their children –"

"Leeanne –"

She sighed deeply, thoughtfully. "No, I'm the one who should apologize."

"Not for feeling what you do."

"It happened again in WW11. Russia wanted farmers in Poland and the Ukraine to work themselves to the bone so their army had enough food."

"It was a terrible time for many people," Kincaid replied softly. "When did you immigrate?"

"When I was fourteen. But many, many of my relatives were left behind. Still, to this day –"

She paused and stared at the pictures. A small tear twinkled in her eye.

"And now, the Maidan Uprising."

Leeanne wiped her eyes. Again she seemed surprised, but only for a second. She glanced at Kincaid's face. This man knew a lot, and probably hid even more. *Who was he, really?*

"Did you ever see –"

"I volunteered to be an Observer with the U.N. contingent."

Leeanne's breath caught. "No. Really? You were there?"

"For a couple of months in 2015."

"Ahh. Just long enough to see –"

"What was really happening. Yes."

"It was the rampant corruption that sparked the revolt, you know. The pro-Western revolution provoked a conflict with the Russian separatists. Kiev was in shambles. Promises to stop the cronyism of Yanukoych, the puppet, went nowhere. Did you know there were still book burnings just twenty years ago? The Russians want us to assimilate at all costs. Be Russian or don't be anything."

The seething anger made her body rigid. Kincaid touched her arm. "Perhaps I shouldn't have –"

"No. No, it's not your fault, it's mine. Sometimes the memories need to re-surface. Anyway, I couldn't believe the sanitized pictures in the media," she said coldly.

"The convoys?"

"Yes. The trucks all in line, purportedly bringing in humanitarian aid – food, clothing, health services. But most of them were empty by the time they reached the border. Did you see that?"

"I did," Kincaid said quietly. "Most of the vehicles in the convoy had actually been carrying materiel, weapons, munitions, and platoons of soldiers. There'd be a couple of bags of food or flour left in the back. Perhaps as a reminder."

"Or a threat. They cut down protesters, you know. My grandparents fled to Odessa, but it wasn't any better there. No food, no jobs, and prices spiraling out of control."

"We couldn't do anything, just observe and file reports. But you're right," Kincaid agreed. "The assistance was a farce." He remembered the trucks slowing down at the border crossings, the soldiers jumping out with their caches of weapons, the grey tarpaulins flapping in the breeze. Then the photo-ops for the Russian officials, standing beside trucks filled with food, medical aid, fresh water, nurses.

"Almost a hundred years after the Holodomor and nothing has really changed. You still have to know someone in order to live properly, safely."

"How is your family?"

"The ones who have emigrated aren't doing badly. But that doesn't mean the Russian government still can't reach out whenever they want and tap them on the shoulder. Come back, they'll say. We need you."

"Still? Today."

"Oh yes."

"So you couldn't go back? See all your other relatives?"

The bitter laugh changed Leeanne's face. Kincaid found it disconcerting.

"Impossible." She shook her head angrily. "They'd never let me leave, Detective. You must know that. I can't go back. No matter how long you've been gone or your current country of status, your citizenship immediately reverts back the moment you touch Russian soil."

"Unbelievable." Kincaid returned her distraught stare. "And the relatives still there?"

"Are the lonely ones. Unlucky. Poor. Like everyone else I try and send whatever extra money I have back to them, but what can I really do?"

Leeanne looked around her little office and then directly into Kincaid's eyes. "The *Old Regime* still has all the files, Detective."

"Will Zelenskiy change anything?"

"Who knows? But I don't really have much hope."

Silence. The office suddenly seemed smaller, denser, almost. Kincaid could see that the pictures were far more than just photographs of another time and place.

Leeanne's sense of professionalism quickly returned. There'd be other moments for the photographs. She exhaled a heavy breath and forced a small smile. When she looked at Kincaid, the smiled deepened. He was knowledgeable and empathic. Perhaps, at another time . . . She tugged her hair back behind her ear. It was a familiar gesture Kincaid had always liked watching someone else do, and it made *him* smile. She suggested they sit in the visitor's chairs.

"I get the distinct impression that's not the only place you've volunteered for, Detective. Have you gone to other hotspots for the U.N?"

"And NATO."

"Where to?"

" I was in the Democratic Republic of the Congo in 2013."

"Peacekeeping?" She straightened out a crease that wasn't really in her dress and moved just a little closer. She watched Kincaid's eyes.

"No, actually. I went to The Congo with a number of officers from a variety of military and police forces around the country. I'd read about the wonderful work that was being done in Zimbabwe by the Akashinga."

Leeanne raised an eyebrow.

"The Brave Ones. They're an all-female group of Rangers that work with non-profit organizations to help stop illegal poaching in the Phundundu Wildlife Area in the Zambezi Valley. They were trained by Australian Special Forces soldiers, led by an officer who's been committed to them for over a decade. The women have made a huge impact on illegal poaching. The project has worked so well it's been initiated in a variety of African parks."

Kincaid's face softened. *Or was it something different?*

"When I saw the pictures of the huge alpha silver back being carried out of the jungle, his paws and head gone, I knew I had to do something. We went to the huge National Park, Virunga, in the north east part of the Congo to help train other female units like the Australians had done."

Leeanne shifted her chair a little closer to Kincaid's. "Teaching them what?"

"Basic training. Close combat. Special weapons. Tactical techniques. There were some fundraisers, so we were also able to bring them tents, material, full fatigues, night vision goggles, things like that. The poachers, you have to understand, have extensive weapons, they're quite skilled and well-equipped, and are motivated by lots and lots of money."

For a moment, Kincaid looked thoughtful, almost lost. Uneasy. He frowned, and gently massaged his right temple.

"Why would someone kill a gorilla?"

"What's one of the primal causes of everything?"

"Greed?"

Kincaid nodded. "Anything on an endangered species list is financially significant. The Chinese say they need parts of the animals for their traditional medicines, although there's no proof whatsoever any component of a gorilla paw, for instance, actually cures cancer or any other disease. The head is a trophy to put on the wall, nothing more. It doesn't matter if it comes from the sea or a jungle – Asians in general think parts like nails or skin or pieces of internal organs can solve all their health problems, especially their incessant need to combat erectile dysfunction. So the animals are worth more dead than alive. Someone needs to protect them."

"That's horrible." Something had touched a chord – tears burgeoned in Leeanne's eyes again. "And the women –"

"We trained are dedicated, and have a collective goal. They're tenacious and reliable."

"It couldn't always have been pleasant, working in the jungle."

"Not always."

"Was it dangerous?"

The question caught him off guard. Kincaid looked away, pretending to scan the volumes of books that were gradually bending a couple of shelves. Images of *Dr. Chadpur and Dr. Torvay flashed through his thoughts. The MRI and CT. The pictures of his left temporal lobe. A steely morning sky filled with bird cries. The darkness turning to light, the sun beating down the mist. The heat, dampening him. And then the sudden burst of a fragmentation grenade launched by a poacher deep inside the tree line. The rumbling silence. The seconds of confusion and uncertainty. Kincaid didn't really remember being hit, or the emergency flight to the U.S. military base in Landstuhl, Germany, the transport home, the months of pain, the surgeons shaking their heads, the fainting, the headaches and searing pain, the threat of surgery that might leave him in a chair for the rest of his life.*

He didn't answer Leeanne's question. Instead, he told her, "I was in Iraq, too."

Kincaid felt a little odd. *More* than a little odd. Why was he telling this kind of story to a woman he'd come to interview about a murder investigation? Something about her – made him want to talk. To let all of those memories he'd left buried inside for so long to find expression, if even for a moment.

"When was that?"

"2012. Initially, we'd been asked to help train the Kurdish Security Forces."

"The peshmerga?"

It was Kincaid's turn to be impressed. "Exactly. Kurdistan needed a professional military. Again, forces from all over the country formed special units, depending on their area of expertise, to provide arms and tactical training to the Kurds. We did a tour with them and U.N. affiliated groups to fight against the ISIL cowards. Then other forces took over."

"Not the best place to spend your holidays."

Kincaid smiled uneasily. "You do what you can."

"What about –"

Kincaid held up his hand. "I appreciate your interest, but that's enough, Leeanne. I really came to talk about something completely different. "

She blushed. "You're right, Detective. I'm so sorry. I know how valuable your time must be. It's just that I find you – it – so interesting. But my God, we can't keep talking like this. Morbidity is just as overwhelming as depression. You're here for a reason and I hope I can help. But first, can I have something brought in? Coffee? Tea?"

"I'm fine, thanks."

Leeanne gestured to a chair with the warmest of smiles. "So, you're here about the information Ms. Meredith promised. I understood someone else was with you." *Was that a hint of sadness in his eyes?*

"My partner. Sergeant MacKenzie."

"Yes, your partner." From what Leeanne gleaned from the grapevine, the consensus in the office was that the young woman wanted to be more than just his partner.

"She's canvassing the outer labyrinth of offices as we speak, trying to drum up as much information as possible. Seemingly inconsequential details might point us in the right direction."

"A lead to a lead."

"Precisely. You'd be surprised what you hear when you keep your ear to the ground. Office politics, rivalries, and the never ending strands of gossip and hearsay that keep the business world churning. You'll probably run into her later."

Ms. Davidivitch walked around her desk and withdrew a large white interoffice envelope from a drawer. *Amazing*, Kincaid thought. Normally he was quite adept at matching people with their age, but this woman was a siren: she could have been anywhere from thirty-five to fifty-five, and either end of that differential spectrum would be a compliment. The pastel blue jacket and skirt she was wearing was provocative and professional at the same time. She chewed at the end of her glasses, her perfume cloying with his senses. Something from the past, yet something timeless. He closed his eyes, drew in a breath, and felt the memories stir.

She sat down in the guest chair next to Kincaid, hesitating for a second before she passed him the envelope. "I assume –"

"We're always confidential, Mrs. Davidivitch. And we're as discreet as we can be under the circumstances."

"Ms.," she corrected him. "But please, call me Leeanne."

"*Windsong*."

"I beg your pardon?"

"Your perfume. I haven't had the pleasure of that scent in quite a while."

"Are you trying to *date* me, Detective?"

He laughed with her. "Not in the least. It's a fragrance that conjures up some very pleasant memories." *Did Kincaid blush?* Refocusing, he took out his notebook. "What's your position with Meredith House, Leeanne?"

"I'm listed as a first reader, but I do a fair amount of editing. I'm also seconded to human resources. One of my jobs is to keep track of communication sent to the staff. Some authors, even if we reject their manuscript, send nice thank you letters back if the reader or editor has shown them how they can make their script better. Unfortunately, they're few and far between. I also have to deal with the aggressive or unconventional kind, the "personal correspondence" you discussed with Ms. Meredith."

Leeanne sighed at her own euphemism. "The proverbial hate mail. What's sent, and what, if anything, the staff replies. For legal reasons, I have to make sure that 'bother' doesn't evolve into 'harassment.'" She wanted to reach out and run her fingertips lightly across the tiny scar etched into Kincaid's chin. She shifted in the chair and smoothed out her skirt. Her legs were nicely tanned.

Kincaid fanned through the folder. Gail Meredith was right: it was much thicker than he'd anticipated. *Bleak House* came to mind.

"This is quite a list."

"I'm sure Ms. Meredith warned you."

"Yes she did, but I didn't anticipate –"

"– Something quite so extensive?"

He nodded.

"We're inundated with letters, cards, faxes, e-mail and texts every day. It's obviously become more prevalent with the escalation of social media, although some of that is relatively easy to block. We even receive a few parcels from time to time."

"Such as?"

"Dead flowers, animal feces wrapped up ever so nicely. Stuffed toys with their heads cut off. That sort of thing."

"Lovely. Does it happen often?"

"More than we'd like to admit. It's the same with most of the larger houses."

Strange. The look in her eyes. The way she moved. Kincaid had the oddest feeling he could confide in her. Trust her. The way she was sitting, her perfume, the intensity of her gaze, her half-smile. Would this be Stephanie in ten years? Strong, sensual, beautiful, educated and independent – yes, she reminded him of Stephanie. More than a little. *And Amy?*

"Detective?"

She shifted her chair closer, leaned over, and pulled her hair back around behind her ears. A delicate move, gentle and precise, one he immediately wanted to see again. "Are you sure I can't get you anything? Something cold?"

"Thanks. But no." He flipped through the pages. "I hope I'm not infringing on your time."

A wry grin. "I'm all yours, Detective."

That was a pleasant thought. "What exactly am I looking at?"

"I've listed every reader and editor who's received something over the past two years. *Something* being at least one piece of hate mail. Practically everyone has. Most of them are harmless. They're from frustrated individuals who've spent a great deal of time working on something very personal, only to have it rejected."

"No one likes the messenger," Kincaid mused.

"Exactly. They're the ones where the person just needs to vent. I've tabulated the manuscripts with the appropriate correspondence, then notated the outcome. Unless, of course, it's an ongoing problem."

"The outcome?"

"If the situation became more intense and we had to utilize a restraining order, or if we had to pursue litigation, things like that. I don't want to sound overly dramatic. In most cases, it just takes a little chat; a phone call from one of the senior editors can reassure the person enough they accept the rejection and move on. We'll even have them in for a quiet talk about their book, point out some good things, but criticize it hard enough so they can see how much more work it actually requires to get it in the running."

"Assuage their egos with a dose of reality." Kincaid frowned and changed positions again.

"Indeed. Gently close the door, but leave it open an inch. Everyone needs a spa day once in a while, Detective. A little one on one, a new perspective, and everybody's happy."

Leeanne thought it would be nice to have Kincaid massage scented oil over her neck and back.

"I assume there's quite a disparity between the staff in terms of who receives things."

"Naturally." Leeanne inched closer and pointed to another tab marker. "I've also cross-referenced the list with anyone who worked on projects with Mr. Turner. He's very aggressive . . . *was* very aggressive."

"Why?"

"I've no idea. Childhood issues, perhaps? Isn't that the old standby?"

The standard plea. *I'm not responsible, it was my upbringing. Or lack of it.*

"He was bold, forceful, and if I may say something acerbic about the dead, the definition of hubris. He was busy to the point he was almost always rude. But he was scornfully successful, and for a lot of people, that's enough."

Kincaid agreed. Power and money: two prime motives for the majority of murders he'd investigated. That, and jealousy, ego, and love.

"Will the list help?" Leeanne asked coquettishly. She crossed her legs and leaned closer until her hand touched Kincaid's forearm. She looked into his eyes. Every time she moved, her perfume daintily curled around his senses.

Kincaid hadn't seen Stephanie in almost three years. He was still getting to know Amy in a personal way that was close but not intimate. It had been so long he'd almost forgotten how to flirt. *Almost.*

"Undoubtedly. I hadn't expected anything quite so thorough. This will help immensely."

"I don't mean to be intrusive, but it seems fairly obvious you're making the assumption that whoever sounded Mr. Turners death knell is directly tied to his work. A rejected writer, perhaps? An unhappy client?"

"It's the most probable place to start. Tell me, Leeanne. Pretend we're at the races, and I want you to pick your favorites."

"By *my favorites*, you mean the ones I'd bet were involved."

A nod. "Your gut instinct. The ones who've been the most persistent and unnerving. The people you believe would have whatever it takes to follow through on their threat. The ones that would bother *you.* Particularly those who've dealt with both Meredith House and Devlin Turner."

She leaned back and closed her eyes. "Walter Croft, for one."

Kincaid jotted down the name.

"Richard Barclay."

Another scribble. "Anyone else?"

Leeanne frowned, then shrugged. "Maybe Lois Gibney, or Peter Maxell. Oh, I'd have to include Brent Jacobs as well."

"Why them?"

"They've all been rather prolific and persistent in their correspondence, with a highly agitated and aggressive tone. And each of them has only written one book."

"Why is that important?"

"Most people learn something from their rejections – and not necessarily from their first one – then they try new avenues. Go to classes, join workshops, meet other writers, seek out mentors, things like that. They try to improve their skills to become better writers. Generally, their writing and submissions get better over time."

"But not always?"

"No. Everyone has limits."

"And the people you've mentioned?"

"They all imagine that the one book they've managed to put together is the penultimate piece of literature they're able to produce. They sincerely believe it's a classic, something that will change the literary world, or at the very least cement their place within it. It's that one book or nothing. Any changes they make are miniscule or unimportant, regardless of what we said initially. When the book's rejected again, they don't have anything else to fall back on. They've got that one novel, and its success or failure is slowly eating them alive."

"If it's all or nothing, the rejections must be insufferable."

Ms. Davidivitch nodded sadly. She gestured at the folder. "The names I gave you can't give up. *That's all they have left.*"

What had Rebecca said? *Depending on the person, the timing, or what else was going on in his or her life, a rejection might be that one final stressor that pushes someone over the edge.*

Leeanne paused. "Detective, you're looking a little piqued. Would you like some water?"

"Please." Even though he kept moving, his spine was on fire.

She poured some ice water from a carafe on a small vestibule behind her desk. By the time she'd turned around, Kincaid had hidden two painkillers in his hand. It would only be a few minutes before the pain dulled.

Kincaid jotted down a few notes. Ms. Davidivitch straightened the hem of her dress, leaned over, and tucked her hair behind her ears again. Did she know how seductive that movement was? *Of course she did.*

"An incredible number of people want to be writers, Detective. Most of them seriously believe they have the ability to produce something of merit. Unfortunately, only a handful have the competency and talent necessary, let alone the time and effort to work at their craft."

She smiled, her teeth perfect and white. She watched his face, her lips drawing him in. "And don't forget, although we don't like to admit it, we're not the only publisher in town. When a writer's rejected, they usually send their work somewhere else, automatically assuming the first publisher was wrong in their assessment. Multiply all those rejection letters by all the other houses and agents. From the small, limited print houses to the multinational corporations that control where the industry is going. When *all of them* tell him his work isn't good enough . . . "

It's a lot of hurt, Kincaid thought again. *A lot of hate.* The idea was staggering and sobering at the same time. How many rejections would it take to make someone leap over the abyss into the darkness? Some people might take it in stride and put up with dozens of rejections before they gave up. For others, the first one could be the last. *How could you tell? And how could people sending the rejections back ever know the kind of monsters they might be creating?*

"But success happens, Detective. Finding those few gems is obviously possible. That's why practically every year, and against seemingly insurmountable odds, a handful of new voices appear that justify all our time and effort."

"And the money."

"And the risk."

"And Devlin Turner managed to find those?"

"Oh, yes. Yes he did. In fact, Devlin found much more than his share, which never ceased to confound industry insiders. And please don't ask me why, because I can't give you any reason other than potions, magic elixirs, and crystal balls, so you'd have to see Harry Potter about that. Which is, in itself naturally, a perfect case in point. It takes an enormous amount of work to write a good book. The rest, however, like whether it's published or not, is generally out of your hands."

Kincaid gestured to the tome. "And Turner? What would his query load have been like?"

"Well, he wouldn't get anywhere near the number we receive, but he'd definitely garner enough to keep a couple of full time people busy. He often shared resources with Ms. Meredith. Secretarial work, readers' hours, that sort of thing."

"So Turners death will have a large financial effect on Meredith House?"

Nodding, Leeanne reached over and picked an errant thread from Kincaid's sleeve.

"You've read a number of Turners' personal replies, particularly the caustic ones that were so aggressive. They were scathing, humiliating, and degrading. What would he possibly achieve by taunting the writers he rejected?"

Leeanne frowned. "I guess we'll never know, Detective. It doesn't make any sense at all. Especially from someone as successful as Turner."

"Tough love?"

"I doubt that very much. They're far too hateful and vindictive."

"Making them reach for something higher?"

"No way. In general, writers are a rather sensitive group. They don't take sarcastic rejection well. Then again, who does?"

Kincaid jotted something down. "Out of all the editors and readers you know, how many send back hand-written replies?"

Leeanne took off her glasses and gently nibbled on one of the arms. She stopped almost immediately, her face red. "Sorry – bad habit. I wouldn't think any more than a handful."

Kincaid pocketed his pen and closed the folder. He was certain he was holding an invaluable lead: chances were that someone in these pages was a bitter, ruthless killer, fueled by vengeance. But he still didn't understand why someone of Turner's ilk wanted to direct that much hatred against himself. What would he gain psychologically by deliberately provoking peoples' rage and anger? The metaphor was lame and puerile, but he couldn't stop picturing someone poking a bear with a stick. He looked down at Leeannes' notes: he had a lot of paperwork to go through. He stood up slowly, consciously aware of his medications' strength.

Leeanne rose gracefully. "Can I help you with anything else?"

"Not now. I'm grateful for your time and all that you've done. I can't tell you how much we appreciate this information. But I may be back in touch, if that's not too much of an intrusion."

"Not in the least, Detective."

Her hand rested delicately on his forearm. Seconds ticked quietly by before Leeanne's fingers slid softly away.

"Perhaps buying me dinner would help justify taking up so much of my time?"

"I'll certainly mention that to my Lieutenant, Leeanne."

She smiled warmly. "Should I have Sergeant –"

"MacKenzie."

"Yes, MacKenzie, paged?"

"No, I'm sure I'll find her." Kincaid turned toward the door, then paused, frowning. "There was one other thing."

"Yes?"

"What percentage of your time do you spend reading first submissions?"

She tilted her head thoughtfully to one side. "I don't know. Perhaps twenty-five percent. Why?"

"I wondered if you've been immune to the threats, or if you've received your share as well?"

Her smile melted, and the sparkle vanished from her eyes. "No one is immune, Detective."

"You don't send personal replies back, do you?"

"Of course not. At least not in the way you mean. Not like Turner. On the rare occasions I do, anything remotely personal would only be sent to help a writer. To assuage feelings I know are going to be hurt, or perhaps to point them in a better direction."

"No dead animals?"

She didn't blink. She thought about the terrible passages she shared with James Lamberton, and a slight shiver tickled up her spine.

"Do they frighten you?"

"I don't let them." Leeanne's stance was bold and strong, but the look in her eyes was unnerving.

Kincaid slipped his hand into his breast pocket and withdrew his card. "Now it's *my* turn. If there's anything *I* can do *for* you, please don't hesitate to call."

Leeanne's demeanor changed instantly. She whispered *thanks*. "And I'm holding you to that dinner."

She struggled to keep smiling, but the anxiousness in her eyes was fixed. She slipped her glasses on, folded her arms across her chest, and watched Kincaid make his way through the maze of little cubicles towards the elevators. She didn't move for almost a minute.

The gossip wheel was already spinning wildly out of control.

But all she could think about was that binder.

*

Slowly making her way through Meredith House, Amy had quietly and methodically been gathering a plethora of information while Kincaid met with Leeanne Davidivitch. Like an untamable river, the stream of office gossip never ran completely dry. Speculation, innuendo and rumor made the office go round. True to form, everyone enjoyed 'sharing' a secret. It was a little like crossing the yellow tape stretched around a crime scene and suddenly being involved in a murder investigation. Your fifteen minutes of fame. Right now, all she had was a pile of theories and conjectures, some absolutely wild. But others had that special sense, that subtle thread of "perhaps" that might just tie some loose ends together. And some were just the usual trash – a staff member trying to get one up on a colleague. She ended up with a notepad full of possible leads. Amy flipped through the pages. She was going to have to shift through all the conjectures and get down to the facts if she was going to be able to give Kincaid anything concrete.

And if there was one thing she didn't want to do, it was to disappoint him.

Chapter Thirteen

Sergeant MacKenzie caught up with Kincaid in the lobby. He was leaning against the large onyx desk, clearly irritating the security officer immensely. Suppressing his OCD, the guard drummed his fingers against his blotter. He re-positioned everything the Detective touched – and Kincaid was touching everything. Amy frowned: she didn't think her partner looked very well. Pale, and already a little fatigued.

"Did you get much, Sergeant, other than a lot of whispered innuendos?"

"And inquisitive stares? I'm afraid not, Sir. The staff had more questions for me than I had for them. Childish, really. *Have you ever fired your gun? Do you carry a Taser? Are we on camera?*"

"Was anyone particularly helpful?"

"Not really. Other than their regular office gossip, they were tightlipped about everything else. And every*one* else. Close the ranks, I suppose. I got the feeling the demand for silence came down from Gail Meredith herself. "

"You're probably right. I think it's time we paid a visit to Turner's partner."

"Cynthia –"

"Baxter. I just checked: her secretary confirmed her flight was on time. She flew in about an hour ago." Kincaid glanced up at a huge silver wall clock behind the guard's desk. "She went straight to the gym. Says it shakes off the jet lag."

"What about your interview with Leeanne Davidivitch?"

"Productive." He showed her the folder. "She's given us a number of potential leads and a few good possibilities. We'll go over my notes later."

Kincaid flipped Amy his keys. "You drive."

The security guard was talking to a courier. Kincaid moved his pen set and log-in book a fraction of an inch to one side.

*

After another spate of recent expansion, the fitness center commandeered almost half a block of retail space south of Yonge and Bloor, one of Toronto's major intersections. Quickly developing over the past year, it incorporated four floors of an old brick building that had sequentially been transformed from a pre-war factory to a warehouse, then a restaurant, and, most recently, a huge army surplus and camping outlet. Now, a trendy health food bar, gym, pool, and an extensive spa area dominated two main floors. The upper levels were saved for condos and expensive lofts with floor to ceiling windows and expansive brick fireplaces. The detectives followed the signs to the *Gym* and *Weight Training* area.

Pushing the doors open, the first thing that struck Kincaid was the smell. Overhead ventilation fans ceaselessly tried to refresh the stifling air, but the gymnasium was impregnated with an intense stench of sweat and body odor. Kincaid stopped at the front desk and asked about Cynthia Baxter. A petite young girl who barely managed to chew her gum while she sorted towels directed him to the back of the room with a lackadaisical wave that might have meant practically anything.

The weight room was immense. Pounding music punctuated groans and metallic *clangs* as suspended weights fell back together. Along one wall, computerized bikes blinked with little scale versions of mountain courses. The adjacent area was littered with treadmills, rowing machines, stair climbers, and a couple of contraptions that reminded Kincaid of iniquitous pieces of medieval torture. Trapped in a sloped-backed chair connected to a stack of weights, a young woman listening to headphones was stretching her thighs so far apart Kincaid was sure she'd dislocate her hips. Her little exercising outfit was skimpier than most bathing suits. He watched her for about a minute before MacKenzie jabbed him in the ribs.

"That's enough for today, Sir. You're not supposed to get too excited, remember?" She turned him by the shoulders and moved on.

Benches and free weights were arranged in front of a long, mirrored wall. Huffing and puffing, men and women watched Amy's reflection pass behind them. Everyone strained just a bit harder, held the curl a little longer. They had a defiant, challenging glare in their eyes as they watched their muscles expand with each rep. They looked like animals ritualistically posturing at some communal watering hole, posing for likely mates and demonstrating their strength to potential adversaries.

The air was tight. Noise came from everywhere: cables, treads, clanking weights, bikes whirring, and the constant *thud thud thud* of what was supposed to pass for music. Like the woman on the "thigh ripper," everyone wore some version of the same chic ensemble. Designer labels, coordinated outfits, logos: the "in" brands of the day. Kincaid hadn't realized you had to be so preoccupied with your appearance when you just wanted to sweat.

When Kincaid saw Cynthia Baxter, the only words he could think of were *stunning* and *stunning*. A head-turner in the worst way. Early thirties, skin alluringly smooth, her features softly defined, with an enticing sense of fierce competitiveness twinkling in her eyes. Full lips, her mouth wide and sensual. Soft auburn streaks highlighted a thick mane of long brown hair she'd tied into a braid that ran down the center of her back. Small but well-toned, she possessed the muscular physique of a tri-athlete. If she had an ounce of body fat it would have been easy to spot: her Lycra body suit was tighter than a second skin. The fluorescent thong she wore overtop was the same blood red as her lipstick. A woman to be reckoned with: Cynthia Baxter would be your prime suspect in an office back stabbing. Or a murder where the motive was jealousy.

Wearing extra wrap-around weights on her ankles and wrists, Ms. Baxter was nearing the end of a hiking trail on one of the Stairmasters. She toweled her forehead and watched the computer screen as her legs pumped vigorously up and down. Without looking, she felt Kincaid's presence behind her. She turned, saw him reach subtlety for his identification, nodded, and gestured that she only had three minutes to go. She barely gave Amy a glance, dismissing her by not acknowledging her presence. Kincaid felt his partner stiffen.

Cynthia Baxter's pace gradually decelerated until her legs finally stopped moving. The pedals hissed. She wiped her forehead, unclasped the extra weights, then draped a fresh towel around her neck. The strain brought a light blush to her cheeks.

Kincaid introduced himself. Cynthia, as expected, had quite a grip. "And this is Sergeant MacKenzie." Their hands hardly touched.

"Bear with me. I have to stretch or I'll cramp up something fierce." She walked over to a matted enclave on the side wall.

"Just get back?"

"What?"

"Your office said you were flying in this morning."

"Vancouver. A little rain, as usual, but pleasant enough." She toweled the sweat from her forehead. "I assume you're here about Devlin," she said, slowly beginning a series of side-to-side stretches. Kincaid realized he was staring when another elbow caught him in the side.

"Haven't I talked to someone else already?"

Sergeant MacKenzie quickly told her about Detective Gerbec.

"Horrible business with Devlin," Cynthia admitted coldly. "Not the most pleasant way to exit this plane."

"Turner owned the agency, isn't that correct?"

Cynthia paused, stared, then answered with a bitter *"yes."*

"You were partners?"

"On paper."

"But not in practice?"

She leaned against the wall and stretched her hamstrings. A couple of weightlifters stopped to watch her thong move up and down. "Turner was obstinate and opinionated, and he always wanted to get his own way. I'm the same. There wasn't much leeway for compromise."

"So?"

"So we established our boundaries and stayed out of each other's way."

"You owned the agency first, though?" Amy asked.

Teeth clenched together. "Uh-huh." She straightened her back, spread her legs until her feet were shoulder width apart, and started a series of knee bends. She stared belligerently at one of the men until he went back to his weights.

"What happened?"

"It was a small agency, but mine. One other agent, a couple of readers and support staff. The industry has tightened up considerably over the past few years, especially with the Internet. Everyone with a laptop can pretend they're a writer." She shook her head. "Fucking vanity presses and DIY publishers. It's pathetic. Open the Writer's Manual. You'll see ads on every page for self-publishers. They practically guarantee your thriller will make the best ten list, or your pathetic volume of poetry will be in the race for a Nobel. The writing's shit but you pay to be published. Makes me want to puke."

Cynthia's face reddened. "We had financial problems, especially after that terrible September day, so I put the word out we'd consider a partner. Someone who could help with our writers and could consistently bring fresh clients on board. Turner called."

"But he didn't really want to be a partner?"

"Never did. He bought in at fifty percent."

"How did you feel about that?"

"How do you think I felt, Sergeant?"

"But you accepted his offer."

"The world of takeovers and mergers. He brought a lot of quality clients and contacts," Cynthia shrugged. "And even more than fame, I like money."

But she didn't say 'more than power.

"So the agency did well after Devlin came on board."

"There's no secret about that. He brought in numerous clients and publishers we wouldn't have had access to." She sneered. "The little agency that grew."

Amy pressed a little more. "What was Turner like to you?"

"I told you. Two alpha males. We kept our distance."

"That's not what I asked."

Cynthia Baxter pretended to muse. "To me? Devlin was a bastard. An erudite, educated, ambitious, self-effacing bastard. A prick with a capital "P."

"And his bad points?" Kincaid asked.

It was the first time Cynthia smiled. Her eyes glistened with a child's impishness, but it disappeared in a moment. "It's how you have to be in our business. And as I said –"

"You like money."

Another shrug.

"Did he socialize much?"

"Turner? Are you joking? Devlin defined "loner." I couldn't name a friend."

Behind them, two huge metal discs clanged together. The noise reverberated through the gym, momentarily blocking out the dull throb of music.

"Enemies?"

A sarcastic laugh. "What kind of fucking question is that?"

Kincaid waited.

"Turner had too many enemies to count."

"Why?"

"Because of the way he treated people."

"Which was?"

"Brutally. Like everyone was trash. As if no one mattered. And to Devlin Turner, I'm sure they didn't. Ask his wife. They were in the middle of a messy divorce. If you had something he thought he could make some money on, fine. Everyone else was an inconvenience. Collateral damage. He was your best friend until the coin stopped."

Kincaid remembered what Rebecca told him. "It doesn't sound like he'd be most writers' choice for an agent," he lied.

"But that's where you're wrong. People lined up for him to represent them."

"Why?"

"Simple economics. Devlin was a highly driven, selfish, motivated bastard who got things done. The agent gets a piece of whatever is placed. The greater the volume he represents and the more they sell, the more he makes. Writers wanted Turner because they knew he'd work to promote them, but he was really interested in publicizing himself. Publishers felt the same way."

"So everyone wins?" Kincaid said. "Especially your agency."

"You're two for two, Detective." She gave him a slow look up and down. "You've spent some time in a gym."

"A bit. But not in any place as upscale as this."

"Liar. Still train?"

"Not much."

"Bull shit. Why?"

"No time," he lied. The look in her eyes said she didn't believe him. The incessant *thump thump thump* of the music was becoming increasingly irritating. *Who actually confused this tautologous banging with music?*

"What if a writer Turner pushed faltered?" Amy wondered. "What if they got writer's block or something?"

"Then he was toast. He'd be off Turner's 'good list' before you could say metaphor. The man had the patience of a ten buck hooker."

Kincaid smiled. "We need your help, Ms. Baxter."

"In what way?"

"We're compiling a list of people who had grudges with Turner."

"You're kidding, surely?"

There was that *'you're kidding'* again. "No, I'm not."

"Aww. Enemies. I see. Because of the way he treated writers? His penchant for sending rather scathing rejections? Is that where all this shit is going?"

"You were aware of that?"

"Hard to miss."

"Why would someone as wealthy and famous as Devlin Turner waste his time sending out personal rejections that couldn't possibly do anything than generate hate?"

"I've already told you. We didn't share. And we certainly didn't play nice together. I knew what he was doing but I really didn't care."

Cynthia Baxter was lying.

"And I doubt it matters now."

Kincaid glanced at Amy. "But wouldn't it damage your relationship with some of your own clients?"

"Not the good ones. And not the ones who dealt directly with me."

Kincaid noticed the tremor in her hands. "We'll still need that list, Ms. Baxter."

"Of *all* the people who hated Turner? Well, Detective, that would include just about everyone he came in contact with. Especially rotund little Dorthea."

Amy winced. "Turner's wife?"

"She was filing for divorce. Or didn't you know?"

"We're aware of their marital discord."

"*Their marital discord*? Oh, I like that."

"Even if you're correct and Turner was awash in enemies," Kincaid interrupted, sensing Amy fume, "there must be a few whitecaps that rise above the other waves."

Cynthia Baxter smiled at Kincaid again. For real. *Almost.* She shrugged noncommittally, but genuinely appeared to be thinking about an answer. "There were some, I suppose. A couple of real nut cases. And some persistent little bastards you wouldn't want sneaking up behind you in a dark alley. If you've done some background checks, you already know he received more than his fair share of hate mail."

"We do. And that's what we're interested in. From what we've pieced together, people hated Turner because of those rejections."

"And –"

"And we need to understand why he sent the ones he did. Sergeant MacKenzie can pick up the list as soon as it's ready."

"You're almost as pushy as Turner." Cynthia eyed Kincaid closely. She leaned forward and toweled the last beads of sweat from her neck. "Tell you what. Come for a quick sauna, leave your card at reception, and I'll email whatever I can find . . . later."

Kincaid smiled. "Thanks for the list. But the sauna is going to have to wait."

"There's one other thing." Amy made a show of checking her notes.

A bored *yes.*

"Did Turner *always* send personal rejections back to his clients?"

"Of course not. The volume of submissions we receive is incredible. That's what the support staff is for."

"If time equaled money, what would prompt him to send personal replies to writers he had no intention of dealing with?"

There was a moment's pause. "Money, greed, vindictiveness, hate. Jealousy. Maybe the day of the week, or if he'd nicked himself shaving. He might have been loaded the night before and had to do his wife."

"What happens to the agency now that he's dead?" Amy's stare was fixed and cold.

Nothing.

"Ms. Baxter?"

Reaching up on her toes, Cynthia stretched her arms back behind her head. Her breasts strained against the bodysuit, her stomach flattened, and the taut muscles in her thighs and calves swelled sensually. She released the stretch, smiling innocently. A mischievous siren.

A siren whose call could lure just about anyone, Kincaid thought.

"Our original contract agreement gives me first right of refusal for his shares. Buying them back is definitely something I'll have to consider. *We'll all miss Devlin deeply,* but I have to think about the writers the agency represents, don't I? I certainly can't leave them stranded."

She smiled and started gathering up her things. "Anything else?"

"Not right now. But we'll be in touch. And we really need that list as soon as possible."

Cynthia Baxter took a step closer to Kincaid. "Bring your suit next time. Or then again, don't."

She spun around without another word and walked off toward the changing rooms. Her hips swayed to the pounding music, and she slowly started unbraiding her hair as she moved around the equipment. Everyone paused as she passed, smiling, staring, or boldly trying to catch her eye with a pose. She pulled the thin band of her fluorescent G-string out from her buttocks, ignoring them all.

But sensed their lust.

Chapter Fourteen

Richardson grinned broadly when he recognized the voice on the other end of the line. He had an odd habit of breathing in just as he started to laugh, so it often sounded like he was choking or snorting.

"God, listen to what the cat dragged in. How they hanging, Kincaid?"

"I missed you too, Richardson." He'd changed his mind at the last minute and decided to drive. He'd known the man forever, so he'd flipped the speaker phone off.

"Where are you, the fucking Parkway?" He could hear the telltale sounds of snarled, stop and start traffic in the background, the grunts and groans from the diesel trucks, the sirens, the constant jack hammering at the construction sites, the new cement meridians being guided into place. It never ended.

"The very same."

"So you're really okay?"

"Sure thing."

Kincaid knew that's how Richardson would leave it, that he wouldn't press. Two days and he was already growing weary of his colleagues' defensiveness and Amy's well-meant vigilance. Like Kincaid, Richardson was a solitary individual who ignored rumors and respected your privacy. A cabbie zipped dangerously by, leaning on his horn and cutting Kincaid off. After weaving in and out for the last ten minutes, the cabbie was about a car length of where he would have been if he'd just stayed in his lane. The man's face was blood-red, the veins in his neck pounding. Kincaid knew the feeling. He'd taken Dr. Chapur's threat seriously, but it had still taken him ages to relax and slow down.

"Sounds like a fucking asshole. Hey, Kincaid. This bear walks into a bar and says 'I want a gin . . . . and tonic. The bartender gives him one and says, 'why the long pause?' and the bear says 'I don't know, I've had them all my life."

Silence.

"So you see, this bear . . . "

"Okay, okay. Half decent. Are you still on the DiMatteo thing?"

"Shit yeah. But not for long. Everything should come together in a week, maybe two. Then again, it might be a month.

You know how it is with these fucking bikers. Triple cross each other, and their best friend taps a bullet in their back. But my gut tells me we're ready to move."

The cabbie honked at someone again. "Are you looking at a turf war?"

Richardson cradled the phone with his shoulder. "The Rock need to re-establish a foothold in Toronto if they want a piece of the human trafficking action before it's too late. The Hell's Angels control the pie and pipeline, and they're not offering anyone so much as a taste. They're making more than they did on dope by selling kids back and forth. There were two bombings in Montreal last week. Another one the month before that. Like the Mafia, they're using gangs to do the real dirty work. You know a shitty little titty bar called the *Pink Carousel*? A crapper on Dundas Street? "

"I've heard of it."

"Someone tossed a pipe bomb through the front window when you were in the hospital. No one wants to see this go south. I'm moving the second that puke of a CI rears his ugly little head. We go deep to ground. See if we can buy in, offer our own "girls." Show them we can move a lot of children quick and see what happens." His voice faltered. Tracking narcotics was one thing – chasing human slaves was another. Kincaid heard the stress in his friend's voice.

It would be nice working together again, Kincaid thought. "Be careful."

"Fucking eh. If you need anything, you know the code. Use it. Anytime."

"Thanks."

"I mean it, Kincaid. I know how far you've stuck your neck out for me. You know I'd break the fucking rules for you, too."

"Now don't go getting me all teary eyed." Kincaid shot through an open space and back into the outside lane. *Why do the slowest cars stay in the fast lane at rush hour?* "Richardson? Can you still hear me?"

He grunted or burped.

"The stuff LT gave us was incomplete."

"Us? Oh right. You're working with MacKenzie. Now that's a hot little number. God, I miss Jeff Healy. Real Blues."

Kincaid glanced at his partner. She was scribbling some notes. "Down, boy. Have you found anything else Gerbec managed to put together?"

"I'm rounding up what I can, but there's still missing pieces. Big ones."

"Forensics?"

"Part. The coroner's sitting on a bunch of info downtown."

"Why have they still got it?"

"No comprendo."

"Do you know if the area was canvassed?"

"Thoroughly. Gerbec and friends talked to everyone near the scene, but I haven't had a chance to read through his notes."

"How much?"

"Maybe half. There's a shitload."

Another honk, this one loud enough to wail through Kincaid's earpiece.

Richardson jumped. "Shit. That *was* close."

"I almost lost my bumper. What's the charge for icing a cabbie?"

"Just points."

Kincaid smiled when Amy pretended to undo the clasp on the dashboard shotgun.

"So this lounge piano player has a little monkey collecting his cash."

"Richardson . . . "

"No wait. All of a sudden, the monkey runs over and jumps onto the bar. He starts running back and forth, dunking his junk into everybody's beer. So this big guy goes over to the piano player and says 'do you know your monkey's dropping his nuts into our beer? And the pianist says, "No, but if you hum a few bars . . . "

"Kincaid? K? You still there?"

"Still here."

"I might have told you that one before."

A hundred times, Kincaid groaned. *And he'd tell it again.* "What about the rest of the crime scene photos?"

"Bagged and tagged. The new photo man went a little overboard. There's a dung load of pictures floating around. Turner in the chair, all the pens. Blood everywhere. He looks like a fucking hedgehog."

"I'll need those photos."

"I'll do what I can."

"Are you sure you've got the time –"

"I said, 'I'll do what I can.' Undercover guys *work*. We don't sit on our ass all day like kids from homicide."

"Richardson? Thanks."

Silence.

"I'll binder it all up neat and tidy."

"I'll hold you to that."

Kincaid changed lanes to get rid of an eighteen wheeler sitting about three feet off his rear bumper. He glanced at Amy, his eyes flashing one of those *that was close* looks. She nodded, the color seeping back into her face.

"Leave the paperwork with Sgt. MacKenzie if I'm not there. You know her now, right?"

"Not in the Biblical sense, but I'd like to. We met briefly yesterday. Word at the house says she's all over you, but I could tell right away she wants me. Big time."

"Don't believe everything you hear. Give her as much as you think she can handle." He looked at his partner. "Then throw in a little more."

"She did the ShoeCam guy, didn't she? Tell her that was a nice collar."

"Tell her yourself."

"Does she know about Stephanie?"

"Richardson –"

"Okay, okay. Subject's over." He paused. "Are you working with her *all* the time? Because if you need a boner to point her in the right direction though some of the tougher stuff –"

"As usual, your diction is unique. I'm sure she'll manage. Anything special in Gerbec's notes?"

"Other than the pens?" Richardson snorted, then was quiet for a moment. Papers rustled in the background. Phones rang continuously. Farther up the road, two idiots in souped up Hondas were chasing each other at about 150 km to see who'd be the first one to wrap themselves around a pole. Amy called in the tags. The cabbie's, too.

"So far, no prints," Richardson said. "It's possible the perp wore surgical gloves. Gerbec jotted a note on the back of one of the pics, something he must have wanted to check later. It says – *'wore something on his feet'* and a question mark. "

"You mean like oversized boots?"

"That's my guess."

"Male or female?"

The Hondas disappeared into the distance. It was bad enough when they cracked themselves up – Kincaid hoped they wouldn't take any innocent people with them. An unmarked car was waiting for them at the next cut-off. Still honking belligerently, the cab was sitting three cars in front of them.

"Unknown," Richardson replied. "But if it's a woman, I don't want to meet her down at the docks one night. She'd be wearing a size thirteen shoe."

"I thought you met all your dates at the Docks."

"At least I date."

"Anything taken?"

"Nothing major. But the puke didn't have to kill the fucking dog, you know what I'm saying?"

"I do." Kincaid caught Amy's eye. "So there's not much to go on."

"You see? That's why you made Detective so quickly. You put things together" – Richardson snapped his fingers next to the phone –"just like that."

"And you're still a funny guy who never stops playing someone else."

Richardson's bravado showed through. "Hell, K. If you can't find a laugh or two in this game then you don't stand a chance, right?"

"Agreed. Are you going to be there long?"

"I'm still on standby. Busy busy busy. Hey, wait. I think there's something moving in my beard."

"You're a pig. If you have a minute, can you put everything you've got together for me? The canvass reports, the victim's background information, forensics, whatever you can find that's got Gerbec's name on it?"

"That's the second time you asked." He paused. He'd almost said, *something wrong with your fucking brain?* "I'll work my usual magic. The binders are getting filed into a couple of boxes as we speak. If I'm not here I'll leave them with The Chipmunk."

"God, LT looks pretty horrible."

"Well the afternoon hasn't done shit for his mood, I can tell you."

"Stay out of his way. And don't forget the photographs and the crime scene report."

"No problem. Hey, Kincaid" – he paused, not really sure what to say, or how to say it – "how's little Ryan doing?"

Silence. A van roared past Kincaid on the right, barely cramming into a space that had momentarily opened up between two trucks, its wheels spitting dirt onto Kincaid's windshield.

"Kincaid?"

"As well as can be expected."

An uncomfortable silence, this time from Richardson's end. "That's good, isn't it?"

Suddenly, nothing in the world seemed to matter. "If I think of anything else, I'll call. And thanks, again."

His friend was only confused for a moment. "Shit on everyone else, Kincaid. People know what kind of a guy you are. Ignore the rumors and do what you have to do." He paused, lowered his voice. "But if you need anything –"

"I will. Now forget you're undercover and pretend you're a real cop. Get to work. I'll be in touch."

"So this guy walks into a bar with a chunk of asphalt on his shoulder and says, "I want a beer for me and one for the road."

Richardson heard the phone disconnecting, and smiled.

The cabbie was finally sick and tired of the stop and start, bumper to bumper crawl up the Parkway. He squeezed into the middle lane, and then pushed his way into the inner one. He pulled up on the shoulder and took off, hurling fresh gravel at Kincaid's car. A large chunk of stone put a chink in his right headlight.

A grin crept across Kincaid's lips. He reached down under his dashboard for his lights and flicked the siren on. This was going to make him feel a whole lot better.

Chapter Fifteen

Parked on the off-ramp shoulder, Amy filed the cabbie's citations into her daybook. There was one more stop they had to make before heading to the precinct. She gave Kincaid the address.

"Did you have any trouble finding the place, Sergeant?"

"None." She'd tracked down the company that used the logo Mrs. Dempsey recognized on the "repairman's" shirt after a couple of calls. Two sub-contractors bore an insignia that was even close. Only one was multicolored and had a little hand-stitched satellite on the front pocket.

Satellite International.

*

Summoned by a receptionist who'd been on a personal call and wasn't pleased with the interruption, the owner of *Satellite International,* Mr. Rommolo, seemed just as put out. Mumbling and cursing, he came out from the back room still doing up his fly. Amy coughed and looked away. *All class.*

Mr. Rommolo was the quintessential stereotype of a dirty old man, the 1970's "Stranger Danger" image who, though well-intentioned, had given the wrong impression of what a pervert looked like to a generation of vulnerable children. Squinty eyes, almost bald but still combing the last vestiges of hair over his crown, grossly overweight, a sweaty, pock-marked face, and filthy hands. He wore a t-shirt that had never fit and someone else's oversized pants. His stomach bloated out over the top of his belt. He chewed the end of a fat, unlit cigar. A lingering stale, heavy odor moved as he did. A quick glance at Kincaid, then a slow once over, up and down, of Amy. Another look at Kincaid told him he shouldn't push too hard. Amy stared at Rommolo until he looked up from her blouse.

"You the young lady that was comin' 'bout the robbery? Of the clothes?"

"Sergeant MacKenzie," she said brusquely. He made her skin crawl. "We need to see one of your work shirts."

"Why?" He rolled the cigar back and forth in his mouth.

"Someone might have used one of your shirts during a felony."

"Shit." The cigar kept moving. He yelled to a man hunched over a desk in the corner. "Jack. Leave the routing crap alone for a sec and call Ivan."

The man sighed, dutifully punching in a number.

"Ivan's our parts guy," Mr. Rommolo explained.

Kincaid asked him whose clothes were taken.

"Lloyd's. Got ripped off a few weeks back. I figured he was just trying to stiff me for an extra shirt, but the kid seems pretty straight. Works hard and needs the job, so I believed him and got him new threads. Shirt *and* pants. All our stuff's done at Crow Cleaners, over on Dupont. The old Indian guy gives me a special price. On time and never wrecks a thing."

He glanced at Amy's chest and gave her arm a gentle nudge. "Keeps the wages –"

She took a quick step inside and jammed her elbow into his ribs hard enough his breath caught. "Don't *ever* touch me *again* or you'll be scraping your junk off the floor."

Rommolo's face blanched. He coughed. "Yes mam." Moving back, he thought about lighting his cigar, but looked at Amy and decided to wait.

The rear door swung open and a small, wiry little man with a thick red beard walked into the room. Rommolo grabbed him and pulled him forward.

"Cops. They want to see your shirt."

Ivan looked dumbfounded.

"Show'em the picture you stupid prick. See? The installer's shirts look the same." He turned to Ivan. "Police are looking for some guy wearing one of our shirts."

The insignia matched Mrs. Dempsey's description.

Rommolo looked at the detectives. "Did Lloyd whack someone or –?"

"He's not implicated at all," Kincaid replied. "Collateral damage. The shirt was used as a disguise."

Mr. Rommolo's eyes brightened. "The shirts that were scooped. Do I get paid back for 'em or somethin'?"

Kincaid offered him a precinct business card. It was lined with a plethora of email addresses for police complaints and civilian issues. "Try them."

The fat man squinted. "Yeah. Sure I will."

"You think I can get the shirt back if the guy did somethun' really bad? Shit, that's a talkin' piece, right? We could hang it out front."

A talkin'piece? Kincaid assured Mr. Rommolo that would be the first thing they'd look into when they got back. The detectives turned without another word and left. Amy brushed her coat sleeves, scattering all of the little crawling things she pictured on her clothes.

*

When Kincaid dropped Amy off outside the underground garage, he told her the day was done and she was free to book off. She offered to stay and see what Richardson had amassed, but Kincaid said he wanted to take a look at whatever had been scrounged up first. She'd done well and held up her own again – he'd catch up with her in the morning. She didn't look pleased. Or impressed.

He wanted to go home too, but had to check in with Davis. He treated himself to specialty mocha at *The Coffee Shoppe* across the street, which gave him a few quiet moments to toy with some ideas beginning to percolate about the case. Twenty minutes later he was chatting with the Sergeants that ran the first floor of the house. Complaints, jail transfers, incoming arrests, bookings – what a ceaseless, thankless, job, he thought.

Upstairs, Davis' face was still badly swollen. Obviously in pain, his words rolled out through a mouthful of marbles. "I went back this morning," he grumbled. "Another hour in the chair while he drained it or something." LT popped more aspirin, grimacing as the chalky pills went down.

"How'd it go at Meredith House?"

Kincaid told him about their visit and the subsequent meetings with Leeanne Davidivitch and Cynthia Baxter.

"And?" LTs words were at a premium.

"The investigation is well under way, and we're currently exploring all possibilities." Kincaid smiled – it was Davis' stock media line.

"Nothing definite?"

"Not until we start going over Richardson's new information."

"How was Amy's second day?"

"Fine. A little impatient and overeager, but that's to be expected. She knows when to move and when to stay back. The morgue was a little much for her. Tough one to start with for my shadow."

"Peter Pan too tight?"

"Not an issue. I know it's part of her job because you're concerned."

"She's wanted to work homicide with you for months. To learn from the best. But you're right – and she'll keep watching. Closely."

Kincaid glanced out the window. He had to watch his distance. It would be hard not to want to get closer to Amy. A lot closer. If he was honest with himself, he had to admit there was something very special about his colleague. But it was the wrong time to get involved with a tracker. *Wasn't that how he lost Stephanie?*

Davis tore off a memo pinned to his bulletin board. "Gail Meredith called."

"I'm surprised she had the time."

"She sounded nice on the phone."

"I'll call her from now on."

LT scowled and touched his jaw. "She wants to send her security consultant over to give you some information. Maybe even tag along to stay in the loop. I told her you'd appreciate her help."

Davis didn't anticipate an argument. Kincaid was one of the only officers he'd worked with who never begrudged an extra pair of eyes or fresh perspective. More often than not it was the various departments' unwillingness to share information, and their innate need to protect their own agendas, that impaired investigations. If he had more people with his friend's tolerance, interdepartmental co-operation wouldn't be a platitude but something that actually worked. Kincaid preferred to work alone, but always accepted his own limitations and acknowledged help when he needed it.

"Did you get a name?"

"No. They'll meet with you tomorrow."

Kincaid watched his eyes. "Come on Reg. What aren't you telling me?"

"Meredith doesn't know you, so she threw out some names, just to be sure you'd be comfortable with the idea." He signed a document then flipped it closed. His mouth tightened the longer he spoke. "Ten minutes later the mayor's office called."

"Just so everyone –"

"Was on the same page."

"Uh-huh. I said it was your investigation and that was good enough for him. Shit."

"What?"

"Just this stupid tooth. If it happens again I'm having them all pulled."

Kincaid sighed. "It too will pass. Anyway, as long as he doesn't get in the way, everything will be fine."

"Amy can deflect him a bit, too. What's on now?"

"Richardson's stuff. Is he still skulking around, or did he leave something with you?"

"You just missed him. Over there." Davis pointed to two large boxes by the door.

"I went through Gerbec's notes last night, so I'll scan these later and see what I can put together. I'll go over it with Amy tomorrow so we're ready for the security consultant."

Davis would have laughed if he could. "You mean the Amy who needs some confidence? She knew you were going for coffee, so she slipped in and copied a bunch of stuff. Said she wanted to get a jump on it so you didn't have to sift through it all yourself. She left out anything she didn't understand, like the PM report."

So Amy copied the files while she reported to Davis. The little devil.

"I saw an old friend yesterday."

"Anyone I know?"

"Rebecca Potterdam."

Davis's eyes widened. "The writer? She's one of Lizzy's favorites. How the hell do you know her?"

"She's my godmother. We've been friends for ages. She was very close to my mom."

"It never ceases to amaze me who you know, Kincaid. Case info?"

"She gave me some background from the perspective of someone who knows the industry inside and out. She explained how the whole publisher-agent-writer thing actually works. It'll help with the interviews. And she offered some insider scoops. I think she narrowed down the motivation for our killer."

"Perfect. Lizzy and I have practically all of her stuff, you know."

Kincaid noticed a number of Rebecca's books on Davis' credenza over the years.

"I do." He smiled, opened his jacket, and slid the copy of Rebecca's latest work across the table. "Autographed and personalized."

"That's great." Davis flipped through the first few pages until he saw the note. While he read it, Kincaid picked up the boxes of files and reports. There was lots to go through. *How much had Amy copied?*

Davis pointed at them. "Remember. Don't make it a late night."

"Everything in stride. But I feel good."

Lt. watched his eyes. There was a half-truth there. "No *pushing the envelope* just yet. And that's an order. You do and you're out. And please thank Mrs. Potterdam." He looked down at the book. "This is really nice of her."

"I will. And I'm not pressing, Reg. See you in the morning."

"Unless I'm at the bloody dentist," he mumbled bitterly. He reached for another file from his 'in' basket.

"Reg? Perhaps you shouldn't take your gun."

Chapter Sixteen

Predictably, the first part of the drive home had been bumper to bumper, the cars pressing in like a vice. The congestion eased once Kincaid passed the city limits, but even then, when the lights were falling away in his rearview and the trees lining the highway started to thicken, the lanes were still clotted like a diseased artery. The cancerous tentacles of the subdivisions kept reaching out farther and farther, strangling what was once beautiful patchworks of farmland with prosaic rows of townhouses, fast food restaurants and strip malls. One day, the world would come too close and he'd have to move again. But Kincaid rarely thought about 'one day'.

Although the country roads northeast of the city were often treacherous, Kincaid rarely bemoaned the drive. When January blizzards hurled their worst, insidious patches of slick black ice often lay unseen beneath shifting coats of snow, and the narrow back roads became perilous smears of slippery rinks. With the autumn harvests long baled, the fields on either side of the road were barren, and with nothing to deflect the squalls, blurry whiteouts were common. In the spring there was mud; in the summer, rain buckled asphalt. Yet despite the seasonal hazards, Kincaid wouldn't have wanted to be anywhere else.

He lived on a little rural route to nowhere, fifteen minutes from the closest town north of the city but years in ambience from Toronto. Kincaid's home was a converted two-story farm house. Constructed with stone from the local quarry and timber from surrounding trees, the original structure was almost a hundred and twenty years old. It had changed hands several times, and had stopped being used as a working farm two families before Kincaid moved in. Parcels of land had gradually been sold off to larger farm owners in the area, but the old house still sat on almost fifty acres of gently rolling hills and valleys, covered with deep thickets of pine and spruce and maple trees. The land butted up against the tip of the moraine, the last vestiges of the receding ice age when glaziers plowed and gnawed at what was left of the earth thousands and thousands of years ago, leaving jumbled slopes of unearthed rocks and boulders behind.

The house was bright and airy, effusing a sense of openness and space. Kincaid never liked feeling cramped or closed in. Not foreseeing a time he'd need all the extra room, he gutted the entire second story of the house, which opened up the main floor and gave him a central cathedral ceiling over twenty feet high. There was a large kitchen, a guest room, a spacious living area that faced the back of the house and was overshadowed by an expansive stone fireplace, and his bedroom. More than enough room for his needs.

After knocking out two adjoining walls, his bedroom took up most of the space on the other side of the kitchen. There was a small raised woodstove in the corner, a couple of old handmade rocking chairs someone left behind, and a wooden four-poster bed beautifully detailed that seemed a little small for the room. The far wall was dominated by a tall, dome-shaped window that bathed his room in early morning light.

It was pitch black by the time Kincaid reached his sanctuary. He carried in the boxes that contained Devlin Turner's effects and piled them on his kitchen table, along with Gerbec's original notes and the information Richardson pieced together. He lit a fire with some cedar kindling, poured himself a short scotch, shook two painkillers from the little bottle, and turned to a fresh page in his notebook. Then, just as he'd done practically all the way home, he tried to force Ryan's face from his thoughts. The child was dying, and there was nothing he could do. Perhaps that's what was making everything feel worse. And what if he didn't outlast his special little friend from the 'Wish Foundation'? No. He couldn't even begin to think like that.

Carefully keeping everything tagged and in order, Kincaid took Turner's things from the evidence box and spread them across the table. Papers, folders, half-finished correspondence, bank records, a bulging accordion file stuffed full, and a box of computer discs and sticks. Could Turner have been tortured for something hidden here?

He glanced at the crime scene photographs and shivered. There was murder, and there was *this*. He couldn't begin to imagine the pain Turner must have suffered. Richardson was right: he looked like a horribly disfigured porcupine covered in blood. Kincaid had seen a lot of grotesque things over the years, but he still couldn't fathom the depths of mans hatred. He stared at the images of Turners swollen lips, the blood, the stitches. He thought about the time it must have taken. Who could possibly do that to someone else? Considering the circumstances, Amy had done pretty well just looking at the photos, let alone being with him at the morgue when he'd pulled the white sheet back and exposed the abject horror of what mankind is truly capable of.

Examining Turner's personal files, one of the first things Kincaid realized was that the man had indeed perversely kept the replies he received back from the officious rejections he'd sent to writers. They were sequenced alphabetically in the accordion file. And there were a lot of them. He cross-referenced the names he'd received from Cynthia Baxter and Leeanne Davidivitch. Turner had kept everything Walter Croft had sent on behalf of his wife, Matilda. There were so many pages clipped together he didn't bother to count them. Brent Jacob's file wasn't as thick, but it looked more *legal*; there were at least two dozen antagonistic and threatening letters in his folder. Comparatively, the files on Lois Maxwell and Peter Gibney weren't as thick and actually rather non-descript. Either whatever was there had been propitiously removed, or there hadn't been very much information filed away in the first place. *Odd.*

Richard Barclays, however, was completely crammed full.

But so was another one. It was so thick that it bulged into the "B" and "D" sections. It was undoubtedly the largest file in the folder. Kincaid frowned and tugged the dossier loose. *Erik Caster.* The man's picture was enough to make you shiver. There was an asterisk beside Casters name on Cynthia Baxter's list, but Leeanne Davidivitch hadn't mentioned him personally at all? *Why?*

*

Kincaid kept Caster's information out. Flipping through the rest of the accordion file, one other name caught his eye. *One he never expected.* He checked Baxter's list: there it was again. He frowned. 'Unexpected' was pejorative. So were eerie and disconcerting.

Sipping his drink, Kincaid read for about an hour. He still couldn't believe someone would be that odious to send back the moribund replies Turner had. What was the point? What could he possibly have achieved by maliciously destroying peoples' hopes and dreams? A simple "no thank you" would have probably been sufficient in most cases, but Turner deliberately pushed people, people who'd sent him their life's work, to the edge of despair. He thought about some of the things Rebecca had told him about the pain and effort writers pour into their work. Even if he absolutely detested their manuscripts or proposals, why had Turner needed to condemn them so spitefully? And *then* taken the time to write something even *ghastlier* back if they contacted him again. Surely he must have realized what he was doing. Why goad them so malevolently?

Kincaid jotted down some notes, filed the first binder away, and pulled another one out of the box. There was no need to dwell over the contents in detail – the letters were just as ignorant and antagonistic as the ones in the first book. A large piece of birch rolled over in the fire, the bark unfurling in a plethora of bright colors. Thinking about Ryan, he tugged out another smaller book. Turner's bank records. Kincaid went back about four years, studying the entries, dates, the credit and balances, trying to recognize any pattern that might have been hidden between the lines. He didn't know if these were Turner's accountant's *actual* books, or the second set he undoubtedly kept for taxes. Either way, the first thing he noticed was Turner's income was even more sizable than he'd expected.

Rights and royalty fees came in every month from numerous writers and publishers. Regardless of how old a book was or when it was printed, Turner still received a piece of the profits from every sale. Each time the book was taken from the library, a few more pennies found their way into Turner's coffers. Kincaid recognized a few of the more well-known writers, but there were dozens of names, publishers, and houses that didn't strike a chord. It was immediately apparent, though, that Ian Nuraki's books provided Turner with the majority of his income. They were a prime component of Meredith House's substantial profits as well.

Kincaid rarely had more than one drink during an evening, but the days stress had exacted its toll and he poured himself another. On his way back from the kitchen he threw two more logs on the fire. One was a thick piece of well-dried poplar, and the instant the flames licked its edges, the white-grey bark uncurled in a blaze of light.

A cursory inspection of the bank records showed something else, too. Despite what she'd said in their interview earlier, Gail Meredith had more than a passing business acquaintance with Devlin Turner. He was undoubtedly her most prolific agent, and they wined and dined practically every week. In fact, most of Meredith Houses' major writers had originally come from Turners' stable of aspiring authors.

And what about Cynthia Baxter? Kincaid lingered over his scotch. Her fortune had taken a rather severe turn for the better when Turner bought the majority of shares in the agency. Her wealth and success had increased drastically with him at the helm. *Then why did she despise him so much?*

A few pages later, Kincaid found one of the patterns he'd been looking for. He double-checked the entries, confirmed the dates, and then pushed himself up from the table with a thoughtful smile. Pacing back and forth, he stopped in front of the large bay window, mulling over his ideas as he swirled the remnants of his drink around his glass. The sky was an oily black, and a thick cloak of dark clouds strangled any starlight. He could just make out the treetops shimmering with the wind. An owl hooted in the distance.

For each of the last six months, Turner had withdrawn a total of $9,999.00 from his personal account. The same amount over the same number of days, but always under different names. One dollar under an even ten thousand – just enough so he didn't raise any flags at the bank.

Kincaid finished his scotch. He was more exhausted than he'd thought. The day had left him physically drained, and sleep beckoned. If he was going to be able to keep up the same pace tomorrow, he had to forget the viciousness of the murder and push the gnawing pain from his mind. At least now he had a few threads to weave together: the entries confirmed there was no doubt Turner was being blackmailed. But the questions of *why* and *by who* would undoubtedly hover around his thoughts like a swarm of stinging insects.

He'd learned something else, too. Turner's agency was apparently being wooed by another publishing company called *Excalibur Books*. Each quarter, Turner had done a little more business with *Excalibur*. Certainly nowhere near as much as he did with Meredith House, but enough that Gail must have started feeling threatened. From what the records showed, Meredith House couldn't afford to lose Turner and his cache of writers – old and new – but especially Ian Nuraki. How far would she go to keep her business intact, he wondered? And what lengths would a rejected writer go to in search of revenge?

Kincaid went to his bedroom and lit a small pyre of kindling in the corner woodstove, then added enough logs to sustain the fire for several hours. He stood quietly in front of the hearth, hands out, savoring the seductive warmth. The day had been grueling: he needed to rest. But another pricking rumination kept digging at the back of his mind, festering, making sleep a distant siren.

When he watched her – when he *really* watched her – Kincaid realized Davis and Leeanne Davidivitch were right. He was Amy's first partner, and he'd been her mentor since she'd been assigned to the House. *Had two years gone by that quickly?* They were friends, close friends. He hadn't noticed it before because too much was going on in his personal life, and he lacked the necessary objectivity to see his own dilemma. But they saw something he hadn't – Amy was a lot more interested in him than he realized. She was definitely hoping for something more than new ideas, some fresh instruction, and a close working relationship. It wasn't something he could ignore. And the truth was, he wasn't really sure he wanted to.

Amy was attractive. Very attractive. She had a special look about her, something captivating and exciting that stirred his deepest passions. She was probably the only person he'd ever seen decked out in a flak jacket and baseball cap who made the outfit look sexy. How could he not have noticed it so completely, so deeply, before? The nights they had dinner. The night in the car . . .

Memories. Thinking back, he realized how much her wardrobe had changed since they started working together, even when they were in different departments. Finer, sleeker, everything showing her off to her best advantage. And that was pretty easy to do. He started remembering all the little things: a touch here, a laugh about some private thing they shared, hands brushing over each other, a look out of the corner of her eye. Kincaid was shocked he'd missed all the little things, the gentle things, the personal things, that should have sent the bells peeling.

Perhaps he hadn't realized how close he'd slipped.

Or maybe he was just afraid of seeing it.

A thick piece of kindling toppled over and sent a shower of sparks into the air. The sudden blaze was a conduit, instantly igniting the two other things he hadn't been able to stop thinking about since he'd been in the hospital. He'd managed to keep the other thoughts in check: Gail Meredith, Cynthia Baxter, the list of suspects already formulating in his mind, the blood-splattered pictures of Turner's study, the pens through his eye, the blood-soaked lips, and the poor dog hanging so listlessly from the branch of the maple tree.

But not these two.

Stephanie.

Rebecca had sowed a seed that kept growing like a kudzu vine, strangling everything around it from the light and eating what was left from the inside out. Amy was wonderful, but God, how he missed the love of his life. *If only* . . .

And no matter how drained he felt, the scotch and the painkillers weren't going to be able to keep Ryan from his dreams. He thought about his own tests coming up, and shuddered. He had to see his young friend again tomorrow. They'd been apart days too long.

No.

He *needed* to see him.

Chapter Seventeen

Dawn.

The final embers in the woodstove smoldered in a bed of ash. Outside, stippled with the last twinkling stars, the sky was streaked a rusty pink. A light, filmy gauze of clouds drifted past the trees like battlefield mist.

As soon as Kincaid started moving, the lethargic hangover that came with the sleeping pills lost its potency, and the medications cloying pull slowly seeped away. For the first time in ages he felt rested and awake, his mind clear as the sunlight glistening through his bedroom window. After a shower and shave, he scrambled a skillet of eggs, diced in some ham, cheddar, mushrooms and peppers, and sipped a cappuccino while he re-checked the notes he'd made before bed. Spoiling himself with a second coffee for the drive, he was on the road before he took his first pain killer. He had two stops to make before he went to the precinct. As long as the highway was clear, he'd be able to interview his first suspect before the night shift ended.

Tree shadows whipped by. Kincaid called Amy just before he reached the downtown core. Still groggy and wrapped up in tentacles of murky dreams, she listened carefully to what he said then jotted down a few points on her bedside notepad. He hung up just before she rolled over, checked the time, and started yelling his name.

*

Strafed with a swath of clouds that stretched across the horizon, morning broke as Kincaid veered off the Parkway. The city yawned awake. The few trees that stole space from the concrete enclave shivered in the wind tunnel between buildings. Countless doughnut shops that infested the streets fired up ovens and prepared to feed the caffeine and sugar zombies who'd be swarming over them like a plague. Planes and helicopters were lifting off the ground to report the morning traffic. Kincaid pulled to a stop in front of the Toronto-Dominion Centre, a collage of high-rise banking and office towers that dominated several blocks in the financial district. The front of the building was speckled with real gold flakes.

He banged on the building's huge glass doors. A security guard ignored the first few knocks, but jolted awake when the second set shivered the window. Yawning and fumbling with his tie, he hustled over immediately when he saw the reflection of Kincaid's badge.

"You're here awfully early, sir. Not even the head brown-nosers are in yet."

The guard smiled – Kincaid didn't. He scrawled his name and badge number on the man's clipboard.

"Where would the cleaners be right now?"

"There's four separate teams, Detective."

"I'm looking for Barclay. Richard."

The guard checked the schedule sheet. "The seventeenth or eighteenth floor."

Kincaid took the elevator to the seventeenth. After a few steps down the hall, he heard someone humming in an adjacent office. Short, squat and preternaturally aged, the woman was stooped over a large oak desk, barely scattering the previous day's dirt with her feather duster. She wore a formless frock over an even more nondescript dress, a black hairnet and threadbare sock-nylons that barely covered the bottom of her calves. A jailer's ring of keys dangled from her waist, jingling like chimes.

"Pardon me."

Jumping involuntarily, the old woman frantically began cleaning the desk. She coughed twice, not accustomed to the smell as the dust disseminated. She glanced up uneasily when she was sure whoever was at the door realized how tirelessly she worked and she didn't have time for interruptions.

"Miss?"

She squinted hard, but didn't recognize the man. Definitely not a supervisor. She stopped working and rubbed the small of her back. He certainly looked nice, though. Too bad Ludmilya was on break – this one looked promising. Mature, handsome face, nice clothes, muscular, polished shoes, clean hands. Not like those no-good bums who were always sniffling around her like a pack of wild dogs.

"I'm looking for Barclay."

The cleaning lady shrugged. She was chewing on something Kincaid hoped wasn't tobacco.

Slower. "Richard . . . Barclay. Can you tell me where he's working?"

The name didn't generate a flicker of interest on the weathered lines of the old woman's face.

"A tall man," Kincaid smiled patiently, showing her with his hands. "Thin, too." Another physical depiction. Kincaid stroked his chin. "A goatee? A little beard?" He pulled the hair back from his forehead. "Balding?" He squinted hard and pretended he was wearing glasses, then pantomimed someone sweeping.

"Yes, yes," the woman nodded excitedly, smiling back. "*Bar*clay." She stressed the first syllable, happy she understood but sad the game was over. "Sixteen floor."

She showed Kincaid with her fingers, then repeated the number in case he didn't understand. All her fingers, plus another hand and extra thumb. "Him mop and polish." It was her turn for charades, and she showed her visitor how hard it was to control the big power polisher that buffed the hallways.

Kincaid smiled and thanked her for her help. The woman blushed and promptly submerged herself in the ritual of appearing excessively overworked. She glanced back at the open door. Poor Ludmilya. For a forty-year-old woman always in heat she'd missed her chance at love again.

Pacing himself, Kincaid took the stairs. As soon as he stepped out of the stairwell he saw Barclay at the far end of the hall. The cumbersome polisher waited idly by an office door while Barclay hastily slapped water back and forth with a sudsy mop. *Was he humming, too? A cleaner's habit?* Drawing nearer, he realized the man wasn't carrying a tune: he was engaged in an animated conversation with himself.

"Richard Barclay?"

Startled, the man instantly fell silent. He peered over the rim of his glasses and looked Kincaid up and down. He turned away, sneering, and started swabbing the tiles again. He muttered *cops* under his breath.

Kincaid introduced himself and proffered his identification, but Barclay wasn't interested in the least. He rammed the mop down into the rusted bucket then squeezed what was left of the bristles through a wringer. The water was filthy.

"I need to ask you a few questions."

"So ask." He had a deep, scratchy voice, the remnants of a smoker's cough. When he spoke he wheezed.

"Do you know why I'm here?"

Wringing out the mop, the man breathed a tired sigh. "Sure. And I haven't called him in months."

"Who?"

"Turner." Barclay leaned over his mop and frowned. "And I haven't sent the prick anything either. I've followed the restraining order to the letter." His eyes narrowed suspiciously. "That's why you're here, isn't it?"

Kincaid stretched from side to side, trying to get the kinks out from the long drive. He pretended to check some entries in his notebook. "Tell me about it."

Barclay coughed. "Like I said. I've stayed away from that asshole, so I don't care what he says. I'd rather stay upwind, if you know what I mean. If he wants to press more charges he'll have to prove it."

He tugged the mop free and slapped it against the floor. He glanced up and realized he was lucky he hadn't flicked any water onto Kincaid's shoes.

"When was the last time?"

Barclay shook his head. "April. May, maybe. I don't know, but it was sometime around then."

"That's when you were served with the restraining order?"

"The prick thinks he's real special."

"And you haven't been near him since?"

"No." Barclay's tone changed and became less defiant. "Why? What's – Richard – saying I did now?"

"Richard?"

"I'm trying to be nice. One of my characters calls people 'Richard' instead of 'dickhead.'

Kincaid suppressed a smile. "I've re-checked your file. Devlin Turner received so much hate mail from you I didn't think I was going to be able to pick it up."

Barclay half-grinned, half-scowled. "Yeah, I figured he kept it all. Obsessive little deviant. I guess that's how he got the Restraining Order."

"A lot of things you sent would have unsettled most people. And we always react in some way or another when we're afraid, don't we?"

Barclay squashed the mop down and tried to return the detective's penetrating stare. He couldn't stand still. "Okay, so I got a little carried away."

"A *little*?"

"I was angry, bitter, frustrated. Everything I'd worked at for so long, everything I'd been dreaming about day after day, week after week, month after month, was gone" he snapped his fingers "just like that."

"But it wasn't Turner's fault, was it?"

Barclay stared at the floor like a chastised schoolboy. "No. But I blamed him more than anyone else." He smashed the bucket into the wall. "I know I shouldn't have called or sent the letters. Or the faxes and e-mail – it got out of hand." Barclay bit the edge of his lip. He held the mop so tight his knuckles started shaking. "But the more I thought about him the angrier I got."

"Did you ever consider following through on your threats?"

His face flushed. "Don't be absurd." He splashed the water around, trying to calm down. "I was angry, okay, plain and simple. And I needed to vent or it would've eaten me up until there was nothing left."

Another harsh cough. Barclay slumped against the wall. Tired. Weary. Defeated. Everything in his posture reiterated that the memories deeply disturbed him.

Were they disturbing enough? Kincaid pushed him a little more. "You threatened to kill him."

"Actually, I threatened to kill his whole family."

"And blow up his house."

Barclay mumbled something.

"Pardon me?"

"And poison his dog." Barclay leaned against the mop. "And you know what? I like animals. Most of them, anyway. But that great big stupid Collie. *Shakespeare.* I've never seen anyone more compulsive about a dog. If there were only the two of us left, he'd publish that fucking dog's prints first."

Kincaid smiled and looked at his notes. "Did you go to his home?"

Barclay sighed and nodded dully.

"How many times?"

A shrug. "Six. Seven maybe."

"After the R.O.?"

"Zip."

"Was Turner the only one you threatened?"

His eyes misted over. "No. Meredith, too."

"Gail?"

"Uh-huh." Sweat dripped down Barclay's face. "There were so many rejections," he added sadly, stroking his goatee and drifting away.

"Why Turner?"

Spite contorted his face. "One, he just happened to be *it*. That one rejection that made *too many*. The one that took away all the hope, the one that finally breaks you here" – he touched his heart – "inside. The thing that pushes you over the edge and . . ."

"And what?"

". . . makes you want to give up. That makes you feel the meaninglessness of it all."

Kincaid cocked an eyebrow. "The proverbial straw that breaks the camel's back?"

Barclay nodded, then pushed his glasses up over the bridge of his nose. "I'd been sending my book out for almost two years. Publishers, small presses, agents, the whole thing."

"No offers?"

Barclay shook his head. "Not a real bite. The worst part of the day was when I picked up my mail. Up until then, there was still a chance, you know."

Kincaid remembered what Rebecca said. The frustration, the loneliness, the anguish, the fear when you opened your mail. The angst when there wasn't any, the anxiety when there was.

Barclay started mopping again but stopped before he finished the first stroke. Splayed and dirty, the scraggly head looked like a mangled wig. One more time through the wringer and the mop was going to fall apart. Like Barclay.

"I got a few positives. A couple of readers asked to see some chapters, but that was about it."

"One was from Turner and Baxter's agency?"

"Yeah. But there were a couple of other ones first."

"Did they want to look at the whole manuscript?" Kincaid prompted quietly.

"No. They all said it needed work. Besides, it's just another scam." He haphazardly washed another few tiles. "The agent or publisher sends you a letter and tells you how much they like your book. It's good, but not quite good enough. They recommend an editorial company who'll evaluate your script and make some changes so it will be more 'saleable.' You send it to the Premier Editing Company or whoever and then six months later you get it back. They charge an arm and a leg, and all they did was make a few red marks on it here and there. Change this tense, indent that, use a different adverb here, change a few clauses, show you where you split infinitives."

He slammed the mop into the water. It looked like he was trying to *drown* it.

"It's bullshit. Like Turner. You pay hundreds of dollars then re-do the script exactly the way they show you, but guess what? The publisher isn't interested anymore, and the agent who recommended the service says he's sorry, but even though it's better, it can't compete in today's marketplace. Party's over. Scam after scam. The Internet is filled with sites warning you about this shit, but people don't want to listen."

Kincaid eyed Barclay closely. It sounded like the modeling scams he worked back in the day. *Oh honey, we're going to make you a star.* Then so much for make-up, new clothes, a portfolio, and an expensive artist shoot – which invariably involved a few semi-nude pictures. Then it was good-bye, out the door, nice to see you. Next? *Oh honey, we're going to make you a star.* Feeding on people's need to succeed. Ego. Stardom. The dopamine maze.

"Sounds demoralizing."

"You can't imagine it unless you go through it yourself. Every day someone sends you a rejection. Half the time they just send the query back unopened. Sometimes they scrawl something illegible across the top, but usually you get a banal little form letter."

"And Turner's rejection?"

There was that fuse of anger again. Barclay palmed his goatee. "Put me over the edge. Like you said: it was the last straw. The final stab in the heart. But you know what? He didn't have to be so fucking ignorant. When I got it, something snapped inside. Everything was . . . gone."

He turned, gave the floor another halfhearted swipe, and stared at the debris floating on the water. "I wasn't a janitor working like a dog because I was really an aspiring writer. After Turner, I was just a janitor."

"What's the manuscript about?"

Barclay's demeanor changed in a flash. He folded his arms over the top of the mop, blushed, and rushed through a cursory outline of his novel's plot and characters. When he was finished, he looked up for support.

Amazing. Kincaid could tell by the tremor in Barclay's arms and the nervous twitch in his eyes that an unkind word could shred the man to pieces. He'd poured his heart and soul into the book, and now, no one wanted to see it. The terrible fragility of ego.

"Sounds like a pretty interesting thriller," the detective admitted sincerely.

Barclay shrugged, but his face reddened.

"Turner always sent you personal replies, didn't he? Not just a note scrawled from a reader?"

Barclay sneered a drunk's lazy, off-centered smile, his teeth clenched tightly together.

"Yeah, he did. That's why I wanted to kill the bastard." His words drifted into silence, but anger festered behind his eyes. He was struggling to control his rage. "What he said, and the way he said it. All he had to say was 'no thanks,' like everyone else."

Barclay jammed the mop into the bucket. Kincaid stopped him with a hand on his shoulder. He settled down a bit.

"He said it was 'bombastically puerile.' That's the phrase he actually used. *Bombastically puerile*. The characters sounded trite and one-dimensional, the plot was prosaic, and the style was completely devoid of substance. He suggested I try another career before I wasted my life savings on stamps."

Bombastically puerile. Where else had Kincaid seen that? He watched a series of emotions flicker over Barclay's face. Fear, anxiousness, loathing, despair, hurt. Anger. Turner's letter had obviously wounded him a great deal, and he carried the rejection around like a ball and chain every day. *That was a powerful motive for murder.*

"He didn't have to say that fucking shit." He whispered *bombastically puerile*.

"So you stopped sending queries?"

"Why the hell wouldn't I?"

"And started working on threatening letters instead?"

Barclay kicked the bucket into the wall and started unwinding the cord for the buffer. "What's this all about? I swear I haven't sent him anything in months. If you checked through all the things he keeps you'd know that already."

Barclay looked down at the machine and sighed. Who cared? The floor, the elevators, the entire building would be scuffed and filthy by ten in the morning, anyway. Everything just kept going around and around. Without meaning.

"I do. Did you keep his rejection letters?" Kincaid knew he had. Every single one.

Scratching his goatee, Barclay nodded dully. Kincaid wondered how often he punished himself by reading that rejection again. "I'd like to see it."

"What's this really about?"

Kincaid watched the man's eyes. "Devlin Turner's dead."

"What? When?"

"About three weeks ago."

The hallway thickened with an unsettling silence. "Good. Serves the asshole right. Don't expect me to shed any tears. You don't know what he was like, how many people he destroyed or the number of dreams he ruined."

"Did he ruin all your dreams?"

"You mean this?" Barclay gestured at the bristly pads on the buffer with a nod. "No. I wouldn't let him. I'm still a writer."

"You said you were 'just a janitor'. That you stopped sending out queries."

"Sure. About *that* book." He returned Kincaid's stare. "A writer writes. It's as simple as that. A writer writes because he has to, not always because he should, or even because he wants to. It's in your blood. It's who you are."

"And now you're a cleaner."

Barclay recoiled at the taunt. "I do this so I can write. Working nights gives me the opportunity to keep most of my days free so I can do what I want. My building's quiet, there's no one around to bother me, and all the libraries are open. It hasn't worked out bad. And –"

"Go on."

"On the nights I need to I can finish here with an hour or two to spare so I can work on my script. You don't have to be a rocket scientist to clean floors. I think a lot while I'm working. Envisioning characters, refining plots, that sort of thing."

Kincaid remembered the conversation Barclay had been carrying on with himself when he first approached. He pictured the starving, aspiring artists that gathered in the little coffee shops along Queen, and mentally listened to the *what ifs* and *if only*s that were always on the lips of the hopefuls. One break, that's all it took.

"So you're not just a janitor. Despite what you said in your letters, you haven't given up your aspirations of becoming a writer?"

"I *am* a writer," Barclay replied. "Just not a published one. Yet. And I won't pay anyone to publish my work. There's lots of people out there who are better writers than the ones with redundant crap lining the walls at the bookstores. But yeah, I stopped for a couple of months."

"Until the muse called you back?"

Barclay smiled genuinely for the second time. "Yes. Yes it did." He breathed on his glasses and cleaned them with the bottom of his shirt.

"What are you working on now?"

"A comedy."

"About?"

"A black farce about a foiled bank robbery. You know, the worst of the worst, the dumbest of the dumb criminals get together to plan the big heist that will put them on easy street for the rest of their lives. But everything goes wrong from moment one. I'm halfway through the first draft."

"Sounds promising."

Barclay tried not to smile.

Kincaid had been standing far too long. He shifted around, trying to release the stiffness in his neck and lower back. "Anything else on the go?"

"Not really."

Kincaid waited him out. Barclay checked the brushes on the polishers. *Should he tell him or not?* "A mystery," he admitted. "About a guy who starts murdering the staff at a publishing house because they rejected his work."

Kincaid noticed the beads of sweat on the back of the man's neck. "Let's go back to Wednesday the third. First week of the month."

Barclay pulled a diary from his back pocket. Most pages were blank, except for a few isolated words scrawled here and there. *Reminders? Plot notes*? "The third?"

"Between six and eleven."

There wasn't anything on the page. "I would've been here by 7:30. I don't like being late."

"And earlier?"

"Do I need a lawyer?"

"Do you?"

Barclay's tone was less haughty. "I guess I had dinner."

"You guess?"

"I wasn't thinking back then that I'd be questioned about it almost a month later."

Fair enough.

Barclay leaned down and pulled something from the buffer's bristles. "That was the night of the Red Sox- Blue Jays game. So yeah. I think I went to that little curry place on Spadina."

"Alone?"

"No. With my usual entourage of fans, hangers-on, and paparazzi."

"See anyone you know? Talk to anyone?"

"Don't think so. Other than the waiter, but he barely knows a word that's not on the menu."

"Do you go there often?"

"Once in a while. It's good food and fairly reasonable."

"And after work?"

"I went to the library."

"Which –"

"The Resource Centre in Yorkville."

"Why?"

"Their material is unbelievable. It's a great place for research and the staff is knowledgeable and helpful. I probably found a quiet little cubicle and worked on my notes. I saw Timothy Findley there one night, you know. He was a great writer." Barclay drifted away for a second. "And no. I didn't talk to anyone." He frowned angrily. "You don't think I had anything to do with Turner's death, do you?"

Kincaid's tone changed. "We're checking everyone he had problems with."

Eliminating them from your enquiries, Barclay whispered. "It must be a long list."

"It is." No smile. Kincaid took out a business card and handed it to Barclay. The man took it gingerly, as if it was on fire.

"Don't lose it, or I'll make you crawl through every dumpster on the block to find it again. I only have a partial list of Turner's correspondence. I need to see a copy of any rejections he sent you that weren't in his files. You can e-mail it to me or bring it in, whichever's easier. Just make sure I have it within the next two days."

Barclay nodded and pocketed the card. He turned towards the polisher and heard his running shoes *squelch*.

"I'll be back if I need anything else," Kincaid said. It sounded like a threat. He started walking away.

"I'll be waiting with baited breath." Barclay turned on the polisher, instantly drowning the hall in a loud buzzing drone.

Kincaid spun around and made a slicing motion at his throat with his hand. Barclay switched off the machine.

"Horrible way to die, wasn't it?"

Barclay stared back. "I guess that depends on how he was killed, Detective."

"You don't read the papers? Watch the news?"

"No time."

A pause. "Good luck on your new book."

Walking back down the hall toward the stairwell, Kincaid could practically feel the hole Barclay was glaring into the center of his back.

Chapter Eighteen

Kincaid pulled into a curbside space next to a small parkette. Sitting in the passenger's seat with the door wide open, he checked his messages: one from Richardson, one from the coroner's office, two from Dr. Chadpur, a reply from Amy, and a garbled one from LT. Davis he could barely make out. And surprisingly, one from Barclay. *Already?* He yawned, stretched, chased a painkiller down with some bottled water, and confirmed the time: seven thirty – ground zero for rush hour. Although 'rush hour' was a misnomer: there didn't seem to be a time, day or night, when the city wasn't strangled with snarled traffic that made the streets inert parking lots. The downtown core was always congested, especially since the city had gone on a vendetta and lanes were being usurped by special bicycle paths. The incessant construction didn't help, nor did the aggressiveness of the drivers or the clots of wayward pedestrians chained to their phones.

Rather than getting frustrated by a trip that would take twice as long as it should, he'd penciled in another interview for nine o'clock. He called Amy. Not home. He tried her cell. She picked up on the second ring, fully alert, the sleepiness gone. He told her about his interview with Barclay. She wasn't happy he'd gone to see him alone. Davis had warned her not to let him out of her sight. Her tone was frosty and brusque.

"Why didn't you wait?"

"At five-fifteen? You didn't sound like you had too much *up-and-at-'em* when I called. Barclay's shift ended at six thirty, and I wanted to see him at work."

"Any particular reason?"

"No. I was up early and decided to catch him before he left. And let you sleep. Did you get the tapes?"

"Yes, I got the traffic downloads for the time periods you wanted. I've been trying to reach you for an hour."

"Sorry. I left my phone in the car."

"So I guessed." She was peeved. And worried. Her directions came from Davis, but her feelings came from somewhere else.

"I was going to call and have you meet me at the next name on our list—you know, from Richardson's information you copied."

"You told me to stay ahead of you. Read your mind. I thought –"

"I appreciate the initiative."

"Walter Croft."

"That's him. Have you read his file?"

"Yes, sir."

"Good. Perhaps we should sidestep the traffic and talk to him later. Hungry?"

"Starved." She shook her coffee container upside down. "Big Max needs a refill."

"Then let me make the morning up to you with a nice breakfast. You know the little cafe just south of Queen on Dundas? Curtains that cover the bottom of the window? Sells all weird pastries?"

"*Bagelicious*?"

"That's the one. Get a uniform to drive you over and I'll see you there in half an hour. I've got some calls to make. If you get there before me, tell Andy, the tall mulatto kid, you're with me."

"Done."

"And Sergeant?"

"Sir?"

"I apologize. I should have told you what I was going to do and kept you in the loop. You're right, you should have met Barclay. Believe me, you will."

"Thanks." Amy needed to hear that. "See you in thirty."

*

Kincaid couldn't reach Barclay, and Richardson's phone went straight to voicemail. He felt a twinge of guilt, but Davis and Dr. Chadpur could wait. The next call was to The Hospital for Sick Children on University Avenue to check on Ryan. The nurse who answered said he had a fairly rough night, but wouldn't elaborate. She told Kincaid he couldn't talk to him right now, so he asked her to tell Ryan he'd do his best to drop in later. *What had made it a bad night?*

Despite the smog and pollution, the honking cars and endless traffic, the morning breeze was fairly pleasant. Kincaid closed his eyes and slowed his breathing down, but his thoughts kept drifting back to what he'd seen at Turner's office. With experience, he'd gradually been able to let the nascent revulsion of a crime scene slowly "mature" and "fade to black." Given time, he'd succeeded in compartmentalizing even the most horrific tableaux. But he couldn't stop picturing all the little things, the horrible things, the phenomena that had almost made him retch. Turner's body practically crucified to the desk. The hole, the wounds, the blood splatters, the cheeks stretched out with crumpled bunches of paper. The pen through his eye. The stitches, perfectly sewn, that sealed the man's lips forever. Even Turner needed closure, didn't he?

*

Bagelicious.

Sergeant MacKenzie was reading through her notes when Kincaid slipped into the booth. He gave her his best 'little boy's' smile. "We're good?"

"Yes. But don't block me again. Sir. You know what Davis wants and expects from both of us."

"Done. Meet Andy?"

She nodded. "He's the tallest person I've ever seen. One look and he said *you with Kincaid?* and took me back here. Says it's *your* booth."

"He can smell a cop from a mile away."

"Trouble?"

"He wore it like a suit. Wrong crowd, wrong path, no hope. Abused at eight, father and mother addicts, a network of broken homes, dealing at twelve, then a gangbanger. He was right on the edge. The bangers didn't want to let him go – a bad example to the others. He was dangling over the pit before he finally turned everything around. Another bust would've been it. But deep inside, the kid's heart was good. He found something he liked more than drugs and b-ball. For some strange reason, despite everything he'd gone through, the guy loved to bake. Started in one of the juvenile detention centers. He was really fortunate – when he got out, a few of the best bakers in the city gave him some placements, and he learned everything he could."

Amy raised an eyebrow. "Just lucky?"

"And finally baked his way into this place."

Amy stared into Kincaid's eyes. "How did he ever get the money to put down on a shop like this?"

Kincaid shrugged, just as a hand slapped him on the back. Not a hand: a paw. Andy's hands were almost twice the size of his own. The big man smiled at Amy. There was a slight gap between his front teeth.

"I knew she was yours, so I put her in your booth."

"Thanks. How's the world?"

"Spinning just fine, Kincaid."

"And how's little Ruthy?"

"Man oh man, not so little anymore, no sir. She's going to be bigger than me, you'll see."

"Maybe she'll play for the National Team one day."

A smile devoured the man's face. "Wouldn't that be something, eh? She sinks a three pointer with 'bout a second left to win the championship." He stopped and looked down at his menus. "That's what makes all this important, you know. Leaving those colors behind, turnin' everythin' 'round." He slapped Kincaid so hard he almost knocked his breath away. "And I got you to thank, my man."

"You got yourself to thank, A.J. That's who you got to thank. And Nola."

"And the Lord, sir. And the Lord. Now, what can I bring you?"

"How about two of those delicious cheddar and bacon bagels you won't give me the recipe for?"

He smiled, showing off a gold tooth that matched his earring. "Comin' right up. Top up that coffee, Sergeant?"

"Please." She turned back to Kincaid. He looked pretty lively. "Did you check all your messages?" Amy asked.

"Nothing earth-shattering."

"How's Ryan?"

His face hardened. "Still fighting. That's all the boy has left, I'm afraid."

"I hear you're taking him to the game tomorrow night."

"There aren't any secrets at the precinct, are there? It should be a nice time out for him, especially since he missed the Disney trip. I've got a special surprise lined up. But the nurse said he had a rough night, so it depends on how well he does today."

"That's great."

"What's great?"

"That you spend so much time with kids like Ryan."

Kincaid sipped his coffee. "It's nice to be able to give something back. Look at the things we see in our jobs. It makes everything more tolerable when you can help someone else."

"Like A.J?"

Silence.

"But you're hurting right now, too," she said quietly. "Maybe you're trying to do too much."

"Leave it, Amy. Please."

"But the word at the house has it you're –"

"We all cope differently, Sergeant. Let me handle what I have to deal with my way."

"I'm –"

A.J. slipped their plates down. "Now is that a great bagel, or what? More java, K? Your partner sucks it back with a hose."

"Just hook her up to an IV."

The gold tooth flashed again as Andy backed away. Two uniforms came in and waved to the restaurant as a whole, smiling at the owner.

Amy didn't press. *Make sure you watch him closely*, the Lieutenant told her. *I can't put people in jeopardy*. But it was an awkward role she still wasn't easy with. She wanted a different relationship with Kincaid, and she was pretty sure he knew it.

Kincaid managed half the bagel before his back screamed for another painkiller. Amy couldn't stop attacking hers. Kincaid started telling her what he'd found out about Turner, but she interrupted him almost immediately.

"Blackmail. Because of those monthly withdrawals for amounts under the radar."

Kincaid was impressed. "And he might have been bailing out to another company. *Ex -*"

"Right. *'Excalibur Books.'*"

She'd done her homework.

Andy topped up their cups. He frowned when he saw Kincaid's half-eaten bagel, but didn't say anything. He a*lways* finished his special bacon and cheese. His friend didn't look right. *Something in his eyes.*

"Sounds like there could be a motive there, Kincaid. If not two."

He nodded and checked his watch. "I believe Mr. Croft awaits."

Kincaid signaled for the bill – Andy brought it over and slipped it under his plate. Cramming in the last bite, Amy noticed that other than a happy face, nothing else was written on it. The men shook hands, and Kincaid whispered something to Andy that coaxed out a broad smile. Andy told Amy to come back any time: the booth would always be reserved for her, too. As they walked away from the table, she noticed there was a trio of fifties tucked neatly under her plate.

*

Walter Croft lived in a small tangle of residential side streets that meandered off Danforth Avenue in Toronto's east end and slowly molded into old Scarborough. It was one of the more archaic sections of the city, where the roads were narrow and awning-covered storefronts fought for meager space. Although the dialects changed every block, the area was predominantly Greek, Italian, and Eastern European. Old school.

Scrunched up tightly between two rather nondescript images of itself, Croft's house was tall and narrow, with a little front garden two graves wide and a car port that looked as if it wouldn't survive another winter. Originally brick, the upper floor of the house had recently suffered some catastrophe or another and had been renovated with an off-white shade of siding that didn't match the rest of the house. One of the sections beneath the front window was already badly dented. There was a solitary poplar at the end of the tiny front lawn, near the sidewalk, its top branches dangerously close to the hydro wires. The lower branches were thick and reached out like fingers – Kincaid couldn't help thinking about poor Shakespeare.

The house was in darkness when he rang the doorbell. Kincaid waited, then pressed it again. A light flickered on somewhere in the back of the house. Another sputtered alive and then the hall light came on. Someone shuffled closer: Kincaid pictured an aged lamplighter in the blackened halls of a medieval castle. A shadow blinked behind the peephole. Two chain locks were unhooked before a dead bolt slid back. The door cracked open but the screen door stayed locked.

"Walter Croft?"

"So?"

"I'd like to speak to you for a few minutes."

"Go away. I ain't interested in what you're selling." He closed the door. Kincaid sighed and rang the bell again.

"Thump your bibles somewhere else or I'll call the police," the man yelled from the safety of the hall. "I don't believe in your God anymore, and it's too late to be saved anyway."

Amy frowned. *Too late to be saved? Why?* She held her badge up to the peephole. "We *are* the police."

The screen door opened a moment later. The old man squinted at Kincaid's shield, then at Amy's.

"You the guy who called a little while ago?"

"I am."

Walter Croft ushered them inside. "Can't be too careful these days."

"It's always better to err on the side of caution." A smile. Kincaid gestured toward the adjacent front room. "May we talk in there?"

Croft nodded and followed them in. The room was small and musty, and as he drew in his first breath Kincaid knew it hadn't been aired out for several seasons. A thick coat of dust blanketed two table lamps that framed a weathered couch. The wobbly little coffee table, the old radiator, and the little wooden book rack hadn't been cleaned in ages. Newspapers and magazines spilled out over the top and across the floor like lava from a mountain. A small round table next to a battered rocking chair was covered with old photographs. Everything was ingrained with the unmistakable, heavy odor of years of cigarette smoke.

Bending down slowly on cracking, fragile knees, Croft gently eased himself into the rocking chair. Kincaid watched him pitch slowly backwards and forwards. If he hadn't read his file, he would have had a difficult time guessing the man's age closer than a decade. His clothes were as old and threadbare as everything else in the room. Heavy woolen pants, a checkered flannel shirt, and a tweed jacket that had probably looked halfway respectable a generation or two before. Croft's bottom teeth were tobacco-yellowed, and his upper plate seemed far too small for his mouth. Cruelly aged, lines of dolor were deeply etched into his face. His white hair was fine and wispy, his eyebrows thick and curly, his hands mottled with yellow liver spots. He wheezed slightly as he spoke with the soft hush of strained bellows.

"Smoke?" he asked, lighting one for himself. Kincaid and Amy declined.

"So you're here about that dork next door?" Croft gestured to the adjacent house with a quick stab of his thumb. "I still want it down. Or at least put in its proper place. If we were in the States it would'a been down already, you can bet your ass. Yanks don't stand for things like that. But those pussies in Ottawa . . ."

He glanced at Amy through a cloud of grey smoke. "Sorry. Shouldn't be talk'n like that in front of a lady."

Amy smiled. "No offense taken, Mr. Croft."

"Mr. Croft was my dad. It's Walter to you."

Kincaid was still confused. "I'm not sure what you're talking about, Walter."

"It's still Mr. Croft to *you*. I'm talking about that *flag.*" Another thumb gesture.

"The one on the front door next to yours?"

"Damn right. I ain't got nothing against people being proud'a where they come from, of the place they was born. But they've come here to live, so they should show respect. If he wants to hang a flag it should be ours." The old man was getting fired up: he had to force himself to slow down so he could catch his breath. As soon as he coughed he took another long drag of his cigarette.

"If he wants to show it, fine. But do it proper, with honor. *Our flag* should be above it. And bigger." Croft shook his head angrily and reached for one of the myriad pictures on the table. "My uncle Jesse didn't die at Vimy Ridge for things like that. And our boys ain't dying in some desert backwater today for it neither. Americans wouldn't stand for it, I can tell you. When you're in *their* country, it's the Yank flag on top, then yours underneath. That's the way it should be."

"We didn't know you'd filed a complaint, Mr. Croft." Kincaid turned to Amy. "Sergeant, can you check on this when we get back to the station?"

"Sergeant?"

"Yes sir. We'll see what we can do, Mr. Croft."

"Walter." The old man snorted, momentarily disappearing behind a veil of smoke. "Sergeant? Well I'll be." He put Jesse's picture back down on the exact spot it had been so that none of the dust moved.

"Thanks. But I bet it don't do much good. Called before about it lots of times."

He started rocking more quickly and his bushy eyebrows crinkled together. "So if you're not here about that"– the thumb jerked up again – "then why are ya here?"

Kincaid explained why they'd come. The old man's eyes didn't even blink when he heard they were working a murder investigation. When Kincaid finished, Croft stayed silent. The only sound in the little room was the creaking noise the rocking chair made against the floor and the traffic thudding by just beyond the window.

The stillness lengthened. Kincaid glanced at the bookcases on the far wall. "It looks like your wife liked to read, Mr. Croft."

"Oh yes, Matilda loved books," he smiled proudly. "She was a real – what do you call it? – a real . . ."

"Bibliophile?" Amy asked.

Another smile. A daub of spittle dribbled down his chin. "Smart *and* good looking." He giggled at some private thought. "I tried to keep'em all, but there were just too many." He paused. Another private thought intruded, but this one was obviously distressing. The old man leaned towards Amy and whispered conspiratorially. "I needed the money, so I sold some. She had some pretty rare ones I hated letting go. But I don't like asking anyone for help. I hate charity. I won't take it from anyone. Not from the government, not from my family. Not from *anyone.*"

Kincaid waited politely as the old man looked slowly around the room. "Mr. Croft?" Nothing. He called again. "Mr. Croft?"

"What?"

"Your wife liked to write her own books as well, didn't she?"

"Sure did. She loved making up stories."

"What kind of books did Matilda write?"

"Fiction mainly. Though she tried her hand at poetry when the mood hit her. Not really what I think of when I think'a poetry, though. The lines weren't even and they didn't rhyme. But –"

Kincaid waited again. "But?"

Croft smiled self-consciously. "Damn brain," he muttered. Where was I? Oh yeah. Matilda's poetry. Even if I didn't understand it all it still made me feel sad."

An old pipe in the basement groaned. The radiator rattled. Something outside caught Croft's eye and he started drifting away again.

"What types of books did she write, Mr. Croft?"

He crushed out his cigarette and coughed. "Romance." He smiled at Amy. "You know. Where a love-torn woman is strong and independent enough to save the day. That sort of thing. Not my type, really. But I read all her stuff, anyway. Yes, I did."

"Was it good?"

"I thought so."

"How many books did she write?"

"After she retired? Let me see now." The old man mouthed what Kincaid thought must have been titles as he counted them out on his fingers. "Seven. No, eight. That's right. Eight."

"But she never had any of them published?"

A bus rumbled by the end of Croft's driveway, shaking the table and making some of the pictures tremble. Croft shook his head. His eyes narrowed and his teeth grinded together.

"But she kept writing them anyway?" Kincaid prompted gently. Rebecca had told him there was a lot of room under the bed, and that's where many novels ended up.

"Tilly – Matilda – enjoyed writing. She liked to create things, to make new people and have them come alive, you know. I don't think it was a hobby, really. It was more like something she *needed* to do. It gave her – I don't know – a sense of purpose. Especially – especially at the end."

Walter's eyes misted as he stared at the old photographs. "I really loved her. Miss her, too."

Kincaid felt a little uneasy going on. Amy kept scribbling. "What was the last thing she was working on, Mr. Croft?"

It was a minute before the old man looked away from the picture. "A book about her illness."

"Her illness?"

"Kind of like a diary. Matilda had the Big C. It was slowly eating her away."

Walter looked back at the snatches of memory frozen in frames. "Something there, inside you, slowly taking everything away and you can't do anything about it except wait. You have no idea how difficult that journey is, how lonely and unforgiving."

Still and silent, Kincaid stared down at his hands. *What could he say?* He took a slow, relaxing breath. Yes, he knew how difficult and lonely the journey was.

"She wrote her last book about what she knew best," Croft continued quietly. "The last battle she had no chance of winning." He smiled sadly and punched out his cigarette.

Kincaid cleared his throat. "Did she finish it?"

The old man whispered. "Barely."

Kincaid could see tears coagulating in the corners of Croft's eyes, but the old man blinked them away. He was grinding his teeth again, and gripping the armrest of his chair so hard his arthritic knuckles were red. His body bristled with suppressed hatred. He struggled to light another cigarette.

"No one wanted to see that one, either. I think – I think Tilly saw that as something more than just another rejection." He slapped the armrest with his hand. Dust scattered. "The other ones were rejections about the book. Maybe the publishers already had too many romances, or maybe it needed extra editing or something. Maybe someone wrote one just like it. Who knows? But those rejections were easier to take. With the one about her illness, it was as if they were rejecting *her*, not the book." He shook his head angrily. "Here she is, struggling every day just to sit up enough to type, trying to tell people about the pain and suffering – the suffering she fought right up to the very last breath, and no-one else cared enough to read it. Except me. And I already knew about everything she was goin' through. She was doing all this for other people, people she didn't know, or wouldn't ever know, to help ease their suffering . . . when the time came for them. And their families. Know what I mean?" He stared back and forth at Kincaid and Amy.

"I do. She was trying to tell others about what the end was like, so her own suffering could help make a difference."

Croft nodded and looked up at Kincaid through a curl of smoke. "And they wouldn't even let her do that. She didn't want to be a millionaire author or anything. She wanted to write something that might'a helped other people when . . . when . . . "

Kincaid heard Amy sigh. She stopped writing and wiped her eyes.

The first few tears trickled down Walter's cheeks. "All those letters. I wanted her to get something good back more than she did herself, you know. Especially before she . . .   Something that would have given her hope, made her feel that what she'd done was worthwhile."

"It was important to her," Kincaid said softly. "And to you."

He nodded, then leaned forward conspiratorially. "I even thought of pretending I worked at one of 'em publishing places and writing one myself. I'd seen enough to do it. Tell her something like "the editorial board thought it was really good and wanted to use it, but they still needed time to think it over because the economy's so tight." Oh, but I knew my Matilda. She would'a seen through that ruse in a second. Would'a made her feel worse."

Croft stamped out the cigarette he'd just lit and fired up another.

Amy waved the smoke away. "Walter, did your wife ever deal with agents?"

"Some."

"What about Devlin —"

"Turner? *Devlin Turner*? That fuc – bastard." He sighed deeply. "Sorry, ma'am."

Sensing his tears, Amy didn't look up. "No need. What happened, Walter?"

"If it hadn't been for his rejections, everything *still* would have been easier to swallow. But no. That pri . . . had to say everything ignorant he could about her book."

Amy's pen stopped in midair. The room tightened with an awkward silence. Another bus rumbled by, rattling the radiator.

Croft drifted away into the photos. "Why would he'd a'wanted to write something like that? It was like he was trying to shove a blade into her dreams and rip'em apart. All he had to do was say '*no thanks*.' Oh, but he didn't. He was so cruel. He criticized *her*, not her book. He told her' – he paused, caught his breath –'he told her no one would want to read anything about an old lady, who weren't a celebrity or athlete or something, dying of cancer."

Croft picked up a picture from the table and mumbled softly. "Nineteen fifty one." A young woman, early thirties, legs crossed on some old patchwork picnic blanket, her blouse billowing in the wind and a few strands of hair being teased across her face. He wiped the dust away with his shirt sleeve, his voice barely above a whisper. "He was cruel. Very cruel. People like that be . . . "

Kincaid frowned deeply. He still couldn't understand what could possibly have prompted Turner's actions. Was he simply everything people said about him? An abject monster, completely devoid of thoughts or feelings for anyone else? A deviant sociopath? Or was there something else, something he wasn't seeing, buried beneath his hatred?

"Mr. Croft, do you still have them?"

"What?" He was trying to prop the photograph back up with the others.

"Do you still have Turner's letters?"

"No. Threw the bloody things away. Especially the last one. Matilda kept reading it, over and over." He shook his head morosely and wiped his eyes with his sleeve. "Why? What's –"

Devlin Turner was murdered, Mr. Croft."

The old man wheezed and crushed out his cigarette. *Were his lips curling into a smile?* "Well, now, that's a real shame. Can't say I'm sorry someone killed the bastard. Whoever did it was doing the world a favor. Yes sir. A favor."

Croft lit another cigarette. "Know what? I've never thought like that 'bout nobody before. But I bloody well hope he suffered. It would be terrible if they just blew his head off or something. I hope they really made him hurt, hurt bad for a long, long, time." Now he smiled.

Oh, he suffered. Kincaid watched Croft's trembling hand touch some of the other pictures, carefully turning them a little more towards him. Then he pointed a shaking, gnarled finger at Amy.

"And yes, write this down, too. I would'a killed the bastard if I'd'a had the chance."

"The letters you sent him, Mr. Croft – "

He squinted.

"The hate mail. The threats. About the things you were going to do to him?"

"*That's* why you're here? I don't God-damn well believe it. You mean the ones after Matilda . . . after I *lost* her? I was angry, angrier than I've ever been, and I wanted him to know it. And I wanted him to know how much he'd hurt her while she was sitting here waitin' to die."

"Those were some pretty vicious threats."

"And that's what they were – threats. Look at me. Can you picture me doing the things I told him I'd do when I got close enough? For God's sake, Detective. Besides. He sent my Tilly some spiteful letters that ripped the hope from her heart. I just wanted to scare him." He was almost shouting and started to cough. He refused Amy's offer to get him some water.

"If the letters frightened him before he died, then good. Maybe he knew what it felt like to have your world torn to pieces. I'm glad somebody shut his mouth up for good. He'll never criticize someone the way he did to my Matilda again."

Kincaid watched the old man closely. *Shut his mouth up for good?*

"Did Turner ever write anything back to you about *your* letters, Mr. Croft?"

"Nope. The little chicken shit. But then again, I didn't sign em' all. He probably thought some were from me, but some he wouldn't have. All he knew was that there was someone out there who wanted to put a stake through his chest. Make him watch his back. Let him know death was right there, and he'd never know when it was coming. Leave him without hope, just like he left my Matilda."

Kincaid kept staring. *It certainly did.*

"So he's dead and you're here because I sent him some nasty letters. Don't you cops have better things to do?" Still coughing, he took a long draw on his cigarette. He looked at Amy. "Thought you were better than that." He started cleaning the photographs one by one.

Kincaid waited until the old man looked up. "Mr. Croft, I have to ask. Did you have anything to do, anything at all, with Devlin Turner's murder?"

The silence was ephemeral but stifling. Walter's eyes narrowed and his face contorted into a spiteful grimace. He looked back and forth at Amy and Kincaid, his eyes in a tight squint. His forehead wrinkled with lines of hatred.

"I wish to God I did. Now get the fuck out of my God-damn house."

Chapter Nineteen

The threadbare curtains hanging so unevenly above the radiator in Walter Croft's front room stayed slightly parted until Kincaid backed out of the driveway and started up the street.

"Is he still watching us?"

"Probably until I make the corner," Kincaid mused.

The cigarette smoke scratched the back of his throat and the dust-covered time capsule of a living room had depressed him. All the pictures, all the memories scattered over the chipped table in the corner: that's what Croft had left, and even those were becoming harder to see as the months passed, the shadows deepened, his pulse weakened, and his eyes grew misty. Yet Turner made sure he got one last dig into the old man, one final twist of the knife. No rhyme or reason. *Why? How would he have felt?* Kincaid visualized the pens in Turner's back, propping him up, the thick fountain one through his throat.

Wheeling out of the side streets and onto Danforth Avenue, Kincaid told MacKenzie about something else he'd pieced together from Richardson's information. Amy listened patiently, suggesting they stop at *The Bamboo Gardens* on the way to the precinct.

Any lead . . .

*

The chimes tinkled whimsically, their dulcet notes calling Mrs. Cruz from the recesses of the kitchen. Her smile quickly faded to a frown when she saw her 'guests.' Turner was just as much trouble dead as he'd been alive.

"Can't this wait, Detective? It's awfully close to the lunch hour rush. My staff have to be prepared."

Only a few tables were being used. A couple of tired white collar workers were bent over drinks at the bar, quietly scoffing about whatever it was they always scoffed about while they worked at their liquid lunches.

"We won't be long, Mrs. Cruz."

She wasn't relieved.

"Perhaps you'd be kind enough to tell us where Martin is now."

The frown morphed into a grimace. She nodded towards the back of the restaurant. "Outside."

Amy followed Kincaid through the kitchen and into the alley. Martin was nursing a cigarette by a stack of half-crushed food boxes. His face mutated through a series of emotions when he saw them. Navigating the garbage, the Detectives stopped next to the dumpster.

"I never lied," the boy pleaded eagerly. "I was with Miguel all night." Hands shaking, he took one last draw before stamping out his cigarette.

"The new bartender?"

He looked down. "Yes."

Kincaid studied him for several seconds. Did this boy have the psychological disposition to do what had been done to Turner? To mutilation? He didn't think so. But could he have done it with his friend, Miguel? Could they have been fueled by booze and drugs? Vengeance? Money? Rejection? Or could something else have generated that level of violence and hate?

"Martin, your name came up when we were checking a list of people who had "special" grudges against Devlin Turner. It turned up again when we tried a publishing company he worked with – Meredith House."

Using the wall for support, Martin sank down slowly and sat on an overturned bottle crate. He buried his face in is hands.

"I wrote a book. Fiction. It's about the trouble in Mexico, where I lived with my aunt and uncle before my mother sponsored me and I came here. The shanty towns, the back alley sex clubs, the constant threat from the gangs and drug dealers, the governments' lies and deceit, and the corrupt police. No offence."

"None taken."

"I tried to tell people about the horrors of child labor and human trafficking."

"And you wanted Turner to take a look at it?"

"After several rejections, yes." The boy fumbled with his matches before he finally got another cigarette going. His hairnet couldn't keep a tangle of hair from falling across his forehead.

"How did you know about Turner?"

"I heard him entertaining people at lunch. Always the big shot. I waited until he was alone one day and asked him if he'd see my work."

"What did he say?"

"Fuck off." A quick glance at Amy. "Sorry, Sergeant."

Amy kept writing, hiding a smile.

"At first he was angry I bothered him while he was eating. He said the agents and editors who came in for dinner didn't talk business until they were finished. So I brought him another drink – a double, on the house – and he said he'd take a look since this was – what did he call it – his favorite watering pit. Or something like that. Hole."

"So you showed him your manuscript?" Amy prompted.

"No, only a chapter. And it couldn't be the first. He said he could tell everything about a book by reading a few pages."

Kincaid asked, "What happened, Martin?"

"He read it the next day at lunch." The boy's face grew cold and he stabbed the cigarette against the wall. "He started laughing. Right out loud. But there was nothing funny about my book, Sir."

"What did he say?"

"He called me over and almost threw the pages back at me. He said my writing was terrible, that I had no chance whatsoever. He could tell right away, and so could any other agent. He said the work was pathetic and that I should stay with my mother and keep making drinks for people who understood what writing was about."

"That must have hurt very much."

The boy nodded, his eyes teary. "It was crowded. Everyone must have heard. I could have –"

"You could have what, Martin?"

"I could have killed him right there." A blotch of red stained his cheeks and neck. It looked like he'd broken out in hives.

"Martin." Kincaid squatted down on another upended crate so he was looking straight into the boy's eyes. "Did you have anything to do with Devlin Turner's murder?"

"No," the boy stammered. The tears came freely. "No. I was humiliated and angry, but I'd never really hurt anyone for something like that. I swear to Christ on my mother's life." He kissed the silver crucifix that hung from his neck.

Amy handed the boy a black and white picture. "Then why was your car photographed near his house the night he died?"

Martin froze. "How did you get this?"

"A street camera on Barrington Road. One block east of the cut-off for Turner's street. But you know that already."

Martin chewed at his bottom lip. He'd taken the plunge: there was no use in lying. "Miguel and I were drinking."

Kincaid pressed deeper. "You're in a relationship with him?"

He teared up even more. His entire world was collapsing. "Oh God. How – how did you know?" He glanced at the detectives. Kincaid waited quietly.

"My mother doesn't know. Please. Please don't say anything."

"As long as you tell us the truth, Martin, your personal life isn't part of our investigation."

The boy tensed, then sighed. "Sometimes I stay at his apartment. That night we smoked some spliff. Miguel was mad and said we should go to Turner's place and do something, like egg his house like we did as kids, or spray paint his garage. Just something stupid like that. But by the time we got there and looked around, I got scared. We went back to Miguel's place, and smoked some more. I went home about 4:00 a.m. I swear. Honest to God."

"Did you send him some letters?"

A guilty nod. "Yes. Bad ones."

"Threats?"

"Yes, Sir. One night he came in and said he knew by the writing I'd sent them. He was really angry. He told me never to bother him again. I haven't."

Kincaid exchanged a quick glance with Amy. She believed the boy, too. He remembered Turner's crime scene photos. The splattered blood, the open wounds, the ballpoint pen through his eye. The stitched lips, and Shakespeare stretched out above the ground. He was sure Martin was incapable of something so vile, so horrible.

He'd known that before they walked into the alley. That vindictiveness was way beyond the boy who'd seeped urine into the front of his pants when he sat down on the crate. But he had to see the truth in the boy's eyes himself.

But what about Miguel? That was something Amy could follow up on. Alone. Discreetly. When Mrs. Cruz didn't have her antennae raised.

An almost paternal tone crept into Kincaid's voice. "It's just my opinion, Martin. But you should tell your mother about Miguel. And about you, the man – the good man – you are, the one you're trying to become. Believe me. You don't want her finding out from someone else. It would hurt her badly. She loves you. She'll understand. And she'll support you, too."

The boy nodded, embarrassed, frustrated, hurt. He tried to whisper *"thanks"* but the word wouldn't come. His hands were shaking so badly he couldn't light his cigarette.

*

Another decrepit room, just like all the others.

Dieter Vollger took a long swig from the bottle, swirling the whisky around like he was gargling. It burned his throat, so he downed another shot right away. He ripped the blanket off the bed, tipped up the mattress, and crushed all the bed bugs he could find with his boots. Pacing again, he stopped at the window, snapped the rusted metal blinds apart, and checked outside. Nothing. Too bad. He felt like killing something. Some*one*. He could almost feel the fucking God-damn birthmark creeping across his neck. Another drink. He opened up his binder. His prayer book. The names of the dead, and the *dead-to-be*, scrolled on every page. Any agent or publisher who'd sent him a rejection letter. His finger moved across the lines again, smirking. More whisky. He picked up a newspaper from the floor.

The *Tribune's* book reviewer wasn't impressed.

"Again, fans of Paul Wheelers latest "thriller" *The Nail Gun* were left on the edge of their seat – waiting for something to happen. Something we didn't know was coming would have been nice. I'm afraid Wheeler, like Michael Jackson's glitter glove and moonwalk, is having a little trouble with the "thrill" part of thriller. After the unprecedented success of his first two books, *The History of a Beretta* and *Down the Sights*, Wheelers' last three scripts have been far less imaginative or tightly written".

Blah blah blah.

Dieter smiled. He was just like his knife: viciously bipolar. Sleek and harmless when it was closed, or open and ready to kill. He sliced the article from the newspaper and taped it to a fresh page in his scrapbook. On the bottom was a picture of Wheeler with his arm draped around his editor and publicist, Shirley O'Donovan, from Chicago's *Marrauder Books*.

This asshole Wheeler pumped out two useless books a year and Dieter couldn't get anyone to read his manuscript. Well, there was Turner. And Shirley O'Donovan. She'd asked to see the first chapter, but she'd sent it back the same day. *Bitch.* Maybe his writing was too good for the commercial market. Didn't they have ghost writers to help you with that kind of shit? O'Donovan made sure they churned out Wheeler's puke, but she wouldn't read his first page. Well fuck him and fuck Shirley O'Donovan.

Dieter couldn't stay mad for long. Not right now, anyway. He kept picturing Roland Steinberg's helmet rolling down the incline, bobbing up and down, his head still inside, his eyes open, blood trailing down the black asphalt. It looked like his head was caught in a macabre chase after the skidding bike. *Bounce bounce bounce.* He closed his eyes and remembered how the flames leapt higher when he tossed the helmet onto the pyre. Roland would never write a rejection again. Another one down. But there were so many waiting, like O'Donovan.

Dieter glanced at another article he'd pasted into his binder earlier.

Toronto police still have no leads in the vicious slaying of prominent literary agent Devlin Turner. Lieutenant Reginald Davis from 52 Division has reiterated "that the investigation is well under way, and that detectives are currently exploring all possibilities."

Good. Dieter wanted – no, he *needed* – to meet his comrade in arms, the writer who'd been rejected just like he had, the purist who'd managed to slip a picture on the Dark Web to show how he'd stuck Devlin Turner so brutally, so brilliantly, and then sewn his mouth into silence forever.

They'd meet soon.

But for now, Shirley O'Donovan was calling. She just didn't know it yet.

She never should have sent that fucking rejection letter.

Chapter Twenty

"Are you going to drop me out front?" Kincaid asked, re-checking his side view. He didn't feel like getting hit by a bike shooting the gap, or door-jam a walker intoxicated with a text.

"I have to come in anyway, so I might as well park downstairs."

"What do you need?"

"Statements, witness reports, the original warrants." Amy sounded tense.

"Why is the DA's office being so pernickety? The ShoeCam op was about as open and closed as you could get."

"Ahhh, but thus Spoke Lawyers. They're questioning the admissibility of various tapes and photos pulled at the raids."

"Now? When the case is heading for arraignment?"

"I don't want this thing going south when we're so close."

"Don't get ahead of yourself, Sergeant. There's no point in second-guessing anything yet."

"I know." *But it didn't help.* Bad timing. She wanted to be there when Kincaid discussed their information with Meredith's security officer. And Davis wanted an update on how Kincaid was doing.

"Call me when you know something."

"I will. Thanks."

*

Kincaid glanced at his watch: it wouldn't be long before he had to meet the security consultant from *Meredith House*. Egos would have to be stroked. He risked a coffee from the vending machine, sealed himself in his office, checked for messages, and reviewed the notes he'd made about Turner's murder scene. He juxtaposed the pictures from the file, rearranging everything like a huge jigsaw puzzle. He tried to put them in the same frame of reference he'd had in Turner's office, images from various perspectives in the room. Every photo seemed more hideous than the next – he'd almost forgotten how truly horrible they were. *Almost.*

Fifteen minutes later, with half the coffee in the garbage, there was a light knock at the door. He looked up and trembled:

that spine tingling shiver that comes before the report of a gun, or the one that claims your senses when you exhale before stepping into a dark alley. He was sentient and prone to a sixth sense: most field operators were the same. A gut feeling, a sudden sensitivity, an innate intuition had saved him more than once. But this was different. He looked apprehensively at the door, overwhelmed by one of the strongest premonitions he'd ever experienced. Anxiety washed over him in waves, bristling the hairs on the back of his neck. It was as if his entire body was physically recalling a memory. He *knew* who was on the other side of the door before he heard a second knock echo through his office behind the softest voice he'd ever heard.

Stephanie.

Kincaid's entire world expanded and contracted at the same time. He started rising but stopped midway, his arms stiff against the desk, his balance suddenly seized by a surge of emotions that made everything spin out of control. The room was a kaleidoscope and he was a piece of glass. His heart thudded against his chest. *He'd heard her, hadn't he?* Everything, every single fiber of his being told him it couldn't possibly be anyone else. *But . . .*

The tender voice called out again.

Of course it was her. *Stephanie.*

Kincaid was prickly warm, sweating, his voice barely above a strained whisper when he invited her in.

The door opened and she peeked in. He could tell by her eyes she was just as overwhelmed by the intense and conflicting feelings as he was. For once she seemed awkward, like she was about to faint. A puppet on a string, a leaf in the wind. She nervously nibbled her bottom lip, frightened to look directly at Kincaid and reluctant to look away, afraid the dream would shatter. He struggled to move, awash in a tide of emotions that pounded the shores of his very soul. He mouthed her name like a caress, then walked carefully around his desk, worried he'd do something that would make the dream disintegrate into a thousand pieces. But it wasn't a mirage. *She wasn't a phantom.*

Stephanie opened her arms like a flower to the sun.

They touched tentatively – two souls adrift who'd found each other again in the same sea of life. Tears coursed down Stephanie's cheeks, mingling with Kincaid's. Every second they embraced grew more passionate, every touch and sensation they shared resurfaced with a vengeance, haunting and promising at the same time, making them infinitely afraid to let go. They explored each other with an irresistible sense of renewal, of reawakening, half-disbelieving the feelings they were experiencing, yet equally terrified it was all a delusion and the other half of the apparition would suddenly disappear, leaving them with nothing but air.

Kincaid held her as warmly as he could, each hug shredding away more years. *Had it really been seven years*? Years, or moments of unimaginable longing? He kept his arms tightly around her, touching her back, head, shoulders, her hands. For the first time in months he was pain free, fear free, his world full of love. He leaned back so he could look into her eyes. Time stopped and hope began. Her peaceful smile could still take his breath away. The fires of passion flared. He drew her closer again, becoming one. It felt as if they'd never been apart. In many ways, they hadn't. *He'd done what was right for both of them, hadn't he?*

"Stephanie!" he finally breathed. "*You're* the security consultant? Davis never mentioned a name. My God, I had no idea!"

"I just learned about the meeting this morning," she confided softly, rubbing her eyes. "I couldn't believe it either. I didn't know what to do, if I should call first or something. My God, K. I've missed you so much."

Their hearts beat as one, their breaths lightened, their bodies melted into one another just like they'd done so many times before. Neither wanted to end the embrace. Kincaid finally stepped away but he didn't let go of her hands.

Stephanie Quan was the most exquisite woman he'd ever known. She had a natural beauty, an inner radiance people spend fortunes on trying to emulate but never have the strength or providence to obtain. An unpretentious beauty that could never be bought or made. Thick and luxuriously black, her hair was a little longer than he remembered, curling inward and resting on her shoulders, and it was speckled with the first few wisps of gray. Her lips were thick and full, her small nose upturned ever so slightly, her cheeks high and sharply defined. A product of three generations of mixed marriages, Stephanie had a small, oval face, and delicate, almost fragile features, mesmerizing in their simplicity. A face you've seen a hundred times and never really seen at all. One you would never tire of watching.

The years had passed kindly, and Stephanie had kept her body incredibly fit. She was thin and slight, almost petite, but well-muscled and implosively strong, like a cobra. That had always been her advantage: no one ever anticipated the damage she could unleash in a heartbeat. She was so small, so slight and delicate. He'd been to a number of her tournaments and knew what she could do. She barely weighed a hundred pounds, yet Kincaid had seen her methodically dismantle male opponents almost twice her size with strength, precision timing and speed.

He offered her a chair, but couldn't let go of her hand. He perched on the edge of his desk. "You look absolutely wonderful."

"And you're more attractive than I remember."

He kissed her fingers. So much had happened. *What could he say?* They were a little stilted at first, but once they began to talk, to share the things that had made the years seem so long, the conversation became fast and furious, like relatives rejoined and playing catch-up at Thanksgiving or Christmas. They laughed, they cried, they listened passionately to everything the other said, trying to make it their own memory too. But most of all, they *remembered* each other, every move, every nuance, every tiny note that tugged a song from their heartstrings.

Time lost its meaning. Eventually, they parted. Reluctant to look away, Kincaid walked around to the credenza behind his desk and made a fresh pot of tea, never turning his back completely towards her. Unnerved, his words were soft and slow. Everything still felt unbelievable and surreal.

"I understand you're helping out with the National team."

"Still checking up on me?" Her cheeks reddened, but she was pleased he continued to make it his business to know what was going on in her life. Did he still have his scrapbook of magazine and newspaper articles that mentioned her name? She'd kept one of her own about him, too, ever since they were first together, always following the time he spent training officers in overseas hotspots, working with NATO, and his meteoric rise to become the 'lead' Detective for all high profile cases.

"Just part-time. I'm working with someone special right now. An angel out of the ring, a panther inside. A middleweight black belt. I truly believe she has the potential to be an international champion. You'll have to come and see her."

"If anyone can take her there, it's you. I've never seen a better martial arts instructor. Or a more beautiful one." Beautiful and deadly – Brazilian jujitsu, karate, Muay Thai, and a touch of aikido and kung-fu, just to be on the safe side.

Her eyes sparkled when Kincaid poured her tea. "And your work? You've been head of your own security firm for about four years now, right?"

She nodded. "It keeps me busy. There's a lot of running around to do, and most of it is really just taking the appropriate precautions to make sure everything runs smoothly. But with all the deviants out there and the way weapons are so easy to obtain, I still get a taste of danger now and then." She smiled impishly and sipped her tea. "But who am I to tell you about getting their hands dirty?"

Kincaid asked how long she'd been under contract to *Meredith House*.

"Almost three years. At first I took on whatever clients I could, but Meredith House put me on a retainer. They've really expanded over the last few years and needed my services more and more. It came to the point I didn't have time for anyone else." She smiled and looked down at her hands. "Except you."

"Stephanie –"

"I've never stopped thinking about you. Or . . . loving you."

"And you know a day never goes by that I don't think about you either, Stephanie. That I don't hold you in my arms again, and wish – and wish it might have been different."

He leaned closer and instinctively started stroking her hair the way he'd done on countless nights that lengthened into mornings in front of his bedroom hearth. Minutes passed before he pulled himself away.

"What do you do for Meredith?"

"General security."

"For the staff? Because of the threats and hate mail?"

"Partly. But it's for the authors they represent, too. Public personae can't afford to be blasé about security precautions."

"So you're with them when they're on book tours or signings?"

"We have to show a presence, but we're subtle and discreet."

"Some writers must be more high risk."

Stephanie laughed. Kincaid remembered how beautiful that sound was, like chimes, how wonderful it could make him feel. *How lonely.*

"I haven't lost a client yet." She cocked an eyebrow.

"You give them personal protection?"

Stephanie nodded. "From the moment their plane lands to the moment they leave."

"Are there many who really need your protection?"

"Actually, they're few and far between."

"But I thought –"

"Surely you don't believe what you read in the papers, K?" she teased. "Yes, some get bags of hate mail. Especially a few of the more controversial, non-fiction writers. Political and business figures. But half the time it's nothing more than publicity stunts. Get in the news, encourage people to talk, jack up the sales."

"Create the market?"

Stephanie smiled, crossed her legs and leaned forward, her skirt moving ever so seductively over her thighs.

"Some books must rattle a few skeletons. Exposes, things like that."

"A few."

"Who's been your most difficult one so far?"

"Ambroseo Tulmanni."

The name twigged something in the back of Kincaid's mind.

"Fictional characters," Stephanie continued, "but the novel's based on the terrible ongoing conflict in Rwanda between the Hutus and the Tutsi."

"*Wadis of Blood.*"

"That's the one."

Stephanie wasn't surprised he'd read it. Erudite, he had eclectic tastes, and always liked to know what was going on in the world. He wasn't the type of cop who slipped off his holster at night and forgets there was a world of problems beyond his window.

"An 'ongoing conflict' is a little pejorative, don't you think?"

She acquiesced with a nod. "It's genocide. Both groups hate each other to the point they'd like to see their enemy completely eradicated. Tulmanni showed the horror of what's happening: the revenge attacks, the retaliation massacres, the rapes, the machete mutilations, the open pit graves. Each group thought his representations of the enemy was justified, but they didn't like sharing the blame for the barbaric atrocities. The Hutus and the Tutsi's both thought they'd been victimized by what Tulmanni exposed. Militant factions on each side wanted him dead. Especially if it could be done on neutral soil. We had to be particularly careful when he came here on a lecture tour. I've never seen someone get that many death threats. I was with him 24/7, but he had his own private bodyguard as well."

"Problems?"

"No. The press coverage actually worked to our advantage, since so many of the world's problems are pushed to the back pages because of the ISIS cowards. The awkward situations were easily handled."

I'll bet, Kincaid thought. He recalled an evening several years before at *Calamari's*, a steak and seafood restaurant on Spadina. Three gangbangers decided to attack an old man who was using a walker to inch along the sidewalk. They knocked him to the ground, kicked him in the chest and took his wallet, just as Kincaid and Stephanie stepped out into the street. She moved before he'd taken out his badge. If he hadn't seen her in action he never would have believed it possible. Then again, he hadn't actually *seen* her move: he'd witnessed the aftermath. The one banger with a modicum of an IQ fled with a broken nose and a few missing teeth. His two companions weren't as fortunate.

"What about the owner, Gail Meredith?"

"Personal protection whenever she needs it."

"When the threats get out of control?"

A nod.

"Has Meredith been on the edge a little more than usual?"

"With Turner's barbaric demise, she has a right to be. In the last month she's been a priority. She's also hired some extra security personnel."

The uniformed guards by the elevators and front desk.

Stephanie sat back and looked around, a pinch insecure. "I hope you don't mind –"

"There's nothing I'd like more than to work with you again, Stephanie." *Or just to be with you. Forever.*

Her eyes twinkled. She knew the feeling. Deeply.

An attentive silence compressed the office, lengthening and deepening the longer they held each other's gaze. Nothing else mattered. Waves of memories flooded back. In their own ways, they were experiencing feelings and emotions that they hadn't felt in years. They saw themselves in each other's eyes. For the first time in ages, Kincaid remembered what love was.

Stephanie knew that if she remained entranced much longer she wouldn't want to move, so she broke the stillness with a little cough.

"So bring me up to speed."

Right, the investigation. He explained about Gerbec's illness, the delays in acquiring evidence, the fact they were really just starting. He pulled a sheaf of papers from his desk, outlining what they had so far.

"Oh, I almost forgot. How's the Wish Foundation doing?"

A half-smile. "We do what we can."

Stephanie knew that look. "Someone really special right now?" she asked softly.

They're all special. Kincaid pictured his friend in the little curtained-off cubicle at the hospital, the monitors blipping and the plastic tubes snaking around the sheets, the constant smell of disinfectant and sterility. "Ryan. Ryan Culliver."

Kincaid sadly told Stephanie about the child's plight: the countless operations, the boy's immutable spirit, his courage, the prognosis that was nothing more than a death sentence, the pain, the incessant worry, the anguish of his single mother.

Watching Kincaid's eyes, Stephanie knew how important the child was to him. "I'm so sorry."

"So many kids," he muttered quietly. "So much sadness."

"Is there anything –"

He shook his head.

"You just have to ask, K."

"I know." A deep sigh, then a forced smile. "So, we don't have much," he admitted. "Gail Meredith thinks you can provide us with some insights that might turn into leads. Inside information we'd miss, not being in the business. Your knowledge of the people who've posed problems in the past, especially ones with the potential to cross the line. And to run some interference for her.

"I'll do whatever I can."

"Great. I've met Ms. Davidivitch. She compiled a list of the people she felt were particularly pertinent. I got a similar list from

Turner's partner, Cynthia Baxter. We cross-referenced the names and came up with this." He handed her the list. "I've interviewed a couple of people already."

Stephanie scanned the pages. "Who?"

"Richard Barclay and Walter Croft. And I'm supposed to be meeting" – he paused and glanced at his notes – "Brent Jacobs around lunch."

"Walter Croft? But he's such a nice old gentleman. Although I did have to see him after he sent in some rather disquieting letters to Meredith and Turner."

Stephanie pulled her hair back behind one ear. A casual gesture she performed numerous times a day, but one Kincaid never forgot. His throat tightened, and he was a schoolboy again on his first date. Odd. A simple but powerful gesture that Leeanne Davidivitch did too.

"I went for a chat. I apologized on behalf of Turner and Meredith, told him how much pressure they were under, and that they often didn't even do their own correspondence. We spoke for about an hour, mainly about his wife. I thought we smoothed things over."

"Someone else writes their rejections?"

"Not always. They get help when the workload explodes and the slush pile reaches the ceiling. What did Walter say?"

Why didn't he mention Stephanie's visit, Kincaid wondered. "How disappointed he was in how they handled his wife's submissions. How hurt. That is was terrible for her at the end because Turner stripped away her sense of meaning. He was vile and caustic, and quite upset at how cruel the rejections had been when "*no thanks*," or "*not right now*" was enough. Turner tore her to shreds."

Kincaid thought about the collage of pictures on Croft's table. "It must have been really hard on him, knowing just a few kind words might have made all the difference before she died."

Something in his tone, or perhaps his eyes, unsettled Stephanie. "You don't really think he was involved in Turner's murder, do you? From what I've read it was extremely brutal."

"*Brutal* is an understatement. And most of the gory details were kept from the media."

"But he's just an old man."

"A bitter old man deeply in love who lost everything. Got a phone? Computer? Revenge is just a mouse-click away. *Anything* and any*one* can be bought in Cyberspace."

Stephanie didn't look convinced. Studying the lists, she said she could add a few more names. One in particular. "I'm surprised no-one even mentioned Erik Caster."

Kincaid jotted down the name. "Why?"

"We've talked several times. If there's someone I wouldn't turn my back on, it's Caster."

Kincaid knew the man had a huge file. Then why the evasiveness? Why ignore him? He'd re-check the folder later. "What's your take on Gail Meredith?"

"Why?"

"Just wondering."

"You never 'just wonder,' K. She's one of the most ambitious women I've met. A fighter, and she doesn't mind getting down and dirty. She's on the mayor's 'A' list, and her company has supported various educational projects he's been involved with."

"Does she support him personally, too?"

"Naturally. *Scratch my back*, and all that."

"And Cynthia Baxter?"

Stephanie offered a slight shrug. She looked for the teapot, but when Kincaid moved to pour her more she shook her head. "We've never worked closely together, so I don't know her well. I've seen her at the gym a few times."

"Enemies?"

"*Enemies?* In the publishing business? *Everyone* in the publishing industry has enemies, Kincaid. People like Gail and Devlin Turner send out rejection letters constantly, and they never know who those dream-breakers are going to. They cut throats and obliterate egos every single day. Without thought or regret."

Before Kincaid could go on, Stephanie posed the question he knew was coming but desperately wanted to avoid.

"How have you been?" She paused, watching him carefully. "*Really*."

A simple query. With a fine point that stabbed him in the heart.

"Pretty good."

"Look at me."

"Not bad."

Stephanie's eyes glazed with sadness. "Ever since I came in you've been massaging your lumbar spine and the back of your neck. The pain and the headaches are back, aren't they? You're seeing Chadpur again." She cleared her throat and lowered her voice. "Same problems as before?"

Kincaid shrugged, then sunk down deeper into his chair. For once he wished there'd be an impatient knock at his door.

"K, please. After all we've been through, and what we mean to each other, you owe it to me."

She was right, but that didn't make it any easier.

Stephanie leaned forward and tenderly stroked the side of his face. Her eyes softened, her lips parted, and her voice was warm and husky. "I could *make* you tell me."

Kincaid felt like he was melting. *Oh yes, she could.* He couldn't resist her.

She laughed softly when he blushed.

He exhaled a slow breath. "Some things have resurfaced. The last six months have been tough, but in the grand scheme of things I'm doing alright."

Her voice wasn't much more than a whisper. "The shrapnel? Or the tumor?"

"They're not sure. That little fragment of steel might have moved. Or the tumor might be growing again."

Stephanie summoned up her courage behind an artificial smile. "What's the prognosis?"

"I'll know in a couple of weeks." There. He'd said it. And to *her.*

The words burned, but Stephanie knew it wasn't the time to press.

She was the only person Kincaid would have admitted that to. No – that wasn't true – he felt quite strongly about how much he trusted Amy, too. He sensed her closeness, her honesty and protectiveness. Did he love her too? Of course he did – just not in quite the same way. He knew Amy would take a bullet for him in a heartbeat, just like he'd done for Stephanie.

God, it seemed like a lifetime ago.

His eyes closed with the pain of memory.

Just like he'd done for Stephanie.

Almost seven years ago. It had been a set up from the start. He'd taken a shot for Stephanie but she'd still been hit. He never wanted to put her in that kind of situation again and had ended their relationship. A ride home after a hurried precinct dinner. A quiet evening, suddenly torn apart by a cry on the police radio. Kincaid, close to the address, wheeling back, yelling at Stephanie to stay down and in the car. A deserted alley, a firefight, with two cruisers already on the scene. Kincaid getting into position, not realizing until hours later after the ambulances sped away that it had all been a trap, a decoy, to get him out in the open. Stephanie ignoring his warnings when she saw the laser beam, creeping through the alley's shadows toward Kincaid. Her screams, Kincaid running, taking a cop-killer in the back of the vest, but leaping over a car's hood and shoving her out of the way as another sniper's bullet ricocheted off the edge of a dumpster, a metal shard slashing his chin and tearing into Stephanie's stomach.

Tearing into Stephanie's stomach . . .

And in a blood-curdling instant their child was only a memory.

Perhaps he should talk to Amy when they were alone and he had the chance. It didn't feel fair, leaving her out of the loop and distancing himself from her. He liked her close. Needed her close. But not at the price he'd already paid that one terrible night . . .

Stephanie looked into her lap so Kincaid couldn't see her eyes. Sensing the redness flush her cheeks, she struggled to slow her breathing down and re-gain control.

"Kincaid –"

"Thanks. And I will." He smiled awkwardly. "I will, Stephanie."

The silence was strained. They both knew they had to move on.

"That's why the investigation isn't up to speed, given the time frame?"

Kincaid nodded, then reminded her about Gerbec and why they were late picking up the pieces.

"How can I help?"

Kincaid stared into her eyes and all the pain, all the fear, gently melted away like the last patches of snow beneath a warm April sun. "You already have," he whispered. "Just by being here."

Stephanie felt the tears behind her eyes. "What's next on the agenda?"

"I have an appointment for lunch with Brent Jacobs."

"Don't forget to duck."

He raised an eyebrow. "And the connotation is . . . ?"

Stephanie giggled. "You'll see."

"You've met?"

"A few times. He's not one of *Meredith House's* favorite people right now either. They've been embroiled in a rather long, messy, and costly legal battle over plagiarism charges."

Kincaid seemed surprised. There hadn't been much about it in the file. "Is it over?"

"Just."

"Who won?"

"Who always wins, Kincaid? The side with the most money and political clout. Ever fight an insurance company? A friend did: they were secretly using a two-part contract for disability claims. The woman proved conspiracy between the insurance company, the banks, lawyers, and half a dozen judges. They buried her, and to this day, people are still losing out on benefits because of what insurers do in their contracts."

"That's a little harsh, isn't it?"

"Not if it's true."

"Meredith writes your checks."

"She employs me – she doesn't own me. Listen. Do you want me to come along?"

"There's nothing I'd like more. But I want to take my Sergeant first."

"Ahh, yes. A female partner, from what I understand. And perhaps something more?"

"Amy MacKenzie."

"You're blushing."

"You're making me."

"Let's see. Petite, attractive, educated with a nice bearing, and certainly wants to learn more from you than just being a Detective."

"Nice little rumor mill."

"I'm paid for surveillance. Especially if there's competition with an old lov –"

"You're not old. And no-one can compete with you." Kincaid nodded at the folders on his desk. "Basically, this is what we've got so far. Just be careful when you get to the pictures. It's not a normal crime scene."

"I will. And don't forget to read the overview I brought on Erik Caster. I'm really surprised no one mentioned him."

"Why the elusiveness?"

"I'm not sure. I'll see if I can weasel anything out. But give him a look – a good look."

"Done." Kincaid paused, searching for the right words. "Stephanie –"

She smiled anxiously, looked down into her folded hands, and mumbled something Kincaid couldn't catch.

"Pardon?"

She whispered back without looking up. "I do too, K."

Chapter Twenty One

Kincaid was more than a little frustrated Amy was still being cross-examined by the ADAs about loose ends in the ShoeCam case and wouldn't be able to attend Brent Jacob's interview. He hadn't taken her to see Richard Barclay, and probably should have. It was the type of experience she needed, and one of the reasons – *other than to watch her partner* – Davis had assigned her to the case. Unfortunately, she was still lugging around one of the boxes with Turner and Meredith's information, as well as her case files on the ShoeCam Operation. Kincaid knew he felt better with someone else in the car, just to be safe, but he'd have to see Jacobs alone and update Amy and Stephanie later. He still wondered about Stephanie's warning to "duck."

Tucked into the end of an industrial strip mall, the restaurant was one more link in the endless chain of roadhouses that had become so popular over the last two decades. *Crace's* was as indistinguishable as all the others: small, sectioned-off dining areas, wooden benches, checkered tablecloths, a standup bar lined with flat screens and a collage of bric-a-brac and pictures without a theme. The banality of the 'music' would have been much easier to ignore if the vapid base hadn't been so obtrusively loud. Cell phones only added to the static, and everyone had one. Or a laptop. A tablet. They had to stay connected. *But to what? Here's a picture of my lunch?*

The staff bustled back and forth, ambitiously trying to placate the lunch hour horde descending from the nearby office towers. With curt directions from a nervous young man who was obviously frazzled by the burst of activity, Kincaid deftly made his way to the far end of the restaurant. He found Jacobs half-hidden behind a daunting plate of food that could have fed three ravenous people. Still chewing, the man smiled as Kincaid introduced himself, then motioned him into the empty seat across the booth. Sliding along the narrow bench, Kincaid had to turn sideways because Jacob's legs hadn't left him any room. Wherever this man went there'd be far less space for anyone else. He pictured him on the subway; legs splayed, knees spread wide, taking up a whole seat during the evening commute.

The man stuffed another forkful into his mouth and mumbled his name. He wouldn't be deemed attractive to very many people.

Short and decidedly overweight, he was dangerously close to being as wide as he was tall – a heart attack or stroke just waiting to happen. Bald on top, Jacobs had thick hair, long at the back he'd braided into a ponytail, but he pulled it back so severely it made his forehead look high, his cheeks woefully elongated. The rest of his face was compressed into a tight little square. With small eyes and transparent brows and lips so narrow they were almost nonexistent, Jacobs looked like he was losing the battle to some esoteric jungle disease.

Brent Jacobs had never been to a tailor in his life, and the one suit he occasionally forced himself to wear had been bought off the rack at one of the sterile men's warehouses that invariably offer the same three dated suits in limitless sizes and colors. Today he wore faded black track pants, an old sweater with a tear in the sleeve, and floppy, lace-less running shoes. He perspired endlessly: a large handkerchief dangled from his front pocket.

Kincaid declined his offer for something to eat. Jacobs recognized the look in his eyes. "I always have a big meal at lunch. That way I don't feel as hungry at night so I can eat something smaller." He glanced down, his stomach squashed against the edge of the table. "I'm on a diet."

Kincaid just nodded. *What had he looked like before?* Something fell from his fork and Jacobs practically lunged across the table to retrieve it. Stephanie's warning was dolefully prophetic. The men exchanged minor pleasantries for several minutes before Kincaid took out his notebook.

"What do you do for a living, Mr. Jacobs?"

"Same as before. Proofread and edit computer manuals and software texts."

"Good job?"

"It pays the rent."

"Who do you work for?"

"I'm self-employed. I thought you wanted to talk about Devlin Turner." No more small talk. "It was all over the Net. Not much of a story, really, but it certainly brightened my day. Can't see how I can help you, though."

Kincaid watched Jacob's eyes. "Your name came up when we looked at people who had hostile relations with Turner."

Jacobs' hand scurried through the bread basket. Empty. He signaled the waitress for more bread. Kincaid asked her for a coffee.

"Ha. 'Hostile relations.' I imagine everyone in the industry did."

"You might be right," Kincaid acquiesced. "He didn't endear himself to many people, but you've also had serious problems with the publisher he worked with."

"Meredith House?" A burp, a hurried slurp of water, then a huge forkful of meat disappeared. "Who wouldn't? Look what they did to me."

"Tell me about it."

The waitress returned with the coffee and bread. Jacobs was tearing a bun apart before she'd drawn her hand away.

"I submitted a query to Turner. He liked it and said it really piqued his interest. He asked for a full proposal, outline, plot summary, and character synopsis, which I sent off right away. Then he wanted the first few chapters. That's when he offered to be my agent."

"Had you contacted any other ones before?"

Jacobs nodded between mouthfuls. "A few."

"Did they ask to see part of your book?"

"Uh-huh." Another forkful of something disappeared. The food was mashed together in one large pile so Kincaid couldn't decipher what Jacobs was eating. *Pasta?* The man had the obnoxious habit of drinking, eating, and talking at the same time.

"Turner was the first to offer you a contract?"

"Yes." Jacobs stopped eating for a second. "One of the worst decisions I've ever made. But I was desperate." He dove back into his meal.

"What happened?"

"Nothing."

"Nothing?"

"Turner said he sent the overview and initial chapters to a couple of publishers to test the market and they were on it immediately."

"Wasn't that good?"

"Of course it was. *At first.*" Jacobs mopped his forehead with his handkerchief. "He wanted the entire book. He said he needed everything if I expected serious consideration."

"So off it went?"

A nod. "Professionally edited – *my dime* – perfect layout, proofed, tightened up a bit, flushed out some character flaws, thorough spell and grammar check. Exactly what an agent would want to see. After he had it for about three months" – Jacobs pointed his fork at Kincaid – "three *months* – Turner said he wanted his own editorial company to take a second look."

"And?"

Jacobs gulped down more water and ripped another bun in half. "After almost *three more months* I got it back, and Turner started sending it out again. The final, perfect copy. *Allegedly.*"

Kincaid remembered Richard Barclay's warning about scams. "Let me guess. None of the original publishers wanted to see it?"

Brent Jacobs gestured at Kincaid's heart with his knife. "Bingo, gringo. I don't think the bastard sent it out at all, or that he had it re-edited. But I'd already paid."

"Does the agent tell you who they're contacting?"

"Sometimes. But no-one comments on anything until a deal's done. If a book's rejected, they tell the agent and he tells you. That's it. Nada. No explanation, nothing."

"Why didn't Turner try to place it? Obviously it's to his financial advantage to get it published."

"Because it was salable, and because it had 'movie' written all over it."

Kincaid sipped his coffee. Jacobs sneered. "He wanted it for himself, Detective. I only had a contract with him for *a book.* I hadn't considered signing with him to represent me for a movie script."

More food disappeared. Jacob's wasn't even beginning to slow down. Sweat beaded on his nose and layered chin.

"You're suggesting Turner saw your book had literary potential –"

"Of course he did."

"But there was a good chance someone would be interested in the film rights?"

"Yup. If Turner sold the book he'd get his fifteen percent, that's it. But Turner wanted it all."

Kincaid stared into Jacob's eyes. "You're saying he stole the book for himself."

Jacobs nodded. "That's why I sued the bastard. And Meredith House."

Kincaid recalled some of the court documents he'd read in Jacob's file. His back was aching. He shifted along the bench and tried to stretch out his legs, but there wasn't enough room. Behind them, a busboy dropped a tray of plates, breaking almost everything. The waiters simply stepped around the mess.

"Is that common?"

"Sure."

"Because?"

"It's so hard to prove." Jacobs's handkerchief was stained with whatever colored his chin. "Look at how many shows have a crime-solving coroner as their protagonist. The all-knowing forensic pathologist. Remember Quincy? DaVinci? Scully, from the X-Files? Bones? SVU? Criminal Intent? Now we've got a boatload of shows about CSI teams. Though I have to admit, if I was a corpse, there's no one I'd want to do the post mortem more than Dana Scully. She can dissect me anytime."

Kincaid had seen the morgue. *How would they get this man on a gurney? Or slide him into one of the wall chambers?*

Jacobs speared something that instantly disappeared. "Eight or nine coroners and a limited pool of stories. How many plots can there really be? That's why period pieces are so refreshing. But it's not the plot, Detective; regardless of whether it's a movie or a book, it's the characters, the writing, and how the story line is handled that separates an intelligent, engaging series from the rest."

Another forkful was scooped up. "My God, how many police shows are on the tube, and how many books are written every year about supposedly unsolvable murders and mysteries? Thousands? No. *Thousands a month!* How many have similar crimes and comparable characters? Good and bad? That's why everything keeps getting more violent and gory and sexual. The audience has to be drawn in somehow."

His face was flushed and his breathing became a little wheezy, but Jacobs continued. "You can substitute the actors – and believe me, I'm using the term pejoratively – and use them interchangeably in most films and tv shows. Are you going to tell me you haven't seen a movie, some standardize 'action thriller,' where you thought practically anyone else could have played the lead just as well, if not better? Yes, there are exceptions, but generally, you can take a "star" out and stick another one in without missing a beat because they're carbon copies of each other."

"So?"

"So someone writes a movie script and sends it in. All the producers have to do is tweak it here and there, just enough to make the fundamentals different, and *voila*. The original writer gets screwed. Happens all the time. Watch CSI shows based in four different cities – they're all written and produced by the same people."

"And the same thing applies to literature as well?"

"Undoubtedly. There's literally hundreds of thousands of books circulating around the world at any given time. Forget all the vanity houses and people who self-publish on the Internet. Take out the top five percent, the real works of art. Are the rest incredibly individual? Naturally, there's always going to be some similarities between them. But like I said, it's *how* the story is told, the way it unfolds, the quality of writing, and whether or not it can draw you in that's so important."

"So it wouldn't be difficult to exploit someone else's novel or screenplay?"

Jacobs dabbed his neck with the handkerchief. "It's not something the industry admits, but plagiarism is rampant. Since there's so many similar story lines disseminating out there, it's difficult to prove one writer copied another. I think the vast majority of agents and publishers are above board. But the others? Those are the ones that put a kink in the proverbial armor."

Kincaid nodded thoughtfully and finished his coffee. The restaurant was becoming uncomfortably crowded. The acoustics were terrible, so he had to lean farther across the table. The thumping base of what was supposed to be music aggravated his pain. He reached for his painkillers.

"Assuming you're correct – "

"I am."

"If so many people come in contact with a manuscript, wouldn't they be taking an inherently large risk of being noticed?"

"No. Like I said, plagiarism is extremely difficult to prove. And it's almost impossible to copyright an idea. Or even 'intellectual property.'"

"Isn't all material copyrighted?"

"Many writers don't bother. And besides, the copyright doesn't actually apply to the entire book, *per se*. What you're really doing is trying to protect the particular characters and relationships you've created. Not just the idea."

Kincaid thanked the waitress for an unrequested re-fill. She looked haggard and sad, and it was only halfway through the lunch hour crowd.

"When you sent your book out to prospective publishers, who'd have access to the material?"

"First readers, the editorial department, agents, proofreaders, researchers."

"What was your book about?"

Brent Jacobs sighed and stared into Kincaid's eyes. It was the first time he let go of his fork.

"I wrote about the deplorable world of human trafficking. It's incredible how many people are affected, but I focused on young children, so it was particularly difficult to write, believe me. It's a universal horror that people can't keep ignoring. It was a fiction novel based on facts, a social expose, if you will."

"That's admirable, and you're right. There's almost as much money being made selling people as there is on drugs and weapons. It's an unspeakable blight on humanity."

"Sounds like you have a little history."

"I've spent some time in Saudi Arabia, Somalia, Cambodia and Central America."

"Doing – "

"Training exercises for local law enforcement agencies. Weaponry. Helping them establish connections with worldwide organizations like Missing and Exploited Children groups to make tracking systems easier."

"Well I'll be." Jacobs smiled for the first time.

"Some places are isolated from global agencies and need support for their programs. We sent relief personnel to bring their enforcement people up to speed with better technology, and helped with their on-the-ground training. I was in Iraq for six months with the peshmerga."

"So you just don't talk the talk?"

Kincaid shrugged. "Child trafficking. So you wrote *The Innocent*." He visualized the bestseller's jacket and the movie poster.

"Oh no, Ian Nuraki wrote *The Innocent*. The *book* and the *movie.*" I wrote *The Essence of Innocence.*"

Kincaid looked confused.

"It's the same book, Detective. Just look at even a few of the similarities between my novel and Nuraki's. Was the story set in Thailand?"

"No. Cambodia."

"Did a journalist, Paul Taylor, help plan raids to rescue children who'd been kidnapped or sold?"

"No. The protagonist was a woman. Dal'Assam Singh, I think."

"Were there three main children followed throughout the story?"

"No, four."

"And did they end up together in the same brothel?"

"No. Two different ones, if I recall correctly."

"You do. Was one child punished for an escape attempt that went awry by losing a limb? Her left arm?"

"Right leg."

"Did the girls in one of the backstreet brothels get a stray cat as a pet?"

"A caged chameleon, actually."

"Were there sex scenes with the oldest child?"

"Yes. Tame, but it didn't have to be there," Kincaid said uncomfortably.

"And I didn't write any sexual scenes with children. So how about that? The list goes on and on. There were just enough minor changes to the plot and central characters to make it a 'different' book. For shit's sake, Detective, their fucking book was four hundred and seven pages – two more than mine. Two pages! Explain that."

Kincaid frowned. "I can't. So both the book and the movie came out as –"

"*The Innocent*. Exactly." Jacobs allowed himself a smug grin – or more of a '*fuck you*' sneer. He seethed sarcastically, his eyes narrowing with anger. The man's hands trembled with barely controlled rage. "Nuraki's novel just happened to come out about six months after I sent my edited manuscript to Turner's agency. The movie, just under a year later."

"So *your* book –"

"Had a make-over by Nuraki, the reigning poster boy for Turner and Meredith House. It just *sounds* an awful lot like mine. It made me want to heave."

Kincaid pressed. "But you've already admitted thousands of proposals are constantly changing hands at any given time. Couldn't he have come up with a similar outline when your novel was circulating? It is a major topic and socially propitious.

"Theoretically."

"But you don't believe that?"

"God, no. I believe he could have come up with it *after* reading my proposal. There are so many similarities I can't even list them all. Once I sent out the manuscript, numerous industry people got a free dose of inspiration. Guidelines, characters, relationships, plot, researched ideas – *everything* – and I mean *everything* – was right there for them. All they had to do was a 'nip and tuck,' and put it together in their own way."

"And simply because Nuraki's name was on the book, it would instantly become a bestseller?"

"Bingo again. Turner and little old Gail Meredith made a ton of money, especially with the movie rights because it wasn't written by a nobody like me."

"Perhaps I should read your book."

Jacobs reached for his handkerchief. "You'd do that?"

Kincaid felt – *sad*. Jacob's reaction was practically the same one he'd received from Richard Barclay when he offered to read his work. Was it pride? Intrinsic hopefulness? A need for respect? Recognition?

"Send me a copy. It could actually help us. And if it assists our investigation, I assume you wouldn't be hurt by all the publicity. Unless –"

Jacobs stopped chewing. "Unless what?"

"You had something to do with Turner's death. Then you're going to get a plethora of publicity you really don't want."

Jacobs didn't bite. "Ahh, the nuts and bolts of it." He looked apologetic. And concerned. Kincaid watched the man's face morph through a series of quickly changing emotions. How would he have felt if he'd been in Brent Jacobs' place?

"Did you approach Turner and Meredith before you hired a lawyer?"

A nod. "I wasn't looking for the world, Detective. But I'd put a lot of time and creativity into that book, and I wanted what was mine."

"Financial compensation?"

Jacobs shrugged. "And a little fame."

"But they wouldn't budge?"

"They didn't have to. Ian Nuraki wrote the book. They were adamant there wasn't any kind of copyright infringement whatsoever."

"So you sued Meredith House?"

"Of course I fucking sued them." Jacobs was trembling, his face flushed red. "Turner had my script for over six months. Nuraki had plenty of time to re-work it and make whatever minor changes they thought were necessary."

"But you lost the litigation." A statement, not a question.

"Naturally," Jacobs sighed, the color slowly seeping back in his cheeks. "Turner and Meredith have an army of attorneys specializing in these kinds of suits. I didn't have a chance. I lost almost everything. House, car, whatever savings I'd managed to scrape together." He grabbed a fork, speared a piece of meat, and threw it down his throat. "Those bastards deliberately dragged everything out."

"To break you?"

"Sure. But they also wanted to make an example out of me, so no-one else would stand up to them. It's like fighting a bank or insurance company."

"Did you appeal?"

He shook his head despondently. "Couldn't afford it. I had to sell my house to pay my lawyer's fees. They bled me dry until I didn't have anything left."

Jacobs finally pushed his plate away. The exhausted waitress brought his dessert a few minutes later. The fire in Jacob's eyes had died. He looked sad and hopeless, his hands trembling with repressed hate.

"Wednesday the 14th, three weeks ago, Brent. Where were you between six o'clock and midnight?"

Jacobs dove into his pie. "At home, working," he mouthed between forkfuls.

"Can anyone verify that?"

"No."

"You hated Turner. The publishing house, the movie script, that was different. He was the one you trusted, the one who sold you out."

Jacobs slurped down some water. "Yeah, he did. But I didn't kill him."

"You wanted to, though. You said as much in your letters. I also read some of the court transcripts. You had to be restrained on three separate occasions. You even tried to get at him outside the federal court house building one day."

A forkful of pie hovered in front of Jacob's face. "And do you know what, Detective? I'd still have to be restrained if I saw him right now. If he walked through that door I'd get up and stick this fork through his fucking chest. Over and over and over. Puncture him to death. Fortunately, someone saved me a lot of trouble."

Jacobs didn't smile. His eyes glimmered with fury. He held Kincaid's gaze for a moment, then turned back to his plate and half the pie disappeared. Crumbs tumbled across the table.

Kincaid was quiet. A purloined book. Years of hard work. Then desperation and ruin. He could understand what had driven this man to the edge of the abyss. He remembered Rebecca's story about Saramago. *What would it have taken to make Jacobs cross over the threshold and into the darkness of the divide?*

Chapter Twenty Two

Maybe Paul Wheeler wasn't creatively lifeless – perhaps he simply needed someone else who'd take the time to work more closely with him to make his writing commercially viable. Or a new ghost writer who could mimic his earlier success. Shirley O'Donovan's time for representing writers who couldn't put two lines together without her was finished. She was tired of spoon-feeding authors who'd managed to pen the one good novel they had inside, then crashed. Fame was fleeting – so were her percentages.

Legs crossed, her foot tapping to an esoteric beat, she spun around toward her office window and sipped a cup of tepid green tea. It wasn't helping. Nothing was. She took off her earrings and pushed her glasses farther up her nose, then smoothed her hair back and sighed. She punished herself by reading the rest of the *Tribune* article.

"The horror that frightened us half to death in *Down the Sights* is gone, along with the gore and wicked humor that made *Beretta* a realistic page-turner. Sources at *Marrauder* – Shirley O'Donovan must wonder who the mole is – confirmed Wheeler's last two books were published solely because of contractual conditions. *At $39.95, The Nail Gun* is a letdown for people who have to wade through an embarrassing five hundred and twenty-five pages."

Shirley moaned. Just what she needed. *An embarrassing five hundred and twenty-five pages.* She'd worked with Wheeler for months pruning it down from six fifty. The tea was useless – just like Wheeler. She needed some weed.

Shirley O'Donovan had been an associate editor at Chicago's *Marrauder Books* for almost ten years. She worked in a slim but esthetically pleasing building on Roosevelt Road, a mainstay in the business area that ran down to the lake. The Miracle Mile and the Navy Pier were close enough for a nice lunchtime walk, and she enjoyed many evenings combing through the finds at the Museum of Natural History. Unfortunately, that had become the bulk of her finds. Shirley knew her earnings were tied like an umbilical cord to the success, or failure, of her stable of writers. And she desperately needed a new thoroughbred. She also needed a break. Job stress and problems in her personal life had been weighing her down more than she realized, but *Marrauder* didn't care about that. The divorce papers were signed and she was single again. Not by choice. There'd been some emotional closure, but the pain and hurt was still there. Anxious, depressed, and wallowing in *what might have been*, she finally decided to listen to her few real friends and take a vacation, the first one she'd had in ages.

She'd rent a small RV, drive west into North Dakota, then north over the Canadian border into Calgary, Alberta. She'd stop in Banff and enjoy the renowned Hot Springs that overlooked Lake Louise and the Three Sister mountains, then camp in Brooks or Drumheller for a few days. Brooks was home to one of the largest dinosaur museums in North America, and Shirley O'Donovan had always been fascinated with paleontology. She longed to go on one of the research projects she'd read about in *National Geographic,* and this was the closest she'd ever get. She'd take a tour through the badlands, see an actual excavation site, and perhaps even help graduate students explore one of the digs. Forget Wheeler, a ruined marriage and stale life. She'd go, damn it. It might just change everything.

*

A week later, when she started on her trip, she was still tense, frustrated, and more than a little impatient about all the things that had been making her life so difficult. But those were the least of her worries. Shirley O'Donovan was completely oblivious to the fact that just a few hours away, Dieter Vollger, a natural chameleon and a man she didn't know but had rejected and hurt very badly, was morphing into a new kind of killer again.

One call to a temp, pretending to be a distant relative who needed to speak to Ms. O'Donovan as soon as possible, got Vollger all the information he needed. She'd left on a trip to a dinosaur park, the young girl apologized with a nasal whine. She wouldn't be back for two weeks.

Oh, she wouldn't be back then, Dieter smiled.

*

Cruising the mall, Dieter Vollger found an unlocked car in less than five minutes. A blue Taurus. He laughed at his own joke. A quick hotwire and he was on his way. He crossed over the border into Idaho, streaked through North Dakota, then veered north. As usual, the Canadian border crossing was almost comic in its simplicity. Despite the abject horror of 9/11, getting in and out of Canada was still pathetically easy. Two hours and Dieter was in Calgary. He ditched the *dino-Taurus* in a city parking lot. Twenty minutes later he had a new car, a five year old Honda sedan with tinted windows and a new set of radials.

Driving north, he skirted the edge of the Alberta Badlands, a desert of snakes and scorpions, withered trees, vast open plains, and dried ground that was sunbaked concrete-hard. Tracks dug into crusty earth like old runes on a cave wall. He drove across a huge expanse of flat, dusty roads, up and over the steep rocky embankments, and down past ancient riverbeds that had cut deep gorges through the mountains. The crevice walls were striated with the geological lines of times long past. Tumbleweed bounced along the highway. Debris left behind from receding glaciers scattered the countryside. Hoodoos, the giant rock formations that looked like ice cream cones balanced precariously on their narrow tips, made him feel at home. He was part of the landscape: inhospitable, deadly, unrelenting, vengeful, and armed with the venom of snakes and the sting of the scorpions that scoured the valley.

It was early evening when he reached Banff and checked into a one-nighter. The room was just like the one he'd left behind, featureless except for the city beyond the grimy window pane. Dieter rubbed a dirty space clean with his jacket sleeve. No elegant restaurants or tree-lined streets, no fashionable leather shops with upscale cowboy hats and boots. No booths selling tickets for the famous cable car rides up the mountains so you could laze in the natural hot springs and watch the sun curl by the breathtaking mountain vista of The Three Sisters and their snowcapped peaks. Not here, not in this part of the city where the tourists didn't go.

But Dieter Vollger wasn't a tourist, was he?

Tired from the work he'd done earlier, he started pacing, the pungent smoke from another joint wafting around his head. Arm down at his side, he flicked the switchblade open and closed. He thought about tomorrow, the things he had to do. But a chorus of yells and curses echoed through the room. Dieter scurried to the window: there was a fight across the street. Each man had a blade. A few quick parries and the larger man had a knife imbedded in his stomach. He dropped to his knees, then fell flat against the sidewalk, half on the street and half in the gutter. The smaller man ripped out his knife then stuck it in again. He wiped the blood on the dying man's back, then quickly disappeared down an adjacent alley, melting into the shadows. Dieter grinned salaciously. Nice. But it was over much too fast.

More pacing. The joint went well with a fifth of Jack Daniels.

Bedbugs called. The routine began again: a half-night of restless sleep, crammed with images Dieter wanted to remember and lies he didn't want to forget.

*

Shirley O'Donovan loved the museum. Her new digital camera never stopped whirring, ceaselessly recording the incredible history as each step walked her farther backwards in time. There were more dinosaur skeletons than she'd ever seen in one place. The guide was excellent, his running commentary informative and fascinating. Witty and bright, he knew his subject: no, he *loved* his subject. Shirley and her little group watched how bones were excavated, and how they were separated from the rock they'd been imbedded in for millennia. They learned how they were categorized, tagged and processed. She watched excitedly as molds were made of bone fragments, no matter how small, then saw how they were dislodged from plaster casts. Behind a glass partition, Shirley stared at the lab technicians, who, with painstaking detail, used drills and brushes and dental picks to get the bones perfectly cleaned. Fossil fragments were catalogued and slowly put together like a huge jigsaw puzzle. It was one of the most interesting days Shirley had spent in ages. *Marrauder Books,* Paul Wheeler and her divorce seemed a million miles away. Almost as far away as the bones.

Tomorrow, she'd have the adventure of her life.

*

Sunrise.

Cleanly shaved, his hair washed, his teeth actually brushed, it didn't take Dieter Vollger long to find a car in the "employees only" parking lot that had fresh laundry hanging in the back, and it took him even less time to take it. He had new khaki pants and an official museum short-sleeved shirt, crested with the *Albertasaurus*, the most prolific species found in the area, with a name underneath: Bryson. All he had to do now was a little more reading and to find Shirley O'Donovan.

*

Shirley rose bright and early. Her excavation tour wasn't scheduled to start for another couple of hours, so she pulled on a hat and backpack and went for a walk in the area reserved for the public. The sun promised a warm day laced with the humidity of a desert landscape. Like everyone else who traipsed through the stones, she wanted to find something – a bone fragment from a toe, or a fossil millions of years old – so she kept her eyes peeled to the ground. But she'd been chained to a desk too long – meandering over the rocks was more arduous than she imagined. After half an hour she'd already finished her water bottle.

The sun warming her back, she walked another ten minutes before something caught her eye. An overlooked piece of bone? An ancient relic? She scrunched down and started picking through the stones, anxiously trying to find the little shard that had glistened with the light. She found it next to a flat slice of shale and carefully brushed it clean. Shirley had no idea what it could be, and that made it even better: it could be *anything*. Her imagination ran wild.

Consumed with her *find*, Shirley O'Donovan didn't hear the footsteps shuffling through the gravel behind her. A shadow moved across hers. Startled, she turned and looked up, but the man's face was hidden by a halo of sunlight. All she could see was a cane and foot cast. She shaded her eyes with a hand and glanced up at his shirt. *Bryson.*

He asked her what she had. She looked at the tiny fragment cradled in her hand, and blushed.

I found it right here, she said, pointing at the ground. She looked uneasy when the man told her that technically, all finds, however small, were the park's property and protected by provincial and federal laws.

Helping her to her feet, the ranger assured her she wouldn't be going to jail. "It's the small bones that lead to big ones," Bryson explained. "Sites often start with one piece and end up as a skeleton, so you never know what you have. But people have wandered across this area for years and swept it clean. The chance of finding something is pretty rare."

The woman looked crestfallen. Bryson took the bone fragment and pretended to study it meticulously.

"But that doesn't mean you haven't found *something*," he continued, reeling her in. "What you have here," Dieter Vollger lied, "is a bone from the foot of the most common dinosaur here, the *Albertasaurus*."

Shirley's eyes widened. "A metacarpal?"

Vollger – *Bryson* – didn't know what that was, but it sounded good. He handed it back, winked, then curled O'Donovan's fingers around the chip. "One more little piece won't make much of a difference. But if you find a skeleton, Miss –"

"I will," she laughed. "And it's Shirley."

"Had the museum tour yet, Shirley?"

"Yesterday. It was wonderful."

Bryson checked his watch and tugged his shirt collar over the bottom of his birthmark. "Would you like to see where some students are working? They almost gave up but they found a little piece just like you. The area's cordoned off with yellow police tape. They set up a tent, made a grid, the whole shebang. They've found a ton of stuff. A bit off the beaten path, but I could show you if you wanted." He tipped his hat down farther over his eyes. "You'll see something no-one else will."

Shirley O'Donovan jumped at the chance. "That would be great. Is it far?"

"Just over that next ridge. About a fifteen minute walk, even with this stupid thing." He pointed at the cast.

"A fall, Bryson?"

He liked his new name. "Hazard of the job, Shirley."

Vollger started talking non-stop, spewing out everything he'd prepared. He'd read the brochures, magazines, and as much of the other material he could understand. He improvised easily. He was a born liar, after all. A chameleon, remember? And a good one.

"This is a World Heritage site. One of the richest places for dinosaur bones in North America. The *Albertasauraus* lived here about 75 million years ago. He was bi-" *Fuck. What was the word?*

"Bipedal?"

"Yes. Sorry. Almost lost my footing again," Vollger smiled. "Strong back legs and little short arms." He paused, stumped again. He forgot the word 'predator'. "A fast hunter."

"Another therapod," Shirley recalled. "They were smaller than a T-Rex, right?"

Vollger was caught off guard. *Fucking bitch.* "That's right, Shirley. Some were thirty feet long."

They ambled past crushed boulders. O'Donovan almost slipped, but Bryson grabbed her arm before she fell. Perspiring profusely, their pace slowed. Bryson's apprehension intensified by the minute. Rarely had he ever spent so much time with a kill. They were well out of sight of the main building and away from any public routes. Shirley's right leg was cramping up. Bryson offered her some ice cold water from his backpack thermos. Shirley drank deeply, never sensing the rohypnol. Heavily laced, it hit her hard.

Bryson pointed to a small hillock about twenty yards away. "It's right there. Can you make it? See something really special?"

Dizzy and unsure of where she was, Shirley O'Donovan nodded and followed like a lamb. Limping down the slope, Vollger sent stones and bits of gravel tumbling down the hill. He disappeared behind a large rock. He called out to her, and a minute later, Shirley O'Donovan, the editor who'd sent him three cold rejections, stepped around the boulder.

*

The first thing Shirley saw was the pit Vollger had dug last night and the fake cast lying beside it. No tent or tape or equipment or bones on a table. She turned, looked up, masked with confusion, the barbiturate confounding her senses. The second thing she noticed was the shovel coming directly at her face.

The handle quivered so hard Vollger's arms shook. All he could think about were those letters.

My writing isn't good enough? But you'll bend over backwards for that puke Wheeler, you fucking slut?

Shirley swayed back and forth, half aware of the blood streaking down her face, the right side of her cheek sliced open and already swelling. Fresh blood splattered the ground.

What's it like to be rejected?

He hit her again, smashing her nose flat. A sickening thud echoed off the rocks and blood streamed down the shovel.

My story failed to grab you, Vollger quoted. *Well, grab this.*

Shirley dropped to her knees, barely able to breathe let alone scream. Vollger yanked her arms away from his legs and swung the shovel again, the blade's edge cutting into the cleft between her mouth and nose so deeply he could barely wriggle it free. A wet sucking sound. Another hit, just above her eyes. What was left of her face was unrecognizable, a mass of bloody pulp and ripped flesh. Teeth littered the ground. One of her eyes was gone, wedged between two crushed stones. She fell onto her side, unconscious, almost dead but still breathing. Good. Blood trails tricked down the rocky slope. Vollger smiled, hit her again, then rammed the point of the blade into her stomach. Once. Twice. Again. He'd always wanted to see someone disemboweled. Her intestines slithered out onto the rocks. No scream, no noise. *Damn.* He'd waited so long and it was practically over.

Vollger panned the little recessed canyon, making sure they were still alone. He chopped at her legs, breaking her knees and ankles so she'd be more bendable. He pushed the shovel against her throat, then stabbed it down in a flurry of hate. It took three strikes to sever her head. Covered in blood and sweat, Dieter pushed her into the open pit. He rolled her head over so it was facing up, just like the one in Roland Steinberg's flaming helmet.

This one's not for me, either, I'm afraid. Better luck elsewhere.

Vollger took off his shirt and tossed it into the hole, then threw in the cast and cane. He changed into a fresh one from his backpack.

Sorry, but I don't think your work has what it takes to crack today's market.

It took him ten minutes to fill in the hole and five to smooth out the stones and gravel. He rolled a couple of basketball-sized rocks over top. Tossing whatever it was she'd found onto the makeshift grave, he wondered how long it would take them to find her. He would have loved to see the look on the kid's face when some smart-ass student finally saw something buried in the stones, and figured he'd found something everyone else had missed.

Oh, he'd found something all right.

Just not what he expected.

Kind of like a fucking rejection.

Chapter Twenty Three

Kincaid had to stop at his pharmacy, so he made a quick call while he waited for his script.

"How did your interview go with Jacobs?" Stephanie asked.

"I don't think I'll be able to eat for a week."

"I warned you," she giggled.

He missed her voice. "Seriously, he's extremely angry and vitriolic. He's lost a great deal, and from what I've heard, he has a right to be upset."

"The plagiarism case?"

"Sure. The people telling the truth don't usually come out on top."

"Sounds like he convinced you, anyway. How you feeling?"

"Good." A whining, high-pitched scream echoed through the phone. He cringed.

"My God, Kincaid. What was that?"

"A little boy's trying the old *if I start yelling when were in the cashier's line mommy will give me anything* routine. I want to ask you something."

"Yes, I will."

"Settle down. You've been with Meredith House for close to three years now, right?"

"About that. But in the beginning it was just part-time. Covering the writers, mainly."

"Have they always been in the same building?"

"On University? As far as I know. Why?"

"There's a lot of money in that building. Some pretty upscale companies. Insurance, investment firms, lawyers. I was wondering about their overall security."

"You mean the uniforms in the foyer and around the building? It's been the same operation since I started. *Security Plus.*"

"I know them. They use a lot of ex-cops and some undercover, too. Low profile, well trained. Do the other companies have CCTV surveillance like Meredith has in her office?"

"From what I've seen."

"And *Meredith House*?"

"Most of the higher ups are on-line. Accounting, the mail department too. Other than that, just a uniform or two per floor."

"Who does the hallways, stairs, that sort of thing?"

"That's the building's responsibility."

"What about the guards manning her floors? Has she always had someone stationed by the elevators?"

"No. The extra power started sometime last month when I was on the coast."

"A private firm?"

"Yes. Synergy."

"It seems odd, doesn't it? That Meredith would take those kinds of additional precautions just before Turner was murdered?"

"Not necessarily. You know how much hate mail Gail receives every week. The company's inundated. 'Nuisance' threats can be daily. Maybe she felt uncomfortable with some of the ones she's received lately."

"Perhaps." Kincaid sounded skeptical.

"And then there's the unfortunate incident last month."

"What incident?"

"A guy was mugged on his way home to the Village – "

'East Liberty?'

"Uh-huh. Coming from a bar in the entertainment district. Word has it that it was pretty brutal. Gruesome really. Some poor guy in the wrong place at the wrong time."

Silence. "There's an 'and' in there, Stephanie."

"Well, it's probably nothing. But he was in the publishing industry."

"When was this?"

"About a week or two before I left on that signing tour."

"Do you remember his name?"

Stephanie paused. "McCabe. I think his first name started with a 'B' Bill, Brian. Bob. Something like that."

"Did he work for Gail?"

"No. I think he was an editorial assistant or something at an uptown firm. *The Book Doctor* rings a bell. Maybe a researcher. Entrance-level type of guy, or on contract. I've never heard of him, but that doesn't mean anything. Someone mentioned he free-lanced – Oh, God, K."

"What?"

"I think he did some part-time work for Devlin Turner. Jeez, it never even crossed my mind. What if –"

"He was mugged?"

"That's pejorative. Evidently *severe blunt force trauma* is being kind. Died at the scene."

Kincaid was silent.

"Anyway, Gail's received more than the usual number of threats lately. Perhaps Turner's death gave her a little spark of fear she couldn't handle. Then, with someone else from the industry being –"

"Possibly." Kincaid didn't sound convinced.

"And don't forget Caster. Have you read his file yet?"

"Just the bare bones."

"Well, he tried to assault Gail outside the building one day on her way to lunch. Maybe she thought it was time to take some extra precautions."

Kincaid frowned when the little boy tried to intimidate his mother with another tantrum. Meredith was taking more than just added precautions – she was insulating herself like a businessman in China. Ethiopia. Russia. Mexico. Or . . .

"Just a second." He quickly jotted down some reminders in his notebook. He smiled at the young woman who was dragging the child out of the pharmacy. Forced to leave empty-handed, the boy was still bawling. Kincaid gave the woman a wink and a 'thumbs up'. She'd survived another battle unscathed in the parenting power struggle.

"Why wouldn't she have asked you, Stephanie? Instead of getting an outsider involved?"

"She knows I don't do much uniform work. And you've seen them. These guys are definitely not rent-a-cop. She's not fooling around.'

Kincaid made a note to check on Synergy. 'Can you do me a favor? I just called the station and Richardson wasn't there. Amy's phone went straight to voicemail. Can you give them a shout in about an hour, and tell them what you've just told me?"

"About the mugging? You think it's important?"

"It's not irrelevant. And it happened in the District?"

"It might have been near one of the writers' watering holes down from Roy Thomson Hall."

"Tell Amy to get me everything she can on it. Incident reports, pictures, the autopsy – whatever she and Richardson can lay their hands on."

"No problem. Where you off to?"

"The hospital." He heard Stephanie's breath catch. "No, it's nothing like that. I'm taking Ryan to the game."

"Oh right. He's going to love it. Anything else I can do for you?"

"*Anything*?" Kincaid teased. "You mean absolutely —"

"Anything *within* reason. And with you, the bounds of reason are rather vague."

"Good." He paused, searching for words. "Stephanie —"

"Yes?"

"It's nice to have you near again. It really is."

"It's nice to be here. More than nice."

"I'll see you in the morning. And thanks again. For everything."

The laughter. The closeness. The protection, touching, sensitivity, the help.   And for all the wonderful memories. Lots and lots of memories.

*

Sleep wouldn't come, but, like love, it never does when you're worried about it. Kincaid rolled out of bed, shuffled languidly to the fireplace, and added another thick piece of birch to the glowing embers. The fire roared alive, flushing him with a squall of heat. He slipped down to the floor, leaned back against the bed, and stretched out his legs so his feet were close to the warmth. Sparks crackled softly as rekindled flames peeled the bark from the wood. Shadows flickered across the walls.

Ryan's image had relentlessly haunted his thoughts for hours. Kincaid stared into the flames, but he was really watching the child sleep. He saw the blue-screened monitors with the jagged white lines, the tangled tubes hanging from the intravenous stand, the metal rungs on the bedside snapped into place, the flimsy curtain that fringed the child's space but couldn't keep the other hospital sounds at bay. And he saw Ryan, tucked in tightly beneath the covers, his little arms down at his sides, the needle taped to the back of his hand, the gaunt face, the shaven head, the plastic tube that disappeared down his throat, his restless eyes fluttering behind closed lids.

Was he dreaming? What did Ryan dream about? Kincaid couldn't fathom the boy imagining the same things into being other children saw in their sleep, like friends and family and magical beasts and games and running, just running, and fields and lakes and forts and creeks and stars that went on forever. *What, then?*

A pinecone cracked apart and hurled orange sparks into the air. Immersed in the shimmering flames, Kincaid remembered the boy's expression at the game as the second period drew to a close. Physically and emotionally exhausted, Ryan was in too much pain to stay for the final period, and they had to leave. Kincaid couldn't recall a moment in his life when he'd seen such pure joy and such agonizing despair etched into a face at the same time.

Yet the evening had still been a dream come true. He hadn't been able to make the Foundation's trip to Disney World, but for Ryan this was even better. The nurses arranged to feed him and have his medications administered early, so Kincaid had picked him up at five-thirty. The boy's intravenous stand was attached to his wheelchair. Another pole held two monitors. Dr. Degatz went over the child's meds, potential problems, and what specific symptoms Kincaid was to watch for.

Ryan's eyes were wide with anticipation and delight from the moment Kincaid lifted him out of the chair and into his car. Panting and practically out of breath, the child's endless questions came fast and furiously. What was the new arena like? What did Kincaid think the teams chances were tonight? Would his hero, Berger, be in goal? Where were their seats? Ryan barked the questions out like gunfire, barely waiting for an answer before firing off the next volley. With Ryan controlling Kincaid's siren, they sped through the city and made it to the ScotiaBank Arena well before the pre-game warm up began. A glossy program in hand, the only time Ryan was speechless was when Kincaid wheeled him to the elevators and they went upstairs, stopping in front of one of the marked doors.

"We're not sitting in the regular seats, buddy. We've got a private box."

Ryan blinked and stared, but he couldn't believe it: all he could do was point at the door. Kincaid smiled and pushed him in.

"Wow," was all the boy could breathe. "Wow."

"You've got your own washroom," Kincaid said, pointing at the side door. "And a refrigerator and snack bar. We can order in whatever we want, and we've got these monitors so we can see all the replays and stuff."

Carpeted steps led down to the railing. "I can carry you down there," Kincaid told his friend. "But we can't get your chair in the first row. This level is a bit higher, so I thought we'd stay here so we can see straight down. Awesome view, right?" Below, the fresh ice glistened.

Still trying to take everything in, Ryan nodded excitedly. Kincaid crouched down, and they looked through the program together. Engrossed in a world he never dreamed of experiencing, the child didn't look up when there was a knock at their door. Kincaid knew who it was.

"Back in a minute. Call if you need anything, okay sport?"

Ryan nodded, reverentially turning another page, a smile frozen on his face.

When Kincaid stepped out into the hall, Darryl Berger was just putting the finishing touches on his flourish of a signature across a hockey stick. Kincaid looked up. And up. Berger was one of the tallest goalies he'd ever seen. Even without his skates he was still a good head taller than Kincaid. Berger wore his socks and sweater, but hadn't donned any equipment yet.

Unlike the goalies of the past, when helmets and masks were future inventions and pulverizing pucks and slapping sticks stitched scars over a goalie's head and face, Berger was relatively unscathed, except for a small jagged wound on his right cheek. He had short dark hair, blue eyes, and a quickly proffered smile. With 'Berg' as part of his surname, and a penchant for being a cool, solid block in net, he'd picked up the nickname "Iceberg" years ago when he played Junior. An audacious prankster, Berger always seemed gregarious and friendly. But those closest to him knew that deep down, he was a temperamental and religious man who never understood why life had smiled so kindly on him while so many people suffered.

In his private life, far away from the rink, there was much more to the young man than most people ever saw. Even as a junior in the Ontario Hockey League with the Peterborough Petes, he'd always been involved with children's programs. A year in the ECHL with the Florida Everblades, two with the Marlies in the American League, and he was called up to the big time as a temporary back-up. He never looked back. Invariably, when he wasn't playing, Berger was helping some charity or other: doing hospital rounds, playing in Pro-Am golf tournaments, or organizing Old Timer games with local firefighters and the police. He spent much of the off-season working with Kincaid at the Children's Wish Foundation, drumming up funds for an orphanage they sponsored in Vietnam for victims rescued from human trafficking rings. He was always doing something, giving something back.

He took his friend's hand. "It's great to see you, K."

"You're looking good," Kincaid smiled. He knew enough not to ask him about the game: that's all most people wanted to talk about. "How's Carol and my little god-daughter?"

"Wonderful. But Amelia's not so little any more. I swear she's grown another inch since the last time I saw her."

"It must be difficult being on the road so much."

Berger shrugged. "Professional hazard. The time we spend together is more special."

Kincaid wondered how many people ever thought about the loneliness of the man behind the mask. "Is Carol still working?"

Berger nodded. "She'll hang in as long as she can before taking maternity leave."

"Is she feeling all right?"

"Yeah, she's doing really well." He patted his stomach. "Although she's carrying around more weight than I do."

"Are you stopping at two?"

"We're not sure yet."

The Iceberg paused uncomfortably. He knew Kincaid didn't like talking about his work either, but whenever they met, Berger couldn't help wanting to thank him for what he'd done. Then again, he knew his friend didn't want to be thanked. Nine years had passed since that cold February night Kincaid risked his life stopping a carjacking that had gone horribly awry.

Carol, Berger's fiancée then, had been the ill-fated driver the two thieves had targeted. Kincaid was forced to use his gun for the third time in his career. He killed the carjacker who'd been holding a .38 to Carol's head. The other guy managed to slice him twice before fleeing into the crowd, leaving Kincaid with a deep wiggling line of stitches above his eyebrow and a tear-shaped scar down his cheek, a small memento none of them would ever forget.

"How's Ryan?"

"God, he's on cloud nine. He hasn't stopped talking since we left *Sick Kids.*"

"Then wait until he sees this." Berger showed Kincaid the goalie stick – it had been signed by everyone on the team. "And this, too." Berger left a parcel by the door. "Give it to him later. I hope it fits. I've got a practice shirt for him, too, to wear during the game."

Kincaid opened the door. "There's someone here to see you, Ryan."

Berger walked in, the huge stick slapping against a chair. Ryan was shocked when he leaned around his monitor to see their guest. His mouth fell open in a soundless gape, his eyes frozen wide, his body rigidly still. He held up a trembling arm, pointed, and mouthed *Iceberg*. It sounded like he was chewing marbles.

Darryl took the child's hand from the side of the wheelchair. It was so small it scared him. "Hi, Ryan. It's nice to meet you. Kincaid talks about you all the time."

The boy looked at Kincaid, pointed at the goalie, and blushed. "You're *The Iceberg*!" he whispered again.

"And I've brought you something special because you're such a big fan."

Berger laid the stick across the arms of the wheelchair. "Everyone's signed it for you."

Ryan stared down in disbelief. Berger's own stick. No, it couldn't be. *One he'd used!* It had actually been in the dressing room, with all the players, and they'd all touched it! Speechless, his eyes were moist, his hands shaking. Any other time, Ryan wouldn't have been able to stop talking. He had a thousand questions for his hero, but now, face to face, he couldn't think of one. All he could do was stare. Stare and smile.

"Here, let's get this on him too, K."

Kincaid took the practice squad shirt and pulled it over Ryan's head. He disconnected the IV's just long enough to pull the boy's arms through the sleeves. The blue Maple Leaf was almost as large as Ryan's chest.

Crouched down beside the wheelchair, Berger asked him about his family, the hospital, how he liked the new rink, and what he thought the team could do to improve. But Ryan only replied in muted monosyllables that made his cheeks redden even more.

Fifteen minutes flew by, and Berger told the child he had to go. He gestured to the ice surface below. "Do you know what I do when I'm down there and there's a break in the play?'

Ryan smiled and whispered. "You skate around the crease and then you touch the goal posts with your stick." He looked down: with *this* stick.

"Right, my man. That's because the posts are the goalies best friend. After brave little boys like you, that is. Do you think goalies are superstitious?"

Ryan nodded seriously. He'd seen Berger do that very thing more times than he could count.

"So I think you'll give me extra luck tonight. Every time you look down and I slap the posts with my stick, I'm going to whisper your name. Okay?"

Ryan couldn't even nod. Berger stood back up, tussled the boy's hair, shook Ryan's hand again, then walked up the stairs into the hall.

"Don't forget the parcel," he reminded Kincaid.

"I won't. Thanks for coming up."

"I wish there was more I could do."

"You've done enough."

"You're wrong, K. This kind of thing doesn't take anything at all." He paused and shook his head. "Look at me. I make more money in a season than most people make in a lifetime, and I make it doing something I love. There are thousands of people out there involved with children or handicapped adults who don't have anywhere near what I have: health, a family, and more opportunities than I could ever need. No. *Those people are the heroes*, Kincaid. And all the volunteers who help kids like Ryan."

Lost in thought, he looked down at the floor. "Tell him how cool I think he is."

"I will."

"Are you playing in our Pro-Am again this summer for the CAMP program?"

"Of course."

"Twenty a hole? To the winner's favorite food charity?"

"Start saving up now. And take some putting lessons." He paused, then put his hand on Kincaid's shoulder.

"Listen, Carol and I just wondered —"

"Not now, okay?"

Berger nodded and didn't go on. He looked into his friend's eyes: he was worried, but there'd be another time. Kincaid watched the mammoth goalie jog toward the elevator. When he walked back into the box, Ryan was still staring open-mouthed at the door. Kincaid handed him the parcel, and Ryan managed to let go of the stick just long enough to open it. It was Berger's official replica jersey, with Ryan's name embroidered on the back. Overwhelmed, the child valiantly tried to hold back the tears. He couldn't.

Ryan had hardly been able to sit still all night. He never stopped smiling, not even for a moment, and yelled as loud as he could whenever a roar went up from the crowd. The boy was overcome by the noise, the brightness of the banks of television lights, the cameramen tucked into their perches, the giant scoreboard that tirelessly urged him to clap. He nibbled at bits and pieces of everything Kincaid offered, ending the evening with his lap covered in popcorn, his shirt smeared with ketchup and mustard, and a remnant of an ice cream bar on his foot. There was so much soda pop over the wheels of his chair Kincaid had to wash them off twice or he would have been stuck to the floor.

Each time there was a stoppage in play, Berger did his ritualistic glide back and forth across his goal crease, tapping each post with his stick. Every time he did, Ryan reached over, tapped his own stick against his wheels, and whispered *save*.

But Kincaid could tell that no matter how deeply Ryan was engrossed in the whole experience, the pain never really went away. He'd smile and frown at the same time, or blink the tears from his eyes when he thought Kincaid wasn't looking. His breathing grew distressingly labored for awhile, but the tightness in the child's chest slowly passed. At one point he closed his eyes for several minutes, and Kincaid thought he'd fallen asleep. But his lips quivered, and Kincaid realized Ryan was praying.

A shrill whistle blast halted the action below. "What were you praying for, Ryan?" he asked when the child's eyes opened again.

"I asked God to let other kids have a chance to come here, too," the boy whispered. "Without having to be so sick."

*

I asked God . . .

Alternating flames of red and orange leapfrogged along the log. The bark smelled warm and sweet. When Kincaid had left Ryan safely tucked in his hospital bed, he folded up his new sweater and left it on his nightstand.

Dr. Degatz had been filling out reports at the nurses' station. When she noticed Kincaid pacing in front of the elevators, she smiled and beckoned for him to wait. They met halfway. Dr. Degatz shook Kincaid's hand warmly. She held on a touch too long, like lost friends found again.

"How did our friend like the game?"

Kincaid didn't answer. "What is it?" he asked, not letting go of her hand. He'd known her long enough to expect her to be honest and straightforward. Dr. Degatz finally let her hand slip away, reached for his arm, and drew him off to the side. She didn't speak until an aide pushing a large metal trolley cart passed by.

"I saw his follow-up test results this afternoon. There's not much time left, you understand."

Kincaid exhaled a breath that seemed to burn his lungs. "How long?"

Dr. Degatz bit the edge of her lip. "A week. Two at the most."

It was what Kincaid had expected, but hearing the words aloud, hearing the sentence passed, hammered a nail through his chest. He remembered the look on Ryan's pale face when they'd had to leave at the end of the second period. The boy had to leave life before the game had really started.

Dr. Degatz had already explained what the child's final days would be like, but Kincaid asked her again anyway. Perhaps something had changed. She squeezed Kincaid's shoulder and whispered sterile phrases about nausea, fever, debilitating cramps, pain, and coma.

Kincaid murmured a terse *thank you*. When he took her hand again, he realized he was shaking. He turned without another word, punched a finger at the elevator button, then walked away and took the stairs just as the metal doors winced open.

*

Licks of fire swarmed around a knot on the edge of the log, and the birch bark flamed alive.

One week, Kincaid, thought. *Maybe two.* Ryan knew, he was sure of that.

He tossed a handful of pinecones into the fire and tried to put everything in perspective. Amy. He cared about her very, very much. The more he thought about Ryan, the more Stephanie crept into his mind. He was feeling it all over again – the pain, the anguish, the fear. And how very much he loved her. Kincaid thought about the people he'd met at the publishing house and the ones he'd interviewed so far: Croft, Jacobs, and Barclay. Shadows from the firelight danced across his face. He held Ryan's image in his mind, and the thought that kept niggling at the back of his mind surfaced again.

McCabe.

He'd managed to talk to Amy between periods at the game. The information she and Richardson had been collecting from Division was still coming in in bits and pieces, but they already had enough to make his skin crawl. It had definitely been more than a random mugging. Yes, the poor young man had worked part-time for Devlin Turner. Yes, it was more than gruesome – most of his upper face was gone.

And yes, it looked like someone had tried to sew his lips together.

Was it really possible, Kincaid wondered, that someone could kill so brutally for fame? Or for being rejected?

What a waste.

But he knew people killed for a lot less every day.

The Devil at the crossroads.

Chapter Twenty Four

Kincaid despised wasting time and refused to be put off again. He made two quick calls: one to Lt. Davis and one to the ADA's office. Words were few, concise, crisp and well delivered.

Leaning against the car downstairs, Amy was smiling when Kincaid stepped out of the elevators.

"You certainly put a bee in their collective bonnet – I was out in ten minutes."

"We're a team and I need you. So do two dead bodies. They can find someone else to play with."

"Thanks. I thought I'd be there forever. You picked some tight strings."

"And I can't even play the guitar." Kincaid tossed her the keys. His back was aching, his temples throbbing. *"Meredith House*, please."

*

Someone must have sent up a warning, because a little elf of a secretary with a bobbed mushroom-cap hairdo met Kincaid and MacKenzie as the elevator doors slid open. She was apologizing before they stepped into reception. Kincaid ignored the guard's proffered clipboard. The man stiffened and jotted down the Detective's name and rank.

"We didn't know you'd be back so soon, Detective. Sergeant. I'm afraid Ms. Meredith isn't here. I'm quite sure she wasn't expecting you. Quite."

Blushing self-consciously, she glanced nervously toward the hall that led to the publisher's office. "Really, she isn't here. And I'm not saying that because she told me to, either."

Twenty-five going on sixteen, the girl shifted anxiously back and forth, like a meerkat guarding the troop while the others fed. Her cheeks puffed out like a blowfish, she gnawed a wad of cinnamon gum that looked like it might choke her if she wasn't careful. Kincaid couldn't count the number of piercings dotting her ears.

"That's quite all right –"

"Darla." A beaming smile.

"Darla. I know Ms. Meredith isn't here."

Confused, the girl snapped her gum. "Oh."

"We'd like to see Ms. Davidivitch."

The young girl kept grinning and returned Kincaid's stare. He waited, she waited.

"Oh, sorry," she suddenly blurted out. "Yes. I'll make sure she's here. Well not *here*, but in her office."

Darla leaned over the consul and punched in a number. Unlike all other millennials, she seemed to find the technology baffling, and looked quite pleased but a tad bewildered when someone answered from another floor. She spoke in hushed tones. Kincaid smiled politely, but all he was really concerned about was assessing the security. Stephanie was right: ex-cop or military. This guy was a mirror image of the one the other day, just a bit taller.

Darla stepped closer. "Ms. Davidivitch is in, Sir. I'll take you to her."

"That won't be necessary, Darla."

She stopped chewing. "You *know* where her office is?"

"I do. Thanks so much for your help."

Darla pushed the gum to one side of her mouth. "Anytime."

Watching her toy with the ends of her hair, Kincaid thought she was going to curtsy. When he glanced back, Darla waved.

Leeanne Davidivitch was opening her door just as Kincaid and MacKenzie emerged from a nearby stairwell. She frowned when she saw he had a partner.

"Claustrophobic? Or you just don't like elevators, Detective?"

"I enjoy getting a little exercise when I can, Ms. Davidivitch."

"Leeanne."

"Yes. Leeanne. This is my partner, Sergeant Amy MacKenzie."

Leeanne didn't offer her hand. "I didn't know you were training someone. It's a pleasure to meet you. Please, come in."

Impeccably dressed in a dark green, knee-length skirt and matching jacket, she'd fastened her hair behind her head with an old-fashioned comb that was the same striking fuscia as her scarf. Amy noticed she walked like a runway model: head erect, legs straight, and a subtle, provocative sway to her hips.

"Feeling better?" Leeanne asked, offering Kincaid a chair. She sat beside him, a little closer than before. She gestured to another chair across from her desk for Amy. "You seemed a little under the weather the other day."

"I'm fine, thank you." Kincaid was staring and looked away. Leeanne was definitely single by choice. She reminded him of Stephanie. And Amy in another decade and a half.

"So, how can I help? Are you any closer to apprehending Mr. Turner's assailant?"

Kincaid pictured Turner slumped across the desk, a pencil through his eye, his hand speared with the letter opener, paper stuffed behind the ragged stitches that sealed his lips. *Assailant* was somewhat pejorative. "We're doing our best. We need your assistance with someone else."

"Yes?"

"Brian McCabe."

"Brian McCabe." Leeanne mulled over the name, then shook her head. "Sorry, but I don't recognize him."

"He worked with an editorial agency, *The Book Doctor*," Sgt. MacKenzie prompted. "Perhaps a researcher."

"Oh, Michael Cormier's firm. Yes, we deal with them occasionally. But he doesn't sound familiar at all, Detective. Ms. Meredith would undoubtedly be more helpful. She deals directly with the editors, and she's worked with Michael Cormier for ages. Perhaps she knows Mr. McCabe."

"Knew," Kincaid corrected her. "He was killed about six weeks ago."

"Oh, how dreadful."

There was a light knock at Leeanne's door, but the interloper was sent away with a curt '*not now*' as the door started opening.

"Forgive me," 'Leeanne apologized, crossing her legs and leaning forward. "I understand your interest in *Meredith House* because of Mr. Turner, but why do you think we can help with Mr. McCabe if he worked at the *Book Doctor*."

Kincaid recalled the notes he'd read. "It appears Brian McCabe free-lanced with Turner as well."

"Ahh, I see. You wouldn't believe the volume of submissions Devlin Turner receives on a weekly basis. *Received.* I'm not surprised he employed additional help. Sergeant, you're taking notes. Should I go slower?"

Amy stiffened but maintained her composure. She stared right back at Leeanne Davidivitch. Subtle. Discreet. They implicitly grasped where the other stood.

"And you found out about poor Mr. McCabe —"

"Ms. Meredith's security consultant mentioned him."

"Yes, Stephanie Quan. My colleagues commented on her visit. She fired a veritable Gatling gun of questions, from what I understand."

"She didn't speak with you?" Amy asked.

Leeanne replied to Kincaid. "No. However, I was out most of the day." She shifted forward and smiled, her grin infectious.

"What?" Kincaid asked.

"I don't mean to sound intrusive, but word has it — well, that you've met Ms. Quan before." Leeanne's eyebrows arched and her smile broadened. She completely ignored Amy.

"That's quite a rumor mill you have turning."

"I like to stay informed about things that interest me."

"I've known Stephanie for a long time."

"I see." Leeanne watched Kincaid's face. "Ms. Quan likes to keep her life private, but you already know that. Everyone got the impression she thinks very highly of you, Detective."

Kincaid didn't bite. Neither did MacKenzie, although she gripped her pen more tightly than she needed to.

"What would Mr. McCabe have done for Turner?"

Leeanne re-crossed her legs. Her thighs and calves were more than just shapely. "If you're correct, other than first reads, he probably did research and fact-finding. Most writers rarely check their information thoroughly, so a researcher goes through a manuscript with the proverbial fine-toothed comb. He isn't focused on grammatical or syntactical errors: he's looking for inconsistencies in the plot and factual mistakes that readers might notice. Am I going to fast, Sergeant?"

"No, Leeanne. I'm completely up to speed."

The tension was palatable. Kincaid hoped Amy would see this baiting as nothing more than informative. She had to distance herself, to stay objective. The thing he found more disconcerting was the intense pulsing sensation in his lower back. Oddly, *his foot hurt.* An almost painful *numbness.*

"To verify a book's authenticity?"

"Precisely. Take directions, for example. A scene is based in London. The researcher checks that all directions – city streets, intersections, addresses, buildings, that sort of thing – are accurate. Ensure a bridge or a river is exactly where it's supposed to be, and not in the middle of St. James Park." A brief pause. "Coffee, Detective? Tea?"

"Thank you, no."

"Sergeant? I'm so sorry – I've forgotten your name."

"MacKenzie. If I need you for anything, I'll ask."

Kincaid tried not to smile. "So a researcher doesn't do editing?"

"Sometimes. Our readers might take a second to correct glaring spelling or grammatical errors." Leeanne leaned a little closer. "Devlin Turner. And now someone else in the publishing industry who free-lanced with him. I assume you think there's a connection between the men? Or their deaths?"

"It's something we're looking at very closely. So if a reader liked a script, he'd pass it on to Turner. If *he* liked it, he might send it to Michael Cormier for editing."

"Exactly. And Mr. Cormier –"

"Would have a researcher like McCabe verify the book's authenticity," Amy interjected.

"Correct. Why?"

Kincaid answered for his Sergeant. "Just wondering."

Early days, but Amy Mackenzie knew Kincaid didn't '*just wonder*.'" And you think Ms. Meredith might know more about Mr. McCabe?" she asked.

"I do. And I can see another *and* in there as well."

"There are certain similarities between the mens' deaths," Kincaid replied, careful not to mention anything that shouldn't be in the public domain. Like the color of the thread or the mouths crammed with paper.

Leeanne sat up straight and smoothed wrinkles she knew weren't there from her skirt. "That's why you're interested in the writers we've rejected who've sent us threatening letters or hate mail."

No answer. Kincaid asked when Ms. Meredith would be back.

"She'll probably be tied up all day."

"She mentioned a court case involving copyright infringements."

"I believe that's still pending." Leeanne showed the first sign of indecision. She lowered her voice conspiratorially. "She's meeting with Garth Danielson."

The name didn't mean anything to Kincaid. He wondered why Gail Meredith hadn't told him the truth about her appointment.

"He owns our largest rival, *Excalibur Books*. I'm mentioning this in confidence, Detective, and it's certainly not common knowledge." Leeanne reached over and touched Kincaid's hand. "But the rumor mill has it that *Excalibur* is positioning itself for a takeover."

That's why she lied.

"We appreciate your frankness, Leeanne." He pictured Gail's bracelets jangling together, the tight smile, the evasive replies, the distressed look.

"Nothing's certain. Everything I've heard has sifted up through the rumor express, so its validity is questionable. All I know is that Ms. Meredith is under a great deal of pressure, and I'm sure Turner's death has affected her more than she's letting on."

That could explain the additional security precautions she'd taken since Turner's murder, Kincaid thought. But where did McCabe fit in? There was a moment's silence, and Kincaid and Leeanne both realized her hand was still resting on his. She smiled insecurely and slipped it away. She glanced at Amy, smiling.

"There's one other thing, Leeanne."

"Yes?"

"The list of people you put together for us? The ones you thought were particularly important to check?"

Suddenly, her tone was brusque and businesslike. "Go on."

"We asked Turner's partner, Cynthia Baxter, for a similar list."

"I see."

"We can definitely rule out Lois Gibney and Peter Maxwell. Mr. Maxwell was in Vancouver giving a three day seminar on financial planning when Turner was murdered, and Lois Gibney was having her gall bladder removed at St. Mike's."

"Two down, then." Leeanne tried for a smile that wouldn't come.

Two leads, or misdirections?

"We found it odd that neither of you mentioned Erik Caster. Next to Richard Barclay, he had the thickest file in Turner's folder."

Leeanne was pensively still. She looked down at her hands and appeared to be collecting her thoughts. "Creative forgetting."

Sergeant MacKenzie twirled her pen. "Creative or deliberate?"

"I'm sorry. But Erik Caster has been quite a nuisance." She held up a hand and smiled guiltily. "Alright. Much more than a nuisance."

"He confronted Ms. Meredith outside the building," Kincaid said.

Leeanne nodded and didn't bother asking how Kincaid knew. "She was fortunate two security men were there. I'm afraid to think what might have happened if she'd been alone."

"Why didn't you mention him?" Kincaid asked pointedly.

"A directive from Ms. Meredith, Detective. Or perhaps, a *dismissive.*"

"When was this?"

"Just after the attempted assault."

"What did Meredith say?"

"That none of his calls were to be put through and fully screened and recorded by switchboard. Anything sent was to be returned unopened. Ms. Meredith filed another restraining order, and had his photograph posted at the security desk in the lobby. She didn't want his name mentioned again, or have any contact with him whatsoever. Ms. Meredith wanted to ensure he was completely and utterly ignored. *Ghosted* is the word, I think."

Kincaid pictured Casters' face and remembered some of the things he'd seen in the man's file. He wasn't the type of person to be intimidated. Not before he'd done whatever he'd started to do.

"Where's the rest of his file?" Amy asked.

"I don't know." She didn't like Kincaid's frown. "I believe Ms. Meredith keeps everything we have on Caster."

Silence. Kincaid returned her passive stare. Something wasn't right and it made him uncomfortable. He had the unsettling feeling Leeanne wasn't telling him everything. *What was she holding back? And for who? Why would Gail Meredith keep everything herself?* He looked down at Amy's notes and saw 'Leeanne, Meredith, and Caster' all circled with a question mark beside the names. Why would Gail be concerned they didn't find anything about Erik Caster that hadn't been in Turner's file?

"I'm sure we've taken up enough of your time, Leeanne," Kincaid smiled. He folded his notebook into his jacket pocket – the subtle gesture telling Amy it was time to leave. If there was anything else she wanted to ask, now was the time. Still staring at Leeanne, she closed her own notebook.

Kincaid started to stand, but a sudden weightlessness in his leg made him sit right back down.

"Detective? Are you –?"

"Sir –"

"I'm fine, thank you. It's nothing." He glanced at Amy a little self-consciously. "It was just an awkward cramp." That sounded much more palatable than *I lost the feeling in my leg.* He stood up again, one hand braced against the armrest, carefully checking his balance. The sensation was gone, but the pain in his back had flared up again. *Damn.*

Amy eyed him closely. "You're sure it's alright, Sir?"

"It's nothing." He turned to Leeanne. "Thanks for your time." *But not for your evasiveness.*

Leeanne looked overly concerned. "Again, Detective, if you need anything else, please call."

She stepped in front of Amy and opened her door. "Or better yet, stop by."

Kincaid walked slowly toward the stairwell, Amy matching him step for step. He paused, then kept walking past the door and on to the elevators. He didn't hear Leeanne's door close until he was completely devoured by the interconnected maze of little cubicles.

*

Caught in the middle of the civilian shift change, the station was relatively quiet, and Kincaid was grateful to have an extra few minutes alone before the late afternoon exploded. But just as he opened his notebook, there was a heavy drumbeat at his door.

"Come in, Richardson."

He nodded hello, put two coffees and a file folder down on Kincaid's desk, then settled into a visitors chair. He hadn't shaved: his face looked weary and impatient. Waiting for *the call* could do that to you. He wore black pants, leather boots, two earrings in each ear, and a Harley Davidson t-shirt with *If you can read this, the bitch fell off* scrawled across the back. Thick chains dangled from his pockets.

"You look a little worse for wear," Kincaid said.

"Feel it, too."

"Thanks for the coffee."

"You haven't tried it yet."

"DiMatteo's still not moving?"

"Nope."

That was bad. With every hour that passed, there was something – a flatbed, a cargo container, some non-descript tractor-trailer, an RV or a boat– trafficking human beings to the next secret location.

Time was money. "What's the delay?"

Richardson shrugged.

"What's your gut say?"

"That someone new is pulling the strings. Or a mole. So how'd it go at the game?"

"Incredible. He never stopped smiling."

"Did Berger see him?"

"Of course. He gave him an autographed stick, a practice shirt, and a little replica jersey with Ryan's name on it."

"That's great." There was a twinge of sadness to Richardson's smile. "And how you doing, K?"

"I'm okay."

"I didn't mean with Ryan."

"I know you didn't. Have you had the chance to talk to Stephanie Quan yet?"

Richardson's face lit up. "I certainly did."

"Down boy."

He smiled. "Gorgeous with a capital 'G'. That's the woman you lost your –"

"Heart to. Yes."

"We got along fine. She's got some more information to give you tomorrow."

Kincaid looked down at the files. "It's not here?"

"Nope. To-*mor-row*. How'd Amy do at Meredith House?"

"She held her own. She's bright and inquisitive, so not much gets by her. She has a lot of questions about Leeanne Davidivitch."

"And?"

"We'll see. Davidivitch wasn't as open this time. And she was trying to play off Amy."

"I guess she's still reporting to LT?"

"That's part of her job."

"How old is she?"

"None of your business."

"Where is my beautiful little Sgt. MacKenzie?"

"She wanted some personal time."

"When she got back from the ADA's yesterday she couldn't stop talking about you. God, does it get any better? Listen, if you need any help, just say the word. Please."

Kincaid wasn't going to let his friend push his buttons "Did you have a chance to check that name Stephanie gave us? He's definitely a '*no-go*' at Meredith House."

"Erik Caster. Yup." Richardson nodded at the file and cleared the hair from his eyes with a quick flick of his head. "Not someone you'd want your daughter to bring home. A real pig. The one judges should have to live with when they decide the poor guy needs another chance. Rehabilitation my ass."

Kincaid scanned the file. Forty one. He'd spent over half his life incarcerated in some form of institution or another. Juvenile detention centers, minimal security prisons that were nothing more than liberal government-sponsored out-reach programs to baby-sit guys doing two years less a day, halfway homes, and psychiatric hospitals.

Caster's list of charges and convictions told the story of a career criminal who'd started off small, then quickly escalated to more vicious crimes. Vandalism and muggings were usurped by pay-for-hire beatings, snatch-and-grab thefts by well-planned armed robberies. Extortion, assault, attempted murder. But Caster was at his worst when it came to sex-related offenses. A charge of sexual assault at seventeen led to a conviction for attempted rape at nineteen. He'd been remanded for psychiatric care for indecent assault, molestation, corrupting minors, gang rape, stalking, and aggravated rape. Each time he'd been released from an institution, his ensuing crimes and attacks had become increasingly fierce and brutal.

Kincaid looked up over the report.

"I warned you,' Richardson sneered. "Each time some bleeding heart finds something redeemable about the bastard he's back out. Been a model prisoner. Shown remorse or found God. It makes me sick, Kincaid. It really does." He crushed his coffee cup into a disc.

"And he was released –"

"Seven months ago. The psych eval's at the back. I wish whoever let him out had a daughter –"

"Richardson."

He sighed heavily. "No, you're right. I wouldn't wish that on anyone. But who gets hurt for other people's mistakes?"

Kincaid didn't have an answer. "Anything major since then?"

"No, he's been a real boy scout. Other than the threats he sent Meredith and Turner. What would a bottom dweller like Caster have to do with an influential agent and publisher?"

"A book."

"*Caster* wrote a *book*?" Richardson asked incredulously. Judging by the man's profile it was difficult imagining he could read, let alone having the faculty to string a couple of coherent sentences together.

"'Book' is a stretch," Kincaid confirmed. "It's an autobiography about his time in jail."

"An asshole's memoir."

Kincaid smiled.

He shuffled through the pages until he found the report he wanted. One of Caster's assessment counselors thought the idea of getting all his innermost thoughts down on paper might be cathartic. Wrong. Kincaid read her narrative about how hard Caster worked on the manuscript, how dedicated and industrious the project made him. Why not? Caster was a narcissistic sociopath who craved attention. Any attention. Letting other people see how vile and disgusting he was would stoke the fire of his ego like dried out swamp grass in a Florida brushfire. He was sure his counselor must have been mentioned in fervent terms.

"He wrote about his crimes and places he was incarcerated," Kincaid added. "The other 'innocent' men he met, how he was treated, and how he turned his life around after being so maliciously victimized."

"So he took his pitiful little treatise to one of the biggest agents in the city."

"And Turner rejected it. He probably sent him one of his special little letters." *The caustic ones that could push someone over the abyss.*

"And Meredith?"

"He represented himself as a new agent from the States and sent it directly to Gail. It would only have taken her a few seconds to realize that no-one in their right mind would have backed it."

"So he tried to grab her after he got the rejection letter?"

Kincaid nodded. "Meredith was leaving her office. She'd left her car at home and was Ubering it. He came out of nowhere, yelling and cursing, right in her face before she could even call for help. A couple of the guards grabbed him before anything happened."

"Building security?"

"No. Two of the new suits. It was just after Turner died."

"But she didn't press charges?"

"No."

"And yet E.E. confronted her and she nailed him right away."

"E.E.?"

"Eddie Etiquette. Brent Jacobs."

Kincaid threw a paperclip at Richardson, who snared it with a quick right hand. "I don't think the intent was quite the same."

"But Jacobs lost everything. And she charged him."

Richardson was right. Kincaid looked puzzled. Why didn't Meredith press charges? Other than her original statement to the investigators, she refused to take the matter any further. She'd taken the time, however, to send in a copy of her rejection letter, just for the record. And yet she'd immediately filed a restraining order against Jacobs.

"What did the rejection say?"

Kincaid flipped over the page. "That the book was pathetic. The spelling was atrocious, it was devoid of even rudimentary grammatical structure, and the entire manuscript was nothing more than a trashy, trite piece of self-serving garbage lacking any form of substance whatsoever."

"So she missed all the good stuff. No wonder he thought she might not want to read it again."

Another paperclip, another nice catch.

"Are you going to talk to him?"

"We'll let him know he's in the frame."

Kincaid skimmed the rest of the pages. Something didn't feel right. Richardson knew what he was looking for.

"It's on the bottom."

"The information you and Amy found out about Brian McCabe?"

"We scraped together as much as we could. Actually, it was all Amy. Stephanie was right about the digital stuff. Pretty brutal. It was almost *too personal*, if you know what I mean. Complete overkill – whoever did it enjoyed it just a little too much. If you need anything else, you'll have to go to forensics and dig for it."

"Thanks." Kincaid winced when he saw the first two photographs of the crime scene. There were beatings, and there was this. You certainly couldn't call this blunt force trauma: McCabe's face had practically been obliterated. There was so much blood it was hard to make out what was left of the man's features.

"So the deaths are definitely related, right?"

"Meredith certainly thinks so. That's why she hired an extra level of protection."

"What are you going to do now?"

He looked up thoughtfully and tried to purge the crime scene photos from his mind. "I think it's time to have a chat with our famous author. Erik Caster."

Chapter Twenty Five

The noise was horrific, the distractions annoying, which made it increasingly difficult to concentrate. Kincaid couldn't wait any longer. He stopped at the water cooler in booking and took two more painkillers. That was four already and it wasn't even noon. He had to be careful: he had to be able to focus, but the pain in his spine was becoming a taxing diversion. Just as he pushed the heavy stairwell doors open, Stephanie called his name. He spun around and smiled. She kissed him lightly on the cheek.

"I heard you were on your way in, so I thought I'd wait." She couldn't help staring: his skin was warm and moist, his eyes dull. "You okay?"

"I'll manage."

"How's your back? The headaches?"

"You look wonderful."

"Kincaid –"

"Later. I couldn't stop thinking about you last night."

She reached up and laid a hand softly against his cheek. "And I've never stopped thinking about you either, K."

He brushed his lips across her forehead.

"How did Ryan like the game?"

Beaming, Kincaid quickly told her everything that happened.

"His own sweater," Stephanie smiled. "That was nice of Darryl."

"Every time he hit the posts with his stick, Ryan –." He tried to keep smiling, but a heavy sense of melancholy veiled his eyes.

Stephanie smiled the smile that always made everything seem right. "Thanks for inviting me."

"Amy had another meeting with the brass about the ShoeCam collar, so it wasn't completely altruistic," he admitted.

"You couldn't pull any more strings?"

"Not this time. Lt. wants –"

"Someone to have your back. I know. But I would have come anyway, even if Davis hadn't asked."

Davis had already told Stephanie about Amy's 'other' role, and that he needed her to be an extra pair of eyes when MacKenzie wasn't available. To protect Kincaid *and* the investigation. Davis didn't want either one in jeopardy. With Amy still tied up with the suits, Stephanie could cover for him –

unofficially of course – if he needed help. That's the role Gail Meredith had expected of her anyway: to be as close to the inquiry as possible. Kincaid still felt guilty about leaving his partner out of the picture. He hoped she understood.

"When are we going?"

"Right now."

Stephanie rubbed her hands together, her eyes glistening with the threat of excitement.

*

Despite the traffic, the territorial problems with the insufferable bike lanes and the incessant construction, the drive was relatively short, and they weaved their way into the city's heart to a labyrinth of over-exploited tenement apartments coagulated around Parliament Street. A drug and prostitute mecca, it was an area where fast love and chemical escape could be rented day and night. Stephanie drove past the target building and parked discreetly a block away. Walking back, they stopped near the corner. Old sheets and tattered laundry flapped in the wind from balconies littered with rusted bikes and old kitchen chairs. Ripped t-shirts hung over the railings, secret signals to the dealers and pimps.

Kincaid checked the street, glanced at the adjacent alley, and studied the rows of windows glistening with reflected light. Stephanie had seen the look in his eyes before. The troubled, *knowing* glare. He was verifying his options. It was like the glint of apprehension in a mother's eyes when she senses that somewhere, her child's been hurt, or the trembling frown that creases your forehead before you tear the telegram open. Stephanie never questioned Kincaid's judgment. He nodded toward the narrow alley that ran behind the nearest building.

"I won't come up, then?" she asked.

He looked into her eyes. Years rolled seamlessly away. They'd only been together for less than two days, and they were already cognizant of what the other was thinking before they were aware of it themselves.

"Be careful."

"You too," she whispered.

*

The elevator reeked of stale urine and even mustier, homegrown weed as it jerked from floor to floor. The walls were splattered with tags, and all of the panel buttons had been gouged away. Kincaid refrained from breathing too deeply until the doors finally clanged open. The hall, however, wasn't any better. More graffiti. The overhead lights had been smashed or had their sockets torn from the ceiling. Any wallpaper that hadn't been defaced was shredded in long, jagged strips. Suffocatingly thick cooking smells mingled with the stench of rotting garbage and dirt-caked floors. Shouts and slaps punctured the stillness. Televisions roared from the nearest rooms.

Kincaid walked down to the end of the hall. He leaned forward and listened at the door for a moment before he knocked, but all he could hear were curses from the apartment behind him. He tried the door, but it was locked. He waited for a second and rapped the door again, harder this time, more insistent.

"Police!"

Inside, a chair toppled over and something fell and crashed into pieces. There was a harsh scraping noise, a muffled yell, and then a flurry of frenzied steps pounded across the floor. Kincaid heard a window being rammed open, and felt a fresh breeze seep beneath the door. Silence. The curses and threats behind him echoed even louder. Kincaid shook his head and briskly retraced his steps back down the hall. Two kids took off as soon as they saw him, leapfrogging down the stairwell. After a glance at the elevator, Kincaid decided to take the stairs, too. Time wasn't an issue – Erik Caster had blown his chance. It had been a long trek to save him some grief. Oh, well.

*

Erik Caster ducked down the fire escape, grabbed the handrail, and swung over the last few steps. He hit the ground with a dull thud, skidded on a discarded fast-food bag, then was off and running before the echo began to fade. He took three strides before Stephanie stepped out from behind a dumpster halfway down the alley. He jerked to a stop, anxiously looking her up and down. A rueful headshake and he licked his lips.

"Such a waste. But I don't have time to make you love the dark side, cutie." A quick glance back to make sure he wasn't being followed. "Nice tits and legs. And those lips! How 'bout showing me your other ones?" He stared at her crotch, rudely grabbing his own.

He didn't wait for an answer. But the second he moved, Stephanie stepped out farther, blocking his path and effectively cutting the alley in half. Her legs were spread shoulder-width apart and her arms hung loosely down at her sides. Caster smiled salaciously. He liked the defiance in her eyes.

"Not now, sweetheart." He re-checked the fire escape. "I know you fucking want me, but I'm kind of in a hurry."

He knew he'd have to move her to get by. And he was going to get by, so that was fine by him. He could feel her skin already. Her tears. The blood.

"Don't make me fuck you over, princess."

Flexing her hands open and closed, Stephanie rolled up ever so slightly onto the balls of her feet.

Caster reached back into his waistband and drew out a ten-inch piece of pipe. The size was deceiving: it was a collapsible baton, with the rest of the weapon telescoped inside. Caster flicked it open. Expanded, it was almost a meter long. The tip had been filed to a fine point. He cracked it down against the pavement, making a spark, then whipped it through the air like a sabre. *Whooosh.*

"You picked the wrong fucking time for this, bitch."

Caster inched closer, palming the weapon back and forth. Stephanie knew he could wield it like a sword or jab it like a knife. She had to be careful until she knew how he moved. And he did. She circled slowly to his right. When they were only a few steps apart, he lifted the metal tip high above his head. Feigning an attack, he faked a swing, then quickly lowered it down in one fluid motion and lunged the point at Stephanie's chest.

She whipped around and blocked the thrust with a side kick. Instinctively moving inside, she smashed her palm into the bottom of Caster's jaw. His head snapped back. He felt the wind being sucked from his lungs and a searing pain in his shoulder so sudden and fierce he thought he was going to be sick. He sensed himself being spun around, his body practically following his numbed elbow and shoulder, then heard the weapon clang to the ground.

He gasped desperately for breath as the alley flickered into darkness.

The next thing Caster was half aware of was a large man leaning over and slapping him back into consciousness. He saw clouds high above the man's head, the corroded bottom of the fire escape ladder, the dumpster's lid hanging at an awkward angle. The alley's buckled asphalt was cold against his head. *Where was he?*

Caster jerked back when Stephanie peered down over Kincaid's shoulder. She leaned in closer, her smile making him shiver, as she twirled the telescoped baton like a majorette at half-time. A *lethal* baton. And a *vicious* majorette.

"Stay very still," Stephanie ordered. She moved his shoulder and he tasted bile again. Caster thought he could see his reflection in her eyes. The man helped him sit up while the woman's hands explored the muscles in his arm and upper back.

"What the fuck hap –"

"Caster," Kincaid called, bringing the man back. Glancing up at Stephanie, he couldn't help smiling. "Boy, this is going to hurt."

Dazed, Caster tried to focus. He felt the woman's hands kneading, pressing. Every touch rekindled the searing fire. "Hurt? What's going to fuc –?"

He choked on a scream as Stephanie popped his separated shoulder back into place. Pain blistered through his entire body, and for a moment, all he could see was a sparkling white light. Waves of nausea pounded his senses, and from somewhere, somewhere far away, he heard the echo of a yell and groan. His muscles turned to jelly as he collapsed backwards. The filth of the alley seemed a long, long way down. He felt the stones, the chill of the asphalt, the fire ravage through his body as the blackness reclaimed him again.

*

Caster sat up, with help. His jeans were scuffed and his denim shirt was stained with sour beer. His long black hair was oily and unkempt. He had a large, ragged scar etched down the left side of his jaw. A dark blue prison tattoo peaked out from the sleeve of his shirt. He pleaded with Kincaid. "You gotta get me to a hospital, man. That fucking bitch broke my shoulder."

"It was just dislocated," Kincaid replied. "There's no such word as 'gotta.' And if you ever call her that again . . ." He squeezed Caster's shoulder, pushing his thumb deeply into the muscle.

Caster groaned and glanced uneasily at Stephanie. Any movement of his arm quashed tempting thoughts of revenge. *For now.* He looked her up and down when she wasn't staring at him. Good looking. And so fucking small! Had she really hurt him so badly, so quickly? Then again, Caster wasn't sure *what* she'd done. His shoulder ached, his stomach felt like his insides had been ripped apart, and his right wrist throbbed painfully. His jaw felt slack and uneven.

"Why did you run?" Kincaid asked quietly.

"I didn't know who it was. There's bad people in the building and I wasn't taking any chances."

"So the word 'Police' didn't mean anything to you?"

"I heard the knock and took off." He glanced at Stephanie. "And I'd still be running if that bi – if it wasn't for her." He jabbed his chin out at Stephanie. *That* hurt.

"You're extremely fortunate she wasn't angry," Kincaid said. "All I wanted to do was ask you a few questions."

Caster kicked out at an empty bottle.

"Where were you Wednesday night, the 14th, between six and midnight?"

"I need a hospital. Bad."

"I need your co-operation."

Massaging his shoulder, Caster stalled for time. "The 14th? Shit, man. That was like three weeks ago. I can't remember that far back." *Yesterday* was often a stretch.

"Try."

"I think – I think I was looking for work. Yeah. Didn't find nothin', so I crashed and watched the tube."

"*'Nothin's* not a word either, Erik. What did you watch?"

"I don't remember. T.V. shit. You know."

"That certainly narrows it down." Kincaid leaned closer. "Try a little harder."

"I don't remember," Caster pleaded. "How the fuck did I know you'd want to know what I watched back then?"

"Did you go out that evening?"

"No."

"Not at all?"

"I said no. Look, what's this all about? Do I have to lawyer up?"

"That depends on how much trouble you're in."

"I've been clean since I've been out. Ask around."

"And I'm sure all the kind souls that would offer you succor would be exemplary citizens of the highest moral turpitude, Erik. But I don't have time for that. Tell me what happened about five weeks ago outside *Meredith House*?"

"*Meredith House*? I don't know what –"

Stephanie rose up and stepped around Kincaid, the threat in her eyes unmistakable.

"Look, I tried to grab her, okay. But I couldn't. The bitch didn't press any charges, right? So what's the problem, man?"

"Man?"

"*Detective*," he seethed.

Kincaid smiled placatingly. "The problem is still your behavior, regardless of whether or not Ms. Meredith refused to take the matter further."

Caster scratched the pavement with his heel. "She fucked me over, ma – *Detective*."

"How did she do that?"

"She promised she'd take a look at something I did inside."

"The book you wrote during your incarceration at Kingston?"

Caster's face brightened noticeably. "Yeah. You know about it?"

Kincaid nodded. "It's an autobiography, from what I understand."

"Took me three years." He glanced at Stephanie. She wasn't smiling, so he quickly looked away.

"And you thought Ms. Meredith was interested in your work?" Kincaid asked, hiding a smile.

Caster nodded excitedly. 'That's what that puke Turner told me. He –"

"Ah. Devlin Turner?"

"Yeah. He's an agent, see. I sent the prick some chapters and he told me he wanted to see the whole thing."

"So in good faith you sent him your manuscript."

"Right. He sent me a letter saying it needed some fine tuning, or some shit like that. Said I could use his editing guys to make it better. Check out the spelling and grammar and shit. Shorten some scenes and – what do you call it? - *flesh out* other crap. It cost some serious coin but I figured it was worth it."

"And?"

"And after I paid him, he told me to re-write it the way they said, 'cause he was going to send it to *Meredith House*."

Caster winced from another flash of pain and gently rubbed his shoulder.

"So you re-wrote your manuscript and he took it to her?"

"Gail Meredith. The publisher cun – *woman*."

"And what did she say?"

He shook his head angrily and stared at the ground. His jaw throbbed and he'd lost the feeling in his arm. A dog crept into the alley, growled, then backed away.

"Fucking bitch."

"I beg your pardon?"

"She didn't want to touch it."

"Who told you? Turner, or Meredith?"

"I got letters from both of them. They said I didn't have a hope in hell of getting it published."

"Despite its inherent literary merit?"

"What?"

"Nothing. You must have been pretty angry. Especially with Turner. He took you for the editing scam. You paid him and re-wrote the whole thing, and he didn't really want to see it at all."

Caster was quiet. He tried to keep an inconspicuous eye on Stephanie. She was twirling the pipe so fast it was making a *hummm*.

"Erik?"

"Sure I was fucking angry. So what? I told you. Things got out of hand. I'd had a few, you know. So I went to see her –"

"Gail Meredith?"

"Yeah. Just to, like, you know, find out where I went wrong, why she wasn't going to pick it up. That kind of shit."

"Yes, I see." Kincaid looked up at Stephanie. "And that's why you threatened her?"

Caster glared smugly. "She did the right thing and let it go."

But why? Kincaid wondered. Why not press charges? He'd met Gail Meredith twice: she certainly wasn't the type to let anything go. He watched Caster's eyes.

"Devlin Turner was murdered almost three weeks ago. Wednesday night."

Caster's face blanched white and a fresh stab of pain ripped through his shoulder and neck. Then a half smile and half sneer crept across his face. "Fucking A," he mumbled.

"So. Back to the original query. Where were you that evening?"

He shook his head demonstratively. "No fucking way. You're not jamming me up on that one. I didn't have anything to do with the fucking puke's death. Uh-huh. No way."

"I guess you were watching television?"

"That's right."

"Alone?"

"Fucking eh."

"Well, that's too bad," Kincaid said, standing up. "That means you don't have an alibi." The smug grin melted from Caster's face.

Kincaid turned, nodded to Stephanie, and together, they started walking down the alley toward the street. She flicked the baton closed and tucked it into her jacket pocket. A drunk in someone else's overcoat was rummaging through the garbage, completely ignoring what was happening.

"Hey, what about my fucking shoulder?"

"It's fine," Kincaid called back. "It was reset perfectly. If you don't move around too much, it should only hurt for a week or two. Ice it and tuck it into a sling."

"But that fucking bitch –"

Kincaid stopped and turned, his eyes narrowed with rage.

"I mean that *woman*," Caster corrected himself.

Kincaid looked around the alley, shrugging when he didn't see what he was searching for. "And what woman would that be, Erik?"

Caster nodded angrily and spit a wad of phlegm across the lane way. "Yeah, stick together, you shits."

"I'm sorry?"

"Nothin.' I mean, 'noth*ing*.'"

"Stay close to home, Caster. We'll be back."

He pivoted around and walked away. Stephanie stared back at Caster a moment longer, took a few strides backwards, then turned and hurried off after Kincaid.

Chapter Twenty Six

The call came early.

"You can do it, buddy. You can do it."

Kincaid shifted impatiently back and forth, trying to ignore the blue lines spiking across the monitor above Ryan's bed, the jagged peaks and valleys that constantly measured the strength in the child's ravaged body. The boy hadn't moved since he'd come in. Did Ryan know he was there, hovering like an expectant father? Was the child dreaming? Sleeping? Or was it something else, something dark and mysterious and infinitely longer, the same place Kincaid knew so well but couldn't remember? Ryan's blankets moved imperceptibly, practically in waves, his breaths so light Kincaid could barely hear them. Fluids leaked through three IVs. A transparent tube disappeared down his throat. Kincaid smoothed a hand over the boy's forehead.

He didn't look back when the heavy metal door winched open. The room immediately succumbed to the aggravating noises from the ward, but the humming silence returned as the door slowly swung closed. Paper-slippered feet padded lightly across the antiseptic floor.

"He had a rough night," Dr. Degatz admitted softly without preamble. "We thought we lost him –twice."

Kincaid nodded without speaking. The bouquet of balloons he'd left by the window shivered.

"He's stable now." Dr. Degatz took Ryan's pulse, felt his forehead, then straightened his sheets, just like Kincaid had done.

"There's a call for you. A woman. She said it's quite urgent."

Here, beside the bed, in the shadows of the monitors, external urgencies lost their meaning. He leaned down, his head close to Ryan's, and watched the boy's eyes flicker behind closed lids. He seemed even smaller than he had the day before.

"Kincaid," Dr. Degatz whispered.

"Has his mother been in?"

"Yes. For a couple of hours early this morning."

"How did she seem?"

"It's taking a severe toll on her. Mentally and physically. She was crying when she left, but I could see it in her eyes – she couldn't stay any longer, no matter how much she wanted to." A deep sigh. "She's reaching her limit, too."

Kincaid knew the feeling. "I'll call her later, and see what I can do."

"Kincaid? The woman said she really needed to speak to you."

Everyone always needs something. "When he wakes up, tell him I was here. That his mother was, too."

Dr. Degatz peered over the rim of her glasses and laid a hand on Kincaid's arm. "I will."

Kincaid followed her quietly from the room, stopping once, looking back, and wishing beyond hope there was something more he could do. But there wasn't, and it detonated his insides with a grenade of anger, fear and resentment. He retrieved his phone from the nurses' station and punched in his department's number. Amy answered on the first ring.

"It's me."

"Where are you?"

"At the hospital."

"Still? Oh no, Kincaid. Is –"

"He's stable." A moment's silence. The calm before a storm of locusts appears in the distance. "What did you need, Amy?"

She cleared her throat. "I'm glad I caught you. I've got something you should see."

Kincaid tried to sound responsive. "That's one of the best offers I've had all day."

"One of the best? Listen. Do you read the Sunday edition of the Gazette?"

"That rag. No. Why?"

"There's a story you have to see. It may be nothing, but –"

"But you think it's pertinent to the case?"

"Yes."

"Then that's enough for me."

"I needed to check out some things, and I didn't want to do it at *Meredith House*, so I used your office."

"I don't blame you. There's no such thing as a secret over there. I'll be there in thirty minutes. Richardson around?"

"He just went for coffee."

"Give Stephanie a call. If it's as important as you think, they both need to hear it."

"Already done. What about Ry –"

"Not now. Please."

Kincaid frowned when three nurses hustled by: another crisis. He snapped the phone closed and watched them rush down the hall. He waited until they passed Ryan's door, then mumbled a silent prayer. But their path led somewhere. More pain. To another child. Another bedside parent. He prayed for them, too.

*

Kincaid felt a palpable sense of unease when he opened his door. Stephanie was at the window, hands clasped behind her back like an orator at a podium. Slouched down in a visitor's chair, Richardson quietly scanned a sheaf of photocopied pages, the ubiquitous coffee at his side. Amy sat in the other one, frowning as she read a crumpled newspaper.

Stephanie's heart picked up its beat when she saw Kincaid's reflection. She turned and smiled, and the frustration and pain that had flared through his body disintegrated faster than a Somalian ceasefire. Amy glanced up, wondering. After nodding and smiling warmly at his Sergeant and Stephanie, Kincaid turned to Richardson.

"What's so important that I couldn't leave you on your own for a while?"

Back in his ripped jeans and battered leather jacket, Richardson looked more like a biker hit man than a cop. He slipped some photocopied sheets across the desk. "I think your Sergeant's found something."

Kincaid gave them a cursory glance. "What am I looking at?"

"Trouble with a capital 'T'," Richardson replied.

Amy walked around his desk and leaned over Kincaid's shoulder. Her skin exuded warmth, and she smelled so sweet he wanted to reach up and touch her. Behind him, he could almost feel Stephanie breathe. Why did Amy have to come along now? *God, life's timing. Or perhaps His lack of it.*

"This is just an excerpt."

"A newspaper article?" Kincaid replied impatiently. "So?"

"Not an article," Stephanie said. "A story. One I think you should read."

Kincaid sped through the first few paragraphs.

Allan Sheedy could have been anything. He excelled in high school and college, consistently placing at the top of his class in every discipline. He had a razor-sharp mind tempered with an intuitive disposition and a need to understand the intricate patterns that lay beneath the surface of all things. But although Sheedy had a natural affinity for the pure sciences, they bored him. There was no excitement, no challenge. Frustrated, Allan had always harbored a deeper interest, an unquenchable thirst, to create something that didn't conform to rules or patterns, esoteric laws or reformulated givens. Allan Sheedy wanted to be a writer.

He could have been a research scientist, a neurosurgeon, or a nuclear physicist. If only he hadn't been infected with such an overwhelming need to write. And if he hadn't been so obsessed with killing, with defining and executing the perfect murder.

"So it's a dime store novel about a man who wants to commit the usual unsolvable crime."

"It was published in *The Gazette* 12 weeks ago."

"That's not the only piece – yet," Richardson said, nodding at the pages. "Keep going."

Amy fanned another couple of pages in front of Kincaid. "This is the next part of the story they printed two weeks later. It's the second installment."

It was only a minute before a troubled frown creased Kincaid's forehead. "O..k... So this Sheedy guy starts sending out his manuscript about the perfect murder to agents and publishers."

Amy handed him another two sheets. "This is the third installment."

"From 8 weeks ago," Stephanie added.

Kincaid quickly scanned them, then looked up with a disconcerted frown, absently squaring the pages back together. "So let me get this straight, Sergeant. That rag—*The Gazette*—started printing this about twelve weeks ago?"

"Judging by the dates, yes."

"And the story is about a man who wants to kill his agent because he stole his work and had it published by someone else."

Amy sighed, "Exactly."

"Hell."

"Shit hell, yeah." Richardson echoed. "But that's not all." He dumped his coffee dregs into Kincaid's garbage can.

"That was the 3rd installment."

"There's more?" Kincaid asked, anticipating where this might be going.

"Lots more. It's possible it's a coincidence," Richardson suggested. His tone implied otherwise.

Kincaid remembered what he'd learned from Rebecca about the sheer volume of manuscripts and story ideas that are constantly circling the literary world at any given moment. *Coincidence?* It was possible someone had written a storyline similar to an ongoing murder investigation. But he shared Richardson's obvious suspicions. *Plausible denial.* However, this was beginning to feel more than similar. He envisioned Turner impaled to his desk.

Stephanie stared out the window. "The story is being done in serial format, the way newspapers used to publish books before they went to print. Like –"

"Dickens," Kincaid interjected.

Amy nodded. "From what I understand it was a great way to sell papers. They published an excerpt every two weeks, for example. People got caught up in the story. The only way they could follow what was happening was to make sure they bought the Sunday paper. I guess it's kind of like reality shows today."

Kincaid agreed. "In London, in Dickens time, it was done with *The Pickwick Papers* and *Oliver Twist." But this was different. A newspaper serial that parallels a current police investigation.* He remembered the book Barclay said he was working on, the one he'd left on the 'back burner.' *Another coincidence?*

Then the proverbial shoe dropped. Kincaid started to stand as he read. Oh God, everything was far too familiar, too recognizable. This definitely wasn't a coincidence. Allan Sheedy's story was a description of Turner's murder. Right down to the coded entry, the smashed computer monitor and *the pen through the man's eye. Shakespeare.* No-one was supposed to know about the God-damned dog. That was definitely information that was supposed to be kept close to the vest, and not for the public domain. Kincaid sat back down, rubbing his temples.

Amy pointed at a manila envelope at the corner of Kincaid's desk. "I made you a copy. It's all in there, sir." She handed him duplicates of some specific pages.

"So, I'm guessing there was another part last Sunday."

Amy, Stephanie and Richardson exchanged glances and almost spoke in unison. "Yes."

Kincaid was sure he knew what that installment would have been about, but asked anyway.

"Last week's piece dealt with a second killing. Graphic, but not enough that it couldn't be included in a daily newspaper. Then again, you can print anything these days."

Kincaid let out a deep breath. "Tell me it wasn't like McCabe's."

"Exactly the same," Richardson sighed. "An apparent mugging. But the police find out later it wasn't as straight forward as it originally seemed." He shook his head. "There's one other thing."

Kincaid looked over at Amy. The other shoe dropped.

She returned his stare. "The murderer stitched the guy's lips together."

"Unbelievable."

"Once might have been coincidental," Stephanie said.

"But not twice," Kincaid murmured.

"No, not twice," Amy added. "The chapter last Sunday describes the crime scene pretty explicitly. Whoever wrote the story was *there.*"

Or knew someone who was, Kincaid thought. *The stitches? That was the other key piece that had been kept from the public.* He pushed himself up from his chair and sat down on the corner of his desk.

"Two murders, both involving a disgruntled writer bent on killing people in the literary field."

"That's what it looks like, sir."

"So either someone knows what's happening and is writing a parallel piece of fiction," Kincaid said with an anxious scowl. "Or someone is duplicating the stories in real life."

Richardson slammed his armrest with his fist. "And no matter what way you look at it, we probably have the biggest fucking leak I've ever seen."

Amy glanced at her partner but it was Stephanie who spoke. "And you'll never guess who chairs the board of governors for *The Gazette*."

Kincaid tried to drag the name from his memory, but it wouldn't come.

Stephanie helped him. "Gail Meredith."

Chapter Twenty Seven

The phone rang once before it was answered.

"Good morning. Lab."

"Morning. It's Kincaid. I'd like to speak to Dr. Tantor, please."

"She's out on a case, Detective. Can I help?"

Kincaid didn't recognize the voice. "Who is this?"

"Kevin Matsu, the new guy."

"Is that 'Matsu' or *'Matsu The New Guy'*?"

"Matsu, Sir."

Kincaid almost felt the man blush. "When did you start?"

"About three weeks ago, Sir. When –." He paused uncomfortably.

When I was in the hospital. Does everyone know?

"Good to have you with us, Kevin. And yes, I need some help. There was an attack in the Entertainment District about a month ago. Pretty messy thing. The face completely smashed in."

"Brian McCabe?"

"How did you know?"

"I was catching up on the backlog, Sir. I just finished scanning the pictures into the data base."

"Perfect timing. I need to see them."

"Of course, Sir. Do you want me to come up?"

"As soon as you can. I'm on –"

"The third floor. Yes, I know. I'll be there in a few minutes, Detective."

The phone went dead.

*

Dressed in a conservative blue suit and lab coat, Kevin Matsu was smaller than Kincaid expected. Thin and wiry, with short cropped black hair and a soft, sensitive face, he looked like he was barely out of high school. Matsu flashed a beaming smile as he took Kincaid's hand. His grip was deceptively strong – and it was easy to sense the power in his arms and neck.

"Tae Kwon Do?" Kincaid guessed.

"Kung fu." A deep bow. "I understand you're not a stranger to the martial arts either, Sir. And you know Miss Quan." His smile was full of admiration.

"Thanks for coming on such short notice."

Matsu waved the thought away. Every movement he made hinted at an enthusiastic eagerness to help. He sat down behind Kincaid's desk and pushed a USB stick into an empty port. A series of quick taps at the keyboard brought McCabe's file into focus.

"What exactly are you looking for, Sir?"

"I'm not sure yet. But Kevin –"

"Yes?"

"Don't call me *sir*. Okay?"

The young man nodded.

"Do you have the PM pictures?"

Another click, and the screen was filled with rows of thumbnail photographs taken during the autopsy.

Matsu scrolled down and scanned the textual information. "Caucasian, mid-thirties, average height and a little overweight. Slight cirrhosis of the liver shows he drank more than he should have, although that's a moot point now. He recently started smoking occasionally – probably marijuana. Heart was fine. Lungs, kidneys, blood work all seem quite normal. Tox screen's clear for a level one autopsy."

Kincaid leaned closer and squinted at the screen. Each tiny picture showed a new incision, another part of the body freshly exposed. They were photographs, but some were just as difficult to look at as an actual autopsy from the glass cubicle downstairs. Kincaid asked Matsu to enlarge various thumbnails that were focused on McCabe's head and upper body. Kincaid studied each one in detail.

"That one. Sixteen. Can you enlarge it?"

Matsu's fingers danced across the keyboard. "I can, but from this point on, each change in size will affect the resolution."

"Go for it. That one, too. Nineteen as well."

Tap tap tap tap.

"And this one."

When Kevin was finished, he looked at the images dominating the screen and groaned. "God, what a mess."

Kincaid was silent. The photograph was a straight-on view of the dead man's lower face and jaw. McCabe's mouth had been smashed in. Viciously. Repeatedly. Kincaid didn't possess the coroner's eye for detail. He peered closer, but all he could make out were the bruising patterns and the left-over shards of the man's front teeth.

"What do you think was used?"

"A bat? Perhaps a pipe? Something with a small, circular end," Kevin replied quietly. There was nothing but a bloodied, gaping hole where the man's mouth had been. And what looked like a clump of shredded paper.

"Shots to the head?"

"I'd guess about ten, give or take."

Kincaid winced. He couldn't imagine the pain. He hoped McCabe had been dead, or at least unconscious, when he'd been hit. "That one. I have to see it even larger."

Matsu grimaced. "What are we looking for, Detective?"

"Anything left of his upper lip."

More keystrokes. The image gradually increased in size, but the picture was becoming blurred and distorted.

Kincaid leaned closer to the monitor. "Stop there. See that?"

"What am I looking at?"

"That tiny perforation. There. Beneath his nose and just above his lip." *At least the section of his nose that hadn't been ripped apart.*

Matsu squinted. "Yes, I see it. Sorry it's so faint and grainy, Detective. I don't think I can bring it in any better without losing it."

"Can you highlight it or something?" Kincaid asked anxiously. "Color contrast it?"

"I can try," the young man answered. "But it will take a while."

"Zoom in on that spot and make it as large and clear as possible."

"You got it."

"Where's Dr. Tantor?"

"She was called away late last evening. A double, down in the Beaches, right by the lake."

"Show her whatever you get, and then have her call me as soon as she can."

"Will do." Matsu stared obliquely at the tiny mark. "Will this help, Detective?"

"It will if it's what I think it is," Kincaid said softly. "I want you to tell her something for me."

The young man frowned as he listened. When Kincaid was finished, he looked up, startled. "You're joking?"

"I'm afraid not, Kevin." Kincaid shook his head. "I'm afraid not."

*

With Erik Caster's folder tucked under his arm, Kincaid and Amy took the elevator up to the twenty-fifth floor of *Meredith House*. Kincaid told his Sergeant to play nice and sign in, then asked her to check later and see if any more security cameras or personnel had been added since their last visit. He took the guard's proffered pen but didn't sign the sheet, sensing the man's forearm tighten as he squeezed the clipboard. Darla, the gum-chewing pixie at reception, recognized him immediately. She tried to speak before he walked by.

"Detective Kincaid. Sergeant. It's nice to see you again. I'm sorry but –"

"We'll only be a moment," he interrupted, disarming her with a wink and smile.

"But –" The young woman quickly followed them down the hall. "Sir – Sergeant –." Darla was obviously aware of Meredith's legendary wrath.

They dragged the anxious girl in their wake. Whispering everything would be fine, Kincaid knocked on the publisher's door.

A cold bark. "Go away."

Amy reached over and knocked harder.

"What part of 'no fucking interruptions!' don't you understand?"

Flitting back and forth like a caged budgie, the receptionist nervously wrung her hands together. "Detective, please – "

After the next knock the door ripped open. Gail Meredith's face was flushed red, the veins in her neck throbbing. She reigned in her anger when she recognized her guests, but her exasperation didn't abate.

"Ahh, Kincaid. And Sergeant MacKenzie. What a lovely surprise." She dismissed the receptionist with a brusque nod. Her eyes told the girl she'd speak to her later. *Yell later.*

Glancing petulantly at her watch, Gail Meredith didn't bother offering them a seat. With a half-finished triangulo dangling from the corner of her mouth, she walked back behind her desk and continued packing a stack of folders into her briefcase.

"Wasn't Ms. Davidivitch able to assist you with whatever you needed?"

Kincaid didn't hear the gentle *coo* from beyond her window, and wondered if she'd had the officious little pigeon removed – *for good.*

"We have a problem. We need to speak to you about someone Ms. Davidivitch didn't mention. You didn't either."

Gail didn't look up.

Amy MacKenzie stepped forward. "Erik Caster."

Meredith's breath caught, but she didn't say anything. She tapped the ember from her cigar and stared at the files strewn across her desk.

"Ms. Meredith?"

"I'm sorry? Who?"

Kincaid smiled. "Erik Caster."

She chewed over the name. "I'm afraid I don't recognize him."

"Are you sure?"

She turned to Amy. "Check your notes, Sergeant. I meet hundreds of people every week. Surely you don't expect me to remember them all?"

Kincaid glanced at his partner. "Let me refresh your memory. Erik Caster is the man who sent you his own folders' worth of threatening letters. The man who tried to assault you when you left your building about a month ago. The guy no-one will talk to me about."

"The persona non grata," MacKenzie added. "The one you issued a restraining order against."

Gail Meredith rubbed her forehead and waved a hand dismissively. "Oh, that horrible little shit."

"Yes, that one."

"If I thought it was important I would have told you."

"The man makes numerous threats on your life, as well as on Turner's, and he has to be physically restrained from attacking you. But you didn't see any importance in his behavior?"

"I don't like your tone, Kincaid."

"And I don't appreciate your evasiveness, Ms. Meredith."

Her eyes narrowed but she didn't respond.

"Why didn't you press charges?"

"I didn't feel the situation warranted it." One of the lights on her phone blinked. Kincaid said her name before she reached for it. She stuffed a number of manila files into her briefcase.

"Look. I didn't bother pressing charges against that piece of garbage because I would have been giving him exactly what he wanted."

"And that would be?" Amy asked.

"Attention. Browser bile. We don't need that kind of publicity. Or any confirmation of those types of threats. And especially *that* kind of *book*."

"Did you read it?"

Gail returned Kincaid's stare. "I don't know. A chapter. Maybe two. That was fucking enough."

"It wasn't something you'd normally consider for publication?"

She laughed derisively. "Are you kidding? Have you seen the masterpiece?"

"No."

"Don't bother." Another purposeful glance at her watch.

"I read your statement about it, however."

"Then that's all you need to know. It wasn't even good enough to be pitiful. Abject, poorly written, pathetic, self-promoting guttural garbage fueled with hubris. Pure and simple."

"But how did you really feel about it?"

Gail looked up and her lips almost cracked into a smile. She exhaled a trail of smoke into the air, then stabbed her cigar into a silver ashtray.

Amy kept her notepad open. "Did you like the concept of the book?"

She paused before answering. "The idea was there, I'll give him that. And the topic is controversial and propitious. The shit that goes on in our over-crowded prisons. Sex, drugs, violence, gangs, religious radicalization. But the script was so utterly repulsive it was inconceivable to have considered it seriously."

"Did Turner agree?"

"Yes."

Kincaid remembered his conversation with Rebecca. "I thought a lot of books were edited and even ghost-written by a publishing house if they had marketable potential. Hit a niche, let's say."

"You're about three decades behind the times," Meredith admitted coldly. "The days when a publisher worked that closely with a writer are long gone. We don't have the time, opportunity, or resources. In today's business, a book comes in as close to being publishable as possible, or it doesn't come in at all."

"I see." Kincaid ignored the perfunctory time check. "But –"

"But what?" Gail interrupted impatiently.

"Isn't the type of book Caster was offering the kind that often outsells better, more well-written manuscripts?"

A glare. "It can be."

"But not in this case?"

"No. It was too ridiculous to even consider."

Kincaid stared back silently. Meredith couldn't hide her irascibility. "You're right. Those kinds of books often do better than ones that actually have a plot, substance, style, and memorable characters."

Amy asked why.

"Two things. One, the subject. It's sensationalistic, confessional, vulgar, and laced with violence and sex. Those things sell. You should know that, Sergeant."

MacKenzie ignored the jibe. "And two?"

"Two, a large section of the general reading public isn't what you'd call particularly erudite."

"So give them a graphic novel covered in blood before a thoughtful exposé, on human trafficking like *The Innocent*."

"You're catching on, Kincaid. But it can still be too offensive, boorish and brutal. Besides, I don't like to provide people like Caster with any kind of forum. It just fuels their vanity." Her bracelets jangled loudly as she shoved another folder into the attaché case.

"So when can we talk?"

She sighed exasperatedly. "Not now. Really, I can't." It was as close as she came to being gracious. The silence thickened. Meredith's hand stopped in mid-air as she reached for another folder. She glanced at an incoming email.

"I'm sorry. I want to help, but I'd appreciate it if we could do this at another time."

Kincaid stood up. No smile. "We need to talk."

"I'd change my appointment if I could, but I'm due in court in less than an hour. We're facing a libel suit and copyright infringement."

"From one of your writers?"

She nodded. "They've subpoenaed all these records."

"So Brent Jacobs isn't the only one who thinks he's been taken?"

Meredith stopped dead. She looked up coldly. "So you've already talked to Jacobs? Did he stop eating long enough to say anything coherent?"

"Actually he did. So when –"

Meredith rubbed her forehead. "Soon."

"Not good enough."

She was startled by the change of tone and bristled. She wasn't used to adjusting her schedule to conform with someone else's, but she could tell by Kincaid's look he wasn't giving her an option.

"Tomorrow?"

"Tomorrow would be fine."

"Wonderful. Now if you'll excuse me, I really have to get this paperwork sorted out."

"Of course. Good luck."

Meredith stopped and glanced back up. Another *almost-smile,* and a mouthed *thank you.* She stopped Kincaid just as Amy reached for the door.

"I understand you've been working with our security consultant?"

"We have. We're meeting again today. She's the reason we found out about Caster."

Gail didn't look pleased. "Well, her office is –"

"On the eighth floor. Thanks."

"And is Ms. Quan everything you hoped she'd be?"

Kincaid smiled at the irony. "She certainly is. You're lucky to have her here." He felt Amy stiffen ever so slightly.

"I'm glad. Now, if you'll excuse –"

Kincaid didn't turn away. "Ms. Meredith?"

She sighed with bored impatience. "Yes?"

"What is it that you aren't telling me?"

"I beg your pardon?"

"I understand you have your own priorities, but you don't seem particularly concerned with helping us with our investigation."

"Forgive me if I don't cry," she replied caustically. "Devlin brought me some good clients and we made each other a lot of money. But if I may be blunt, Detective, that was all he was to me. And as I've reiterated, I have more pressing problems on my plate right now."

Gail Meredith rammed the last few folders into her briefcase, grabbed her coat, and hustled past Amy and into the hall without another word. People scattered out of her way as she stomped past their little glass cubicles. Kincaid wondered if she ever relaxed, if she ever stopped the merry-go-round for even a few moments and sat down on the grass to savor the sunshine and let a warm, summer breeze caress her cheeks.

He didn't think so.

But he didn't really care.

He'd rather know what she was hiding.

Chapter Twenty Eight

When Kincaid walked through the double-doors leading into *The Gazette's* Sunday edition department, he thought the sudden blast of noise would physically propel him back into the hallway, like the repercussions of a faulty IED.

"And I thought *our* office epitomized sheer bedlam."

"It's always like this," the young woman who'd led him from reception replied. "But you get used to it." She wore two matching ponytails that hung down to her waist, skin tight jeans, and boot-style red running shoes that were popular in the sixties.

"I doubt it," Kincaid murmured. Careful where he stepped, he followed her through a minefield of desks and cables. Oblivious to the pandemonium unraveling all around, lemmings raced about in a frenzy. Orders were barked from one side of the huge office to the other, and papers and files changed hands faster than a South American bribe. The office was smothered by the incessant drone of a hundred keyboards and the *whirr* of incoming faxes.

The woman stopped in front of a small, glassed-in cubicle tucked into the corner of the room. "This is the editor's office." She knocked once, ushered Kincaid in, and disappeared.

"Detective Kincaid," the man said, rising and offering his hand.

"Mr. Stevens."

"Frank. What can I do for you?" Frank Stevens sat down and pretended to ignore the jumbled array of papers that masked his desk.

Kincaid gave the editor an appraising eye. Mid-thirties, an intrusive beer belly he didn't bother to fight, eyes red with fatigue, nicotine-stained fingers, and a pensive alertness that probably made him seem impatient even when he slept. Kincaid wondered when the man had time to breathe. Balding, Frank Stevens clutched at youth by keeping his uncombed hair absurdly long at the back. Nervous hands. A heart attack waiting to happen. Stevens eased a drawer closed, hoping his visitor hadn't seen the crusted glass bong. He eyed the papers scattered across his desk.

"I want to ask you a few questions about one of your articles."

"Sure."

"A story, actually. The one you're doing as a serial. *'Writer's Revenge.'*"

"Ahh." Stevens smiled, leaned back, and interlocked his fingers behind his head. "Wouldn't everybody."

"Sorry?"

He unclasped his hands and rummaged for a cigarette. "Everyone's interested in that one. An old fashioned fiction serial. I don't know why it hasn't been done much before."

Stevens tried the lighter three or four times before he got a flame. He jammed his little window open and made an apologetic shrug with his shoulders, curling the smoke outside.

"Know how much sales have gone up since we started publishing it? Nineteen percent." A cloud of smoke momentarily obliterated his features. "Nineteen percent! Increased sales means more advertising revenue. You don't expect me to tell you the ending?" Stevens smiled.

"Who's writing it?"

Stevens' smile disappeared. "No can do, Detective."

"Why's that, Mr. Stevens?"

"Frank." He crushed out half the cigarette and immediately lit another. "Because I don't know."

Kincaid raised an eyebrow, disbelief reflected in his eyes. "You're publishing a serial piece but you don't know who's writing it?"

The editor shrugged. "The age of modern technology, Detective."

Kincaid looked confused.

"It comes in via e-mail, right to my terminal. I get tons of junk that's supposed to be screened. But one morning I was scanning messages and there it was. Hooked me from the start. It's got everything: danger, mystery, a vicious murder." A conspiratorial wink. "We had to tone it down a bit. It's got enough diversions to whet our readers' appetites without giving too much away."

"And there wasn't a name attached?"

"*Nada.* No place to reply, either."

"So where do you send the author's remuneration?"

Steven's exhaled a cloud of smoke. "The cover letter wanted it sent to a numbered account. *Nineteen percent*!"

"And you never found it?"

"The IP and Proxy bounced around everywhere, enough that our tech team couldn't trace it. And to be honest, I don't care where it's coming from."

"What's the address?"

Stevens frowned. "I'll have to consult our legal department on that one, Detective."

"Do it. I can have a warrant here in an hour." He took out his phone and texted Amy. "Has each part come in the same way?"

Stevens nodded. "From different locations." His smoker's cough returned, and it was a minute before he managed to clear his throat. "Sorry. What was I saying? Ah, yes. Perhaps one of your computer experts might have better luck."

"So you wire the money, and someone sends in the next segment."

"More pieces of the puzzle," Steven's smiled. He chuckled to himself. "Each new segment brings us more subscriptions."

"How many installments are there?"

"Hell if I know. I only get one at a time."

"You don't have a synopsis? And you don't know how it turns out?"

Stevens nodded sheepishly. "Yeah, I know. It's not usual, and the whole thing could backfire. But the way sales have been, I'm willing to risk it. Besides, I can always have the ending rewritten. I've got a room full of writers out there who could finish it any way I want." He winked. "Why is it important, anyway? What difference does it make to the police?"

"We're working on a murder investigation."

"And?" Stevens lit a fresh cigarette off a half-finished one.

Kincaid glared. His back was hurting again. "Put it out."

Stevens thought about leaving it lit, but not for long.

"There are a number of disturbing parallels to what's happening in your serial."

The editor clicked the lighter on and off, rekindling the flame over and over. He looked deep in thought. "In what way?"

"The details I can provide are limited."

"Naturally." Stevens was frustrated. This could be a real scoop. Big time.

"The occurrences can't just be a matter of coincidence."

"You're saying that whoever is involved in your murder investigation might be writing the serial?"

No answer.

Stevens sat forward excitedly. "To taunt you? To tell you what he's done? Or going to do?"

"It could be that your author has information about the investigation that he shouldn't be privy to."

"I see."

Kincaid could almost visualize the dollar signs in the editor's eyes. Stevens spun around in his chair. He was dying to light the cigarette dangling from his lips. "What do you want?"

Kincaid knew Stevens already had the answer. "I want you to stop publishing the story."

"Out of the question," Stevens snapped. He lit the smoke, took a long, drawn out breath, then crushed it out.

"Lives may depend on it."

"No can do."

"Perhaps you didn't hear me clearly about lives depending on it."

"Doesn't matter."

"Because of the financial gain?"

Stevens shifted uncomfortably. He picked up a paper, defensively scanning it without reading it. "Partly. Then again, you haven't given me anything that would confirm what you're saying."

Kincaid stared back. "And I can't, now can I, Frank? Unless you're hoping another body shows up?"

"I don't know what you —"

"Sure you do. Whatever information I'd offer you would find its way into your paper. Once people thought your serial piece was mimicking an actual murder case, your sales would rise exponentially. So would the killings. Two so far. But there'd be more."

"Detective, I can assure —"

"I'll need to see a copy of whatever is sent to you — *before it's printed.*"

The cigarette drooped from the side of his mouth like Bogart's did. "I'll see what I can do."

"Not good enough."

"I'll talk to the board. And the legal rats."

Kincaid sat stoically still and stared into Stevens' eyes.

"I'll speak to them this afternoon."

"Fine. I'll also need a copy of whatever you get." He wrote down Amy's email and cell number. "Send it to my partner. I'll be in touch."

Kincaid rose to leave, but didn't turn around. He loomed over the editor's desk. "Have you seen the next piece yet?"

"No."

"You'll tell me as soon as you do."

The editor nodded coldly.

"Good. I know you wouldn't want to jeopardize anyone else. Or have your paper held responsible for a reader's death. Check with your legal department on the ramifications of that. Two men have been murdered, and our killer − like yours − is targeting individuals in the publishing field. I know how uncomfortable it would make you feel if, for some reason, *you* were on the list."

Kincaid smiled as he left. He could tell by the man's eyes and the sudden tremor in his hands that Steven's didn't want to even consider the thought.

Perhaps he'd be some help after all.

*

Dr. Cecelia Tantor called just after lunch, propitiously catching Kincaid at his desk.

"Thanks for getting back so quickly, Cecelia."

"You sound a little jittery, Kincaid. Are you all right?"

"Fine."

"How are your meds?"

"No problem."

She knew he'd tell her if there was. "So you've met our new intern?"

"Yes. *Matsu the New Guy*. He seems quite pleasant."

"Top of the class, enthusiastic, and so young it makes me sick."

"You were in the Beaches?"

"A side street near Fallingbrook and Kingston. Murder-suicide. A young couple. Too much too soon. Messy business, really. Ever read Future Shock?"

"Alvin Toffler?"

"The same. They put way too much pressure on themselves. So did everyone else."

"I'm sorry."

"So are they." Silence. "I had a look at the pictures Kevin said you wanted to know about."

"Did he manage to enlarge the images?"

"No. But he cleaned them quite a bit."

"What did you see?"

"What you expected. A puncture mark."

Kincaid closed his eyes and rubbed his forehead.

"It's a neat hole, probably made by a carpet needle."

"I checked with Hoyt from 52 Division."

"He handled the investigation?"

"Yes. He thinks the killer was short on time. Someone came by minutes after McCabe was attacked."

"Ahh. So your assailant started –"

"But had to leave. He had enough time, though, to smash McCabe's face in with a piece of pipe and gag him with paper."

Silence. Kincaid's thoughts were racing. He finally whispered. "Different method, but the message is still the same."

"As your second vic. Turner."

"You're sure about the dimensions of the puncture mark, Cecelia?"

"I checked it three times, K. The hole is exactly the same size as the one that stitched Turner's lips together."

Chapter Twenty Nine

"Do you remember the last time we were here?"

Kincaid smiled, but there was a hint of sadness in his eyes as he folded his napkin. "I remember everything we've done together, Stephanie." He felt a tangible sense of awkwardness as he eased Amy from his thoughts. He sampled the Riesling, nodded, and the waitress poured their wine. The silence was uncharacteristically intransigent. Touched by Kincaid's melancholy, Stephanie took a long, thoughtful sip.

Queensbury Avenue. Scrunched down between two larger buildings with old, frayed awnings that dotted the street corner with a patch of sunlight, the tiny bistro was almost deserted. Twenty tables were packed together, but only four were occupied. Sparsely decorated, the restaurant didn't really have a theme, just a collection of pictures and bric-a-brac designed to break up the monotony of the dark walls. A couple of bored waiters lounged together at a table in the back, and the young girl from the front counter had ambled over to the window to look outside and drift away on distant dreams.

Kincaid quietly went on. "I think everything's changed."

"Because of McCabe?"

"Yes. It puts a whole new perspective on Turner's death. There's no doubt they're related. If it hadn't been for the puncture mark on McCabe's upper lip, the only other thing that connected them was their work. But since the wounds were caused by the same kind of needle and their mouths were stuffed with paper –"

"The same person is responsible for both deaths."

Kincaid paused when the waitress returned with their dinner. She smiled perfunctorily and left without a word. Kincaid looked down at the expansive plate of pasta, wishing he'd ordered something *smaller*. He toyed with the noodles. "McCabe, then Turner. Their mouths virtually obliterated and choked with their own letters. The message is clear. Someone wanted them to literally eat their own words."

Stephanie twirled a length of fettuccine against her spoon. "Could it be a warning? Shut up, or else?"

"Shut up about what, though? I think it means our perp didn't like something they said."

"The rejections? Did they work together?"

"Not daily, but it seems like they had regular contact. Turner referred a number of his clients to Michael Cormier's agency, and McCabe did a fair amount of editorial work for him."

"So they both could have seen the same manuscripts?"

"Some of them, anyway."

"That must have bothered Gail to no end."

Kincaid agreed.

"How are your interviews progressing?"

"Caster hasn't filed any charges."

Stephanie blushed and sipped her wine. "He had it coming."

"You popped it in nicely. You were behind him – you should have seen his face."

"I was glad to help."

"Something about Barclay makes me uncomfortable."

"What?"

"I'm not sure yet. And I know you're sympathetic to Walter Croft, but you have to admit the man has a lot of pent up rage he's desperately trying to control."

"But not enough to kill two men half his age, surely."

"Killers are a keystroke away. Like whoever's taunting us by writing the pieces for the *Gazette*."

Stephanie was enjoying her pasta. "The service has always left something to be desired, but the food is still wonderful."

Kincaid had hardly touched his meal. She looked worried. "What about Jacobs?"

"He's manipulative and controlling, no question. Bright, too. And he certainly has motive. The man's lost everything."

Stephanie watched his forehead crease. "What?"

"It's not even the material things he's lost. Jacobs wanted more than money. He wanted fame, and he's been cheated out of that, too. He's been emotionally devastated."

"Do you think it might have pushed him over the edge?"

Kincaid sighed, leaned back, and daubed his lips with his napkin. "You'd be surprised what rejection can do to people."

The waitress came back to see if everything was fine, but didn't look like she was interested in whether it was or not. She disappeared after a cursory smile.

Kincaid lowered his voice. "I know this isn't dinner conversation –"

"Go on."

"But it's taking the time to sew the vic's lips together that bothers me."

"Is it possible it points to something more than wanting to keep them both quiet? A warning or something?"

"Perhaps."

"You're not eating."

"I'm not hungry."

"Are you feeling all right?"

"Fine." He pushed his plate away and poured them each another glass of wine.

"I'd like to have another word with Cynthia Baxter, too. She certainly didn't seem very upset about his murder."

"Shock?"

"No way. Not with that one. And she stands to gain a good deal financially." Kincaid remembered Cynthia provocatively posing at the gym. "I'll have to wade through the papers Gerbec found at Turner's again. If I feel awake enough, I'll start tonight. Maybe I can find something that can point me in the right direction."

"Can I help?"

Kincaid checked the time and shook his head. His heart ached when he thought about seeing Stephanie in his home again. "Thanks, but I've got something else I have to do first."

"Another woman?" she teased. But it wasn't really kidding. She didn't need her women's intuition to notice the depth of Amy's fondness for Kincaid. She was blunt. "I've seen the way you look at her. And the way she looks at you. Something's there. Something deep."

Kincaid struggled with his feelings. He wanted to be as honest as he could without betraying either woman. "She's wonderful and I respect her deeply. I like her very, very much, too. But I don't think there can ever be anyone else as long as you're here, with me. I've never loved anyone the same way."

Stephanie looked down sadly, her stomach in knots. "If you need her, Kincaid, we can still –"

"This isn't the time, Stephanie. I'm still shocked at seeing you, with being together again." He looked around the little restaurant. "Here. At the office. Working with each other. It's a bit overwhelming."

"It's the same for me, K."

"So let's not make any emotional decisions we might regret."

"I've never regretted anything we've done. Other than letting each other go."

He leaned forward, reached across the table, and took her hand. "Nothing's changed, Stephanie."

"Yes it has. We've had discussions like this before, and all we've really done is lost the time we might have had together. If you can live your life better with someone else, I understand. I do."

He sighed. "I can't do this, Stephanie. I've got a double homicide, Ryan is battling for his life, and all I can —"

He left the thought dangling. He didn't want to admit how concerned he was about having Dr. Chadpur's tests. Concerned? Even that was a denial. For one of the first times in his life, he was afraid.

"Are you seeing Ryan tonight?" Stephanie asked softly, squeezing his hands.

"Yes."

"Give him my best, and tell him he's in my prayers."

"I will. And thanks."

"For what?"

"Just for being here."

"And remember."

"Yes?"

"You'll be in them, too."

*

"I can't believe you had the fucking guts to answer the phone, bitch."

Despite the tension, Gail Meredith managed to respond with a bored sigh.

"Do you know how many times I've called? How many letters I've written?"

"I do, yes."

"No you fucking don't. So don't patro – patrai –"

"Patronize."

"Patronize me, bitch. Or . . ."

"Or what?"

"Or you'll get what Turner got. Only worse."

Gail Meredith knew she had to be careful. Careful, but in control. "That's what I need to talk to you about."

The voice chuckled. "I wouldn't doubt it. You're scared shitless, Meredith. And you should be."

"You haven't gotten through since your little tantrum outside, have you?" she challenged. "Then why did I bother taking this one?"

Silence. Then a slew of curses and something kicked over. "No, you're scared. That's why you got extra security. That clown from the other place. McCabe. Then Turner. Maybe I'll do the puke from *The Gazette*. Then you."

The Gazette? Frank Stevens? Gail's thoughts were racing again. He could kill and mutilate, but couldn't write a line worth shit. Someone else had to be sending in the story. But *who,* and *why?* And why didn't he take the credit? Gail stayed calm. Her business voice was back.

"I don't think so."

"You're a cocky bitch."

"A very wealthy one."

The voice was agitatedly silent. This was Meredith's moment, and she instinctively lowered her voice. "And one that can help you."

"Help me! What the fuck for? You sure as hell haven't helped me before, bitch."

"Call me 'bitch' again and you'll never know what I was going to offer you."

The man muttered something.

"Pardon?"

"I said, 'you never helped me before'"

"No, no I didn't. But then again, I was taken in, just like you."

"What – what do you mean?"

"By Turner."

"He paid the price."

"He certainly did. But I trusted Turner. I admit it now, and it was probably foolish, but I always listened to him. No matter what you think, he knew the business. He helped make me a fortune."

"By stealing scripts."

"Perhaps." *How the hell did he know that?*

"You were fucking in on it."

"No, I wasn't. I swear I didn't know anything about that side of things."

"Bullshit."

"I'm not trying to convince you of anything. That's the honest truth. I never knew where the scripts came from." Meredith knew what buttons to push. "What difference did it make to me *who* wrote *what* as long as I published them and the change kept rolling in? Lots and lots of change."

She heard a grunt.

"Okay, I never asked. And that's on me. I let Turner hide Ian Nurakis' identity and played along with the little mystery. But in the end it added more interest and made us even more money. All of us were happy."

"Good for you."

"Turner controlled some of the best writers around. If he brought it in and said it was good, I bought and sold it. And when he told me something was worthless, I believed him. I realize now that was a mistake."

"Fucking right. A big one."

"I never even saw your book. So I'd like to make amends."

"Amends?"

There was a moment's pause while she lit a fresh cigar, her dangling bracelets tinkling some esoteric tune. She smiled. He didn't know what "amends" meant. This was going to be easier than she thought.

"Make things right."

"How?"

"Not here. And not on the phone. Grab a pen and listen."

Chapter Thirty

A short, muscular youth with elephant-sized pants, the boringly ever-present Nike shirt, and brand new high-topped running shoes leaned against the wall a few stores up from an alley that joined Yonge to a backstreet. Slouching in the shadows, he kept his back to the laneway, his face to the street. Each time a car slowed by the curb, his antennae quivered and he looked for the signal. Staked out in an unmarked car parked near the corner, Kincaid watched in his side view as the boy sauntered to the idling cars. No, not saunter – it was more of an eclectic mixture of dancing, shuffling, and weaving like a prize fighter.

Most transactions took less than thirty seconds. Kincaid had to admit the kid was having a good morning. Three cars had stopped in the last five minutes – gram bags in, money out. He stretched from side to side, trying to release the pain in his lower back. He rechecked the time and gave himself another five minutes. He didn't need it – his CI was right: in less than two minutes the car he'd been waiting for pulled around the corner, idled in a parking space, and signaled the runner. The kid checked the street. The moment he moved, Kincaid slipped out of his own vehicle and hustled toward the car parked a few spaces behind him.

The boy instinctively looked up just before he poked his head into the driver's window. The instant he picked Kincaid out from the crowd he was gone, racing down the alley, a cloud of dirt in his wake. By the time the driver turned around, Kincaid was standing in front of the car, hand on his gun.

"Get out."

"What? Here?" Horns blared impatiently.

"We're going to talk, Mr. Caster, and we're going to talk right now."

Caster shut off the engine gesticulating angrily to several people driving past. He led Kincaid into the alley, anxiously looking around.

"She's not here."

"I don't give a fuck." The Detective wasn't here because of the dope.

"How's your shoulder?"

"You're lucky I'm not pressing charges."

"You didn't have to run."

"I don't trust cops."

"Yes, and you're a paragon of virtue. Who helped you with your book?"

The question caught Caster off guard and his eyes narrowed. "What do you mean?"

"I assumed the question was obvious to a writer with your latent potential and innate command of language."

He frowned. "No one helped me. I wrote it by myself. You better not have stopped me for that. I told both of you I was at home when that piece of shit was cooked."

"I'm sure Devlin would have wanted to be described that way. You sent your book to Turner after you sent if off to *Meredith House*, right?"

"So?"

"You wanted someone to take a good look at it. See where it came up short, how you could make it better."

Caster nodded. "Everybody does that. It's a writer's thing, yeah? It's fucking hard to change your own work, you know."

The kid in the baggy pants peaked around a dumpster, then disappeared faster than a politician's honor.

"I'm afraid I don't. Did Turner say you should have it edited?"

Another nod.

"Who was supposed to do the work? Many of Turner's clients used an editor called *The Book Doctor*."

Caster mulled over the name. "Yeah, that was it. So what?"

"Turner kept a file on all his clients. I read yours. There's a long and rather unflattering analysis from the researcher who checked your work."

Caster's eyes flashed with anger, but Kincaid didn't let him speak. "The researcher told Turner it would take a lot of work to do all the fact-finding because it seemed as though you made up a great deal of information. When the correctional institutions were built, their histories, the stories of infamous prisoners held in various places, riots – that sort of thing. The researcher said that he'd have to do more background work than usual."

Caster flexed his fists down at his sides.

"Do you think that was one of the reasons Turner rejected your manuscript so aggressively?"

He seethed through clenched teeth. "I wouldn't know."

"Well, maybe you're right. Perhaps that wasn't the only thing. I guess it could have been the editor's report as well. That was one of the most scathing rejections I've ever read."

Kincaid watched the hate fester in Caster's eyes. He knew what was going on in the man's head. *If only there weren't so many people around. If only I could get this fucking cop deeper into the alley. If only . . .*

Raging inside, Caster didn't hear Kincaid's next question. "What?"

"I said, were you at Devlin Turner's home at any time on the night of his murder?"

"No."

"We have a fairly good description of someone who was seen around his house several times that evening. The man was just about your height and build."

"A lot of people are," Caster sneered.

"You're right. Does the name Brian McCabe mean anything to you?"

"No."

"Think about it."

"I said no."

"Unfortunately, a little more than a month ago, Mr. McCabe was murdered. Violently, and not unlike poor Devlin Turner. So, where were you on the night of the fourteenth, Erik? Near Bloor and Charles? Say, between ten and twelve?"

Caster crossed his arms over his chest and shook his head. "I don't do gay bars. No LQB – FTG –"

"LGBTQ. I see. No homosexual experiences in all the time you've spent in prison?"

Caster rocked forward, unfolding his arms and squeezing his hands into tightly shaking fists. He recovered quickly when he saw Kincaid's challenging look and managed to stay in control. Barely. "That's not gay – that's staying alive." He took a haughty stance. "My spigot ain't no bigot but I don't do dandy candy." He looked quite pleased with himself.

"Brian McCabe was beaten badly enough his face was practically caved in."

Caster snorted. "Then he shouldn't have hung with queers."

"His teeth were smashed in. All of them. We think he was struck repeatedly in the mouth with some kind of round, blunt object. Like that telescopic pipe Ms. Quan took away from you the other day. Why do you think someone would do that, Erik?"

Caster stared back as defiantly as he could.

Kincaid tried to look *beyond* the man's eyes. "Obliterating his mouth? It's almost as if his killer was sending a message about something McCabe said. What do you think?"

Caster kicked a liquor bottle across the alley. It clanged against a rusted trash bin but didn't break.

Kincaid's voice was suddenly dull and flat. "Who did the editing on your script, Caster?"

"The company you said before. *The Book Doctor*."

"Yes, Michael Cormier's editing service. Did you know Brian McCabe worked for Cormier?"

"Nope."

"Are you sure? Wasn't he the researcher who examined your script?"

"I don't know."

"I think you do." Kincaid pulled a folded letter from inside his jacket pocket. "This is a copy of Michael Cormier's letter to you about your book. Third paragraph. See? Mr. Cormier indicated the editing would be delayed because his researcher needed more time due to the number of serious errors. He went on to say Mr. McCabe would contact you directly if he wanted additional information."

Caster shrugged and handed the letter back. He tried to look indifferent but his hands were trembling. "He sure as fuck never called me."

Kincaid stared into Caster's eyes. "One last thing."

"What?"

"Do you have a computer?"

"No."

"How did you write your book?"

"I used one at the prison. The halfway house had some, too."

Kincaid watched him silently for a moment. "Stay where I can see you, Caster. Oh, and I'm sorry about your deal." Kincaid smiled and nodded toward the far end of the alley. The kid in the baggy pants wouldn't be back today. "Word on the street will be you're the one to blame there wasn't any action down here."

Kincaid turned, took a step, and stopped. "And just so you're not surprised or upset, the meter maid came by while we we're talking and ticketed your car. Have a nice day, Erik."

Chapter Thirty One

Kincaid paused at the water fountain next to the elevators and took more painkillers. They weren't helping as much as they had been: he needed them earlier in the day and later at night. He'd thrown the cruise control on this morning until he hit the city limits. If Lieutenant Davis knew, he probably wouldn't be driving any more. He didn't want to put Amy in an awkward position, but he didn't want to have her drive him every time he needed to go out. A constant chauffeur and no independence: he couldn't function like that. Stephanie could help, but that didn't make the situation any easier.

As usual, no-one in the elevator spoke: they stood quietly apart and watched the floor numbers pass by. When Kincaid stepped out onto the eighth floor, he felt his whole body sigh. His anxiousness over the messages he'd ignored from Dr. Chadpur dissolved as soon as he walked into Stephanie's office and saw her smile. Even if it was just for a moment, the world was right. She rose and met him in front of her desk, taking his hands in hers. He marveled at their softness despite her training. The fusion of delicacy and strength.

She kissed him lightly on the cheek, then studied his face. "You look tired. Did you get much sleep?"

"A bit."

"How's Ryan."

"Hanging in there."

"I dreamed about you last night."

"Did you need a cold shower?"

Stephanie giggled. "Have you spoken with your doctor yet?"

"I'll call him later."

"Kincaid – "

"You look wonderful." He gently brought her hands to his lips. She'd combed her hair back behind her ears the way he'd always liked it, and tied it with a dark green ribbon that was almost the same shade as her eyes.

"Call him. For me."

Kincaid nodded. He'd never been able to refuse her anything. No, that wasn't true. He'd refused her once, and he'd never forgotten the repercussions of that night. "Coffee?"

Stephanie said no. "Where were you this morning? I called you at home."

"I came in early. I haven't had time to go through all the material Richardson and Amy put together. And I had an informal appointment with our friend Caster. He says he misses you."

"I'll bet. Where's your partner?"

"She's trying to find out if there's anything in 52 Division we might have over-looked about Brian McCabe."

"Your text said you needed some information about *Meredith House*."

And I needed to see you. He sat down and opened a file. "The rumor mill has it someone's initiating a takeover."

Stephanie nodded. "It's not a rumor. At least for the insiders."

"Are you sure?"

"Positive."

"How's Meredith reacting?"

"Clinging to the ledge. She's a tough competitor, and I can't see her going down without a fight. I'm not sure how many shares she owns of *Meredith House*. Or how that changed when Turner died."

"The takeover bid isn't common knowledge."

"The main players are still trying to keep it hush-hush. But you know how quickly gossip sweeps through a company."

"Amy and I saw Gail yesterday, and she looked pretty stressed. She had a meeting with the board."

"I think she's trying to work out a deal, or at least get some leverage."

"Who's the predator?"

"Everything points to Excalibur Books. That's the problem."

That was the name Leeanne had heard being bantered about. And the one Gerbec had jotted down with a question mark in his last file.

"Why?" Kincaid watched the light from the outer office glint in Stephanie's hair. Two slender strands of gray shone above her temples. He wanted to touch them.

"Being in security, I get quite a bit of inside information. Not just about our House, but about some of the other companies as well."

"I assumed as much."

"So that's why you want me here," she teased.

Kincaid couldn't quite manage a smile. "You know that's not true."

"Word has it –" She stopped dead. "Kincaid – your eye."

"What about it?"

"Ever see someone with 'lazy eye'?"

"Where your eyes don't seem to be in sync? Sure."

"That's how your left one looked just now. Like it was following the other one." She leaned forward, staring. "It seems fine now, though. Call Dr. Chadpur."

"I will."

"Please?"

Kincaid felt his resolve slip away. If Stephanie ever interrogated him, he'd tell her everything she wanted to know. "I'll call him today. Now, what about *Excalibur*?"

"It seems as though they shouldn't be in a position to instigate a takeover bid right now."

"Why not?"

"A couple of things. The last three quarters haven't been particularly good for them. Turner had a couple of blockbusters come to print at *Meredith*, while *Excalibur* backed a few books that were financial disappointments."

"So Turner was still a large part of Meredith's success."

"*Excalibur* would have loved to have him on their side. Anyway, they're involved in a great deal of in-fighting. That's not usually the best time to have your company exposed, is it?"

"No. What's the issue?"

"What it's always about: greed and control. The majority of the company is in the hands of Garth Danielson. His two sons are also involved. I think the boys own somewhere around twenty-five percent."

"And?"

"Danielson is ill. Cancer. Late stages. It doesn't look like he'll be around much longer."

"So the sons are scheming to see who comes out on top," Kincaid mused.

"Precisely. They're spending a great deal of time and money jockeying for position. And like I said, their resources are limited. They haven't had a number one bestseller in almost two years."

"Then where's the money coming from for the takeover bid?"

Stephanie arched an eyebrow. "My point exactly."

"Could it be another publisher? Someone expanding who wants them both?"

Stephanie shrugged. "Perhaps. I've been keeping my ear to the ground, but nothing's surfaced. Although *B and W* from down in Carolina has shown some interest. I'm not sure how serious they are, but I think they're putting together a few merger options."

"Would Turner have jumped ship?"

"Leave *Meredith House* for *Excalibur*? I couldn't say for certain, but I doubt it. He'd worked with Gail for years, and they always seemed to get along quite well. They helped each other, and from everything I can gather, they both profited handsomely from their relationship. But he could always use that friendship as leverage. Why?"

"Just wondering."

"You never 'just wonder', Kincaid."

He leaned forward and returned her smile. "So someone behind the scenes wants Meredith House. They want control, but they don't want to be in the limelight. Does that put *B and W* in the frame?"

"I'm not sure. But if they wanted in they'd want the world to know about it. They wouldn't be backseat players."

Kincaid interlaced his fingers, his thumbs sparring. "Why do you want to take someone over?"

"For profit of course," Stephanie answered. "To reduce the competition and get a bigger piece of the pie. To gain an asset the other company owns. Lots of reasons." She watched Kincaid's eyes. "But that's not what you're thinking, is it?"

He shook his head. After all this time he still couldn't keep anything from her. It seemed like a nice mantel of vulnerability to have.

"What did you find out from Caster?"

"Not much."

"Did you have any trouble without me?"

"I always do," Kincaid smiled. "I'd like to have another chat with Jacobs. Feel like a drive?"

Stephanie was already rising. "I thought you'd never ask."

Chapter Thirty Two

They stopped and picked up Sergeant MacKenzie on the way. She slipped into the front seat and rode shotgun – literally. She looked relaxed and relieved. The first thing she told Kincaid was that she'd found some more material related to McCabe's murder. The second thing she confirmed was that the ADA's office was sufficiently placated, and the ShoeCam Operation was now officially in the can. He congratulated her with a beaming smile, and for a moment, their hands laid together on the console.

"I knew it would all come through for you."

There was a light cough from the rear seat. "Nice job, Amy. I hear it was a pretty scary bust."

Her hand slipped away from Kincaid's. "Thanks." *Awkward.*

Kincaid asked Amy to punch in a speed dial number – it was a private one she didn't recognize. He told her to wait: it wasn't picked up until the seventh ring.

"Oh, Kincaid. It's nice to hear from you again so soon. Miss me?"

"I certainly do, Rebecca."

"The line isn't particularly clear."

"I'm in the car, on speaker. Sergeant MacKenzie and Stephanie are with me."

"Busy, busy, busy. Hi ladies. I trust you're keeping him safe. How's the case proceeding?"

"It's slow, Rebecca, but it's coming. It's why I called, actually."

"Well, before *that*, how is the *other* problem?"

It took Kincaid a moment to catch her meaning. "Fine."

"'Fine' isn't an answer."

"You'll know when I know, remember?"

"Good. I'm worried, K."

"I know. But try not to be. Everything's going –."

"*To be fine.* Yes, I understand." Static cackled on the line. The endless construction hampered the signal. "So. More queries. Fire away."

"Did you manage to find out anything else about Devlin Turner? Anything personal?"

"Well, yes, I did, and it's rather exciting," she said with a whiff of canniness. "I was surprised to learn I'm still in the loop. I haven't been as active lately as I used to be in writer's groups, forums, or anything like that, but I certainly haven't been forgotten by the core, either."

"You'll never be forgotten, Rebecca."

"Promises, promises. Anyway, I put a few well-placed feelers out, and my phone hasn't stopped ringing. I've been talking so much I got a crook in my neck. To shorten the proverbial long story, not many people had anything nice to say about him, I'm afraid. He fostered enemies everywhere. Rumor has it he actually started out as a writer. Lives ago. Evidently, he wrote two suspense novels he was sure were destined for the bestsellers' list back in his twenties."

"What happened?"

"Nothing. He couldn't get anyone to represent him, and he didn't have any luck with editors or publishers either. I imagine –"

"They're shoe box material under his bed?"

Rebecca chuckled. "Precisely. What's the old adage? If you can't do it, teach? If he couldn't be a writer, Turner chose to stay close to the business by becoming an agent."

"A very influential one."

"Yes. But apparently not your most loyal representative."

"What do you mean?"

"You know he was involved with that recent court case along with *Meredith House*, don't you?"

"Against Brent Jacobs? Yes. He sued them because he believes they stole his manuscript."

"They probably did. And it wouldn't be the first time."

"There were others?"

"*Numerous* others. His name – excuse me." There was a slice of silence before Rebecca spoke again. "Sorry, had to sneeze. I think I might be allergic to Adolphus. Anyway, Turner and *Meredith House* have been cited and charged in several writer's lawsuits."

"For plagiarism?"

"Uh-huh. A number of books have been published by Turner and Gail after a similar novel was rejected by *Meredith House*. There were slight changes, naturally. Protagonist modifications. Character and plot designs. But anyone reading them could see they were basically the same books. Except the lawyers and the judges, of course. None of the writers ever won in court. In each instance, the allegedly pilfered books that went on to become bestsellers and movies were 'written' by the same author. Ian Nuraki. Publicity, fame, and money. All triggered by the legal challenges."

"Well, well."

"His name's always right up there. He sells enough books to finance a small country. And that doesn't include the movie rights or royalties, either. It's odd, don't you think?"

"What?"

"That Ian Nurakis' meteoric rise coincides with Turners'?"

"That wouldn't be unusual," Kincaid replied. "A writer's success often depends on having a good agent. And vice versa."

"Sure. But Nuraki never published anything until Turner came along."

"There's an 'and' in there, Rebecca."

"There sure is. No one knows Ian Nuraki."

"It's a pseudonym?" Kincaid asked surprised.

"A *nom du plume*. Whoever he is, he's risen to dizzying heights in the literary world with Turner. Well, 'rose.'"

"Could Turner have written – "

"No way. That opinion is based on his first foray into the literary world, and a subsequent effort a couple of agents have seen."

Kincaid slowed to a stop at the intersection. Interesting. Rejected as a writer, Turner built his career on the work of others, authors he probably deeply resented. *Was he jealous*?

The light changed. Kincaid sped past an idling delivery truck, skirted around a weaving line of black and orange traffic cones, and took the next right onto Jarvis. "Go on."

"I want to hear how much you've missed me."

"With all my heart."

Kincaid slowed down and waved in a signaling cab parked by the curb. A cabbie *signaling*: must be a newbie.

"Nothing concrete, and it's all hearsay, but it's intriguing nonetheless, don't you think?"

"Undoubtedly."

"So, Jacob's book – *The Essence of Innocence* – was taken out of the editorial frame just before *The Innocent* hit the bestseller list and Turner announced it was being made into a feature film, just like the others. Have you had an opportunity to read it yet?"

"A quick scan."

"And?"

"He certainly seems to have a case."

"Ahh, but he didn't win, and that's the important thing. The only thing, I dare say. Scat."

"Pardon?"

"Not you —Adolphus. But that's not all."

"My goodness, you're a gold mine of information."

"Like I said, no one seems to have liked Turner. Everyone he's slighted wants to pass along whatever they can."

"So?"

"So each time Turner and Meredith were sued, it was because a writer accused them of stealing a book or script, correct?"

"Right."

Kincaid pulled to a stop in front of Brent Jacob's house. "Rebecca, have I told you yet today —"

"No."

"I love you. How about dinner?"

"Anytime. Will the information help?"

"Indubitably."

"Good. So now you can do something for me."

"Anything."

"Keep me posted, and let me know as soon as you hear something."

"I will. But I can't let you in on everything, Rebecca."

"I wasn't talking about the investigation."

"I know. I'll call as soon as I hear something. Don't worry."

"Ha! Of course I'm going to worry. That's what Godmothers do. And if I hear about anything else, I'll make sure to give you a call."

"Thanks. And you ladies listening in make sure he follows up with his doctor. Call me if he reneges — I have a friend in the police department downtown."

Kincaid mouthed, *LT. Davis.*

Stephanie and Amy almost replied in unison. "We will."

"Good. *Scat.*"

Aaachooo.

Chapter Thirty Three

It took Brent Jacobs several minutes to respond to Kincaid's insistent knock. Lumbering down his front hall, he reached the door just as Amy was ready to try again. Glancing through the peephole, Jacobs paused when he saw who was waiting. Passively aggressive, he seemed to be considering whether or not he was going to let them inside. Not bothering to hide his impatience, he finally ushered them in with a heavy sigh. He stared at Amy as she squeezed past, his stomach almost pinning her against the wall. A slow look up and down.

"This is my partner, Sergeant MacKenzie." Kincaid stressed her title.

Jacobs nodded and backed off ever so slightly. He was troubled. Dressed in an old shirt and baggy sweatpants, he looked even heavier than he had at the restaurant. His pocket was stuffed with a profusion of pens. He held half a doughnut aloft, his pudgy lips white with icing sugar.

"I didn't think I'd see you again, Detective."

"You know what they say about a bad penny."

"I do." He leaned over and gave Stephanie an appraising glance. Like the Sergeant, she was quite attractive, but something about her made him uncomfortable.

"Neither of you were with the Detective the last time I was 'interviewed,' he said, licking a dollop of jam from his finger. He stared pointedly at Stephanie. "But I know you."

"Stephanie Quan." She smiled and held out her hand.

Jacobs didn't take it. "You're with *Meredith House.* I'm sure we talked outside the courthouse after a hearing."

"We did. We also had a quick coffee one night before that. We had an informal chat about the material you sent Ms. Meredith."

"Yes, that's it." He looked her up and down again. "You're one of her little pit bulls. A petite little intimidator."

Stephanie stopped Kincaid with a subtle wave. "I sincerely believe that's a stretch. I was only trying to make sure things didn't escalate at a difficult time."

"A *difficult* time. Oh, that's pejorative."

"Is there a problem?" Kincaid stared petulantly into Jacobs' eyes. He wasn't satisfied.

"There is. I assume you're on official business. I'll talk to you and your Sergeant, but this 'woman' doesn't come past my front door."

"And that's because –"

"We have history, don't we, Miss Quan." He smiled placatively. "We haven't always managed to see eye to eye. So she stays out."

Stephanie nodded at Kincaid, her glance assuring him everything was fine. "Perhaps I'll go for a walk, Detective. I'll join you when you're finished."

Kincaid was displeased, but he didn't want to make the issue confrontational. He needed Jacobs as compliant as possible.

Jacobs slammed the door closed when Stephanie walked down the porch steps. He gestured for his remaining guests to follow him along the hall and into the basement, waving noncommittally to the room with the doughnut.

"My office," he muttered, taking another bite. He cleared off a pair of folding chairs, then held one out for Amy. "Sergeant –"

"Thank you." She smiled demurely. *Tactically.*

Jacobs' office took up most of the little basement. Metal shelves lined the wall behind his desk. They were crammed with monitors, keyboards, packages of discs, sticks, printers, and the most impressive collection of the thickest manuals Kincaid had ever seen. Tangled cables snaked across the floor. Everything was littered with food remnants: used coffee cups, crumpled bags of chips, candy wrappers, and the cardboard insert with the corresponding pictures of what had been inside a box of chocolates.

Jacobs could barely sit down without perspiring. "What new information do you wish to regale me with this time, Detective? As you can see, now that the court case has reached the inevitable money-pit of an impasse, I'm quite busy. I have to get back to making a living."

"I understand you've changed your mind, that you're going ahead and appealing the court's ruling," Kincaid said quietly.

Jacobs smiled thoughtfully at Amy. "As is my constitutional right. Of course in Canada, 'rights' are only granted to the special interest groups that scream the loudest. Judges and insurance companies' lawyers dictate what 'democracy' and 'truth' means."

He quickly turned his attention back to Sergeant MacKenzie. "Besides, I haven't got anything to lose. They might as well have rammed me down into a commercial shredder with all of my documents and ended the proceedings even quicker. But that's not their style is it? They'd rather fillet you, bleed you to death, piece by piece. Just ask your lovely Ms. Quan."

"Finance isn't my area of expertise, Mr. Jacobs."

"Oh, that's grand. And it's Brent. Or *The Wizard*."

MacKenzie raised an eyebrow.

"Because of what I do with computers."

"So you've come into additional funding or support?" Kincaid wondered aloud.

No answer. Jacobs reached for the doughnut box. He picked a chocolate dip for himself and offered what was left to Amy. She declined: so did Kincaid.

"How is your business going?" Kincaid asked.

"You didn't come all the way here to make sure I was recovering nicely from being trampled upon, Detective. All you had to do was call my bank to see if I've declared bankruptcy."

A smile tugged at Kincaid's lips. He offered two words: "*Writer's Revenge.*"

Jacobs paused mid-bite. "I think most writers want revenge at some time or other. Rejection is extremely difficult. We've gone over all this. Check with little Ms. Quan."

"That's not what I meant," Kincaid countered impatiently. "'Writer's Revenge' is the title of a serialized story *The Gazette's* running."

Jacob's face went flat. Expressionless. *Was he surprised? Honestly?* "An old fashioned serialized story? Like Dickens? My heavens, I'm impressed! Good for them! There's hope for humanity yet. What? Bi-weekly, perhaps? And by *The Gazette*, no less. Tell me it can't be sent straight to your phone, that you actually have to pick up a paper and *read it*? I hope they haven't dumbed it down too much. Unfortunately, I don't read tabloid rags."

"The story is strangely familiar. It's echoing circumstances revolving around Devlin Turner's murder. A writer who goes on a killing spree after his work is rejected."

The rest of the doughnut disappeared. Jacobs listened quietly while Kincaid explained some of the things he'd learned at the newspaper.

"Is it difficult to trace e-mail submissions, Mr. Jacobs?"

The question caught him off guard and there was a moment's delay. "Not usually. Unless they're extremely savvy, you can usually track down an originator."

"But not always?"

Jacobs acquiesced with a shrug. "It's not hard to bury yourself if you know what you're doing. Especially if you're not using the same server. There are literally hundreds of addresses in this area alone someone could use and not care whether or not it was traced."

Kincaid frowned.

"Coffee houses, school labs, libraries: they all have Internet access, and you don't need a personal access code to log on. Then you can rout your IP address all over the world. It would take a good hacker to find you."

"So someone could send the installments in from anywhere?" Amy asked.

"Sure. By the time you traced it back to its point of origin, dozens of people would have used that same terminal."

"Could it be done from a home or office?"

Jacobs sneered. "You mean someone like me, who has much more than a working knowledge of computers?"

Kincaid nodded. "Sure. Someone like you."

"Yes." He offered Amy another syrupy smile.

Kincaid glanced at the books rammed into the metal shelves. "You're still editing computer manuals?"

"When I can."

"Have you been following the newspaper story, Mr. Jacobs?"

"I already told you, no."

Kincaid leaned forward and pulled him in with his eyes. "Have you *written* any segment of the story?"

"Nary a word. I wish I'd thought of it, though. What a precocious way to undermine someone. But why would I?" His eyes brightened and he stared at Amy. Everything clicked in. "Ahh, so that's why you've pasted on that sweet smile and followed our intrepid king of murderous conundrums into this veritable den of inequity." Jacobs shook his head, grinning. "Could that troublesome but erudite bear of a man seek his revenge not through the courts but by a supposedly well-written serial that would gradually expose what Turner and *Meredith House* had done?"

Amy stared back. "You certainly have enough to be angry about, Mr. Jacobs. You're convinced your script was plagiarized. You've lost a great deal financially. You lost the movie rights, and . . ."

"And," Kincaid interjected, "you've been denied the notoriety I believe is quite important to you. And now you appear to have come into some money that's given you the opportunity to attack *Meredith House* from a different angle and with a real lawyer at the helm this time."

Jacobs bristled.

"That gives you motive, Mr. Jacobs. And whoever is writing the serial knows a great deal about publishing. They're also cognizant of some of the things the industry would like to keep quiet, and they have inside information that would be difficult to obtain if you weren't close to the main players. You fall into all of those categories."

Jacobs rubbed his mouth with the back of his hand. Beads of perspiration glistened on his forehead. "I've already told you, Detective, that I had nothing to do with Turner's death."

Amy inched forward. *Attack time.* "Or with Brian McCabe's demise?"

"McCabe? Who's that?" Jacobs looked genuinely perplexed.

"Mr. McCabe worked part-time for a fairly well-known local agency," Kincaid explained.

"An editor? I've never heard of him."

"No. His specialty was fact-finding. He validated the information in a manuscript."

"A researcher. So?"

"He was found murdered just over five weeks ago."

Jacobs reached for another doughnut. A maple glazed was gone in a second. His hand was shaking. "And?"

"And when he wasn't working for the agency, he freelanced. In fact, he worked on a number of books for Devlin Turner."

Jacobs choked back a burp and tapped his stomach with a fist. He popped open a soda and gulped back a long draught that helped him recover. "I'm telling you, Kincaid. I've never heard of him."

"Who edited your script?"

More sweat. Another shrug.

"Mr. Jacobs?"

"Michael Cormier."

"Did you get a personal reply back when he finished his analysis of your book?"

"Of course."

Kincaid waited silently. Flustered, Jacobs sighed loudly, then started rummaging through his desk drawers, finally withdrawing a ringed binder. "This was my second draft," he muttered, flipping to the front page. He stabbed a bulbous finger at the name on the bottom of the third page of the editor's report. "Here it is. Michael Cormier. Satisfied? Like I said, I've never heard of the other guy."

"Brian McCabe."

Kincaid squinted, his vision suddenly troubled by a blurry haze that crept across the outer edge of the visual field of his left eye. It also felt like a needle was pressing into his lower spine. He must have looked uncomfortable because he felt Amy tense beside him.

"You don't have an alibi for the night of Turner's murder."

"I've already told you I was here, working." After a disparaging smirk, he reached for another doughnut, angry there weren't any left. He tossed the empty box onto the floor.

"But your statement can't be corroborated."

"That's too bad. I assume it's up to you to prove I wasn't here."

Kincaid smiled at the challenge. "It is. And for your own edification, Mr. McCabe worked at *The Book Doctor*. Michael Cormier's agency."

Jacobs sank back into his chair. He looked like he'd been hit in the stomach with a baseball bat. Fidgeting nervously, he wouldn't look Kincaid in the eye.

Kincaid had a hunch and let the silence thicken for a minute. "And what about Erik Caster?"

Jacob's breath caught. His eyes narrowed and his fat lips pinched tight. "Never heard of him either."

"He's a frustrated writer, just like you. In fact, although I admit I'm not a literary critic, a character in *The Writer's Revenge*, the newspaper serial, bears a remarkable similarity to Erik Caster."

"A great many people are really quite similar when you get right down to it, aren't they Sergeant?" Jacobs scoffed.

"Of course," Kincaid replied. "But it seems to me that whoever is writing the story probably knows Mr. Caster, and identifies with some of the things he's been through trying to get his book published. The things he's done. The threats he's made. The things he could do."

"I don't."

"Well, that's probably for the best, Jacobs."

"*Mr. Jacobs.* And why is that?"

Kincaid leaned forward across the desk and whispered. "Because Erik Caster isn't the type of person who can easily be controlled. It would be a *dangerous liaison.* You might *think* you're in control, but he's the kind of person who'd use that against you. There's no telling what he might do if something doesn't go his way."

"I'll bear that in mind if I ever meet him."

"You do that." Kincaid rose to leave. Amy stood, too. "Don't bother getting up," Kincaid said, scrunching around past the desk and then holding the door for his Sergeant. "We know our way out."

He stopped with one hand on the basement door and turned around. "And we know our way in, too."

And we'll be back, he thought, smiling as he walked up the stairs.

It wasn't Jacobs' denial of knowing anything about the newspaper story or having any involvement with Caster or McCabe that caught Kincaid's attention. It was the instantaneous and uncontrolled glimmer in his eyes the first time he mentioned *Writer's Revenge.*

Chapter Thirty Four

Brent Jacobs' screen door banged closed as Amy followed Kincaid down the driveway to the car. Before the shivering stopped, the inside door slammed shut even harder. Neither officer turned around.

"God, does he ever stop eating?" Amy shook her head. "Do you believe him? About not having anything to do with the *Gazette* piece? He really lit up when you mentioned the *Writer's Revenge.*"

"I'm not sure. The technical aspects are obviously well within his computer capabilities. He certainly has motive, and there's no doubt he's emotionally unstable." Kincaid drifted away for a moment. "Mind if we take a little drive?"

"I'm all yours."

Kincaid couldn't help smiling.

Just then, Stephanie turned the corner down at the far end of Jacob's street. Head back, body erect, she was walking briskly, meditatively, her arms pumping up and down with each stride, her hair bouncing in the soft breeze. She was barely perspiring. Kincaid met her at the bottom of the driveway.

"Thanks for leaving your phone on '*speaker.*'"

"I thought you'd want to listen."

"You're right—he's hiding something. But what?"

Kincaid tossed her the keys. "Feel like driving?"

"Should I?"

"Probably. But it's not something Amy needs to know about right now, okay?"

"Kincaid –"

"Not yet, anyway."

"She's got a job to do too, remember. Orders from Davis. And I don't want to get in the middle of it. That's not fair to her – or you."

"I'm not asking you to. Amy's doing what she has to, and she's doing it professionally. But she doesn't have to know everything I feel and do throughout the day. I can't work like that. It's stifling. I'll turn to her when I need to. You have to trust me on this."

Stephanie stared down at the ground. She didn't feel comfortable about what Kincaid was asking, but she'd never mistrusted him before and she wasn't going to start now. She'd wait and watch, just like Amy was doing, so they'd both have his back. Just like Davis wanted *her* to do, too.

Grey clouds were slowly massing together and covering the horizon. Amy frowned when Stephanie slid into the driver's seat, but she didn't say anything to Kincaid. *Was it a hint?*

"I realize it's not protocol, Sergeant, but I didn't have an inch of space in front of that metal desk to move."

"How are your legs? *Sir*?"

"I need to lean back and stretch out as much as I can."

"And the pain?"

"I just need a break. And we don't seem to have a hot tub back here." No smile. "I also want you to look up something on the way."

Amy swung the computer around. "What am I looking for, Sir? And where are we going?"

"Bring up as much as you can about Jacob's financial statements for the last year. Pull anything together that you can."

"Because there wasn't anything in his '*in*' basket?"

"Exactly. And I want to know why he can afford legal counsel —"

"Now? When he couldn't before?"

Kincaid nodded into the rearview. "Good. You're one step ahead of me again. And we're off to Walter Croft's house."

"But you and the Sergeant have already seen him," Stephanie said. "Do you really think he warrants another shot?"

"I do. But we have to make a stop first."

*

Stephanie sliced through the city by jumping on the Parkway, then veered under the newly-lit Viaduct before pushing her way onto the Bayview Extension. She curled up to Bloor and joined the cavalcade of cars crawling towards Parliament. After a long wait to make a left at Church Street, she scooted south to Wellesley. Another quick right. It was a step back in time. Dark streets, dilapidated and restless. Sad streets, forgotten with every suburb that exploded outwards from the city's core and each new condo that blotted out the sky and buried the world in shadows. Where *those* kinds of people lived now.

Stephanie slowly circled the block while Kincaid searched the transparent faces for one he recognized. A banger leaning against a metal fence coldly eyed his car. Two old men hunched against a wall handed a brown bag back and forth. There wasn't much to see. Profiles melted together, half-images blurred, expressions sifted into each other like fractured pieces in a kaleidoscope. Alternating languages capped storefronts, and most windows were barred. People festered at corners, eyes dull with the sense that something was going to happen, but not really caring if it did or not. Hookers, a couple of transients sleeping one off in a bus shelter covered with graffiti, a group of ten year old wannabees acting like their older brothers in the parkette.

One more pass, Kincaid thought, starting the third sweep – there was always later. Then, halfway up the block, he spotted the familiar leather bomber jacket he'd been searching for – fringes hanging from the arms, a bright red that bordered on fluorescent, and a dragon crest on the back. Kincaid told Stephanie to slip into a parking space across the street.

The woman in the jacket was slim, too slim, but bled the part: seamed nylons, long black hair, a tight miniskirt with a side slash of a thigh split, high heels. Sauntering along the curb, she stopped dead when a late model BMW wheeled up. She moved in a bit closer, but not too close, one leg straight back, the other bent at the knee and braced against the car door. She leaned in, listening behind an artificial laugh and half-smile, scanning the car's interior for trouble. It was a sad pose, Kincaid thought, the scene oozing with suppressed anger, trepidation, and needy mistrust on both sides.

Kincaid told Stephanie and Amy to stay in the car. He waited for a gap in the traffic, then cut a quick diagonal across the road. He tried to merge with the pedestrians hustling back and forth, but he was an easy spot for street people who needed to recognize danger before it happened . . . if they wanted to stay alive.

The woman reached for the door handle, but sensed something, and stopped. She glanced up and spotted Kincaid before he reached the corner. Off and running, her heels *click-clacked* against the pavement. The Beemer did a quick U-turn, its tires squealing as it sped away from the curb. The woman slipped through the jostling crowds congesting the sidewalk like a dolphin through waves. Even on a good day Kincaid would have been hard pressed to catch her, so he didn't bother making the effort to run. He walked back to the car. Contact had been made: he knew where he'd find her.

*

Three blocks over, Stephanie pulled the car to a stop. "I'll be in the doughnut shop. And I don't want to hear anything smart from either of you."

Amy looked concerned. "You're sure you don't need me?"

"No. I'll just be a few minutes, and this isn't what it seems."

His partner didn't look convinced.

DodoDoughnuts.

Paint peeled from each waning alliterative letter, and the small overhead awning was torn in three places. In each corner of the window there was a small, weather-faded picture that was supposed to represent the extinct bird of fame in the title. *Supposed to.*

Perched on a stool and still panting to catch her breath, Kendra was hunched over the counter when Kincaid came in, jingling the wooden chimes above the door. Her world expanded and collapsed at the same time.

"The Beemer looked fine."

"You don't need it."

Chairs scraped back and a couple of people left as inconspicuously as they could. Kincaid had already filed their faces away.

"Look Kincaid, I've been really good lately. It's just –"

"You're talking to *me*, Kendra."

Kendra. Or, on other days, when the mood hit hard and the punters needed something different, *Kenny*. In a world increasingly accustomed to transvestites, cross-dressers, and transsexuals, Kendra/Kenny was the only true hermaphrodite Kincaid knew. Androgynous in the purest sense of the word, she'd been beaten by her mother for what she was and by her father for what she wasn't. Kincaid felt genuinely sorry for the young man. He was caught between worlds: physically, emotionally, and psychologically – not a woman or a man, but a *man and a woman.*

Caught in limbo, Kendra was on the list for gender surgery, but the process was extremely long and costly. The tests she had to undergo cost a small fortune, and weren't covered by standard medical benefits. Demonized by emotional and psychological problems, Kenny hid behind drugs, so she rarely had much money for long. Besides, even though she'd spent years in gender therapy and psychiatric counseling, there was still a touch of ambivalence lurking deep inside. Which sex was more overwhelming? *Surgery to become what? To become who?* Some mornings when she looked into the mirror she wondered *where* am I, not *who?*

Kincaid leaned closer: no smell of weed and her arms were clean. "Let's take a window seat."

The young girl behind the counter had so many facial tattoos it was hard to tell her ethnicity. Kendra signaled for two coffees and pointed to a table up front. The chimes tinkled again. A guy came in smiling, took one look around, and left. Kincaid wasn't good for the doughnut business.

"Black, right?"

"Yes, thanks."

"You look awful, Kincaid."

"Kendra –"

"You do. You didn't even pretend to run. So what's up?"

"I'm just tired."

Another non-believer. They caught up with some small talk, rolling with each other but not crossing the line that would have made it *too* close. Then, without going into details, Kincaid explained as much as he could about Brian McCabe. He told her there'd been a fight in the alley behind *The Tavern* a little over a month ago, and that someone was seriously injured. No need to mention homicide just yet.

But Kendra read the papers. "The guy who was beaten to death?"

Kincaid sipped his coffee.

"Word on the street said it was old-time bashers. Monkeys three to the left of Darwin."

"It wasn't. I need to talk to anyone who might have seen something that night. Anything. No questions asked, no follow-ups, but a bit of thanks. Something's missing."

"Other than that poor man's face? What?"

"Whatever was used to kill him. I need to tie it to something else."

Kendra blew the steam from her cup. "So there's two. I'll keep my ears to the ground and see what I can pick up." Staring again, she touched his hand. "Come on, Kincaid. Are you –?"

"I'm fine."

"I remember what you said last time, Kincaid, and the time before that, and I'm clean. Honest to Christ." Her thoughts drifted back to the Beemer. The guy was probably seventy-five and needy as hell. Who was really worse off? "Old habits are hard to break."

"If you're not clean and straight there's no program, right?"

"Right."

"So no more *meet-and-greet*. Every day you do sets you back one."

"I know, but –"

"But '*nothing*', Kendra. Do I have to start swinging a car by?"

She shook her head.

"So don't forget. No matter who you are, or who you want to be, you'll always be beautiful to me."

A small tear glistened in the corner of her eye.

Kincaid pulled a fifty from his wallet and eased it under Kendra's hand. "Call me if you hear anything." He pulled out two more, slipping them under her saucer. "Promise me you won't smoke it. Put it away. It'll all add one day, and then you can decide, okay?"

Nodding, Kendra folded the bills into her purse. The chimes tinkled. Leaning her head against the window, she watched Kincaid walk down the street and slide into his car. People were with him, but she couldn't make out the faces. She sighed wistfully. Someone lucky. Kincaid was the only cop who'd ever had time for her and treated her as a person. Real time. Real concern. If only he'd been his father . . .

Did it always hurt this much to smile?

*

There were two things Kincaid detested in his job. One was the desultory demands of the incessant paperwork that inundated him throughout an investigation. The second thing was putting all that seemingly never-ending paperwork into the computer. He leaned forward from the back seat.

"Sergeant, have I told you yet today how lovely . . ."

"No, you haven't. But yes, I'll stay here and make sure everything's caught up. And I'll keep digging into Jacob's financial situation."

Kincaid passed her his notebook. Seconds later, Amy's slender fingers returned to their rhythmic dance across the keyboard.

*

Standing on the little front porch, Stephanie watched Kincaid glance up and down the street as they waited patiently for Walter Croft to make his way to the door. Nice, simple houses lined both sides of the road. Most had small front lawns spotted with well-sized elm or maple trees, nicely-tended gardens and beckoning stoops swept clean. A pleasant place to grow up, Kincaid thought. He imagined every house had a dog or a cat. Maybe even a bird.

"You're right," Stephanie whispered.

"Pardon?"

"It seems like a very pleasant place to live."

Kincaid touched her lightly on the cheek. He was just about to speak when Walter Croft called out from behind the door. "What?"

"It's Detective Kincaid, Mr. Croft. We spoke the other day." He held his warrant card up to the peephole. A moment later, the locks slid back and the door creaked open like a medieval dungeon.

"Find out anything about the flag?" the old man asked, gesturing them inside. Croft stopped when he saw Stephanie, and squinted. "Don't know you, do I? You're not the cute little officer who was here yesterday, or whenever it was."

Kincaid introduced his 'associate'.

Stephanie tried to put him at ease. "Actually, we met a little while back, Mr. Croft. I spoke to you about some of the letters you sent *Meredith House*."

If Walter Croft remembered anything, his face didn't show it.

Kincaid followed the old man back into the little living room. The rest of the house was obviously off limits. "I'm afraid I haven't heard anything about the flag yet," he said. "But we passed your concerns along to the sergeant on duty."

Stephanie frowned. Kincaid mouthed *later*.

"Hope he bloody well does something. It's not right, you know. Flags are important. I don't like seeing them in truck windows neither. Or made into shirts and shit."

Walter Croft slumped down into *his* chair, the one next to the table sprinkled with old photographs. "Yeah, you were here," he mused, giving Kincaid a lingering glance. He seemed reluctant to look at Stephanie.

"We talked about Devlin Turner."

"Yes," Croft remembered. "With that nice young woman. What was her name?"

"Sergeant MacKenzie."

"Yes. Amy, wasn't it? Can't see too well but she was a cute little thing. I thought if anyone was going to fix the flag nonsense it was her."

"I'm sure she'll do her best."

"So you're back about Turner? I told you before I can't say I'm not glad he's dead. My wife carried his evil words to her grave. I'll never forgive him for that."

"You loved your wife very much, didn't you sir?" Stephanie asked quietly.

Turning with a groan, Croft stared at one of the frames. It held a black and white picture of a young woman's face. Even though it was grainy and probably fifty years old, the woman's beauty was unmistakable. When he answered, he spoke to Kincaid. "Yes, I do."

He turned toward Stephanie. Something in his mind clicked, and the past become whole again. "I remember your face now. You came to tell me to stop sending letters, didn't you?"

Stephanie nodded. "They were getting a little aggressive Mr. Croft. And I think it was really Mr. Turner you were mad at, sir. Not *Meredith House*."

A bus rumbled by outside, honking and swerving around an erratic cyclist who thought he owned the road.

"Don't go and start telling me who I was mad at, missy."

Kincaid quickly interrupted. "We need to check something else, Mr. Croft. Did your wife do her own editing?"

"What? Her own editing?" He turned back from the picture. "Hell no. She said writers can't correct their own work."

"Who did it for her?"

He frowned and tried to remember. "I don't recall." He looked back at the photograph with an intensity that made his body rigid. He rubbed the front of the picture. Dust motes flew everywhere.

"What about *The Book Doctor*? Does that name sound familiar?"

The old man shrugged noncommittally. "Might. Then again, might not."

"Did your wife keep records about her book?"

"What kind of records?"

"Where she sent her queries, who she contacted for her research, who did her editing – that kind of thing."

"Probably. Matty was always neat and tidy about everything."

"Is it possible we can have a look at them, Sir?"

The old man wavered. "And I said you could if I found them. And I haven't. I've been busy." He coughed, scrounged through his pockets for a lighter, and lit a fresh cigarette. He blew a cloud of grey smoke between his guests.

Kincaid leaned forward. "Do you think you'll be able to locate them? It's quite important."

"Why?"

Kincaid was a tad ambivalent about how much to tell him. There was something evasive about the old man that troubled him, but he couldn't quite put his finger on it. Walter Croft knew his wife had kept all the correspondence she'd received from Devlin Turner. And Walter had probably kept his own. Why didn't he want to show it to him? What was he hiding? And why was he purposefully ignoring Stephanie? Was it really just because she'd talked to him about the letters he'd sent *Meredith House?* He knew she wouldn't have been aggressive or rude to the old man.

"Another man has also been murdered, Mr. Croft. Brian McCabe. He worked part-time with Devlin Turner."

"Serves him right, then." Croft stared past Kincaid and out the little front window of his little house. The glass hadn't been cleaned in ages. Two blue jays foraged for food at a feeder hanging from a thick maple down by the street. He took a long draw and crushed out his cigarette.

"Mr. Croft?"

"What?"

"Your wife's papers. When can I see them?"

"Like I said, I'll have to find 'em first. It might take some time, and I don't want to keep you."

He smacked his lips together and folded his hands in his lap. All of a sudden he looked terribly tired and gaunt.

"Perhaps you'd be kind enough to call me when you do," Kincaid said, standing. He put one of his cards on the table with the photographs. "Did your wife type her manuscript on a computer?"

"Of course. We may be old, but we're not stupid."

Kincaid couldn't help smiling. "Do you still have it?"

He nodded, took out another smoke, then left it in his shirt pocket.

"Do you ever use it?"

"I don't write books."

"But do you use the computer, Mr. Croft?"

"I know what a keyboard is, if that's what you mean." His eyes narrowed and his forehead wrinkled with a troubled frown. "How the Hell do you think I sent the letters to Turner, and what's her name? That snotty little publisher?"

"Gail Meredith."

"Right. *Her.* But I just wrote letters on the thing. None of that computer mail stuff. Can't be bothered learning, now. Not with Matilda gone."

"I see. Do you ever talk to anyone on your computer, Mr. Croft? Go into chat rooms, use the little cameras built into the top of the screen, or anything like that?"

"Now just who would I talk to?"

"News groups, people who share your interests, hobby clubs, that sort of thing."

Croft shook his head.

"Perhaps your wife chatted with other writers when she was working."

"I wouldn't know." Croft's voice was gravely, but his tone was curt and dismissive. He took the cigarette back out. He lit it slowly, and another cloud of smoke tinged the ceiling yellow. And his lungs.

"Well, thanks for your time. Please let me know when you find your wife's records. I'll have a patrol car swing by to pick them up so you're not inconvenienced."

Even though Kincaid said they'd show themselves out, Walter Croft pushed himself up from the chair with a heavy sigh and followed them to the door. He didn't return Stephanie's smile when she thanked him for his time and said good bye.

"And don't forget about that flag," he called, as they walked down the front steps. But he slammed the door shut and started sliding the locks closed before Kincaid had turned around to answer. He felt like a missionary offering bibles.

The car doors were open, giving Amy a nice warm breeze. She was scrolling down the screen, studying the incoming mail.

"Anything?"

Kincaid shook his head. "He's still pretty evasive. And he certainly doesn't like Stephanie."

"I'll follow-up on the situation with the flag – perhaps that might make him a little more responsive."

"It couldn't hurt."

Kincaid asked for his keys back. Stephanie hesitated for just a second. She sensed he was driving for her benefit, just to prove he could. When they turned off Walter Croft's street and back on to Bloor, Stephanie watched the compact little store fronts pass quickly by. Kincaid had just started speed dialing Richardson's number when an incoming call rang through first.

Before he barked his name into the receiver, he knew something was wrong. He flipped off the speaker. He stared straight ahead, listening attentively without interrupting. As the moments passed, his face blanched a dull white and he flexed his fingers open and closed tightly around the steering wheel.

"I understand. Thanks. I'll be there as soon as I can."

He took a deep breath, checked his mirrors, and then calmly suggested Amy should hold on. She managed to brace her hands against the dashboard just as Kincaid started his turn. Aggressively palming the wheel, he jerked the car out of his lane just before the next intersection and careened around in a sharp 'U' turn. The car leaned awkwardly to the right, crunching down on the shocks, the momentum throwing Stephanie heavily into the back door. The rear end fishtailed and skidded into the curb. Horns blared from both directions.

Caught against the curb, the back wheels screamed savagely for a moment, grinding into the road and showering a pedestrian with a cloud of debris. Cutting off the oncoming traffic as the light changed, Kincaid tramped the pedal to the floor and tore off down the street. Gray smoke ballooned behind them.

Staring straight ahead, Amy let her arms fall back from the dash. Awnings and newspaper boxes blurred past. "What is it?"

He whispered softly. "Ryan."

Chapter Thirty Five

The hospital was a hard fifteen minutes away.

Kincaid made it in nine.

The car screeched to a jerking stop by the ER doors. Waving people out of the way, he ran inside and hurdled up the stairs, dragging Stephanie in his wake. Amy raced to park the car. The first thing Kincaid saw when he pushed the stairwell door open was Dr. Degatz slumped against the far wall, head forward, elbows against her thighs, her stethoscope dangling in front of her chest.

He touched her arm, but before he managed to blurt out the myriad questions thrashing through his mind, Dr. Degatz smiled. Softly, sadly, a little insecurely, but it was still a smile.

"He's all right, Kincaid. He's out of danger." She repeated *'he's all right'* for her own benefit as much as his, but the words *for now* hung between them like a scythe.

Kincaid struggled to catch his breath. "What happened?"

"He started slipping into a coma, but we got to him with the crash cart in time." She shook her head, always amazed at the tenacity and spirit people could muster. "God he's a fighter." She explained what precipitated the crisis and what the team had done as quickly and as simply as she could.

"Can I see him?"

"No, he needs to rest, and his mother's with him now."

"Carolyn? When did she get here?"

"About an hour ago. She was in the cafeteria when I was paged."

"How is she?"

"As well as can be expected."

"When can I go in?"

Dr. Degatz smiled gently. "Give them some time. Okay?"

Kincaid nodded. A hand touched him lightly on the shoulder, the warmth more reassuring than he could have hoped. He turned and hugged Stephanie tightly to his side. It was hard to let her go.

"This is Dr. Degatz, Ryan's physician."

He paused for a second, unsure of what to say about Stephanie. *An old friend* sounded ridiculous. "Ellen, this is that special someone I've told you about."

"I'm sorry we had to meet under these circumstances," Dr. Degatz said, accepting Stephanie's hand. "Do you know Ryan?"

"Only from what Kincaid has told me. He seems like quite a remarkable little boy."

"He is." Kincaid and Dr. Degatz had spoken at the same time, and they smiled awkwardly. Kincaid reached for the doctor's hand. "Ellen –"

She took his hand between her own and stopped him with a smile. There was no need for words. No matter how difficult it was to think about, they both knew there was going to be a 'next time'. And soon. Ryan had walked this road before, and Kincaid's steps had never left his side. They never would.

"Go have a coffee," Dr. Degatz said quietly. "I'll page you after I check on him."

Kincaid reluctantly let her hands go. He wrapped his arm around Stephanie's shoulders and slowly walked toward the elevators. He stopped at the nurses' station and turned back, but Dr. Degatz had already gone into Ryan's room.

The cafeteria was nothing more than a dream, a spurious veil of suits and nurses and uniforms and families sitting together without eating and students weighed down with books and surgeons crumpling up paper slippers and masks while they stared at untouched meals as patients passed by, tugging i.v. stands behind them, and old men and women staring off into the distance and wondering what they were going to do now.

A hand touched Kincaid lightly on his neck. Amy tried, but a smile wouldn't come.

"He's good, right?"

"Yes. For now."

Kincaid pulled out a chair for her and quickly brought her up to speed. Absently tearing her Styrofoam cup apart, Amy watched his eyes as he spoke. Then, silence. Lives unfolded all around them. Leaving half-finished coffees, they got up together when they heard Kincaid's name crackling over the intercom, and quickly made their way back to the ICU ward.

Carolyn was sitting on a chair outside her son's room. The frown etched into her forehead was a deepening crevice that would never go completely away. She was a slight woman, almost elfish, with the formlessness of a young girl's body and small, delicate hands. Redheaded and freckled, her skin was more pale and gaunt than usual. She didn't look sickly, just tiny and fragile. Carolyn briskly rubbed the tears away when she saw Kincaid, then rose anxiously to meet him.

"God, K, I'm glad you're here," she mumbled, collapsing into his embrace. "I thought – I thought that this was – this was –." More tears.

"Shhh. He's all right now." Kincaid was surprised at how hard she was trembling. He stroked her cheeks and whispered gentle encouragements into her ear.

"I'd gone to get a coffee, when – when *it* happened – when he –."

"Softly, Carolyn. Take it easy." Kincaid helped her back down into the chair. She wouldn't let go of his hands. It seemed strange, but it was a thought Kincaid had had many times before staring into the bathroom mirror: all he could see was that the woman's eyes were filled with – *nothingness*.

"We know how strong he is."

She looked up, sniffling. Kincaid reached into his jacket pocket, took out some tissues, and daubed her eyes. The tears wouldn't stop. *What could he say*? What words could he offer, what comforting murmurs of hope could he whisper that would soften a mother's fear and pain?

Carolyn looked at the women standing so stoically behind Kincaid, consciously noticing them for the first time. Names wouldn't come. She sobbed into her hands. "I don't know how much more of this I can take."

The weak confession brought another deluge of tears. Kincaid wiped her cheek.

"Carolyn, –"

She squeezed his hands with desperation and stared into his eyes. "I have to talk to you. I *really have* to."

"Of course. Come downstairs . We'll have a coffee –."

"No." She shook her head vigorously. "No. Now. It has to be here and now. Just – just in case." She glanced at the women. "Alone."

Kincaid gently pried the woman's fingers from his wrists. "Give us some time, okay?"

Amy looked uncertain – something didn't feel right. Stephanie felt a shiver of worry when she saw the look in

Kincaid's eyes. She'd seen that pain before, that sense of despondency and abandonment.

"We'll be in the cafeteria," Amy whispered. She wished there was something more she could do.

Side by side, Kincaid and Carolyn walked down the corridor and into one of the small rooms reserved for families anxiously waiting to hear the prognosis about a loved one. It was germane and sparse. They sat together on a weathered vinyl couch. He slipped his arm around her shoulders and pulled her close. Carolyn didn't look up when she finally started to speak.

"He loves you. You know that, right?"

A whispered *yes*.

"I don't want him to suffer. At – at the end."

"Neither do I, Carolyn. I'm sure Dr. Degatz will do everything she can."

"That's not enough."

Kincaid tensed. He knew what Carolyn wanted to say, and knew he had to let her say it.

She drew a sleeve across her cheeks. "How long has the poor kid been in the hospital? It seems like all his life. And what kind of life has it been?"

Not waiting for an answer, Carolyn took a deep breath and went on. She'd obviously been preparing for this moment for a long time. "For most of his life he's been in pain. I don't want him to – *to go* - that way, too."

"Carolyn, –"

"No, let me finish." She paused while two orderlies wheeled a gurney past the little waiting room. A heavy white sheet was drawn over the face of a motionless form. Empty bags dangled from an IV stand. The wheels squeaked. An emaciated foot was just barely visible beneath the corner of the bedding, a bloodless foot that would never take another step.

"Dr. Degatz says there's a good chance he'll lapse into another coma before –"

"Shhhh." They swayed softly together, eyes half-closed, listening and feeling each other's heartbeat. Carolyn knew part of Kincaid's story, about how much he suffered, and suddenly, waves of guilt washed over the shores of her heart.

"If I lost him when he was in a coma I don't think – I don't think it would seem so horrible. But to see him suffering and full of pain and fear at the end . . ."

Her voice trailed off and she shook her head despondently. "I can't imagine that. I – I can't live with that."

"Dr. Degatz won't let him suffer."

Carolyn spoke through clenched teeth. Her grip on his hand tightened. "I know she'll do whatever she can. But I don't want it to come to that."

There, she'd said it. *Out loud.* Carolyn choked back the bile rising in her throat and collapsed into Kincaid's side, weightless, formless, and deeply afraid. She was tiny and frail, but the heaviness of her anguish forced the breath from his lungs.

"He's my son. He's all I have left, all that keeps me alive." She chewed on words of glass shards. "One switch. That's all it would take to set him free, to let him go without pain. But I don't think" – she started sobbing again – "I can tell them to do it."

Kincaid rocked her gently back and forth.

Carolyn whispered through tears. "If he goes into another coma they – they say he won't come out K. I . . . would you . . . will you help?"

Silence.

He wrapped his arms tightly around her quivering shoulders.

"Sorry," she sobbed. "I shouldn't have asked. Forget it. Forget what I said."

But he couldn't forget. He pictured Ryan at the hockey game, the stick balanced against the side of his wheelchair and the dog-eared program clutched tightly between his hands. He remembered the anguish on the boy's face when they had to go, and the incessant pain simmering behind his eyes. Didn't Ryan have the right to slip from one darkness to the next without fear, without suffering? And didn't Carolyn have the right to let him go like that?

Kincaid had seen others die. Many others. He remembered the things his father told him after his own mother's death. The frustration of standing impotently by. The anguish. Watching her loneliness and pain swallow up everything that was left.

The only thing Dr. Degatz could really do now would be to soften the suffering. But even by tempering the pain, wasn't she prolonging it and making it worse?

Kincaid closed his eyes and brought his chin down softly against the top of Carolyn's head.

What would Ryan want, he thought. *What does Carolyn need?*

He felt the blood pounding through the woman's neck and face, felt the quiver in her limbs. Her face was flushed with warmth but she was freezing inside.

And who – who am I to judge?

Chapter Thirty Six

Dieter Vollger was dreaming again. But he was anxiously awake.

Watching the morning unfold in shadows across his ceiling, he couldn't stop the haunting images of prison from coming back again and again: Redman's eyes after Dieter shived him through the throat; the pulp that was left of Minter's face after the fight in the yard; the long nights listening to men scream, the putrid shit the bosses called food; the hacks always there, watching, never letting him rest, watching him eat, shit, or tear the semen from his throbbing pole.

He toyed with his knife. The images were really his friends, the only ones he'd ever had, the ones he didn't *want* to forget. After all, he'd had eight years to remember. This time.

He flicked the blade open and closed. All that was behind him. For now. Because now he could remember each new killing, and somehow, that always made him feel safe. He liked reliving every one, right down to the finest, bloody detail. But he didn't have time. He had to get going. He had a lot to do today. He needed a shave, a professional haircut by an actual stylist, and buy one of the knock off suits in New York's garment district. Tonight, Dieter Vollger had another part to play.

Gerhard Dormer. That's who Dieter was going to be tonight. Gerhard Dormer.

It seemed like a nice name to put to a new profile. *How did it sound?*

*

Hours later, Dieter splashed some more Jack Daniels into his glass and re-read the articles he'd pulled off the Net about the Devlin Turner murder case in Toronto. Not murder – mutilation. He still thought the dog left hanging from the tree had been a nice touch. He scanned through the notes in his binder, searching for the researcher – *what was his name* – oh yeah, Brian McCabe. There they were. He'd sent two different queries to Devlin Turner. Both had been returned with nothing but a series of angry black slashes through the letter. In a separate note, McCabe added his two cents as well. Dieter smiled. The guy got what he deserved.

Dieter finished reading an article from the *Seattle Gazette* about the tragic death of Roland Steinberg, the headless biker. Two pages later was the piece from the *Chicago Tribune* about Shirley O'Donovan, the missing editor from *Marrauder Books*. It would be a long time before they dug up the *buried dinosaur hunter*, he smiled. Bones on bones on bones. Dieter took a long pull at the JD, sneered, and started a fresh page in his scrapbook. A few more sentences to fan the flames of his hatred. He read it again, his lips moving slowly. After tonight, he'd make his way north to the Peace Bridge, then east to Toronto, and finally find his companion in arms, the guy who did Devlin Turner so beautifully and that asshole McCabe. A rejected writer, just like he was. Someone who felt what he felt. The humiliation. The scorn. Once he found him they'd be blood brothers, bonded by rejection, and the killing would never stop. Nothing would get in their way. The things they'd do together.

Agents, publishers, editors, researchers . . .

He turned to McCabe's note.

There were just too many errors to make the book a viable project.

Best of luck elsewhere.

Luck wasn't fucking going to have anything to do with it.

*

Although phones, faxes, e-mails, scanners and visual conference calls had revolutionized most industries and made it possible to set up offices practically anywhere, the publishing industry, as a whole, was still focused around four main centers: New York, Chicago, Los Angeles and Toronto. Apart from their European counterparts and subsidiaries, the majority of the larger houses had offices in at least two of the cities, but New York was still the nerve center. The city was rife with publishing companies, agents, ghost writers, producers, and aspiring authors. It seemed like everything above 32nd street had something to do with books. Selling, buying, distributing, publishing. The age old adage still applied: if you could make it in New York you could make it anywhere.

Chamille Nasson was an associate editor at *Hollow Road*, a medium sized publishing house in one of the towers that fought for space along the Avenue of the Americas. She had a small cubicle that was far more than a stone's throw from a window, so she never knew what the weather was like unless she checked her tablet or went outside for a quick bite at one of the vending carts that jammed the sidewalk for space.

Her mole-hole was cluttered with folders; huge mounds of paper clipped together or wrapped in elastic bands, brown bubble mailers, or manila envelopes. Writers didn't need to send so much. Chamille had an eagle's eye for a manuscript's potential, and could usually tell after only a few pages the chance a particular book might have against others in the same genre. Erudite, smart, prescient and industrious, she was every publisher's dream. If a book got an 'okay' from Chamille's desk, the editorial department knew it was something they should take a hard look at. She didn't have Devlin Turner's expertise, but she was close.

Unlike Turner, Chamille Nasson wasn't the type of person to send a caustic reply back to the hundreds of people who sent her manuscripts each month. Her rejections were polite and professional. She'd never forgotten the novel she'd tried to sell about a year after graduating from NYU. Her book never made the cut. Even though she still worked with some of the publishing houses that hadn't wanted to see her novel, she always remembered how she felt about her manuscript – *and about herself* – as the rejections dribbled in. She never wanted to inflict those feelings on anyone else.

But this was something completely different.

It was the third time she'd received the same query in the last two months. Each submission had been written under a different name, and although they'd been slightly altered, it wasn't enough to make them instantly recognizable. She shouldn't have opened it. It was the last one of the week, a terrible one to finish with. But she felt sorry for Dieter Vollger, whoever he was, and despite her impatience, she'd tried to be empathetic but direct at the same time. Why did she have to read it again, tonight of all nights? Dieter Vollger wasn't on her mind.

Gerhard Dormer was.

*

Dear Ms. Nasson -

I rote a book about prison. I've been in a few. It's about a guy (me) who gets sentenced for something he didn't do and the stuff that happens when he goes to a maximom security prison. Fights, drugs, sex, and the constant vilence and hatred. If you're not bad going in you are when you come out. The book goes over the problems of beeing released into the regular comunity, and how hard it is to ajust. If you're readers want a doze of reality, they would love to read my book. The real thing by somebodys who's been there, by someones whoes walked the walk and just not talked the talk.

Dieter Vollger.

Sighing, Chamille Nasson jotted a quick note on the bottom of the query.

Hollow Road only deals with literary submissions. I'm sorry, but this isn't the type of book we're interested in. You've sent the same query in under different names, so I understand how hard you must have worked on this. If you want someone to look at your novel, make sure you check the grammar and spelling. I wish you luck placing your book.

*

Dieter Vollger had followed Chamille Nasson for two weeks and probably knew her routine better than she did herself. She didn't have much of a social life. Didn't date. Her life was orderly: the little Jewish bakery she stopped at Wednesday mornings; the unisex salon where she had her hair touched up after work Friday; the after dinner walk with that ugly little thing she called a dog; where she parked; when she lit the candles in her bathroom for a long soak in the tub; the drinks she sipped alone in a nearby club, hoping someone would finally join her. Although she liked her job, she had a prosaic existence and a boring schedule that rarely changed. Dieter found her as easy to reel in as all the others, the ones who filled up his thickening black binder.

Chamille craved attention, but felt she wasn't attractive. Plain, quiet, almost mousy, she was the classic wall flower. Nevertheless, she refused to stay holed up in her little East Side apartment and let the world slip by. She'd been thinking and dreaming about tonight for the last two days, ever since Gerhard Dormer's first call.

Chamille had been working for *Hollow Road* for almost seven years, and was quite surprised when a man phoned from a headhunting firm in lower Manhattan. Gerhard Dormer told her that one of the largest and most prestigious houses, *Books Unlimited*, had solicited his help in getting her to come and work for them. Flustered and completely off guard, she hadn't known what to say. Chamille knew she was good at what she did, but *that* good? Although she relished her position, she knew offers like this didn't come along very often. Perhaps this was the type of challenge she needed at this time of her life. She certainly wasn't getting any younger. Besides, she didn't owe *HR* a lifelong commitment. Time marched on. It wouldn't hurt just to meet the representative and listen to his pitch, would it? The proverbial *road not taken*.

But she wasn't sure. It took two more calls before she finally agreed to meet Mr. Dormer after work on Friday. Drinks and dinner. Although he'd teased and said he wouldn't be leaving without an answer, he'd promised there'd be no aggressive, hard sell. Just an offer for a wonderful opportunity. She countered that she'd need adequate time to consider anything put on the table. Behind a sneer, Dieter Vollger agreed wholeheartedly. 'Gerhard Dormer' would give her all the time she wanted, as long as the evening ended with a "yes." She'd blushed on the other end of the line.

*

Chamille looked herself up and down in the full length mirror behind her closet door. She felt awkward and a little embarrassed. It had been so long. She almost felt sorry for herself. Age, God-damn it. But she still had a nice pair of legs, a fairly small waist, breasts that weren't too big they hadn't gone too far south yet, a face that might not launch a thousand ships but could still turn a head or two. Not too bad for forty six. Okay, forty nine—but who's counting. Shit – fifty-one, now leave it! She'd slipped on new matching black panties and bra, and had chosen her red dress with the plunging neckline. High heels, and a scarf that swung wistfully around her neck. Maybe tonight everything would change and she'd meet someone she liked. Would this be the night that changed her life? But she couldn't help feeling depressed and more than a little doubtful. She could pick out a manuscript easily enough, but not a man who might become a partner.

She finished a glass of white wine and told herself that tonight was going to be different. All she had to do was pretend. Pretend and hope.

*

Although Chamille had left room for a delayed decision, she was writhing inside at the possibility of working for *Books Unlimited*. And, if she was honest with herself, meeting Gerhard Dormer. She didn't know anything about him, but he sounded so forceful on the phone. Like he wanted *her* more than the placement. *Needed* her. And that only made him more attractive when they actually met.

They'd arranged to meet at *Barranger's*, a trendy little martini bar near Fifth and Lexington, but it was packed, so they'd grabbed a cab and settled for *the Practical Horseman*, the new club over on Ninth. Except for a few studs and fillies at the bar, *The Horseman* didn't really have anything equestrian about it at all. The four piece combo, with the young girl crooning half-forgotten lounge ballads, wasn't that bad. The distraction would help.

Chamille was more stressed and nervous than she thought she'd be, but Gerhard Dormer's constant attention put her at ease, and she liked that. And his accent. Something about him tugged at her emotions from the moment they met. No ring, which was nice. Strong and well-built, he looked pretty good in his soft, pale blue suit. Sure, he hadn't shaven too closely, and he looked a little rough around the edges. The scar kind of balanced that out. He certainly wasn't quite as polished and professional as she'd imagined for having such a high profile job, but she still found him ruggedly attractive in a bad-boy sort of way. He slouched a bit, and was undoubtedly a little self-conscious about the birthmark that marred his neck. But who knew what his story was? Just like she did with books, Chamille made it a point never to judge anyone too hastily – that's how the good ones got away.

And maybe that's what had drawn him to her in the first place. What the hell? She slid her hands slowly down her thighs, smoothing her dress out, and ordered another drink.

Halfway through her second chocolate martini, it was obvious Gerhard Dormer was more interested in talking about her than he was about the position at *Books Unlimited*. Maybe that was his style. Or maybe it wasn't. Chamille was having a little too much fun to care. She sensed his interest in her went far beyond head-hunting. *She didn't realize just how much.*

They talked over dinner, and although Chamille was unabashedly flattered, she was slightly unnerved Gerhard Dormer knew so much about her. He'd certainly done his homework – and it made her feel a little special, too. Listening to the band, their discussion about the possibility of her new position slowly faded into the background. His pitch for the placement could wait, but his need to touch her couldn't. He asked her to dance again and again. Weakened by the pulsing music, the attention, the strength of his arms, the hotness of his breath on her neck, Chamille was enthralled.

And Gerhard was patient. He waited until she left for the ladies room to spike her third drink. There'd be time for more later. He remembered the edge of the shovel blade slicing into Shirley O'Donovan's face and shivered with pleasure, then mentally watched Roland Steinberg's head and helmet roll down the hill after his burning motorcycle with glee. This one would be just as much fun.

Their meals were barely touched. Gerhard kept taking her hand and leading her up to the dance floor. It wasn't long before Chamille's thoughts began to get fuzzy. It was as if they already knew each other. Regardless of the song, they danced slowly to it, like lost lovers, Chamille boldly seductive, pressing her body hard against him, her hips against his groin. She felt him uncurl. More like *unfurl*. Her breathing deepened. It had been so long! The more they moved and swayed together the harder he got. Chamille felt his heat against her thigh, and sensed her own wetness. Image that. A man with a brain, a high class job, the most threatening cock she'd ever felt, and he was interested in *her*. What a find. Four or five dances and another spiked drink later, Chamille forgot about dinner altogether and invited him home for a nightcap. They could talk about the contract in the morning over coffee and a bagel.

*

Twenty minutes later, her drink on the living room table, Chamille was already in the shower, bending down to turn up the hot water. Steam covered the four glass walls. The little room tasted humid, like a rain forest. Gerhard came in and quietly took off his clothes. When he stepped into the enclosure they immediately melted together. Chamille slid her hands gently over Gerhard's neck, his shoulders, his back, his ass. Water coursed down her arms and legs, her face, her spine. Gerhard turned her around, wrapping his arms around her waist. The hot water pulsed against her chest making her nipples rock hard. He trailed light kisses down the side of her neck and across her shoulders, then slowly licked his way down her back, one vertebra at a time. Then it was down one leg, and slowly, gently, up the other. He licked the water droplets from her ass. He turned her around again, staring boldly, drinking her in – the perky breasts, her flat stomach, the small patch of hair between her long legs. He squatted down on his knees and started teasing her sex with kisses, licks, little bites and pulls, his breath hot, his tongue and lips always moving.

Chamille was squirming. She tilted her head back and let the water splash down over her breasts, then reached down and took a firm hold of Dieter's head, moving it how and where she needed it.

Moaning, her tongue tracing her lips, she never saw him reach down behind his foot, never noticed the light glimmer off the razor blade, never felt it rip into her skin until it was too late. It sliced through her left leg, then the right. A scream froze in the back of her throat. She reached down, helplessly trying to staunch the flow, but the blood spurted wildly against the steamed walls. Gerhard was moving up her body, catching her before she collapsed, licking the rivulets of warm blood that coursed down her skin. He reached around her, brought his body even closer, and sliced the razor through her neck. She gurgled, and her mouth filled with blood. Chamille's eyes started closing, the bloody water pouring down her throat, her stomach, between her legs. She could barely stand.

Gerhard kissed the cuts and showered in her blood.

*

Chamille was fighting her way to consciousness. It was like coming out of a deep, dreamless anesthetic sleep after surgery. She felt thick and dopey, heavy and unbalanced. A stab of fear. Somehow, from somewhere, she could hear things. She knew she had to wake up. But each time she thought she was almost free the drugs pulled her back, took her awareness away again. Caught between dreams and a kaleidoscope of sights and sounds, she finally stirred from a series of nonsensical and unrelated images. Suddenly, her face was freezing. She was sitting in a chair in her living room, naked, her body shivering as the warm water droplets quickly turned cold.

Not water. Blood.

Gagged, she couldn't even scream.

*

He was humming softly to himself. The ragged sound brought her a modicum of lucidity. This time, though, one look into his eyes told him she wasn't going to slip away again. He started talking as soon as he realized she was on the verge of wakefulness. Outside, pelting rain slashed against the window.

Gerhard – *Dieter* – started talking, his accent gone. She watched his lips move when he brought his face close to hers, but when he moved back or away, behind her, tugging on the ropes, she couldn't put all the sounds together into real words. Whenever her head nodded he grabbed her roughly by the throat and held her still. *Listen. Listen*, he kept warning her.

"The good news," he whispered, checking another knot, "is that I'm not going to rape you."

He gave the ankle rope a pull. "The bad thing is you'll wish I had."

*

Gerhard kept humming and cutting, piercing and digging. His pace quickened. He couldn't help singing that old, pathetic disco song. *What was it?* Something about shaking your *booty?*

Dieter leaned closer, smiling, finally remembering the tune.

- 322 -

Stab stab stab,
Stab stab stab,
Stab your *booody.*
Stab your *booody.*
Stab stab stab . . .

Dieter wanted to play a game. Each wound was inflicted with a purpose, a thought, a recollection, a vengeful reminder. Everything that had been said or written was worth a small stab, a gentle twist of the knife, an almost innocent slice of the razor. The marks were practically non-existent. Well, not to Chamille. Just enough to break the skin or draw blood. Another slash. A poke. A slice. Penitence. Payback.

What had one of them said?

Your grammar needs work. Computer programs come with a grammar check – use it.

A small pinprick, then he cut her again.

There must be a definable plot.

A twist of the blade just enough to open the skin.

Your writing isn't strong enough to compete in today's market.

Chamille's blood beaded over Dieter's wrists. He liked the warm-cold feeling. He drew the knife along the inside of her arm, tracing some intricate pattern only he could see. Every now and then he'd prick her skin, encouraging the tiniest of holes. Sometimes he stretched the skin without breaking it. Chamille shivered, not from the pain but from the *expectation* of the pain. When he was finished, the line curved up one arm, across her chest, and down the other. Acupuncture paths. Chamille was a pincushion. Bleeding from every site, she was covered in tiny tears, nicks and cuts that oozed blood.

You must have a dictionary tab in your program.

He gave the letter opener a slow, hard push, turning it ever so slightly, widening the wound between her breasts.

Dieter started on her back. The same marks, the same small pinpricks, the same kind of pattern, but in a different shape.

The room reeked of blood.

Still gagged, Chamille was staring to choke. The pinpricks bled faster now, tiny rivulets that trickled down her arms and back, her thighs and throat.

Crying, she shook her head.

Your characters are banal and stereotypic.

Dieter knew Chamille hadn't sent all the letters, but she was still *one of them.* When it came right down to it, they were all the same. Like lawyers. The guy who hanged the dog knew it, and so did Dieter. He leaned closer and whispered in her ear. "I felt like going to that little ivory tower of yours and ripping the tongue out of your head."

She squirmed as hard as she could but her head was spinning and the blood-drenched ropes were too tight. Through the stupefying haze of the keratin, Chamille tried to follow the pattern of the pinpricks. They weren't random. He wasn't just picking a spot and opening a wound. He was spearing her with cuts and dots that actually made sense.

He was making letters.

No sound, not with the gag. But somewhere inside she knew she was screaming.

Dieter smiled. *She knew.*

The game was 'connect the dots.'

And the dots spelled . . . *Rejection.*

*

Obviously, this wasn't Dieter's first dismemberment.

Cut into relatively small pieces, what was left of Chamille fit quite nicely into five large garbage bags, which proved to be a little lighter than Dieter anticipated while they'd danced. One less would have been hard to carry.

Dieter felt quite at home in Chamille's new Prius. Taking Bronx Park E., he stopped in a secluded part of the forest that edged the east side of the zoo, just south of the Parkside project. Dragging Chamille's body parts from the car, he carried them over to one of the places where the top of the fence leaned back into the zoo's interior. The idea was to make it almost impossible for the animals to get out. There was a wide moat directly beside the fence. Beyond that was a small but definite incline on the other side of the water so that an animal attempting to escape had to run downward before it actually made its leap upward toward freedom. The incline and the moat together, let alone the height of the fence and the barbed wire, made it virtually impossible for one of the lions, cheetahs, or wolves to escape. Besides, the animals were all penned in their own separate quarters. The system assuaged the public's fears. *If* the cages stayed locked.

But all the defensive precautions didn't make it difficult at all for someone wanting to *get in.*

*

Tonight was over-due payback time. The whole thing took one call.

Dieter had done three years in New Castle, Indiana. So had Ramone Ramirez. He'd helped Ramone twice – the second time saved his gut. Then, as fate and fortune would have it, Dieter did time near Tallahassee at Franklin, where Ramirez's brother Carlos was doing a sawbuck. The Latino gangs didn't get along very well with the black bangers. For once, Dieter had picked the right side to be on, and he'd given Carlos a sign just before he was shanked. The Ramirez brothers owed him – big time. Their cousin Ricky worked the night shift at the place Dieter needed to go. A debt paid.

*

Dieter tossed the bags into the enclosure. He draped an extra sheet across the barbed wire, donned a pair of thick gloves, and climbed the chain link fence. Just missing the nearest edge of the moat, he dropped to the ground, barely making a sound.

Someone whistled. *Ricky stepped out of the shadows.* A quick handshake. Oaths sworn.

Blood was seeping through the blankets and extra linen Dieter had used. Ricky smelled it and smiled. Dieter knew they didn't have much time. He grabbed three bags and Ricky took two. Somewhere off in the distance, a lion roared, making the hairs on Dieter's neck stand up. An elephant trumpeted a lonely call, and something, somewhere, squealed or wailed.

Dieter liked to share. They dumped one of the bags into the lion enclosure, then tossed another one down into the fenced off tiger cage. He told Ricky to leave one for the hyenas, and the jackals got the rest. God, he would have loved to be there when the keepers opened the cages in the morning.

The two men skulked back to where Dieter left Chamille Nasson's car. A parting handshake. Ricky helped Dieter get a hand-hold on the fence, held his foot, and gave him a quick push back up and onto the blanket. Dieter rolled over onto the ground. Another whistle and Ricky was gone.

Dieter scurried away into the darkness, giggling to himself. He wondered who was going to be lucky enough to get some head.

Rest in pieces.

Chapter Thirty Seven

Kincaid met Amy and Stephanie outside the emergency department main doors. He drew Amy aside and whispered something that made her frown deeper and her eyes seem even sadder. She held his arm, pulling him close, then nodded, cupped his hands in hers, and slowly, unwillingly, walked away toward the doors that led to the adjacent wing. Kincaid didn't say anything to Stephanie until they were back at the car. Carolyn's words still haunted him.

"I need some time alone, Stephanie."

"Kincaid –"

"I know you don't want me to be on my own right now, and I'm grateful you care."

And that Amy does, too. He leaned over and squeezed her hand. "But I have to think some things through by myself."

Stephanie kissed him on the cheek. "Are you –?"

"I'm sure." He couldn't even convince himself.

"What time is your appointment at the clinic?"

He frowned: he'd completely forgotten about it.

"I want to be there."

"Stephanie –"

"I want to be there."

A somber smile. How could he turn her away? "Around seven. I asked Amy to wait for you. A uniform will be here in ten minutes. They'll drop you off wherever you need to go."

"Thanks." She paused, searching for the right words and the gentlest way to say them. They didn't come, and she looked more distressed than Kincaid had seen in her in a long, long time.

*

Caught perusing a travel magazine and dreaming about what *might have been* while he scanned another query, he didn't reach for his phone until the fifth ring. "James Lamberton."

"James, it's Gail."

"Yes Ms. Meredith." He instinctively sat up straighter. "What can I do for you?"

You couldn't begin to imagine. "I'm late for an appointment with – oh, never mind, it doesn't matter. Just more legal run-around, so the sharks can justify their fees. Anyway, I'm up on Bloor Street and the traffic's a bitch."

"What do you need?"

"You're always thinking, James. There's a folder on my desk with a lawyer's letter paper-clipped to the front. Can you get it for me?"

"No problem."

"Good. I should be back in about twenty minutes. Have it ready."

"Should I meet you out front?"

"No. I don't want to be bothered coming inside. Everyone will want something and I don't have time. Meet me downstairs."

"I'll be there." As he hung up, James glanced back down at a picture of a seaside pool and bar. Half-clad women lounged on the beach and palm trees swayed in a gentle breeze that tugged puffs of clouds across a deep blue sky. He sighed, shelved his dreams again, and walked toward the elevators. He tried to imagine the *click clack click clack* of the keyboards as melting ice cubes tinkling in rum-drenched glasses, but it didn't work.

*

Gail Meredith sat stiffly in her car. She hated waiting for anything, and kept glancing anxiously around the parking garage and checking her watch. She looked down into her purse and made sure the mace was within easy reach. Five minutes passed. Eight. Where the hell was he?

A sudden knock at her window startled her and made her jump. Caster leered through the glass, pleased she'd been frightened. He'd crept up from behind the car, and Gail chided herself for not picking him up in the side view. That was the kind of mistake that could cost her her life. She took a deep breath, steadied herself, and unlocked her door.

Caster leaned back against the Audi parked beside her and pointedly looked Gail up and down as she stepped from the car. He grinned salaciously at the momentary flash of her exposed thighs. Gail pretended not to notice, but still felt her neck muscles tense. Could she really trust him? They were alone, and if anything happened, it would be several minutes before someone responded to her screams. What if James was late? A lot could happen in a couple of minutes. Just ask Turner. Or McCabe.

"Erik Caster," she said, staring back.

"Ms. Meredith." He slurred the 'Ms.' sarcastically.

Seeing Caster face to face was very different than listening to him rant and rave on her cell. Gail's heart raced and her palms were lined with sweat, but she did her utmost to appear in complete control. It was a talent she'd fostered over the years that had always served her well in the sordid world of back-room meetings and under-the-table business transactions. She knew she couldn't afford to let Caster see any trace of vulnerability, any crack in her stoic armor, where he could strike. He had to know she couldn't be intimidated.

"I'll get right to the point."

"You do that."

"I read your book. *Inside*. It was a lot better and more insightful than I anticipated, especially after what Devlin Turner told me."

Caster's lips curled at the name. "Bull shit. That's not what you fucking said before."

"As I explained on the phone, that's on Turner. I'd never read a page of your manuscript before."

Diffusing the stress and the tension, Gail offered Caster a thin cigar. She lit his, then her own. She continued talking, her voice quiet and reassuring.

"I'm not saying it's perfect by any means. It needs work, there's no doubt about that."

She watched a flame of hate flicker in Caster's eyes.

"But so does every other script I've ever published. You don't really think a book comes in and we just go ahead and print it, do you?"

Caster looked uncertain. "No, I guess not."

"We're not a vanity press or some little pay-as-you-go ego booster. We have to make sure that everything's perfect: tense, grammar, syntax, spelling, plot, characterization. We have whole departments of other writers who do that."

Caster frowned. He hadn't really thought about it.

"Turner sent your book to an editorial company, didn't he?"

The anger resurfaced. "That was a fucking scam."

"Yes, you might be right. But I'm just beginning to understand how Devlin actually worked." Gail Meredith blew two perfect smoke circles into the air. Her lips toyed with the end of her cigar just enough to make Caster start to unfurl in his pants.

"But he was correct about requiring professional editing. As a writer, you must realize how difficult it is to amend your own work."

Caster shrugged. Gail could tell by the look in his eyes he liked being called a writer. And liked watching her swirl the spit on the end of her cigar. Wait until she changed it to '*author*'. This was going to be easier than she'd thought.

"Writers write, Erik. May I call you Erik? But other people better qualified should always review their work. Do you think we publish Nurakis' books right from his manuscript?"

Caster was smoking too hard and the embers of his cigar burned a bright red. "I don't know."

"Well, we don't. Your book has potential, Erik. I can see that now. Yet it still needs extra work. And believe me, not all editorial agencies are there to scam you."

Caster spit a wad of tobacco onto the ground at Gail Merediths' feet. She smiled condescendingly and ran her tongue over her lips.

"Your story is a fascinating exploration into a normally unseen world, Erik. True prison life, from a real criminal's perspective."

Gail paused, studied her cigar, then stared straight into Caster's eyes.

"I think it should be published. And I'd like to be the one who does it."

Although he did his best not to show any hint of anxiousness or surprise, Gail heard Caster's breath catch. She practically felt it.

"I can help you a great deal, Erik." Gail let the thought sink in, the lure catch. She lowered her voice and held out a world of possibilities to him the way travelling salesmen in the Old West waved the magical elixirs of life under so many eager eyes.

"I could do the promotional roll-out myself."

Caster raised an eyebrow.

"Book signings, radio shows. Perhaps a book tour."

She tapped a long, gnarled ash from the end of her cigar and smiled inwardly. Caster had forgotten his cigar completely and it dangled down at his side, coloring his pants with ash.

"What's the catch?" he finally muttered.

"The catch?" Gail tried to look nonplussed. It didn't work. Caster's eyes narrowed into a probing, unsettling glare.

Gail Meredith took a quick look around the garage to make sure they were still alone, then leaned closer. "It's not a catch, Erik. It's a proposition."

Caster breathed heavily. He liked having her this close. Tasting her perfume. Her lips toying with the end of the cigar. All he had to do was reach out and . . . No, he had to control himself, fight the urge. *Until later.* "What kind of proposition?"

"I publish '*Inside'* and set up a promotional tour, along with readings, interviews, magazine spots, the whole nine yards."

He looked skeptical. Excited, but skeptical. "And what do I have to do, Gail? Mind if I call you Gail?"

She stamped her cigar out with her shoe, and slowly blew a lazy cloud of smoke into the air. "Something you're very, very good at, Erik."

Caster leaned back, widened his stance, and crossed his arms over his chest. "I'm listening."

"I know about McCabe. The researcher found in the alley."

Caster didn't speak.

"And you seemed to have had quite a bit of fun with Turner."

"That fuck had it coming. Get to the point."

Gail had done a lot of things before, a lot of things she'd been afraid to do the first time. But like everything else, it got easier. She took a deep breath and tried to slow the frantic pulse of her heart.

"I need you to do one more."

Erik Caster didn't move. He nodded and uncrossed his arms as a vindictive sneer crept across his face.

"Who?"

"Does it matter?"

Caster shook his head.

"He's in the industry. So you just have to make it look like the others. The police are certain they were murdered by a disgruntled writer they cheated or rejected. Ram some paper down his throat, a stitch here, a stitch there, and bleed him out. Killing a publisher would only fuel their suspicions. Same MO, same motive, same kind of victim. Voilà."

"A publisher?"

"A rival. They can't nail the other two on you, Erik, so I'm sure one more won't be a problem. I'll make certain you have an air-tight alibi, and the police will still be looking for a serial killer who hates the publishing industry for rejecting his work."

Caster rubbed a hand thoughtfully over the stubble lining his chin. "So I do this prick . . ."

"And your book gets a promotional roll-out most authors would die for."

They both grinned at her choice of words.

"It's one thing being a writer, Erik," Gail whispered. "It's something else to be an *author.*"

Caster's eyes sparkled. "When?"

Caught. The lure of fame had reeled him in. "As soon as possible. Tonight would be perfect."

"Tonight?" He kicked his cigar away. "No fucking way."

"I've arranged a private meeting with my . . . rival. He knows we need to talk. But I won't be showing up and he'll be all alone, so you shouldn't have any problem."

"I need more time."

"And I've got my own agenda."

Caster was sweating. "I can't do it that fast. I need a couple of days. Two nights from now."

Gail deliberated for a moment. "Okay. I'll tell him something came up and we can't meet until Thursday. I'll make sure everything's ready for you. But I can't wait any longer than that." Garth Danielson's lawyers at *Excalibur* were already circling like underfed sharks. It wouldn't be long before Gail was nothing more than a remora, floating along and sucking and feeding at Danielson's side.

Caster watched her eyes. "I want a real contract."

"You'll have it the next day. Signed, sealed and delivered, with a nice advance for good faith."

Caster's eyes narrowed as he smiled. What was two more days? He'd be famous and rich in a month. "No problem, partner."

"Good." Gail took a quick glance around the parking lot – she knew they wouldn't be alone for long. "I need you do one more thing to help me set this up."

She stared at the bank of elevators. "But if you fucking dare to get carried away, you're history. So's your book."

*

James was humming the refrain from *Margaritaville* and thinking about *searching for my long lost shaker of salt* as the elevator descended, but the song died in his throat the moment the doors opened and he stepped into the garage. He dropped the folders he'd retrieved from Meredith's office, yelled, and broke into a quick run. He called out again as he picked up speed, half jumping and half rolling across the hood of a car blocking his way.

"Stop! Stop right there!"

Two rows over in her double-spaced spot, Gail Meredith was beside her Benz. She wasn't alone. A man held her tightly by the throat. Her head was being pinned down against the car's roof and her body was arched back painfully against the driver's door. Thrashing from side to side, she flailed wildly at her attacker, which enflamed the man even more. He pulled one hand back and was ready to punch her in the face just as James shouted again.

"Gail!"

He careened around the last car at the end of the row and raced toward her. The man cursed and threw Gail to the ground. Keeping low, he took off toward the exit ramp, adroitly dodging through the rows and zigzagging between the parked cars. When James reached Gail Merediths' car, he'd completely lost sight of her attacker.

Gail was on the ground, slumped against the door. Her eyes had the wild sheen of shock and she was gasping for air. She touched her throat with quivering hands, then ran her fingers over her face, searching for blood. Her left eye was a little swollen. Her blouse was torn, a sleeve ripped. The strap on her purse was broken and the contents had spilled onto the ground. James pushed it away and sank down beside her.

"Gail? Gail, are you okay?"

She looked up at James, confused, as if she was seeing him for the very first time.

"Gail? It's me. James."

He smoothed the hair back from her face and quickly looked for any bumps or scratches.

Her throat was bruised red, and James could see the faint traces of the man's fingers on the back of her neck. When he said her name again, the first hint of recognition flickered in her eyes. She was barely breathing.

"James?"

"Yes, it's me. Are you okay?"

"I think so." She glanced at the scattered papers.

"Here, let me help you up."

James tucked his hands beneath her arms and gently lifted her to her feet. She reached out and tried to steady herself against the car. "My purse?"

"It's right here, Gail. There's nothing to worry about." James quickly gathered up her things and shoved them back inside her purse.

"She glanced around uneasily. "A man came up behind me –"

"Shhh. I know. I saw him. But he's gone now, so let's get you upstairs. You need to sit down. I'll call the police. And you should have someone look at your neck."

Gail gently touched her throat.

"Can you walk?"

She nodded, but a glint of uncertainty dulled her eyes. She looked like she was afraid to move.

"Here, let me take your arm."

Stumbling slightly and still groggy, Gail took James's arm and let him guide her past the rows of cars toward the exit sign. She kept looking back over her shoulder. James did, too. Gail exhaled a heavy, breath-filled sigh when they reached the bank of elevators and one set of doors winched open. She slumped back against the rear wall and closed her eyes.

She whispered anxiously, her voice strained and hoarse. "Did you see who it was?"

James nodded and mentally pictured the man's face in the second before he fled. "It was that puke, Erik Caster."

Chapter Thirty Eight

Led down the hallway by the elfish young girl with the mushroom cut, Kincaid wasn't surprised by the quiet unease that gripped *Meredith House*. The guards looked tense – edgy and on heightened alert. Subdued, everyone cloistered in their little cubicles went about their business with automated indifference. It was like being at a wake; dreary, with a stifling sense of anticipatory anxiety. Darla wasn't her usual jovial self. After a hurried knock and even faster glance inside, she backed away without a word or pop of her gum.

The company nurse was completing a perfunctory examination of Ms. Meredith when Kincaid walked in. He took a chair and watched the woman pack her things into a small black carrying case, but he was really studying Gail. *A remarkable woman.* She'd recovered quickly, and any trace of fear about what just happened had melted away. The trauma was gone. So was the shock. It gave him an uneasy feeling that everything was a little too neat.

The nurse wound the blood pressure cuff into a roll. "You'll have to take it easy for a while, Ms. Meredith. And that bruise –"

"I'll be fine." She stared at Kincaid testily. "Why are the police never around when you really need them?"

The nurse tried again. "You should have a doctor look –"

"I understand what you've told me, Evans. You don't need to repeat yourself."

The woman gulped down a retort and looked at Kincaid. "She appears fine. No breaks or lacerations. Her neck might give her a bit of trouble. She was pushed back pretty hard."

"He was fucking trying to choke me to death. Of course it was bloody well pushed back."

"A cold liniment may help. It will probably feel worse over the next few days."

"Great," her employer sighed petulantly.

"You were lucky, Ms. Meredith," the nurse said, snapping her bag closed. "If Mr. Lamberton hadn't come along when he did, there's no telling what might have happened. Fortunately, the man didn't have time to do any serious damage."

The nurse nodded at Kincaid and quietly left. Gail stared angrily at the door as it closed. "*'You were lucky, Ms. Meredith,'*" she parroted in the woman's sterile, nasal tone. "Lucky my ass."

"Not everyone escapes an attack like that," Kincaid suggested a little coldly. "Especially in the recesses of an underground parking lot. You really are fortunate someone happened by."

Gail offered a condescending nod. It was a sobering thought. Already bored, Gail started massaging her neck and asked Kincaid what he wanted.

"Were you leaving the building?"

"No, I'd just come in. I'd asked one of the readers to bring down some legal papers I needed so I didn't have to bother coming up to my office. I won't do that again." She opened a desk drawer and took out her cigars, paused, then put them back.

"How long had you been there before you were attacked?"

She shrugged. "I don't know. Five minutes."

"Did you see him coming?"

"Don't be ridiculous Kincaid. If I had, I wouldn't have gotten out of my bloody car."

"Did he say anything?"

"Nothing."

"Not even after he grabbed you?"

"I said *no.*"

"Did you know who it was?"

"Not until he actually touched me. I wasn't facing him until then."

"Did you hit him back in any way? Scratch him, punch him, leave any kind of mark?"

Gail shook her head.

"Did he take anything?"

A frown. "Not that I'm aware of. James Lamberton picked up my things. I only had my purse and a small briefcase. I think James dropped some folders by the elevators."

"And he definitely didn't say anything at all?"

"How many more times do I have to tell you? The piece of shit didn't say anything. He grabbed me and started choking me."

Kincaid stared back silently. "Are you going to press charges this time?"

"Of course I am."

"Good. And your nurse is right," he said, standing and turning toward the door. "You should have your physician look at your throat."

"Sure, I'll get right on it. Anything else?"

Kincaid shook his head. "We shouldn't have any problem picking him up. Thanks for your time."

Ms. Meredith didn't bother looking up. She was already texting.

Kincaid watched her for a moment, and looked at the nascent bruise on her neck. He was sure she was lying.

But why?

*

The leaves on the few lonely trees outside the office tower scattered with the wind.

Gail Meredith troubled him, Ryan made him desperately sad, Stephanie ignited the deepest desires in his heart, Amy confused his feelings, the blood at Turner's house made him sick, and the pain in his temples and back pounded viciously. Yet his lips curled into a small smile when he checked his watch. He expected Richard Barclay to be early for work, and here he was, lumbering down from the corner bus stop thirty minutes before his shift. Barclay wasn't punctual, just mildly obsessive. As usual, he was oblivious to the world and was immersed in an animated conversation with himself. His lips waggled feverishly, but his voice was silent. Whatever he was talking about smothered everything around him and commanded his undivided attention.

"Barclay."

The man bolted to a sudden stop, instinctively cowering against the wall and shielding his face with his hands. His cheeks flushed when he realized who it was.

"Shit, you could've given me a heart attack," Barclay mumbled defensively. "I thought you were a mugger."

"Life in the big city, Mr. Barclay. No wonder people are so stressed. Got a minute?"

Barclay squinted with uncertainty.

"It's here or inside," Kincaid said impatiently. "I thought you might want to protect your privacy."

Barclay inched back toward the wall as people hustled by. Each time the front doors of the office complex opened another glut of prosaic suits were expunged onto the street. Same shirt, same tie, same black shoes, same face.

"What do you want?"

Kincaid studied Barclay's face and let him think. He couldn't picture the thin, rakish man standing awkwardly beside him to have the strength and ferociousness to have executed the things done to Turner. And McCabe. But then again, Kincaid knew that rage and hate had the power to unleash the horrors that lived in the darkest corners of our soul. Especially a writer perched on the edge of the abyss. The thought flew by: what would he do to someone who hurt Ryan? Or Stephanie? Amy?

"Your office said you were working the early shift. I went to the Metro Resource Centre and spoke to Mrs. Turecki, the head librarian. She says she knows you quite well, that you're always researching something or other. She confirmed you're polite and quiet, and that you always return materials on time."

"And that's a crime?" It didn't come out quite as forcefully as Barclay would have liked. He scratched his little beard, deftly avoiding the glances of the people hustling past.

"Of course not. But Mrs. Turecki also told me she's sure you weren't at the library the night Turner was murdered."

"I was."

"She didn't see you."

"So? Hundreds of people use the Centre at night. I – I didn't need anything that evening. I just wanted a quiet place to work, that's all. I didn't have to go to the reference desk, so she wouldn't have seen me. Or she just forgot."

Kincaid watched Barclay's eyes dart back and forth and let the anxiousness fester. "Mrs. Turecki doesn't seem like the type of person who forgets things, Mr. Barclay."

Silence.

"Where were you that night?"

"At the library." A group of clerical workers hurried by towards the subway. A blast of wind blew out of the tunnel. "I was working on some notes."

"What time did you get there?"

Barclay had to think. "Around four."

"What time did you leave?"

"Just before closing, which is nine thirty during the week. The bus ride's about half an hour, which gets me here twenty minutes before the late shift."

"Did any of the other staff see you?"

Barclay was getting agitated. "How the hell should I know?"

"Did you talk to anyone?"

"I don't remember. It was almost a month ago. But – but I don't think so."

"Are there computer terminals at the Resource Centre?"

Barclay looked momentarily confused. "Sure."

"Do they have Internet access?"

"Obviously. Why?"

"Wouldn't you need someone to help you log on to a computer?"

"No. I have my own card."

Silence. Kincaid tried to visualize Barclay sitting down at Turner's desk and pushing a pen through his eye. Or making him gag on wads of paper before painstakingly sewing the man's lips together. Could he actually have been able to smash McCabe's mouth into oblivion? Hitting someone is one thing – hammering them to death after they're already unconscious takes something else.

"Turners' housekeeper told us she saw someone in the driveway a couple of hours before he was murdered."

Barclay was beginning to sweat. The front doors of the building kept revolving, spewing more weary, drawn out workers out onto the street. Half of them were bumping into each other because they were already attached to their phones, thumbing through apps or playing games.

"I need to know something about your book."

"What?"

"Was it finished when you sent it to Devlin Turner?"

"As finished as I could make it."

"Did Turner decide to have a serious look at it right away?"

"No, he just wanted the first three chapters. He wrote back later and said I should send the manuscript to an editorial company that would clean it up. Correct the grammar, tighten the plot, and make it flow better. Things like that."

"Did you send it to 'The Book Doctor'?"

Barclay was surprised. "Yeah. How did you know?"

"Do you remember who worked on your script?"

"No. Someone who worked for Michael Cormier. He sent me a fairly detailed letter about what I could do to make the book better – more stylistic and concise. Why?"

"Because we've recently ascertained that someone who worked for Mr. Cormier's agency has also been murdered."

The color drained from Barclay's face. Vigorously shaking his head and backing away, he managed to blurt out a mumbled reply. "I didn't have anything to do with him. Him, or Turner."

"You said 'him'."

"What?"

"You said you didn't have anything to do with 'him'. How did you know it was a man?"

Shaking, Barclay self-consciously shoved his hands down into his pockets. "I just assumed it was, that's all."

"I see. And you're absolutely certain no one can corroborate your story that you were at the library the night Turner died?"

"Not that I can think of. But that doesn't mean I killed him."

"Mr. Turner's housekeeper got a fairly good look at the person she said was lingering around the house, Richard." Kincaid looked the man up and down. "He seems to have been about your height and build. No really distinguishing features, and no facial hair, from what she recalled." Kincaid looked at Barclay's chin. "The goatee looks new. It hasn't completely filled in yet. When did you shave the other one off?"

Barclay nervously chewed at his bottom lip. He spoke quietly, slowly enunciating each word through clenched teeth. "*I – was – at – the – library.*"

Kincaid waited for a group of secretaries to pass. They were all talking at once. A tall brunette smiled at Kincaid, then giggled to her friends. "You said 'wanted', before."

"What?"

"You said you 'wanted' your book published. Not *want*. Have you found a publisher?"

"No," Barclay stammered. "Not yet."

"But you're still hoping to?"

"Yes." He couldn't stop shaking.

"It's been a dream for a long time, hasn't it?"

Barclay sighed and looked down at his feet. Remembered all the negative responses. The years of frustration. The envelopes with the rejection letters from some first reader who couldn't put two lines together. "Yes it has."

"And just how far would you go to make that dream a reality, Richard?"

He mumbled something toward his shoes.

"I beg your pardon?"

Barclay looked up, his eyes wide with anger. "I said, 'I'd do whatever I had to'."

Chapter Thirty Nine

Back at the House, Kincaid parked underground. He couldn't stop thinking about Ryan. The images were disturbing and haunting: the tubes, the iv's, the monitors, the white sheets framing his body a little too tightly, Carolyn leaning into his side and whispering between tears. Amy had left a message on his cell saying she had some new information he needed to see as soon as possible. If it had been about Ryan she would have said so. Nothing was more important right now than his little friend.

Coming up the back stairs, Kincaid met Lieutenant Davis on the second floor landing. Hurrying down to the garage, Davis had a bulging stack of files under one arm, and his briefcase dangling from the other. He looked like he had a million things on his mind, but came to an abrupt stop when he saw Kincaid. He frowned uneasily.

"Clocking out early, Lieutenant?"

"No. Meeting with the brass."

"The swelling's really gone down. How does it feel now?"

"Better, thanks. With any luck I'll be eating solids tonight. I've lost almost ten pounds. I heard what happened. How's Ryan?"

"He's trying his best. So's his mother."

"If there's anything –"

"Thanks."

Davis paused and stared at his friend. The "*boss*" was back. "I left a few messages for you upstairs. From your doctor. Three of them. And one from yesterday."

"Thanks."

"'*Thanks* shit.' He wants you to *call him back* this time. So do *I*."

"I will, LT."

Kincaid went to take a step, but Davis blocked his way. There was a genuine look of concern in his eyes. "Do it, K. He said he's had a problem reaching you. I warned you from the start you follow my rules or you're out."

Kincaid nodded apologetically. "Understood, Sir."

"And that's not all." Davis readjusted the folders. "I just called you."

"I was walking the underground, thinking a couple of scenarios through. You must have caught me between phones."

Davis looked suspicious. "Where's your cell?"

Kincaid patted his pockets. "I guess I left it in the car."

He'd known Davis for a long time, and hated lying to his friend. But he didn't want to tell him a headache had resurfaced with his back pain. It came with a blinding tenacity that made him so weak and dizzy he thought he was going to be sick. He'd leaned over the car for several minutes before the nausea passed and he felt well enough to walk. His steps had been slow and unsteady.

Davis was skeptical. "You better not be shitting me, Kincaid." He closed his eyes and exhaled a heavy sigh. He needed him now more than ever. "Thing is, you've got another one."

"*Murder?*"

"Afraid so. Garth Danielson."

"From *Excalibur Books*?"

"One and the same. How do you know him?"

Kincaid explained the connection between Danielson's company and *Meredith House.*

"*Excalibur* seems to be positioning itself for a take-over bid, although the timing isn't the best for them. Evidently they want to buy Gail right out."

Davis looked troubled. "Did Turner have anything serious to do with him?"

"I can't say for sure. But he was pitching more contracts to Danielson's company for the last year or so. Moving some new writers with potential away from *Meredith House.*"

"So fucking find out." Davis tried to slow his breathing down. "Sorry."

"No problem. Same MO?"

"Apparently. Everything's on your desk. Richardson and MacKenzie have already been briefed so they can fill you in."

Kincaid glanced at the papers Davis was carrying. "Is that what the brass wants you for?"

"Partly. Gail pulls a lot of weight downtown. Do what you can. As soon as you can."

Davis moved out of Kincaid's way and started back down the stairs. He stopped again after two steps.

"And Kincaid?"

"Yes?"

"You sure you're up for this? I don't want either of us to hang."

Kincaid nodded. "Forget the rope."

"Call your doctor. And make sure MacKenzie and Stephanie are stuck to your side with Velcro or you won't be working the case." He didn't wait for a reply.

Garth Danielson. Shit. Nice message. The only one he'd been hoping for was something from the hospital. Or the *Gazette*. Even the morgue. But not something about another murder. An agent, a researcher, and a publisher. *Who was next?*

Kincaid sighed, turned, and walked up another flight. He stopped when he reached the next landing, confused and chagrined. *Was he hearing music? Where was it coming from?* Suddenly, the stairwell seemed obnoxiously bright, and he had the debilitating feeling his knees had become disjointed from the rest of his legs. He tried to speak, to blink the blitz of pain away, but his calves were melting and he started slipping down the wall. Before he realized what was happening, the curtain inched down and the darkness descended.

Chapter Forty

Debbie Michaels, homicide's senior secretary, met Kincaid at the door. "Ah, Detective, glad you're back. I'm sorry our paths didn't cross earlier. LT wanted me to give –"

He nodded at the papers in her hand. "Is that about Danielson?"

"You *know* already?"

"I passed him on my way in."

Just before I passed out.

The middle aged woman gave him the notes. Just back from a much needed vacation, she was nicely tanned and relaxed. Both effects would fade soon enough. "There's not much here, I'm afraid. They only found the body a couple of hours ago."

"I'll go as soon as I can."

"I left your messages on your desk."

"Thanks. Is Richardson in?"

"No."

"Then would you page Sergeant Mackenzie, please?"

In his office, Kincaid took two painkillers. After a moment's hesitation, he took two more. There were seven messages tucked under the phone: one from Stephanie, one from Davis, three from his doctor, and two from Brent Jacobs. He frowned. Why would Jacobs need to call him? Strange. He'd worry about that later. He was more concerned about what had just happened in the stairwell. He hadn't had a headache like that in ages – the one by the car paled hopelessly in comparison. Another one could jeopardize everything. He'd have to tell Amy. Stephanie, too. That would have to be later, too. As he scanned the preliminary reports about Danielson from the first officers on the scene, he dialed Stephanie's number. Busy.

There was a knock at the door. "Come." No time for niceties. It was Amy.

"You heard?"

"From Davis. I saw him in the garage."

She took a seat and studied his face. "What's the matter?"

"I've got another dead body on my hands and you ask me what's the matter?"

She ignored his tone. "No. I mean what's the matter with *you*?"

"I'm sorry, Sergeant. Just tense."

"Kincaid –"

"Not now, Amy." He looked up into her eyes. Thoughtful and expressive, they'd always drawn him in. Relaxed him. "What do we know about Danielson?"

"Not much more than what you have from LT. CSU is still there. The only thing I know for sure is that it's pretty brutal."

"Brutal? Tell that to Turner."

"This might be worse. Reports say the scene is absolutely horrific. One of the first responders booked off the rest of his shift."

Kincaid remembered how rough Amy had found the morgue, but needed her to try. "Are you up for a walk-through?"

Amy took a deep breath and nodded.

"You don't have to. I can see if Richar – "

"No. I'll do it."

"Don't push. Just do what you can."

He paused, watched her body language. Ryan's image punctured his thoughts. "You drive." He tossed her the keys and tried Stephanie's number again. She picked up on the first ring.

"I tried you earlier but –"

"Garth Danielson's been murdered."

"My God."

"Do you want us to pick you up?"

"I'll be out in front of the building in ten minutes."

"I know I might be out of line," Amy said softly. "But are *you* up for this Kincaid?"

He stared back, his face blank. She was perceptive alright. *Should he tell her? No.*

"I have to be. Let's go."

*

Amy swung off the Gardiner and left the jammed cars and angry motorists behind. But this was just as bad. City construction: it never stopped. Orange barrier cones cut three lanes down to two, then one, making her merge into another stagnant line. Turning along Adelaide, a red light stopped her at Spadina. Circling the sidewalk on a pair of in-line skates, a boy raised his squeegee like a sword. He scooted toward the car the instant Kincaid waved. His hair was braided halfway down his back and his chest and arms were covered in tattoos. Two white patches were still untouched, waiting for ink.

While the windows were cleaned, Kincaid picked up the explanation he'd been giving Amy and Stephanie as they crawled off the ramp.

"Cecelia. Her husband is Ralston Tantor. He's a physician and professor. He also works as a consultant to home health care facilities to examine ways to improve their general overall quality of assistance."

"Busy guy," Stephanie agreed. "But he's not the coroner now?"

"He can't be."

"What happened?" Amy glanced at Kincaid. It was a story he'd never shared before.

Kincaid paid the squeegee kid just before the light changed. He saluted him with his wiper.

"He was one of our finest coroners. Ralston had that special knack, that innate sense you couldn't teach, to know when he had to revisit something, or take a look at something deeper. He was always looking outside the box. His colleagues teased him and called him the 'psychic pathologist.'"

Silence.

"And?" Amy prodded.

"And one day, I'd partnered with a rookie so I could finish his evaluation. We heard there was a domestic in one of the housing complexes on Jane Street. The uniforms were there, but I'd dealt with the couple before, and I thought we'd swing by and try to quiet everything down. But things changed fast. As we were pulling up dispatch said the guy had shot his wife, wounded both officers, and was off and running. The ambulance arrived just as we were making the corner. One officer was down: his partner was suffering from a shoulder injury. The man's wife was on the front lawn, bleeding heavily."

"How terrible," Stephanie said softly.

"Ralston just happened to be on his way back to the House after finishing up another coroner's call when he picked up the info on his scanner. He veered back to our location to see if he could help. We didn't know he was on his way."

Kincaid paused while Amy wheeled around the corner.

"We started setting up the crime scene, called for back-up, and instigated a house to house for the husband just as Ralston arrived."

He sighed. "The husband hadn't gone far. He was hiding on a rooftop across the street. Ralston and I were both bending down over the woman's body when the shots rang out, pinging off the sidewalk and the metal rungs of a fence right next to us. I knew the shots were coming from above and behind, but I couldn't get a bead on the shooter. I grabbed Ralston, yanked him over to the curb, and pulled him down between two parked cars. That's when I saw he was bleeding."

"He hadn't cried out?"

"He was still in shock. I don't think he even knew he'd been hit."

Amy slipped in front of an idling bus. "It was bad, wasn't it?"

"Two in the wrist and one through his palm. His hand was shattered so badly they had to amputate."

"Oh God."

"Why did the guy shoot him?"

Kincaid turned around and looked at Stephanie, his eyes heavy with the sadness of the memory. "He just wanted to kill a cop. He was aiming at me."

"Any particular reason?" Amy wondered.

"Do they ever need one?" Kincaid sighed. "I know he misses the morgue. But Ralston's one of the universities' top lecturers, and his expertise has helped hundreds of surgeons improve their skills."

"And his wife became one of the coroners?"

"Odd, right? Cecelia was in research, but she applied for the position before Ralston was out of the hospital. She wanted to help keep him involved. I'm sure they go over every case together. She doesn't have Ralston's special gift, but she's very good at what she does. Cecelia's a little on the eccentric side and has a weird sense of humor, but I think that's her defensive safeguard for the work. And just like Ralston, she has a level of empathy you don't usually see in a coroner. Just don't use any abbreviation of her name. She really hates that."

Amy wound her way along Castlefield until she hit Elm, then followed Glen Road down into the heart of Rosedale. It was one of the older and more prestigious sections of Toronto, a patriarchal throwback where name, financial worth, position and renown were the criterion everyone was measured by. Or condemned. Like Mayfair in London or Westmount in Quebec, the hidden enclave of majestic homes and august mansions was a little world unto itself, where trash was still picked up at the rear of the houses and foreign nannies met visitors at the front door with apprehensive smiles and downcast eyes.

Amy weaved through a labyrinth of tree lined streets framed with stately havens, well-tended gardens, upscale automobiles, and ancient elms that intertwined branches over the road. A left, two quick rights, and then she saw the cruisers and subdued commotion at the end of the street. Kincaid glanced up at the nearby houses – phones would be ablaze with the fiery potential of scandal. Curtains were parted in several residences, but no one ventured out to take a closer look. *That* simply wasn't *done*.

Tires crunching over the gravel driveway, Sergeant MacKenzie pulled to a stop under a canopied entrance way. Kincaid greeted several officers by name as he walked up the stone steps and under the portico. No one was smiling. Someone he didn't recognize was leaning against the wall being sick.

Kincaid stopped at the door and turned back to Stephanie. "You don't have to come in," he whispered. "Every crime scene is different, and each one can affect you in a multitude of ways you can't anticipate."

"I understand. But I'd like to see what we're up against."

Her stance told Kincaid cautioning her any more was futile. He glanced at Amy. She was breathing slowly and deeply.

"Are you okay?"

She nodded and took out her notepad. Her stomach growled. They donned personal protective equipment: disposable gloves, shoe covers, hairnets, masks, and gowns that were offered by a young man at the front door who seemed fixated on the contents of a sealed plastic bag.

Deceptively modest from the outside, the interior of the house was spacious and well-appointed. A large chandelier hung demurely over the central hallway, highlighting a running fountain and small natural pond that dominated the foyer. Lilies floated peacefully on the water. On either side of the pond, an oak staircase wound its way up to the second and third floors. A suit of dull, gunmetal gray armor stood stoically off to the side.

The main hall was lined with ornately framed paintings that continued upstairs, and every available nook and cranny offered some unique piece of sculpture or exorbitantly overpriced *object d'art*. Kincaid recognized several pieces and nodded appraisingly. Whatever other characteristics defined the owner, he had a refined taste in art. All the rooms off the vestibule were screened with heavy wooden pocket doors.

A thick, overwhelming stench of blood strangled Kincaid's senses the deeper he walked into the house. *Thick* blood. *Raw* blood. *Splattered* blood.

Scratching out information in a notebook, a young man immediately approached Kincaid. Short and compact, he had a thick neck, almost colorless eyes, and teeth that seemed too big for his mouth.

Kincaid shook the man's hand. "Crandell." He introduced Stephanie and Amy, but the detective barely mumbled a greeting. His face was blanched white, his lips pale blue.

"You okay?"

Crandell tried to nod. "Been in yet?"

"No."

He glanced uneasily at the study, then back up at his senior officer. "It's a fucking mess, sir."

Crandell cleared his throat with a couple of dry, hacking coughs. "Garth Danielson. Fifty six. Lived here alone."

"'Moe' to his friends," Kincaid added. "Although no one is really clear about the etymology of the moniker."

"You know him?"

"Not personally. He owned *Excalibur Books*."

"The big publishing house on Bay Street?"

"That's the one."

"Well, it seems as though –." Looking back towards the study, Crandell lost the composure he'd been trying to maintain. "Sorry sir. But I've got to get –"

Kincaid touched him lightly on the shoulder. "Take a walk, get some air. We'll go over your notes later."

Crandell closed his book and hurried down the hall.

Stephanie's trepidation soared with her anxiousness. Notepad ready, Amy's hands were trembling so badly she thought she'd broken her pen. She took a deep breath and followed Kincaid to the study.

When he slid the pocket door into the recessed slot, Kincaid gagged.

A combination study and office, the room was larger than he expected. The walls were covered in a deep, rich mahogany paneling that would have effused an inviting sense of warmth any other time. Ornate etchings framed the door, and florid, intricate designs were carved into the wood throughout the room. The ceiling was deceptively high, and the slightly curved dome was adorned with a hand painted fresco of a Renaissance scene. An expansive desk framed by oversized leather tub chairs dominated the far wall. Two easy chairs faced a corner fireplace, and another suit of armor, this one French and smaller and more highly polished than the one poised in the foyer, guarded the hearth.

The CSU team was quietly going about their various jobs. An older man dressed in full whites who was on his way out reminded them to make sure that nothing, absolutely nothing, was touched or moved. He was covered in blood.

Following Kincaid, Amy and Stephanie barely managed to make it past the door.

All the usual office amenities were arranged along the wall adjacent to the desk: a fax machine, computer, recharging laptop, printer, iPod, tablet, and a multi-lined telephone console. A lovely, quiet space to relax or work in.

If it hadn't been for all the blood. It felt like the entire room was *bleeding*.

It was *everywhere*. Practically the entire room was defaced with copious stains and smears. Garish splotches adorned the walls, and splattered dollops decorated the floor around the desk. There was a large, gelled streak down the wall behind the chair, and dark black rivulets had congealed on the keyboard. Blood, torn flesh, tattered bits of muscle, bone, and sinew. Even the suit of armor was flecked with black streaks and blotches. The stench numbed Kincaid's senses, forcing his fear back down with the bile.

Kincaid looked slowly around. The room had been methodically ransacked. The office was littered with bloodstained files and loose papers. Books yanked from shelves were scattered across the floor. All the desk drawers were upended and piled on top of each other. One of the chairs was knocked over, a leg snapped off, and most of the desk had been swept clean. A poker from the fireplace was sticking out from the shattered front of the laptop monitor like a spear. It was as if the whole room had been turned upside down and shaken, like one of those little snow globes, covering the miniature world with bloody snowflakes.

What was left of Garth Danielson – *and it wasn't much* – was crumpled against the wall next to his desk. He was hunched over the industrial shredder in the corner, kneeling on the floor like he was praying. Maybe he had been. But not for long. Avoiding everything he could, Kincaid stepped closer, retching. The room started spinning and his breath was strangled from his lungs.

Danielsons' hands had been forced into the shredder. He'd probably been pushed down from the back. The force of the thinly honed, whirling blades had slowly pulled his hands in, deeper and deeper, then his wrists, elbows, biceps. The blades had cut his shoulders right through, and sliced his throat and neck into flapping strips. The mans' head was split wide open.

Kincaid fought the nausea, took a quick breath, and looked into Danielson's mutilated face. The top of his head had been completely obliterated, the left side of his brain . . . *gone*.

What was left of his mouth was stuffed with paper and was hanging in front of his chest.

Chapter Forty One

Half choking on vomit, Amy stumbled out into the foyer. She ripped off her mask, leaned against the wall, and forced herself to breathe. Slowly. Slower. She was chalk white, but with each deepening inhalation the blood started seeping back into her cheeks. She seemed smaller, somehow, more fragile, than she'd been just moments before. Something inside had changed. Amy started pacing back and forth, silently praying she'd be able to forget what she'd just seen, but she knew the image would always exist in its pernicious gore, just a thought or dream away.

It had been too late to warn Stephanie. Gasping, she stared down in horror and wretched disbelief, her small face colorless with shock. Kincaid reached out and took her arm just before her eyes flickered and she swooned. Staggering from the den, she kept her hands cupped over her mouth. Kincaid led her gently toward the fountain and helped her slip down into one of the Queen Anne chairs. Stephanie brought her knees up to her chest and curled back as deeply as she could. Amy kept pacing, eyes down, her hands trembling.

They were both safe. Kincaid let them be: he knew it was what they wanted and needed. He went back to the study. It was at least five minutes before the stench of the bloodied, voided corpse wasn't so horribly overwhelming. He'd never seen anything like it, but he forced himself to stay. He had to check for stitches, but he couldn't find Danielson's lips. He backed out of the room, leaving the pocket doors open just enough so the CSU team had unrestricted access. *How could they do it?*

Stephanie was still scrunched down into the chair, distractedly watching the water trickle down the fountain. Kincaid tried to say something reassuring, but nothing came. He leaned down next to her and took her hand, her skin cold and clammy.

"How are you doing?"

Her frown deepened. She shrugged uncertainly, her eyes dull and vacuous.

"Can I get you anything?"

"My time back," Stephanie whispered. "I should have listened to you."

"You'll be alright."

"I had no idea a body held that – that much blood."

Kincaid squeezed her hands. She needed more time alone to assimilate the things she'd seen. No matter how she dealt with it, Kincaid knew she'd never forget the terrifying images. He kissed her hands then gently laid them back in her lap.

Amy was still pacing, looking everywhere but *back there*. Kincaid stepped closer but she quickly waved him away with a shaking hand. She'd have to handle it in her own way, too, without simply relying on Kincaid's experience. This was her battle.

He looked up: Dr. Tantor was coming down the right side of the staircase, covered in light blue throw-a-ways. With smooth, luxurious skin the color of polished onyx and fine, delicate features, it was almost impossible to guess her age. Thirty? Fifty? Her short, black hair was bobbed just beneath her chin. She had a broad smile, beautiful teeth, and the well-proportioned body of someone who took care of herself but wasn't obsequious to diets or exercise. Her fingers seemed unnaturally long, like a pianist's. She played a little, but death was her music and scalpels her keys.

Kincaid met her at the bottom of the stairs, warmly accepting the coroner's outstretched hand. They spoke in muted whispers.

"Text and emails. What a blight. It's so nice to actually see you again, Cecelia. It's unfortunate we always have to meet like this."

"You should come around more often when you're not working," she smiled. "Ralston misses you, too."

"How is he?"

"Very well. Busy as ever."

"And the boys?"

A pathologist's objectivity melted into a mother's beaming pride. "Leonard's at the top of his class."

"He's third year pre-med, right?"

"Uh-huh. And Devon starts his final term in veterinary medicine this fall."

"Wonderful. God, it seems like just yesterday –"

She raised a hand. "Don't say it. Everything makes me feel old these days."

"I hope I age as gracefully as you."

"Still the kidder." She gestured to the young woman fixated on the fountain. "Who are your friends?"

Kincaid quickly explained about Stephanie, why she was here, and where she'd just been.

"You should have stopped her," Cecelia said.

"I tried. But she's as tenacious as you."

"Then you should get on famously." She paused thoughtfully. "Just a minute. Not *the Stephanie*? The one who almost stole your heart?"

"No, she stole it all right," Kincaid smiled.

"*She's* the security consultant I heard you were working with? Well, isn't *this* just effused with poetic justice." Dr. Tantor gave the woman a closer look. "She doesn't look like someone in security."

"That's one of her strengths."

Cecelia walked over and quietly introduced herself. Stephanie's eyes were misty, her lips still trembling. A smile wouldn't come.

Cecelia gestured toward the study. "Did you know him?"

"Just to say '*hi*' to. He's involved in a takeover bid with my employer, *Meredith House*." Her voice was light, distant and weary.

"What do you think, Cecelia?" Kincaid asked, surreptitiously glancing down at Stephanie. It was an act they'd played before. The pathologist took the hint, and shrugged.

"Naturally, it's all conjecture. But in my professional opinion, I don't think suicide can be ruled out just yet."

Stephanie only half-heard what the woman said, and it was a moment before the idea sank in. *Suicide? How could someone –?* She smiled – almost – then sighed and scrunched back deeper into the chair. She took a quick look down the hall toward the study, but she was still shaking. It was a start. Perhaps the worst was over. *But he'd been shoved into a shredder, his arms gone. And his head . . . How long had he been – alive?"*

Dr. Tantor squeezed her shoulder, her grip surprising strong. "Don't go in unless you absolutely have to. Promise me."

Stephanie nodded, then reached over and touched Kincaid's hand. After all of the things he'd seen, he still believed that time was the great healer. She'd be fine.

Kincaid asked Dr. Tantor to wait.

Sergeant MacKenzie was in the portico doorway, slipping on a new pair of slippers. She'd thrown up on her other ones. Tiptoeing around some errant blood transfers, she walked back around the fountain, gave Stephanie a half-smile, and slid up beside Kincaid.

"Sorry."

Kincaid hugged her. "There's no need to be sorry, Amy. Believe me – I haven't seen much worse. Cecelia, this is our new Sergeant, Amy MacKenzie."

Smiles and handshakes. "I heard you nailed the ShoeCam case. Nice collar."

Amy blushed. "I had a lot of help."

"Modesty won't get you anywhere, Sergeant. Davis must have a lot of faith in you to partner you up with this guy, especially for something so high profile." She glanced at Kincaid. *Was he blushing?*

Cecelia was well aware of his long, off and on again relationship with Stephanie Quan. But she still sensed the – *tension* – between Kincaid and his 'Sergeant,' and she'd even heard the whispered rumors down in the catacombs of the morgue. It was obvious they could be more than just partners. *Or were they already?*

Time to move on. Kincaid flipped to a new page in his notepad. He pictured the den: the body parts ripped off; splattered and dripping down the walls; facial skin clinging to Danielson's chest; the shredded arms. He'd seen his share of violent death, but this one was hard to even imagine.

Sergeant MacKenzie took out her own book.

"Amy . . . ?"

"No, Sir. I'm good. I'd tell you if I wasn't."

"Okay, then. There's two palm prints on his shoulders. The killer was standing behind him at some point, pushing him down from behind with all of his weight."

"How long has he been there, Doctor?"

"Several hours, at least. There's not enough blood left in his body to make an accurate estimation of lividity."

"Algor mortis?"

"Same problem, until we can get him back to the lab."

Amy grimaced. "Are you going to have to –"

Dr. Tantor nodded and lowered her voice. "Take the shredder with him? Yes."

Kincaid glanced at the study. "Any other viable prints?"

"I haven't talked to the CSU, but with the amount of entertaining this gentleman evidently did there's probably hundreds of useless sets."

"How did he get in?" Amy wondered.

"He *or* she. Through the kitchen door in the back. Perfect timing. The staff had the night off and he was all alone."

Amy frowned. "How many?"

"Two. Both females. Full time housekeeper/cook, and a combination companion/assistant so he could work at home or from wherever he went. The other Detective —"

"Crandell?"

"Right. He said they're already accounted for. All of the lights were off except the ones in the den. A decanter had been knocked over, and two glasses were on the floor. The collage of papers thrown off his desk were *on top* of the wine spills and the decanter, so he was working on something. I'm fairly certain he was expecting someone he knew when he was blitzed. He's also got a needle puncture on his upper back. Deep. We'll do a screen, but I'm sure you'll find it's succinylcholine."

Kincaid frowned. "A muscle relaxant? So he couldn't struggle?"

"It would make everything easier."

"Was he dead before —"

"No, God bless him. He was alive when his hands and arms were jammed inside. Both elbows are severed. Each stump lost more and more pieces."

"Unbelievable." It was almost beyond comprehension, especially if it was premeditated. Kincaid tried to imagine the fear Danielson must have felt in those final moments when he was half-paralyzed.

Amy bundled up her courage. "You found – *you found his face* – right?"

Dr. Tantor lowered her voice again. "Just parts of it, I'm afraid. It will still be a while –"

"What about his lips?" Kincaid asked.

"I thought you'd ask me about that. We found part of his mouth – the part stuffed with paper" – she paused, waiting – "hanging down onto his chest. And yes, despite the horrendous mutilation, I think it's safe to say his lips were sewn together."

Kincaid stretched from side to side. With the presence of such horrifying death it was hard to feel his own pain. "Can you tell us yet if they resemble the stitches on Devlin Turner and Brian McCabe?"

"I can guess, but you don't like me doing that, so let me get him on the table. At first glance they look rather haphazard and a bit cruder. I'll make sure to check if the needle's the same size." She shook her head.

"What?"

"I think – *I think* – the sewing was done *first*. Before he got the shot."

"Oh my God," Kincaid muttered.

"The person who did this is never going to see God."

Silence. Amy forced herself to breathe. She looked at Stephanie. They were both listening to the soft pulse of the water tumbling over the ornamental rocks and cascading down the edges of the fountain. It was obviously soothing Stephanie, and bringing her *chi* back to normal. Amy tried to match her own breathing to Kincaid's slow, deep rhythm.

"Anything else?" Kincaid asked.

"Not yet. You'll have to wait for the PM."

"When –?"

"For you? Priority one."

"Thanks. Amy, I want you to sit on the CSU team until they come up with something."

"Yes, Sir."

Dr. Tantor touched Kincaid's arm and gestured toward Stephanie with her eyes. She'd finally stood up and was studying the suit of armor. "Will she be okay?"

Kincaid nodded.

"I don't care about her background. It's still going to be a long time to make this just a memory."

She turned to Amy. "You won't be immune to the shock either, Sergeant. Don't push yourself today. Or tomorrow. And my office is always open if you need to talk." She smiled. "The real one, upstairs." A wink.

Amy appreciated the gesture.

"The notes should be on your desk by morning, Kincaid." She turned to Amy. "You're still keeping an eye on him, right?"

Does everyone know?

"I am."

"Good. Davis is worried. And this isn't going to help." She glanced at Stephanie. "So listen, both of you. You saw what's in there. Keep your eyes out for each other. We're talking sociopath with a capital 'S.' Don't let your guard down for even a second."

Cecelia leaned up and gave Kincaid a quick kiss on the cheek. She smiled at Amy. "And –"

"I will."

Dr. Tantor had no doubt Kincaid would be in safe hands with this one. They were close – that was obvious. But what about Stephanie? Fate had thrust them together one more time. Would this be their last chance at staying together? Or would their lives part forever?

Cecelia would have to think about that later. For now, she had to put a body back together.

Facial reconstruction took on a whole different meaning.

*

Stephanie was uncomfortably quiet in the car. She stared out the window but didn't really look at anything. She fidgeted nervously with her hands. Kincaid suggested they drop her off at home.

"No. No, I'll be fine," she sighed dispassionately. "I'll go back to the office."

"You should really try and –"

"I can't just sit at home. I need to do something. To keep going."

Kincaid knew what that felt like. He told Amy to swing by *Meredith House.* Twenty five minutes later, she wheeled in front of the main door. "Are you sure we can't take you home?" Amy asked again.

Stephanie shook her head. She cracked the door open, and paused. "The doctor's right. Be careful. Both of you." She reached forward and gave Amy's shoulder a squeeze. "And if you need anything, call."

Stephanie tried to smile, but there was simply too much sadness in her eyes. All she wanted to do was turn back the clock, to wipe her memory slate clean, to forget. But she knew the horror of what she'd seen would stay with her forever.

Kincaid walked around the car and slipped into the driver's seat. Amy didn't protest. It was only after they started pulling away that Stephanie realized she'd forgotten to ask him about Ryan. Her eyes teared. You never know when you were going to get another chance to show you cared, to tell someone you loved them.

Or *if* you'd get another chance.

*

Kincaid dropped Amy off a few blocks from the station.

"Take a walk," he said softly. "Slow and easy. Grab a coffee, get some air. Go home. Take as much time as you need. I'll see you later whenever you're ready."

She nodded without thinking. Without *remembering*. Kincaid wished he hadn't taken her to Danielson's house. There'd be conscious day dreams and nightmares, a scene she'd never be able to erase, and it made him sad. He thought about Ryan. Pain and sorrow.

And a man, still alive, pushed into a shredder.

Chapter Forty Two

Arriving at the dinner hour, Kincaid found a parking spot close to the kiosk at the hospital's main entrance. He looked up at the glass front of the imposing entryway, took a deep breath, then walked inside. *Magnetic Resonance Imaging* was on the third floor. He'd had two MRIs within the last year, so he negotiated his way through the labyrinth of narrow, interconnected hallways without bothering to check the color-coded paths that lined the floor. At the end of the hall he took the stairs.

It had been another hectic day, and although she couldn't put a name to the face, the receptionist remembered Kincaid. Smiling broadly, she slipped a mint into her mouth, ran her fingers through her hair, and hoped she looked alright. When he leaned over the counter and proffered his heath card, Kincaid's jacket opened, and his holster gave the woman an inadvertent start.

"Back again?"

"I'm afraid so." He handed her Dr. Chadpur's requisition slip.

"You've cut your hair since the last time. It looks nice."

A smile and a blush. "I'm sure you know the routine, Detective. Do you need to see the movie?"

It was a ten minute film that explained the MRI to the uninitiated: the machine, the process, what was going to happen, and what the patient had to do. Unless you were claustrophobic, the process was actually quite benign. The part of the machine the patient saw was nothing more than a long, cylindrical tube. It was just wide enough for someone large framed to be slid inside. When he was on his back with his arms down at his side, Kincaid almost touched the walls of the tube. Some machines had a window cut into the side so the patient could see out, but this was an older model, and, except for the front opening, was completely sealed. Inside it was bright, almost too bright, tight and close. It was like being a human piston inside a cylinder casing. Unfortunately, a lot of people thought it was more like being in a coffin. The most difficult part of the entire experience was lying completely still: once you were inside the tube, any movement could potentially disrupt the images.

"Let's see," Kincaid said. "An MRI doesn't use ionizing radiation or radioactively labeled dyes like traditional x-rays do. It can see through bone, and produce images of blood vessels, muscles, ligaments and spinal fluid. It's often used to detect tumors in the posterior fossa."

The woman looked impressed. "And where's that, Detective?"

"The back of the brain between the ears."

"Anything else?"

"The cylinder contains a strong magnet. Radio waves introduced into the cylinder – and I don't know how that happens – causes atoms to resonate. Each type of tissue emits specific signals. The computer in the next room translates those signals into a two-dimensional picture."

The nurse gave him an admiring eye. "So the film's a 'no.'" She handed Kincaid a gown. "Call me when you're ready. Do you want headphones? Any music?"

The only other uncomfortable part of the process was the noise. It was a little like being in a huge metronome stuck on high, or perhaps in a church bell tower when the ringer has a fit. It started with a rapid *tick tick tick* that quickly escalated into a dull, monotonous, metallic clanging that seemed to go on forever. *Heavy metal rap.* That's why many people opted for the headphones. So did Kincaid. He changed, followed her to the MRI room, then laid down on a narrow bed and was slid into the tube. Why couldn't they make the metal a little warmer? Technicians in a glass booth would issue him instructions via an intercom. The noise started almost immediately: that's when the pictures were taken. Each stage of the procedure lasted a little longer than the one preceding it. The longest episode was about twenty minutes, and the entire test usually lasted about an hour. Kincaid found it quite easy to ignore the pernicious sound this time because he couldn't push the image of being in a coffin away. It wasn't being in the coffin that bothered him: it was that the casket reminded him of Ryan.

What was he going to do?

He understood Carolyn's fears about her son being left in a coma: it was like death without an ending. He'd always argued vigorously for an individual's right to die when and how they chose. He admitted there were a great number of variables involved, like the person's age, their illness, their pain, the possibility of any kind of recovery, and whether or not they possessed sufficient faculties to make the decision. But it was still their life and their right. Society, however, didn't agree.

He pictured Ryan at the hospital, tucked into the bed and held in place by thick white sheets, tubes in his mouth and nose, his side, his stomach and his groin. What kind of life was that? Kincaid knew that if he was the one clinging to a thin thread of life solely dictated by something beyond his own control, he'd make his own decision in a heartbeat. But this was someone else. When, and if, the time came, he'd want to help Ryan and his mother. *But could he?*

The deafening *clangclangclangclang* subsided after a few minutes, and Kincaid was slid out of the tube for a brief respite before the next series of images were shot. Huddled behind a bank of monitors, a technician looked over, gave the thumbs up sign, and Kincaid glided back into the chamber. He stared up at the dull whiteness above him. It was only inches away, but since everything was blank and featureless, like a Ganzfeld, it might have been a hundred feet high. The irritating *tick tick tick* was quickly usurped by the *clangclangclang*. He knew he'd hear it for hours.

Kincaid's thoughts drifted aimlessly. Grabbing fragments, he mentally juxtaposed bits and pieces to see if they fit, to see if something could tie some of them together. It was as if invisible hands were plucking them out, putting them onto an invisible screen, and trying to assemble them together into a coherent whole. Some made sense; others didn't.

Who was the third party involved in the takeover bid of *Meredith House*, and why was it happening *now*? Why was Gail so reluctant to be associated with Turner? Was Turner the only one guilty of stealing books and having them published under a name he knew would sell? That he'd *make* sell? Did Baxter or Meredith know what Turner had been doing, or had they been duped from the beginning? Or did they know where the novels were coming from and had conveniently looked the other way as the money poured in? And who was Ian Nuraki, the mysterious writer who poked his head up from the underground every time a blockbuster hit the shelves, and then vanished until Turner needed him again? No limelight, no interviews, nothing. Was Brian McCabe in the loop? Danielson?

Clackclackclackclackclack. Louder. Louder.

Kincaid knew Meredith was lying about what happened in the underground. She wasn't badly hurt and nothing was taken, so *why?* And what about Turner? He was obviously being blackmailed when he was murdered. But who had uncovered his secret? If the case against Turner could be proven, then countless of millions of dollars in rights and royalty fees were at stake. The domino effect would topple everything. But if you were blackmailing Turner and the money was still coming, why murder the proverbial "cash cow?" It didn't make sense. Unless . . .

The *clangclangclangclang* grew obnoxiously loud, effectively drowning out Kincaid's thoughts in a sea of ringing buoys.

*

Kincaid was just leaving the MRI unit when he saw Stephanie walking along the hall toward him. Like an eel through kelp, she slipped through the shuffling throng that was congested by the elevators.

"Sorry I'm late. I wanted to be here when you went in."

"No problem." He ran his fingers through her hair, then took her hands between his. "Everything went fine."

"Good." She leaned up and kissed him lightly on the cheek. She looked a lot better than she had at Danielsons' house. Not quite *Stephanie*, but the shine was back in her eyes, the confidence in her demeanor.

Kincaid returned her stare. "What? You look like the legendary cat that swallowed the canary."

"Coffee first. How about the cafeteria?"

They managed to find a table for two by the window. The sky had been darkened by a thick mantel of black clouds that threatened rain.

"I did some more digging," Stephanie began. "Called in a few favors." She looked into her cup. "This looks worse than the stuff back at the station."

"It's a gourmet taste you have to acquire. What did you find out?"

Stephanie leaned forward conspiratorially, and a teasing smile crept across her lips. "I think I know who's financing the takeover of *Meredith House*."

"Who?"

"Not so fast." She pouted coquettishly. "I want a home cooked meal for this."

"Done."

"Dessert, too. I want your famous chocolate and raspberry tartufo."

She rested her chin on an upraised hand and looked Kincaid up and down. "And then after . . ."

"Stephanie, –"

"Walter Croft."

"Walter Croft?" Kincaid couldn't hide his surprise. Or his suspicions. Something bothered him about the old man, but a takeover threat? "Are you sure? You've seen where he lives. I can't see him as any kind of player to throw money around. He's barely hanging on."

"You're right. But I was referring to Walter Croft *Jr.*"

Kincaid frowned. "His *son?*"

Stephanie nodded. "If I was a man, I wouldn't have wanted to go through life having *'Jr.'* after my name. Anyway, Walter Jr. isn't much like his dad. He's alive and kicking, and he's worth an absolute fortune."

Kincaid looked impressed. "How did you find out?"

"Sources," Stephanie smiled evasively. "You wouldn't give up yours, would you?"

Kincaid didn't press.

"Remember *Saphh -2*," she asked.

Kincaid thought for a moment. "Wasn't that the company out west that allegedly found one of the largest ruby deposits in the world? In Myanmar, I think."

"The same. Sensing something big, thousands of people took a legitimate chance on a little local company. Invest in a dream and see what happens. Everyone was jumping in, begging *Saphh-2* to take their money. A few months later the company hit the mother lode – potentially the greatest ruby cache in history. Perfect rubies, remember, are even more valuable than flawless diamonds by carat. The early investors thought everything was wonderful. They just took the ride, watching the stocks rise. Before the company went public, however, all hell broke loose – because there weren't any rubies. The press got wind the companies' core samples were fake." The savvy investors got out early and made millions."

"It was one of the biggest mining scams ever."

"Sure was. And I'm not saying the investors and developers knew that. But some did. And thousands of others lost a great deal of money."

"But those early ones didn't. And?"

"And Walter Croft Jr. was one of the quick hitters, and one of the largest."

"Insider information?"

"Probably. He and a few friends cashed out before anyone had 'fallen' out of a helicopter in the middle of the jungle. Their profits were somewhere in the six or seven hundred percent range."

"What did they do with the money?"

"The smart thing. They formed a consortium led by Walter Jr. and diversified. Put hundreds of millions into some very lucrative pies. "

"Such as?"

"They bought huge chunks of small start-up companies that were into software programs. Lo and behold, a lot of them were top-end Internet service providers. A couple of nice little dot com enterprises, too. Their profits grew exponentially. I don't know the actual stats, but from what I've heard Walter Jr.'s worth about a billion and a half. Easy."

Hefty numbers, Kincaid admitted. "But why attack *Meredith House*? Surely they can't be a money maker of the same magnitude, especially when you take Turner out of the equation."

"No, they're not. But just like Dad, Jr.'s other passion in his life is his family. He loved his mother very much, and does everything he can to make his father's final days a little easier, even though Walter Sr. isn't the kind of man to accept charity. That's why he still lives where he does. Remember what he said through the smoky haze?"

I don't take help from anyone. No matter who it is.

"He could have that house next door blown to smithereens and get rid of that stupid flag without a second thought."

Kincaid was quiet for a moment. "So Walter Jr. is backing the takeover bid for personal reasons, not financial ones?"

Stephanie started to answer but was drowned out by a coded call that crackled over the intercom. *Code Blue. Code Blue. ICU. Stat.* Chairs scraped back and several people rushed from the cafeteria.

"What better reason is there than love?"

Kincaid shook his head. "It doesn't make sense, Stephanie. Let's say you're right, and Croft Jr. just wanted his mother's books published, especially the last one that was so personal about her illness. Why not just pay to have it published?"

"Himself?"

"By one of the vanity presses. Or why not have someone like *Excalibur* publish it for him. For a price, of course. Pay them to market thousands of copies, and do a professional roll-out. His mother could have seen them in all the bookstores before she died."

"I said love was *a* reason," Stephanie replied. "But not the *only* one."

The crease in Kincaid's forehead softened. "Revenge?"

"Why not? It was Turner, and through Turner, Gail Meredith, who caused Mrs. Croft so much pain before her death. Neither the son nor the father has forgotten that. Or forgiven it."

"So by backing *Excalibur's* takeover bid, they'd end up owning everything."

"And the first thing they would have done was fire Gail Meredith."

"And Turner?"

"The merger would make *Excalibur* the largest publisher in the country. They would have blackballed Turner, and he would have been back dealing with small independent presses."

"And off the gravy train for good. No more bestsellers for him."

"Exactly. The new company would already have his prime writers under contract. If he hadn't died, Turner would've probably wished he had. I think Croft Jr. is gunning for Meredith now."

Kincaid leaned back and watched two bleary-eyed interns fall into a couch beside them.

"You've done well, Stephanie."

"I had a good teacher."

The cafeteria was getting busier. Pockets of conversation competed with the sharp sound of cutlery against plates. Kincaid couldn't help watching an older couple at a nearby table. Heads bent together and seemingly oblivious to everything around them, the man was offering soothing whispers to the woman as she repeatedly daubed a tissue to her eyes.

"Even if Croft's motives are love and revenge," Kincaid wondered, "there's still a viable chance he's going to make money out of this new business venture, right?"

"Sure. His consortium will own one of the largest publishing houses in the country. And everything that goes along with that."

"Then there'd be no reason to have Turner or McCabe murdered. He'd want to see Meredith and Turner be humiliated and suffer financially. Killing them takes all the fun away."

Stephanie sighed. Kincaid was right, and that put a serious dent into her theory. "Then Walter Croft and his son can be ruled out as suspects?"

"Not necessarily." He looked back at the elderly couple: the woman was still crying, and it made him sad. *What was Ryan doing – or feeling – right now?* "It doesn't tell us who the murderer is, so let's not reject them too hastily."

Stephanie checked her watch. It had been a long, grueling, horrifying day. One she wanted to forget. "So. What about that dinner?"

Kincaid looked a little uncomfortable. He fumbled uncharacteristically over what he wanted to say.

"Stephanie, I think –"

She smiled and interrupted him. "I'd love to."

*

Emotionally stressed and psychologically strained from what she'd confronted at Danielsons' house, Stephanie was oddly relaxed and animated during the drive to Kincaids'. Bursts of conversation clashed with reflective silences. She melted into the memories of past drives, and the farther they left the city behind, the quieter she became. She wondered what changes Kincaid had made to the house over the years, but when his car finally crunched to a stop on the gravel driveway it was too dark to see anything clearly. She paused uncertainly at the front door. You can float away on oceans of memories, but you can drown in them, too.

"What's wrong?" Kincaid asked gently.

"Memories. Too many, all of a sudden." She tried to smile. "I guess I wasn't as prepared for this as I thought I'd be."

Kincaid wrapped his arm around her waist and led her inside. Her pangs of anxiousness drifted away with each step. She put her things down on the kitchen table and tried to take everything in, but it was all too much. She closed her eyes and breathed in years of yesterdays.

"Everything seems so comfortingly familiar," she whispered. "But a little overwhelming, too." She'd been here so many times, shared so many things, dreamed so many wishes and wished so many dreams.

"Can I get you something? A glass of wine?"

"That would be lovely, thanks."

The tannins in Reds gave her a headache, so Kincaid opened one of her favorite Rieslings from Niagara.

Stephanie wandered slowly around the main room, picking up this, touching that, reacquainting herself with countless sensations and feelings that had been dormant for a long time. Dormant, but not forgotten.

"The place looks wonderful."

"It does now."

They clinked glasses by the woodstove. Kincaid tucked some crumpled newspaper under a small tepee of cedar strips. One match and everything flared alive in translucent bursts of gold and orange and red. He added a quarter piece of birch to the burgeoning flames, glancing at Stephanie as she took everything in.

"It's so open and comfortable," she said. "Such a nice place to relax. What more can you ask for?"

Just for you to be here, Kincaid smiled. And Amy? She kept creeping into his thoughts, too. She'd made her own little wedge somewhere in the back of his mind, prying open sensitive feelings and longings he didn't know he had. He tossed a handful of pine cones onto the fire, and they exploded in dazzling colors.

Stephanie felt the warm glow against her skin. "Do you still have those toss cushions you used to put down here?" There was a teasing lilt to her voice.

He nodded.

"You're blushing. How sweet."

He arrayed them out on the floor, and they lay down together. Stephanie held a pillow to her chest. She touched Kincaid lightly on the shoulder, listening to the wood crackle. She looked at the little knickknacks on the mantel and reminisced about some of the places they'd come from.

"What did Ryans' mother say that made you so upset?"

Kincaid reached down and took her hand. He sipped his wine and watched the fire peel the bark from the birch log. There was a long silence before he answered. "Ryan. About not wanting him to suffer at the end." There was a sense of finality to his words that made his heart skip a beat.

"That's what I thought." Stephanie started kneading the muscles in his neck. They felt like cords.

"I think it's unfair. I understand how she must feel, how horrible the decision must be, but it's not right to ask you to be a part of it."

"I'm already a part of it."

"It's something she should resolve for herself."

"I don't think she can."

"Maybe not." Stephanie ran her fingers across his shoulders. She looked thoughtfully away, then whispered. "Does she know about – *you*? About *your* situation?"

"No."

He closed his eyes tightly, like he was trying to force some unsettling thought away. He got up and retrieved the wine from the kitchen. He refilled their glasses and watched the fire split a log in half. Power touched with beauty and gentleness.

"She wants you to help, doesn't she? To make the decision for her?"

Kincaid stared at the fire.

"What are you going to do?"

He stretched slowly from side to side, gently trying to release the fierce pain in his lower back. "I'm not sure. But Ryan doesn't have much time. It's not something I can afford to dwell on."

Stephanie inched closer. "What does your mind tell you?"

"That everyone has a right to choose their own end. That the kid's going to be in more pain than a lot of people feel in their lifetime. That his mother's going to suffer for a reason I can't understand." Another small log crackled and split. "Part of me thinks it's wrong. But when I stand there and look at him in bed –"

His voice trailed off. "The thing that bothers me most is that if I were a pet owner, I wouldn't think twice about having an animal put down to stop its suffering."

"We look at humans differently," Stephanie said softly.

"Why? It's okay for Ryan to suffer, but not a dog?"

"You know that's not what I meant."

"I know. And it's obviously not as simplistic as that." He leaned over and kissed Stephanie on the cheek. He didn't pull away. He didn't *want* to pull away. Kincaid kissed her again and slipped his arm behind her neck.

"What does your heart tell you to do?"

"That I should do anything to help him. And his mother. To save them whatever pain I can. If she needs me to help her decide what to do, I'll do it," he said softly. "I'll be whatever she needs me to be."

"And do you feel that's wrong?"

"No," he whispered. "No, I don't."

Kincaid watched the smoke curl up in fleeting, phantom shadows. Stephanie nestled into his side like a cat burrowing into a cozy blanket just out of the dryer.

"Then you'll do what you think you have to do when the time comes."

Outside, the wind bent the trees, and the first few raindrops of an approaching storm trickled down the window. The fire slowly burned down, one warm color gently giving way to another, until the birch was just a memory and the grate was alive with glowing embers.

Everything seemed so far away. The deaths, the people who'd take a life for profit or anger, the crowded hospital wards, the technicians in the little bluish rooms pouring over fates on their monitors, Ryan. And somewhere, Kincaid imagined a harried doctor he'd never met, or who'd never know anything about him at all, was looking at strips of MRI images and making a pronouncement that would change what was left of his life forever.

Finally, they moved, rising together without speaking. Arms around each other, they walked quietly into Kincaid's bedroom, pausing just long enough to seal their pact with a lingering kiss that rekindled something inside neither of them ever wanted to lose. The longer their lips touched, the more they realized nothing had every really been lost. It was there. It always would be.

Later.

Later, their bodies entwined and Stephanie's head softly against his chest, Kincaid listened to his lover's breaths. *His lover.* No matter where he'd been or what he'd been doing, she'd never stopped being anything else to him. He thought about all the times they could have had together, all the things they might have shared if he'd asked her to stay that night so long ago. Was he wrong, thinking like he did? Had he taken something from both of them, something they could never get back? Kincaid closed his eyes. Somewhere in the back of his mind, he heard the rapid *clangclangclangclang* of the MRI machine pounding against the fear that was always part of his dreams.

Stephanie was part of his life again.

Perhaps the tumor was, too.

Had he found her again, only to lose her once more?

For the last time.

Chapter Forty Three

God, she looked so beautiful when she was sleeping.

Stephanie was on her side, one arm tucked securely under Kincaid's pillow, her eyebrows soft, her lips parted ever so slightly, her face glowing gently from the flickering light of the dying embers in the woodstove. Outside, the storm had stopped, and rain beads bathed the picture window in gray rivulets. The last filaments of moonlight streamed across the bed.

Kincaid watched her sleep, felt her breathe. He leaned down and kissed her ever so tenderly on the cheek. *Again.* Her lips curled into a dreamy smile and she squeezed the blankets to her chest. He pulled the sheets up over her shoulders and tucked them around her feet.

Morning broke far, far too quickly.

*

The info was good: fuck, the guy was up early.

Dressed in fatigues, the man knelt down in the underbrush about a hundred yards south of Kincaid's woodpile. The distance was nothing with the night scope: eradicating the shadows from the early morning darkness, it would be like standing face to face. The rifle was mounted on an open pod, the metallic butt form-fit into his shoulder. The glass in the big picture window was thick and double glazed: it would spider out, splinter, but it wouldn't smash and crumble. Adjusting for the effects wasn't a problem. The breeze was light, barely moving the branches of the nearest trees. Kincaid was at the table, drinking from a mug, reading something spread out across the table.

Smiling, the shooter squeezed off two fictitious rounds.

Seconds later, the larger trees had already reclaimed his shadow.

*

Kincaid had been on the highway since five thirty. Fitful and restless, he'd hardly slept at all. He couldn't stop the memories and emotional uncertainties from coming, to stave off the myriad feelings of doubts and fears that plagued his thoughts, the incorrigible stress that kept niggling into that muddled time between dreams and consciousness that refused to let him sleep, but wouldn't let him wake.

Dew drops glistened off the wheat in the farmers' fields, and thick patches of purple Loosestrife that covered the highway's edge stretched awake. Stains of mist wafted through the thick forests of evergreens that separated the fields, gray waves rolling over the hills and valleys like wizard's fog. Dark clouds slipped through distant treetops. The signs were all there: a warm day with low humidity and a sky that would share sunshine with heavy clouds, but no rain. Two cars whizzed past. Even at this hour and far beyond the city limits the traffic was coagulating. How sad. Sad? No. He had to stay focused. No signs, no interpretations, no speculations of what he might be facing.

But . . . was it moving again? *Now?*

No. Forget it. He'd have the test done. Then he'd start worrying.

*

An hour and a half later, the collage of faces from last night still cycling through his mind, Kincaid pulled into the hospital's parking lot, then walked into the new wing that housed the CT department. He undressed in the curtained-off cubicle, neatly hung up his clothes, then struggled to tie up the paper gown behind his back before sitting on a narrow bench to wait. He didn't have long – it was only a moment before a technician called from beyond the curtain.

"Ready, Detective?"

"I am."

The woman slid the curtain back and smiled perfunctorily.

"You can bring in anything personal. Wallet, keys, phone, that sort of thing. I'll check them in at the front desk."

Kincaid handed everything over. He reached back and tried to hold his gown closed as he followed the woman into the testing room.

The routine was exactly the same as before. He couldn't believe two months had passed so quickly. Kincaid slid up onto the metal bed and stretched out. The woman talked while she worked.

"This is just so you don't move," she explained, snapping wrist restraints over Kincaid's arms and drawing the Velcro snug. "Any twitch can ruin the pictures." She secured his feet the same way, with fasteners wrapped over his ankles. Another strap was buckled across his chest, and Kincaid had the fleeting sensation of what those poor inmates in the old asylums must have felt like when they were all trussed up before their electroshock therapy. Did people in Victorian England really pay to watch the mentally ill be shocked into oblivion, or see them go through their sickening compulsions and horrible desecrations? Did they pay more for fights and self-mutilations? Hangings? Then again, it was common today for ISIS beheadings to go viral over the Internet. Women who refused arranged marriages were still publicly stoned. Gangs raped women who didn't cover themselves in fabric cocoons that blotted them from existence. Modern athletes ran blood-thirsty dog fights where animals were shredded to spectators' delight, and kids wore the puke's jersey. How much had we really changed?

"Now for your head." The technician slid a two-sided support underneath his neck, buckling it tightly so his head was immobilized. She checked the straps. "Okay? Nothing's too tight?"

"It's fine."

"Good. You've done this before, right?"

"I have."

"Then just close your eyes and relax. It'll be over in no time."

The metal table was irritatingly cold against his back. Kincaid felt the gurney move. The tech was at the foot of the bed, pushing him forward and angling him beneath a large, circular arch. Cameras were embedded along the inside of its frame, which would rotate while numerous pictures were taken of his head, spine, and lower back. The scan would give the doctors a sequential series of three-dimensional images.

There was nothing to see or hear, so Kincaid closed his eyes and let his thoughts drift away. The collage came back almost instantaneously, pictures and images colliding and circling around each other. Ryan. Stephanie. Danielson hunched over the shredder, his arms . . . gone. The paper stuck in Turners' throat, the pen through his eye, the stiches sewing him into eternal silence. Amy. Ralston. Caster and Meredith. Barclay. Croft. And Stephanie again. He would have shuddered if he'd been able to move.

Blood pounded through his temples. The headache was back, digging into his frontal lobe like maggots on a corpse. *Could the CT scan show an image of a headache?* The large wheel turned, snapping picture after picture, the cameras quickly repositioning themselves. Would the images be any different this time?

Kincaid opened his eyes and watched the revolving arch. It made him feel strangely alone. It was a feeling he knew well, but now it was different – a little deeper, and more intense. He felt more alone since Stephanie had come back into his life. And what about Amy? Could he have some sort of life with her . . . if Stephanie . . . ? Whose hand would he want to hold if they had to wheel him into the operating room, the ceiling lights passing by, the intravenous poles holding swaying bags of blood and saline and pain medication that would keep him alive when the unearthly darkness of anesthesia descended? Amy was here, and she was trying to be *here* and *now*, but had Stephanie ever really left?

The arch wheeled around, smooth and effortlessly, the cameras imbedded inside the track snapping picture after picture.

*

Richardson gave a quick rap at Kincaid's door. Dressed in scruffy jeans and a black leather jacket emblazoned with a motorcycle insignia, he looked like a loan shark's enforcer. He leaned back against the wall and fanned his face with a large manila folder. Kincaid finished reading a report, signed the bottom, closed the file, and looked up.

"Did you pick up Stephanie?"

"Right on time. I think she wants me."

"Undoubtedly."

"She's so slight I had to keep checking to see if she was still on the back of the bike."

"Where did you drop her off?"

"*Meredith House.*"

"I owe you one." Silence. "What?"

Richardson's smile was infectious and Kincaid felt himself start to grin.

"Come on." Kincaid nodded at the folder. "Give."

"So this guy's walking by a farm and he sees this three-legged pig running around the yard . . . "

"Another time."

Richardson's smile faded. "You don't look very good. How'd the CT scan go?"

"They'll have the pictures in a couple of days."

"And?"

"I'll go in and they'll tell me everything's fine," Kincaid lied.

Richardson watched his friend carefully and wondered what he *wasn't* telling him. What *wasn't being said* quickly made the silence stilted. Richardson recognized the file Kincaid had been reading.

"So you went to Danielson's? Unbelievably gruesome, from all accounts. I hear Crandell tossed his cookies."

"We'll keep that to ourselves for the kid's sake. I was there – he doesn't have to answer to anyone about not handling it. Not many people could. It was one of the most horrible scenes I've ever witnessed."

"What do you think?"

"I'm not sure yet. There are a couple of things I didn't like."

"I'll bet there were a couple of things Danielson didn't like. Well, at least I've got *some* good news." He tossed the folder down with a flourish. "Isn't modern technology wonderful?"

Kincaid started untying the envelope. "Forensics already?"

"Yeah. Amy kept them motivated. But this isn't about Danielson. It's from young Mr. Matsu."

"About McCabe?"

"Uh-huh. And a statement from a walk-in."

"Who?"

"A middle-aged gentlemen who was coming out of the Yonge Street subway station the night McCabe was murdered. A man came flying down the steps –"

"When?"

"Just after midnight. He bumped into our startled passer-by. When the man looked down, his coat had blood on it."

"Did he get a good look at him?"

Richardson's smile broadened. "Crystal clear."

"You got a sample?"

"Do I look like a rookie? The man wanted to make sure he hadn't been infected or anything. SARS, Ebola, Hep C, whatever. Amy tracked him down through hospital records."

"And . . ."

"And we were able to track down another witness."

"From the alley?"

"A reluctant one, but he'll talk. He saw McCabe arguing with another man behind the club that night. And by golly –"

"By golly? When do undercover guys say 'by golly'?"

"And by golly, his description just happens to match the one given by the man in the subway."

Kincaid pulled a composite sketch out from the pages and studied it thoughtfully. He leaned back in his chair and swiveled from side to side.

"That's great, Richardson. Thanks. I owe you two. Perhaps I'll solve your problem with DiMatteo and the human trafficking ring."

"Sure, you do that. So?"

"So what?"

"Don't you want to hear what else we got?"

Kincaid stopped swiveling and perched forward.

"The guy in such a hurry at the subway station?"

"Yes?"

"Was Richard Barclay."

"No." Kincaid exhaled a deep, satisfying sigh.

"I guess you're going to have another little chat with him."

"I think that would be in order."

Richardson rubbed the stubble on his chin. "Well, instead of just talking to him, you might want to bring him in."

"And why's that?"

"I told you. Because I've got something else. Well, *I* don't have *it* now, actually. But –"

"Richardson?"

"Huh?"

Kincaid folded his hands together on the desk and smiled gratuitously. "*Please* tell your humble servant what else you've got?"

The larger man shook his head. "No." He turned and walked out. Kincaid counted to five, but Richardson made him wait three or four more seconds before poking his head around the door.

"Well, since you asked so nicely. We've got the pipe used on McCabe."

"No!"

"Sure do. Forensics puts McCabe's blood all over it."

"Where'd you get it from?"

"Your – CI – Kendra called, and put us on to a guy. Hans Toller. No sheet, but pretty well-known in the area. A real tough train. It turns out he saw a couple of punks out for a night of bashing."

"Real vigilantes. Outside *The Tavern*?"

"Not at first. Apparently they were making the rounds, checking out the hood. Toller was at another bar over on Church Street, and when he came out, the punks zeroed in on him. He kept walking as fast as he could. There were a few cat calls at first. A couple of threats."

"Naturally."

"Then some cursing and yelling. Things heated up pretty fast, and one of the guys started mouthing off about what they were going to do to him. Toller took off. Figured he could cut through a couple of back alleys and make it to The Tavern, but he fell. The punks moved in and put the boots to him. Toller rolled up next to a dumpster. He figured that was it, they were going to kill him, but then he saw the edge of a pipe sticking out from under the dumpster. He grabbed it and started swinging for all he was worth. Smashed a few shins and a knee."

"And the heroes?" Kincaid asked.

"Backed right off. They weren't so tough when the guy had a weapon. They put up a front and followed him for a bit, but Toller's been in situations like that before and kept the pipe to make sure the punks stayed away. He skirted down a few laneways and lost them. He didn't even realize he was carrying the thing until he was almost home. That's when he noticed all the blood. He knew he hadn't actually torn one of the little pricks, so he ditched it. The only trouble was, he told Kendra he'd forgotten where."

"Until yesterday?"

Richardson grinned. "We got lucky. They retraced his steps, and *bingo*. He came in last night with Kendra. The lab eliminated both their prints."

Kincaid's face broke into a weary smile. "So we finally got a break."

"If only I could get lucky with DiMatteo."

"Still nothing?"

Richardson shook his head. He looked worried. "You hear what happened yesterday?"

"The stabbing down on Queen's Quay?"

"Stabbing? That's an understatement. It was a gutting. Pierre Desroches. The hole was too big to push his stomach back in. Dr. Tantor called it as close to a disemboweling as you can get. He was a fringe associate with the Rock Machine. A couple of Hell's Angel's picked him off alone. Like I said, human cargo's more profitable than a lot of dope, so they want to kill each other for the territory."

"So DiMatteo's starting to sweat?"

"Big time."

"But you're still not on?"

Richardson shook his head.

"Do me a favor, will you?"

"That's all I seem to do. But sure."

"I couldn't reach Amy. Can you have her take a couple of blues and pick Barclay up?"

"No problem. Where you off to?"

"Brent Jacobs."

"The guy who's been banned from the *Oriental Buffet?*"

"The same. He's left me several messages, but I haven't been able to get in touch with him. It's worth a look."

"I'll have Mr. Barclay ready and waiting," Richardson winked.

Kincaid dialed Jacobs's number once more. Still nothing. He frowned. It was just a few missed phone calls, but something didn't feel right. He'd been a Detective long enough to know he should always trust his gut instincts.

And his gut told him there was something terribly wrong.

Chapter Forty Four

Niagara Falls.

Crouched beneath umbrellas and shouting in a cacophony of languages, tourists from all over the world smiled and laughed beneath the sun shower that never stopped. They snapped an unending collage of photographs, entranced with the floating rainbow that hovered over the precipice where the mighty Niagara River plunged between countries and down into the gorge. Mothers stayed close as their children scrambled up onto metal and stone fences to have their picture taken at the very brink of the roaring Falls, just a step away from death. The swirling water was hypnotic and seemed far too close: one false move or a slip on the wet pavement and the child would be gone forever, their horrified screams deafened by the raging water.

Dieter Vollger snickered at the two cops walking their beat while the vaporous, colored rain sparkled over the crowd.

Jurisdictional shit.

Vollger had checked the papers: the Washington State Police, where Roland Steinberg's head followed his bike into the flames, didn't know what happened in the dinosaur park in Calgary, where Shirley O'Donovan had been freshly buried, and both departments had been left out of the loop and didn't know New York cops were still trying to identify what was left of Chamille Nasson. Nothing would tie the brutal murders together – not yet, anyway, not until more links were forged into the chain and someone, somewhere, realized that three more people in the publishing industry had been named on tombstones.

Fuck, they hadn't even been able to find Dieter's comrade-in-arms yet, either, the writer just a few short hours away who'd brought three other publishing careers to a brutal close. Stupid cops. They were probably out carding delinquents, street profiling, or using their new tasers on someone who was already unconscious. *As long as they remembered to turn off their body cameras.* And these two *Mutt and Jeff's* were no different. Heads down, they were talking about something that made them grin, not even looking at the kids standing on the stone promontories that were so close to the ravaging clutches of the racing river and the jagged rocks below.

Lips stitched closed. A head without a face. A headless rider. And dinner at the zoo. . .

Dieter felt a tingle all over. Three less rejection writers.

He smiled. All he had to do was offer to take a picture for any of the people clustered around in little groups so they didn't have to stage an insipid selfie like the Prime Minister would. When he handed back the camera, all it would take would be a quick push and one of those snotty little brats would be in the water. *In the water* then *under the water*, bouncing up and down at the edge of the Falls where the water curled, screaming, the pointed rocks reaching up like hands from below, waiting, waiting for the offering.

The cops would finally look up and run towards the fence, but they'd be too late. Little *what's his name* would be free-falling into the void as everyone scrambled over to the railing, not to try and help, naturally, but to snap away with their cell phones, their videos mere seconds from going viral.

*

The day was dragging on forever. Kincaid glanced at his watch as he took the elevator down to Dr. Tantor's second office – the morgue. After what he'd just seen, and how he felt, he couldn't believe it had been only two days since he'd been at Croft's house with Stephanie and Amy. But then, staring at what was left of Danielson's body stuffed down into the shredder felt like a lifetime ago. Amy . . . he hoped she was fine. Stephanie's face nudged its way back into his thoughts. He gently eased her image away, hoping she was doing better than he was. My God. So much blood. Turner. McCabe. Danielson. And now . . .

Would it ever stop? He closed his eyes . . .

*

He closed his eyes and was back in Jacobs' basement, standing at the door of the tiny office that was so cluttered with manuals, boxes of discs, folders and computer parts, there wasn't a place to sit down unless a temporary space was cleared. He pictured the fast-food bags crumpled on the floor, the candy wrappers, the doughnut box, the pyramid of coffee cups teetering on the printer stand. Daily rituals. Parts of the man's life. How quickly things changed.

The first thing he saw was Jacobs' body sprawled across the desk like a breached manatee. Blood streamed over the edge, coagulating in red-brown patches on the floor. The gun was in the man's hand, and the room still smelled of cordite and burnt smoke. A quick glance confirmed Jacobs held the barrel close, probably right on the edge of his mouth, literally eating the barrel. The explosion had ripped his entire head apart. There was almost nothing left of the man's face, and there was a gaping hole where his eyes and frontal lobe had been. Bits and pieces of bone and flesh were clumped on the wall. They almost looked like they'd been spray-painted across the ceiling. Behind his desk, slithering entrails of blood and sinew and torn tissue slowly slid toward the floor in dark streaks.

Kincaid felt his body sigh. *Poor Jacobs.* All he really wanted was what was his to begin with. Everything he'd done, everything he worked so hard for had been taken away: his book, his fame, his savings, his house, his literary dreams. Now, there was just his novel death. Everything shredded into nothing – just like Danielson's arms and shoulders. Turner's savage bloodletting. The back of McCabe's obliterated head.

No note. Just the little box Jacobs clutched protectively in his other hand and the envelope on the corner of his desk with Kincaid's name scrawled on the front. Jacobs had managed to access the *Gazette's* files, and the next installment of the Sunday edition's serial piece of the *Writer's Revenge* was spread out beneath him, splattered with blood and shredded tissue. Frank Stevens – *that bastard of an editor* – had never called to warn Kincaid. But then again, revenue was up nineteen percent! This weeks' episode was about a writer who'd had a manuscript stolen, and it outlined the author's descent into hopeless despair after he found out he'd been cheated by the publishing company and Ian Nuraki. Mimicking his own situation to the last detail, the story had been too much for Jacobs, too close to the heart. Now, in his own mind at least, everyone knew his shame: it was there for the world to see. He'd lost everything, and the story made him realize how ridiculous he was, how pathetic he'd been in his pursuit of fame and glory. He'd never write anything again.

What did he have to live for now?

What a waste, Kincaid thought, opening his eyes as the elevator slowed to a stop. The heavy metal doors winched open. The morgue's hallway was unnaturally quiet.

*

Dr. Tantor was leaning over her microscope when Kincaid slid the glass doors open and walked into her lab.

"Kincaid? What brings you down into the subterranean bowels of the earth where the Reaper waits and walls are filled with the dead? *Me?*"

"Nice thought. But you're married."

"But *I'm* not dead."

Dr. Tantor was wearing a long, hooped dress from the early 1900's and a starched white shirt covered in lace that was buttoned up to her neck. Her hair was piled fashionably high and held in place with two ivory combs. No make-up and a slim tie tucked into her blouse.

"You'd be way too much for me, Cecelia. You look absolutely beautiful."

"Liar. But thanks anyway. It's actually because of the whale-bone corset," she smiled mischievously.

"You're kidding –"

"You should have seen Ralston trying to do it up with one hand."

"He certainly won't have any trouble taking it off."

A shared smile. Kincaid glanced at the rows of metal boxes, their aluminum handles gleaming beneath the overhead lights, the little name tags on the front always changing, always announcing someone new, if only for a few moments of silence.

"You want to know if the PM's done," she said, suppressing a yawn. She looked gaunt and more than a little tired. "It is."

"Great. Rough day?"

"From what I can remember. I hear you've brought in a suspect."

"Amy picked up Richard Barclay. I'm going to let him sit upstairs and think about things for a while."

"How's Stephanie? Better than when she left Danielson's house?"

"Much. I wish I could wave a magic wand and wipe it all away. As soon as I start imagining it again I feel so nauseous I could be physically sick, and Stephanie and Amy haven't seen the things I have. Hopefully, they never will."

"Amen."

"What did you find out?"

Cecelia fussed with her glasses and pulled a file folder from a stack. "There's not much more I can tell you that you probably don't already know. I can narrow down the time of death to somewhere between ten and one."

"That helps."

"But just like the Turner scene, our perp was careful not to leave any prints."

"Did he wear something on his feet?"

"Some kind of plastic bag. Probably tied over his shoes, and then crammed with newspaper or something to affect the apparent dimensions."

"No hairs? Fibers?"

"Nothing we've been able to trace."

"How long do you think the killer was there for?"

"An educated guess? More than likely about an hour. I'll talk to Ralston later about some of the variables and see what he says."

"An hour's a long time."

"Especially if you're Danielson. All of the normal drug tests have come back negative, but I did find a needle mark on Danielson's upper back. My guess would be succinylcholine, like we talked about earlier. There's one other thing."

"Yes?"

"I found a small indentation on the outer edge of – well, what was left of Danielson's *jaw*."

"An indentation?"

"It's more of an imbedded mark. I'd say it's probably from a ring. Because of the gloves it's not as clear as it could have been, but it's there. We might get lucky and get an impression."

"That's something. Did you check –"

She nodded. "At this point I can't be one hundred percent sure, especially because of the indentations from the ring. But yes, there's needle marks on the outer edge of his lips. His mouth was stuffed with paper and what was left of the skin around his lips was stitched like Turner's."

"Conjectures?"

"Two. One, your perp is pretty strong, but so was Danielson, despite his illness. He was definitely alive when his arms were shoved into the shredder, even with the succinylcholine. The killer might have misjudged the dose" – Cecelia let out another deep breath – "so Danielson might have been semi-conscious when the blades started reaching his face."

God. Kincaid tried to force the image away. "And two?"

"If Danielson was struggling as fiercely as I think, there's a good chance he injured his attacker. I found traces of blood on his neck, scalp, and the back of his shirt that weren't his." She paused for a moment. "Kincaid?"

"Sorry. Just thinking. Anything else?"

"Not yet, I'm afraid. I'll call you when the tests and toxicology reports are back."

"Thanks."

"Kincaid? You look and sound exhausted. Are you all right?"

Other than a headache that feels like a knife wound, and a spine that's on fire I'm just great. "Sure. Just tired."

"You're pushing yourself too hard. Don't."

"I won't," he lied.

"Did you have your CT scan?"

"Yesterday. No. This morning." It seemed like a week ago now.

"Tell me when the results are in. And take it easy."

"I will."

Kincaid could tell by her eyes that Cecelia didn't believe him.

Chapter Forty Five

Barclay leaned forward, stabbed his elbows down against the table and covered his face with his hands. Kincaid had been questioning him for half an hour, and the man was showing the unmistakable signs of frustration and stress. He couldn't sit still, was perspiring profusely, and he kept pausing and gulping the dryness from his throat while he talked, stammering over his words. He tried to avoid looking directly at Kincaid. Whenever he glanced at Amy she stared back blankly. She only looked at her notes when Barclay's eyes were on Kincaid.

"I swear to God I didn't have anything to do with Turner."

"But you hated him."

"Yes, I hated him. And I'm glad he's dead. But I didn't kill him. You've got to believe me, Kincaid." Barclay ran his fingers through his moistened hair. His forehead glistened with sweat. "I didn't kill him."

Kincaid walked around the table to where he'd left the file. He looked up quickly at the one-way window as he shuffled some photographs together. Richardson and Stephanie watched from the adjacent room.

"Here," he said quietly, tossing them down in front of Barclay. "Take a look."

The second Barclay pulled his hands away from his face and saw the top picture, he covered his eyes and swept the photos away.

"God, that's horrible." He choked back the tears and retched dryly.

Kincaid pushed the photographs back. "I said, 'take a look.'"

Barclay peered under his hands. He studied them silently for a few seconds. Kincaid turned a few more over. Barclay picked one up with a quivering hand, frowning, grimacing in disbelief. "His lips," he muttered quietly to himself. "They look like they've been –"

Barclay couldn't even mouth the word *sewn*. Is that what they were? *Stitched together*? He glanced down again, still unable to believe what he was looking at. "Who could do that?"

"Anyone who has as much hatred and frustration as you."

"No. No way."

It was easy to tell Barclay was horrified by the images. More than horrified. But people often were when they were confronted with what they'd actually done. There wasn't any place to hide any more: just fear and loathing. His face was deathly pale and he was barely breathing. Kincaid slowly gathered up the pictures and left them face-up in a conspicuous pile on the side of the table. He pulled a chair out and sat next to Barclay. The man was whimpering softly. Kincaid looked up at the window – *what was their perception?*

"Richard."

He yanked a tissue from his jeans and wiped the tears away. His eyes were red, the rest of his face almost colorless.

"Richard. I don't think you had anything to do with Devlin Turner's murder."

If Amy was startled, she didn't show it. She jotted down her notes as the tape recorder kept whirling.

Barclay took a jolt. Frowning, he started trembling. "Then why am I here? I don't –"

"Richard." Kincaid waited for him to look up. "I want you to tell me about Brian McCabe."

If a person could faint and keep sitting up, Barclay did it. His lips vibrated with a slurred explosion of words, but there wasn't any sound. He slumped back into his chair, struggling to breathe. "I don't know what you're talking about."

Kincaid sighed deeply. "I can put you in that alley, Richard."

Barclay stared at the table.

"A witness came forward," Amy said coolly, her voice barely above a whisper.

Nothing.

Kincaid wasn't surprised by the initial lack of information, or the paucity of help. Another story had been on the radio that morning. A variety clerk was shot and killed for a couple of cartons of smokes and a handful of lottery tickets. There were at least fifteen witnesses, but not one person stepped up to identify the shooter. Everyone was an interested bystander, afraid, reluctant, or just apathetic enough not to want to get involved.

"No-one at the clubs told the original investigators anything. I've talked to someone since then, however. People often don't talk simply because they're afraid. Sometimes it's for personal reasons. That's what happened in your case."

Barclay combed his fingers through his hair again. Somehow, from somewhere deep inside, he'd known this moment would come the second he decided to follow McCabe into the alley. Fate had fucked him over again.

"The witness came out of the bar with a friend," Kincaid went on. "The man's married, has a family. He didn't want to admit being at the gay club, and assumed his life would be ruined if his wife found out. I assured him his information would be confidential, and he gave us a fairly good description of the men he saw arguing in the alley that night."

Kincaid moved around the table, sat down across from Barclay, and read Amy's notes. "Just under six feet, dark hair, high forehead, glasses, a goatee, no tats, and no particularly distinguishing facial features. He also indicated the man bothering McCabe was wearing a pale blue windbreaker, just like the one you wore the other day when we met on your way into work."

"A common coat and color," Barclay managed to breathe.

"Yes, it is." Kincaid started pacing. He realized he'd moved too fast and a warm surge of blood flushed his cheeks. He waited a second for the nausea to pass. He hoped Amy hadn't noticed. Or Stephanie.

"The man picked you out quite easily when I showed him some photographs."

Barclay tensed.

"I've also checked the cab companies that had calls in the area that evening. A driver for *'City Wide'* definitely remembers picking up a fare around eleven o'clock, just two streets over from the club. He said the man was pretty nervous and kept glancing around, like he was making sure he wasn't being followed. The cabbie said you had blood on your jacket."

Amy looked Barclay in the eyes. "He picked you out too, Richard."

"And if that wasn't enough, we have physical proof."

Barclay was startled.

"The cabbie dropped you off at the Yonge Street station. You probably don't remember running down the stairs, but before you reached the kiosk you bumped into a middle aged man exiting the station. He ended up with blood on the sleeve of his jacket and a smear on his hand. He panicked. People often do when they come in contact with someone else's blood because of the fear of infectious diseases. The man went into an *After Hours* clinic just off Yonge to get tested. They called me. We've already identified one bloodstain. It was McCabe's."

Barclay slumped down into his chair and covered his face with his hands.

"I'm sure the lab results will confirm your blood's there too, Richard."

Silence.

Kincaid leaned over the table. "And we have the pipe."

Barclay shuddered and retched, but managed to choke the bile back down. His face looked painfully tight. He glanced at the pictures piled on the desk but quickly looked away.

Amy stopped writing, her tone soft. "Tell us what happened, Richard."

Kincaid put his hand on Barclay's shoulder. "We'll help if we can. But you have to be honest about everything."

Barclay closed his eyes and took a few deep breaths. He started to taste real air. He hadn't said anything, but he was already aware that the enormous, oppressive weight that had slowly been smothering him for the past month was beginning to ease. Barclay knew it would never go away completely, that it would always be there, like his guilt.

A coarse whisper. "I just wanted to talk to him."

"McCabe?"

A nod. "I followed him one night after work."

"Where?"

"To a club on Richmond." He shrugged. "A gay bar."

"How did you know where he'd be?"

"I watched him for a few days. And besides –"

"Yes?"

"I'd seen him there before."

"So you followed him?" Kincaid prompted.

"He didn't see me. I waited until he came out." He shook his head vigorously. "You've got to believe me. I only wanted to talk to him."

"And?"

Barclay was on the edge. Kincaid didn't want to press too hard but he didn't want to lose him, either.

"What happened, Richard?"

He seemed surprised at the sound of his own name. "I stopped him and told him I wanted to talk about my book."

"Did McCabe know who you were?"

"No. He said he saw hundreds of manuscripts a month and he didn't remember mine or who I was. I told him I thought he was lying, that he was the reason Turner hated my book."

"What did he say?"

"That I was wrong. McCabe said all he did was research and fact-finding, and that whatever editing or criticism he offered was incidental. Things he noticed readers might have missed."

Barclay let out a deep breath. His body stopped shivering, but his eyes clouded over with the distant, far away glaze of passivity that often comes before you release a heavy burden of despair. Kincaid waited. He felt Stephanie's presence behind the window.

"Everything happened so quickly. We started arguing. McCabe told me he didn't have anything to do with the rejection, that if I had a problem I should see Turner. But I wouldn't let him go. Each time he tried to walk away I got in his face. We started pushing. He yelled and said he was calling the police, that he'd have me charged with assault. He started walking back to the club so I grabbed his arm. I spun him around and slammed him into the wall. I've never felt so angry in my life."

Barclay put a hand against his heart and closed his eyes. Tears welled behind his eyes.

"When I shoved him into the wall he hit his head. I heard a dull thud. I guess that's when I cut my knuckles." He looked at his hands, imagining the stain. "He slumped over and felt the back of his head. His hand was covered in blood."

Kincaid waited. Barclay gulped. "He started swearing and shouting. Garbled, kind of. He took a swing at me, but missed. So – so – I hit him again. And again. He kind of slouched down the wall, trying to – trying to cover his face and head with his arms."

The tears came freely now. Barclay choked on anguished sobs. "I saw a pipe by the wall. I grabbed it and swung it at him. Once, maybe twice – I'm not sure. It happened so fast. I heard –"

"What? What did you hear?"

"I think I heard his head crack."

Barclay stopped. His hands shook uncontrollably, his voice barely above a whisper. "You wouldn't have believed the blood. It was everywhere. It was – unreal."

He turned and grabbed Kincaid's arm. "He didn't get up. He crumpled down and didn't move. I was afraid to touch him, but I shook him a bit, to see. Gently, almost. He didn't move."

Kincaid didn't pull away. "Then?"

Barclay frowned deeply. Half of him was trying to remember, half was trying to forget. "I didn't know what to do, but I couldn't stay there. There were people walking past the end of the alley. It wouldn't be long before someone came by."

He yanked his hand away and started rocking back and forth. "Oh God, I just left him there. I killed him and just left him there, bleeding in the alley. I can't believe I did it. I can't believe it. Oh God, the blood."

"But you called the police," Kincaid said softly, guiding him back. "911 says it was your voice."

"I called from outside the subway. I knew the call could be traced, but I couldn't leave him lying in the alley like that. What if – what if he was still alive? I thought they could save him or something." He glanced at Amy. "That it wasn't too late."

Trembling like he was freezing, Barclay collapsed forward and buried his face in his arms. Kincaid squeezed his shoulder and gave him a little shake. He glanced up at the two-way mirror, his eyes sad. This was something else he never liked. Amy kept jotting down notes while the tape recorder whirled, sealing someone else's fate.

"How did you know about McCabe?"

Barclay looked up, his eyes glazed with confusion. "He made a bunch of corrections on the script I sent Turner. I thought it was why he sent me such a terrible rejection."

"How many times did you hit him with the pipe?"

"Once, maybe twice. I'm not sure. It's all just a blur."

"What did you do with the pipe?"

More confusion. "I – I don't remember."

"Did you take it with you?"

He shook his head. "No. I think I threw it away."

Amy looked up at Kincaid.

"In the alley?"

"I think so."

"And then you ran away? Hailed the cab."

Barclay nodded. He stopped crying and slumped back into his chair as the world caved in.

"I want to show you another picture."

"No. No, I don't want to see any more. I killed him and that's it."

Kincaid handed a photograph to Barclay. "Look at it."

Even seeing it upside down, Amy still shuddered.

It was a moment before Barclay looked. The instant he focused on the image, he dropped the picture as if it was on fire. He shook his head and muttered into his hands. "No, no. Oh my God, no. His mouth. His mouth is –"

He couldn't even whisper the word *gone*.

Kincaid took the picture back. It was a facial shot of McCabe at the morgue. Barclay wrapped his arms over his chest and started rocking back and forth again, mumbling incoherently between sobs. Kincaid glanced up at the window and thought he saw shadows move. He shook his head.

Barclay attacked McCabe all right. But he hadn't killed him.

Chapter Forty Six

Tired and in pain, Kincaid walked into the viewing room. Stephanie was talking as he opened the door.

"What do you mean he didn't kill McCabe?"

Kincaid watched Amy review specific details of Barclay's confession, confirming the same information from different perspectives. She wanted to make sure they hadn't missed anything that could blindside them later, and that nothing in Barclay's statement was vague or contradictory. Or suspicious.

Kincaid started massaging the back of his neck. He couldn't deny there was a part of him – albeit a very little part – that felt sorry for the man. Richard Barclay had stepped far beyond his normal boundaries, and had fallen into that dark, primordial abyss where he couldn't control himself, his feelings or his fear. But when all was said and done, he was still the one who'd inched closer to the edge, the one who was responsible for everything he did.

And for what? A few dollars and his name on a book jacket? How many people would actually have read his manuscript? There wouldn't be a huge roll-out, and any promo would be short and sweet. Nothing at all like the ones done for the writers who'd found a niche, who had an audience, regardless of how well – or poorly – written their work was. Anticipatory praise wouldn't come from the New York Times – the reviews would be from paid Internet sites or Podcasts and Facebook friends. It would probably still be true if Barclay's book was ten times better than the cardboard cutouts that line the bestseller shelves, or the ones with a 'famous' author's name dominating the cover but was actually 'co-written' by someone else scrawled across the bottom. How long would it have been before his book was tossed into a remainder bin, or jammed into the bargain table with countless others whose publishers had mistakenly given them a chance? It didn't seem like much to Kincaid – but could it have been enough for Barclay?

"Where's Richardson?"

"He got a call and had to go"

"DiMatteo?"

"No idea. Come on, K. What's this about?"

"He didn't do it, Stephanie."

"He said he did. I watched him confess."

Kincaid stared at Barclay through his own reflection in the two-way mirror. "He attacked him, but he didn't kill him."

"I don't understand."

"You're even more beautiful when you frown."

"Stop it."

"There's no question they argued, and that Barclay knocked him against the wall and hit him with the pipe. The physical evidence is pretty clear. But there are two problems."

"One?"

"One, forensics show that only one blow hit McCabe on the back of the head. The other one actually struck him on the shoulder and left a large, deep bruise that only surfaced during the autopsy. Dr. Tantor confirmed that neither blow – alone or together – would have been enough to kill him."

"Head wounds bleed profusely," Stephanie argued. "So he died because Barclay left him in the alley and he bled out. Or maybe it was internal bleeding? A clot?"

"Cecelia ruled that out. CSU says the pipe was clean, except for some smeared blood."

"So?"

"Remember Kenny and his friend? They guy who was attacked by the bangers? They both touched the pipe when they brought it in. But everything had been carefully wiped clean."

"So someone held the pipe *after* Barclay. Someone wearing gloves."

"Probably surgical."

Stephanie leaned against the glass and watched Barclay daub his eyes as Amy walked him through his prior statements.

"And you saw how Barclay reacted when I showed him the pictures."

"Sure. But most people are devastated when they have to confront what they've done." Stephanie bit at her lip. *Danielson's house*. How could . . . how could anyone . . .

Kincaid acquiesced with a nod. "But McCabe's mouth was smashed in, correct?"

"Correct."

"They still found a tiny puncture mark on his upper lip."

A shiver tickled up Stephanie's back. "And two?"

"Someone else must have used the pipe and then tried to sew McCabe's lips together. *What was left of his lips.* Whoever started couldn't finish. Something, or someone, scared off the attacker. Perhaps someone else came out of the club or people walked into the alley. It doesn't matter: Barclay was already gone. But there were no fingerprints on McCabe's face. Whoever started working with the needle and thread wore gloves, and everything was wiped completely clean."

"So the same person who used the pipe after Barclay —"

"— was the one who'd started sewing his lips together. But he ran out of time, and decided to smash McCabe's mouth in with the pipe instead and stuff it with paper."

Stephanie sighed. "So Barclay attacked McCabe, but someone else finished him off?"

Kincaid took Stephanie's hand. "It's a wonderful world, isn't it?"

Stephanie watched Barclay sob into his hands. She reached over and flicked off the intercom. "What else do you know you're not telling me?"

With a heavy, sullen sigh and downcast eyes, Kincaid told her about his visit to Jacobs.

The blood, the huge body slumped over, the note crushed in his hand. When he was finished, Stephanie could only mumble something inaudible and shake her head. *All this over a book?* She couldn't believe it. Kincaid pulled her back from her morbid thoughts.

"Amy's going to be a while. I want her to take Barclay through the assault charge and file all the paperwork. She'll see if he decides to go the legal route, and if he gets bail. In the meantime . . . "

"Yes?"

"I know it's late, but do you feel like another drive?"

Stephanie nodded, took one last glance at Barclay hunched over the table, and followed Kincaid outside.

*

"Thanks for seeing us on such short notice," Kincaid said as he walked into the small, rather nondescript office. "I apologize for disturbing you so late."

Cynthia Baxter didn't bother hiding her displeasure at the impromptu visit. She kept tidying things up on her desk. "You're lucky I was still here."

Kincaid turned and introduced his companion. "I think you know Ms. Quan, Gail Meredith's security consultant?"

Cynthia Baxter nodded impatiently. "Yes, we've met. We talked about security at the Publisher's Convention last spring, I think."

"We did. At the Royal York."

"Well, now that the pleasantries have been exchanged, Detective, have a seat and tell me why you're harassing me again."

"Harassing?" Kincaid frowned, settling into one of the tub chairs facing the agent's desk. "That seems rather hyperbolic. I find it odd you see a couple of informal conversations as harassment."

Cynthia stared at him coldly. "I really don't care what you find odd. I'm busy. When you called you said it was important, so get on with it."

"I can't argue with that, Ms. Baxter. From what I can ascertain, you've been very busy indeed."

"What are you talking about?"

"Well I assume it would take quite a while putting the story together. It has been pretty good so far, although I'm certainly not a literary critic."

Cynthia tensed noticeably. The veins in her neck pulsed. She glanced at Stephanie then quickly looked away.

"Look, Detective. I don't have time –"

"You've been writing the serial story for *The Gazette*, Ms. Baxter. *Writer's Revenge.* About the murders in the publishing industry." Kincaid instinctively lowered his tone, his words slow and precise. "So indulge me and make the time."

Cynthia Baxter offered a short laugh. "You're joking, surely."

"Do I look like I am?"

She shifted uncomfortably and immediately began searching her purse for a cigarette. "This is ridiculous," she muttered. "I'm going to sue your ass off, Kincaid."

Any trace of sensuality displayed at the gym was gone. Her eyes were cold, her tone bitter and caustic, her lips in a tight sneer. Kincaid waited while Cynthia fumbled with her lighter. "Look," she began. But Kincaid interrupted.

"There have been three murders, Ms. Baxter, and I'm really tired of people lying to me." He couldn't picture her in the skintight leotard she'd been wearing at the gym now that she had a cigarette dangling from the corner of her mouth. Her hands were shaking. Kincaid stared into her eyes, refusing to let her look away and regroup.

"You wrote the serial, Cynthia. Perhaps on your own, perhaps with some help. But you've been submitting the bi-weekly pieces to *The Gazette*."

"You're crazy."

"That's the least of my problems," Kincaid smiled. "You submitted one segment of the serial from the Metropolitan Library. I didn't think it was possible, but we managed to trace the submission to a specific terminal and time."

She scoffed. "Come on, I'm always there. There's got to be at least forty terminals in the resource center alone. And then there's all the WiFi areas on the various floors. You can't possibly link someone to a particular terminal, let alone time." She took a long pull on the cigarette and smiled smugly.

"Normally, you'd probably be right. And you're also correct in assuming I can't *unequivocally* put you at a certain computer."

"Then what the hell –"

"But a witness can. The editor at *The Gazette* received the next installment yesterday morning. He needed it early enough to have time to polish it up for Sunday's paper."

"So?" she said haughtily. "That doesn't mean anything."

"So, with a little prompting and a tip from inside our own House, Ms. Quan decided to keep an eye on you yesterday."

The color drained from Baxter's face. She stabbed her cigarette into the ashtray, struggling to stay in control.

"Ms. Quan followed you to the Resource Centre. Not only did she watch you copy the fourth installment of the serial into the terminal, she also managed to read a section of it as well."

Cynthia looked up dumbfounded.

Stephanie smiled. "There was an announcement a car in the underground parking garage had its alarm activated. They gave out your plate number so you went down to turn it off. You took the stick but forgot to log off the computer."

Cynthia's eyes narrowed into a hateful glare. "You bitch."

"Now, now, Ms. Baxter, there's certainly no need for name calling. The point is that we can trace the submissions right to you."

Cynthia was seething inside. "All you can prove is that I wrote a newspaper story." She leaned back arrogantly. "Even if I *had* been involved, there's absolutely nothing to connect me to any of the murders. And I'm not." She crossed her arms over her chest and tried to dismiss Kincaid with a bored, drawn-out sigh.

"I never suggested you were. And the leak's been fixed."

"Taylor," Kincaid explained when Stephanie frowned. "The guy responsible for putting up the photos from Amy's ShoeCam operation. The brass and the blue in his veins won't be able to save him this time."

"Where did you know him from?"

"The gym," Baxter sighed resignedly. "He wanted me bad, and was prepared to do just about anything to make it happen." A half-smile.

"He gave you information from forensics, the canvasses, interviews, everything."

"Anything I said I needed for a special story. One that might hurt you, too."

"And you paid him –"

"In kind. But my lawyer will twist that into entrapment," Baxter grinned vindictively. "Then I'll have your badge for –"

"C62TP784694."

Cynthia tensed forward and frowned. "What?"

Kincaid slowly repeated the random sequence of numbers and letters.

Baxter looked up uncertainly. "I don't understand," she mumbled.

"I think you do," Kincaid said softly. "We know you serialized *The Gazette* story. But I don't believe you were aware of the ramifications it was going to have."

Silence.

"You had an idea, a good one. Write a serial piece for the newspaper, just like Dickens did with the *Pickwick Papers*. You're an agent, but you've been exposed to writers all your career. If I had to make an educated guess, my assumption would be that you've dabbled in writing before. Short stories, perhaps. Newspaper articles. General freelance stuff. You were never really happy with the ten or fifteen percent you were getting for doing all the work for a bunch of knock-off writers. You always thought you could be *more.*"

Baxter sank back into her chair, her forehead deeply creased.

"You didn't think it would actually incite anyone to murder, did you?"

She sighed, almost sadly. "No. No I didn't. I hated Turner passionately. But I never wanted him dead. Just . . . gone."

"The story was meant to put pressure on him, wasn't it?"

No answer.

"You were losing him, and you knew it. You assumed the story would frighten Turner just enough, didn't you?"

Cynthia couldn't sit still. Her hands trembled as she tried to light another cigarette. She looked like she'd aged since they'd first come into her office.

"You leaked out enough details so that someone who knew what was really going on – someone like Turner – would believe the story could be about him. An agent who hurt and cheated writers. An agent who used an unknown writer for his meteoric rise to success by plagiarizing scripts. And Turner bought it. He thought his story was going to be exposed and everything would be over, right when *Excalibur Books* was wooing him for the takeover bid. He would have lost a fortune."

Kincaid glanced at Stephanie. "All the people he'd ever cheated would know what he'd done. He'd always be looking over his shoulder for a writer he viciously rejected, or for someone who could prove he stole their manuscript and file another lawsuit. His time was up."

Baxter lost her composure. She slumped forward, ran her fingers through her hair, and tried to stop shaking. She couldn't. Her face was red. Sweat glistened on her upper lip. She stabbed her cigarette into the ashtray, burning her fingers as she crushed it to dust.

"I had no idea anyone would ever act on the things I'd written," she whispered. "It was just supposed to be a threat. Something to get him going, wind him up, to let him know his dirty little secret could be exposed."

Stephanie looked quizzically at Kincaid.

"The series of numbers," he explained, "are from an offshore bank account in Grenada."

Baxter didn't even bother asking him how he found out. Nothing was going to surprise her now.

"The deposits match the withdrawals from Turner's account."

"So *you* were the one blackmailing him?"

Cynthia just sighed and shrugged her shoulders.

"Why?"

"Revenge. Power, too." She glanced at Kincaid. "And money. It was always about the money."

"You hated the fact Turner bought your agency. You liked the new clients and the funds they kept generating. But the agency wasn't yours anymore, and I think that bothered you the most."

Baxter whispered hoarsely. "I wanted it back."

"Turner must have finally balked at paying those monthly sums."

Cynthia nodded. "Ego can only take so much. And he was giving more and more to *Excalibur*."

"He didn't know it was you, did he?"

"No."

"How did you find out what he was doing?"

Baxter almost smiled. "He was always on liquid lunches. I went through his personal papers and found his access code. It was only a matter of time before I found his computer records. He didn't even bother to encrypt them. It was like putting a bull's eye on his back."

"So you knew all about the manuscripts he'd been stealing and publishing under another writer's name?"

"Yes. Ian Nuraki. The Japanese wonder."

Stephanie frowned. "You don't know who it is, either?"

"There was nothing in his notes," Cynthia glared.

Kincaid told her to go on.

"So I decided to write the serial when he tried to stop paying. I assumed when he saw himself in the plot line, he'd get scared, and then one of two things would happen."

"So?"

"He'd pay the blackmail again. If I kept draining his personal reserves, he'd have to sell the agency back to me eventually."

"Or?"

"Two, I figured if he thought the story would tip off a few of the writers he'd rejected and cheated, he just might pack up and leave. Get out of the business before he was caught. Either way, I'd be rid of him for good and the agency would be mine."

"As well as all the lucrative contracts he'd brought in."

Baxter nodded. "But I swear to God, that's all I wanted. I didn't think someone would kill him. Or McCabe."

Kincaid glanced at Stephanie. She could tell he believed Baxter's denial of any involvement in the murders.

"The account," Cynthia asked uncertainly. "How did you find –"

"It was traced through a complex web of electronic transfers, holding companies, and offshore accounts set up under various names. It took a good deal of time and effort, but the pieces finally came together. No matter how far you bury things, Ms. Baxter, there's usually someone with the skills to dig them back up."

She squinted. "You?"

Kincaid couldn't help laughing. "Heavens no. I have enough trouble logging on. I went to a real expert for that. A wizard. Even then, he had to be motivated. You apparently disguised your tracks quite well."

"Who was it? A computer expert with the police?"

He shook his head. "Brent Jacobs. And believe me, Cynthia, he certainly had the motivation. He also helped getting the information from the library, and accessing your computer. It was a cake walk for him."

Kincaid stood up and straightened his suit jacket. "The officers are waiting outside. I'll tell them to give you a few minutes to put your papers together and call your lawyer."

Kincaid thought back to when they met. That skimpy little leotard and thong were going to attract a lot of attention in the correction facilities' gym. "*Lights out!*" was going to take on a whole new meaning for Cynthia Baxter.

*

The day had finally worn him down, and after leaving Baxter's office, Kincaid dropped Stephanie off at her condo. Physically and emotionally drained, he had to rest: everything else could wait. Stephanie had wanted to go home with him again, but Kincaid desperately needed to be alone. He didn't like her seeing him in pain.

When he hit the city limits, Kincaid veered off on the back roads so he didn't have to deal with the steady stream of traffic congesting the highway. He was only twenty minutes from home when his phone rang. He pulled over onto the shoulder, braking the car to a rocking stop. Fear tightened his chest. He closed his eyes and tried to stay calm, but he couldn't. He knew it was Dr. Degatz before she spoke.

"It's time, Kincaid."

Chapter Forty Seven

Carolyn stopped wiping her eyes and looked up the moment Kincaid said her name. Barely blinking, she stared down the hall, squinting through eyelids glued with tears, trying to remember the face and bring it into focus. Her lips trembled and she fidgeted nervously with a wad of tissue crumpled between her hands. She looked like someone coming out of a dream who's not sure whether she's awake or not. *And not sure if she wants to be.*

"Kincaid?" she asked tentatively, her voice thick and slurred.

"Yes, Carolyn. I'm here." Careful not to move too quickly, he eased down beside her, sensing the fear in her eyes. And in his own.

"Thanks for coming."

Kincaid put his arm around her shoulders and drew her closer. "How long have you been here?"

"What?"

"How long have you been here?"

Staring through the fog, she mechanically checked her watch, although Kincaid could tell by her puzzled frown time had lost its meaning for Ryan's mother. What would moments mean now? *Moments filled with nothingness?*

"Carolyn? Carolyn?"

She looked up slowly.

"Have you seen Dr. Degatz?"

"Dr. Degatz?" *Another confusing name from the past.* "Yes. She called you, didn't she?"

"Yes."

"Where were you?"

"In the car," he whispered. "Carolyn, would you like to come in —."

"No." She shook her head vigorously. "No. I was in before and" — she looked up insecurely at the door — "I don't think I'm ready to go back in. Maybe we could wait a minute." Carolyn stared at the wad of tissues. "He might feel better by then."

Kincaid hugged her to his side. Tears welled behind his eyes, tears he didn't want her to see. He replayed the phone call in his mind, listening again to what Dr. Degatz told him. *It's time, Kincaid. We're losing him, and there's nothing else we can do.*

"Will you be all right for a few minutes?"

She jolted forward and anxiously looked up. "You're not leaving, are you?" She grabbed his arm as hard as she could, digging her fingers into his flesh until it hurt.

"I'm not going anywhere. I just want to check on Ryan."

"Oh."

"Will you stay here?"

"Yes. I guess so. Did I tell you the minister was here? She seemed nice, but she was very sad. I don't think I'd want to be a minister."

"When was that, Carolyn?"

She gestured faintly with a haphazard wave. "Before. Sometime before. She was worried about me. I told her not to be so silly. I wasn't the one in *there*." There. *Where was that again?*

"I'll get her, too."

"Yes. But Kincaid –"

"What is it?"

"Don't wake him up if he's sleeping. He was in – quite a lot of pain and needs his rest."

Kincaid gently squeezed her shoulders. "I'll only be a few minutes." The pain in his chest tightened, squeezing his breath through constricted arteries. His head ached, his back was knotted with pain, his . . . But what did any of that matter now?

When Kincaid pushed Ryan's door open, he couldn't remember a time when he'd felt the silence so heavy, so demanding and still, like he did now. There were noises in the room: the static *blip blip blip* of the monitors, the hum of the oxygen machines that forced the child to breathe, the ceiling fan, the filtered moans from other rooms, the tread of his own footsteps. But they only made the stillness, the other silence, more brutal.

Kincaid couldn't move, so he stared at Ryan from the door. He looked at the bed, the tubes, the tentacles of wires, the machines that did everything the boy's small body was supposed to do. The hockey stick was propped up in the corner, and Berger's sweater was draped over the end of the bed.

Kincaid willed his legs to move and slowly stepped closer.

Did Ryan know he was there? In some way, with some sense that Kincaid couldn't quite fathom, was the boy able to feel his presence? And if he did, was it a blessing, or a curse? Was he partly *here*, and partly *there*? *Now*, and *then*? What? *Where?*

Kincaid pulled a chair up next to the bed. He sat down quietly, never taking his eyes away from Ryan. The boy's skin was translucent, and there wasn't so much as a trace of movement behind his eyelids. Kincaid thought about how often he lay in bed, with Stephanie curled into his side, wide awake in the middle of the night, watching the tiny ripples and spasms behind her lids as she slept and dreamed. If only Ryan . . .

The pale blue lines on the monitor rippled across the screen in slow, staggered waves.

It's time. There's nothing else we can do.

He reached over the metal bars and took the boy's hand. Was he imagining he could feel a frantic pulse? He was surprised at how cold Ryan's skin seemed. He remembered the boy's face at the hockey game, how excited he'd been, how the smile had rarely left his face unless the pain had been too much. Kincaid knew in his heart he would have given anything to see that look of happiness and wonder on the child's face again, even if it was just for a few precious moments. He leaned his head against the railing, closed his eyes and did something he hadn't done in a long, long time, something he'd almost forgotten how to do. He prayed for something he didn't understand. He didn't know why and he didn't know who he was trying to speak to and he didn't know if it would help or not, but Kincaid opened his heart and prayed for Ryan and his mother until the tears came, glistening his face and wetting his fingers and slowly dripping from his cheeks and onto the bed's metal rungs. He prayed every night – but not like this. Those were a different kind of prayer.

He didn't know how to end this one, so his mumbled words finally just drifted off into silence. He stood up uneasily, bent over the railing, and gently stroked the child's hair. He kissed him softly on the forehead and each cheek, then gave his tiny hand a last, reassuring squeeze.

He stepped soundlessly from the room and took his place beside Ryan's mother.

She kept staring into her hands. "How does he seem?" she asked quietly.

"Carolyn, –"

She reached for his arm, frowning uncertainly. "It's happening, isn't it Kincaid?"

He stroked the back of her hand. "Yes. Yes, it is."

An orderly pushed a large metal trolley cart by. Pill containers rattled noisily. Down the hall, doctors somberly compared notes at the nurses' station.

Kincaid kneeled down in front of Ryans' mother. "Carolyn," he began softly. "Come in with me."

She looked up, her face distorted with a confusing miasma of fear and frustration and anger. She tensed and arched back like a cobra, caught between striking and slithering away, anywhere, but Kincaid wouldn't let go of her hand.

"We have to do what's best for Ryan," Kincaid said softly. "Because we love him so much. I think it's time to let him go."

She stared back through streaming tears that blurred her vision.

"I think if we could ask Ryan, he'd say it was what *he* wanted, too."

"He's always been so brave, hasn't he?"

"He has." Kincaid's lips curled into a fragile smile. "Brave, and content with what he had. I think that's the way we have to be now."

Trembling, the woman pulled her hand away from Kincaid's and leaned forward. He took her in his arms, hugging her as tightly as he could and trying to soothe her fear away with hushed whispers.

"I think I should find Dr. Degatz."

"No," Carolyn cried, shaking. She sank back down, defeated. Kincaid could tell by her eyes that meant everything was really over. It was a finality she couldn't face.

"We have to," Kincaid whispered gently.

Carolyn nodded numbly. "I'll never forget what you –- you've done for him."

Kincaid shook his head, his eyes swollen and red. "I'll never forget what *he's* done for *me.*"

He helped her stand, carefully keeping her in his arms. He kissed the back of her hands, brushing the salt away from her tears with his lips.

"Wait here. I'll find her."

Kincaid walked slowly down the corridor. He didn't find it odd in the least that he wasn't aware of anything else that was going on: the overhead speakers barking out instructions, nurses scurrying back and forth, breathless visitors peering anxiously into other rooms, paper-slippered patients shuffling along and pulling i.v. stands in their wake. None of it mattered, none of it meant anything. Kincaid leaned over the counter and asked one of the nurses to page Dr. Degatz.

"To what room, sir?"

"To here," he said. There would be papers to sign, forms to initial, waivers that needed to be documented. "I need to talk to her first."

He glanced back down the hall. Oblivious to everything around her, Carolyn had slumped into the chair and was sobbing uninhibitedly.

Later, much later, everything was a dream. Not a dream, really; a haunting nightmare of jumbled shadows Kincaid saw wherever he looked. Time passed, but time, strangely, *without time.*

Dr. Degatz had explained everything slowly and carefully. Again. Quietly. Again. Kincaid realized that no matter how often she'd been forced to do this very same thing, it had never become any easier for her. He wondered if saving a child's life overshadowed the pain of losing one. He doubted it.

They went into the room together. Kincaid stood next to Carolyn on the far side of the bed. He put one arm around her waist and held the metal railing with his other hand so he could steady himself. He didn't know what to say, or if he should even speak at all. What *could* he say? He'd already said what he needed to pray. He squeezed Carolyn against him, certain he could hear the pounding pulse of her heartbeat. He watched Dr. Degatz move slowly around, doing this and that, examining a wire and then rechecking a monitor, and wished beyond hope that there was something more he could do.

There was a light knock at the door and the minister came in on silent steps. Her fingers trembled around a well-used Bible and crucifix. Old and stooped with the tragic weight of her own years, she shuffled over to the child's side. She ran her gnarled fingers lightly over Ryan's face and hands, then moved down to the foot of the bed. That's when Kincaid realized he hadn't looked up into the child's face yet. When he did, he shuddered with conflicting and ambivalent feelings of wonder and fear. He reached down and touched Ryan's arm just as Carolyn leaned forward and stroked her palm over her son's forehead.

Kincaid felt the strangest sense of warmth, of warmth and pain, of warmth and pain and fear and hope, and somewhere, somewhere deep within the hidden recesses of his mind, in a place he didn't really know or understand, he realized he was praying again.

Chapter Forty Eight

Gail Meredith jolted to an anxious stop.

Her hand poised inches over the cutting board, the knife was aggressively still. It took her a second to catch her breath. She leaned over her kitchen's center block and scanned the dining room and as much of the front hall as she could see. *What had she heard?* She pulled her hand away from the lime and stepped back, tightening her fingers around the knife's hilt, the blade menacingly upright. She closed her eyes and listened. Nothing. No footsteps. No sound of anything being opened or closed, no creaks or groans from the floorboards in the foyer. She opened her eyes and stared at nothing, rationally examining a list of possibilities.

Mrs. Dellvecchio was off for the evening: once a week she visited a group of domestics at a little apartment downtown where they traded their employers' gossip and didn't have to pick up after anyone but themselves. Sterns, the gardener, had used some vacation time to visit his sister in Montreal. No business appointments, and she never met associates at home. Names flashed through her mind – Turner. McCabe. Danielson. Gail Meredith brandished the knife, and waited.

Seconds passed. The house was quiet: all she heard was the gentle hum of the furnace. She shook her head and forced herself to relax. *It was nothing,* she thought. Nothing at all. She'd been edgy since her "meeting" with Caster. She pictured him again: it wasn't just his eyes that made her skin crawl, but how he moved, his smell, the way his lips curled up angrily every time he spoke that tugged at her deepest fears. A man to reckon with, and one she'd never, ever turn her back on. But he had a purpose and had to be dealt with, and she'd made pacts with people far worse than Erik Caster. She turned back to the cutting board and picked up another lime. The knife pierced the peel, splattering juice over her fingers.

Bang.

She stopped in mid-slice and looked nervously toward the hall. The noise was clearer this time – it had come from the front door.

Gail slipped quietly from the kitchen, the knife stiffly out in front. She leaned down in a defensive crouch and crept toward the door, carefully keeping her back to the wall. She paused in the foyer, took a deep breath, and glanced out each of the long rectangular windows that framed the door. Nothing. Closer. Another look. She pressed her face against the glass and peeked as far as she could to the left and right. Nothing.

Meredith quietly unlocked the door. She waited, listened, then eased the door open just a crack. She paused, then pried it back a little more. The blade at her side, she stepped out onto the portico and scanned the yard. It was almost fifty yards to the street. The darkness *breathed*. No hint of movement. *No scent.*

She hurried back inside and locked the door. She darted into the kitchen and grabbed a glass from an overhead rack. *Settle down*, she thought. *I've got to settle down.* And then she froze. She'd heard it again. A light, metallic, scraping sound. An echo. Someone was trying the windows.

Her heart pounding, Gail moved away from the counter and eased up against the pantry. *Don't panic.* She looked up and caught the edge of a shadow drift by the kitchen window. *A man?* Gail steadied the knife and held her breath. Then she heard the lock on the back door jiggle. Someone was trying to get in.

She flicked off the overhead lights, instantly shrouding the kitchen with murky shadows back-lit from the hallway. She inched her way toward the back door, her body tight to the wall, the knife thrust out stomach high. Tentative steps. It took her half a minute to reach the edge of the kitchen. Gail poked her head around the corner: everything was quiet. Bending down, she scurried on her knees until she reached the door. She leaned up carefully and risked a quick glance through the window. Nothing but emptiness. After a deep breath she flicked on the outside lights. The glare bathed the deck in a shimmering whiteness that made the rest of the yard seem even blacker. Gail peeked out from the edge of the window and gasped. A cry caught deep in her throat as she mouthed a silent scream.

Caster!

He jumped but didn't move away. For a second he looked just as startled as she did. But the surprise faded quickly and the salacious grin she detested so intensely crept back across his lips. Glancing down and nodding at the upraised knife, he held up his open palms.

"What the fuck do you think you're doing?"

Caster smiled impishly, pleased she was still panting for breath. Her breasts strained against her blouse, her nipples hard.

"You Goddamn well scared the shit out of me."

"I tried the front door bell," he answered, watching the blade. "And the lock. But I didn't get no answer."

"Shit, it's broken," Gail muttered, remembering what Mrs. Dellvecchio mentioned before she left.

"Nice knife. Think you could point it . . . ?"

Gail looked down, momentarily confused. "I was cutting some lime for a drink."

"Better it than me." He wasn't smiling.

Gail scanned the yard before she told him to come in. Letting Caster go first, she turned on all the lights as she walked back into the kitchen.

"Quite the house," Caster nodded appreciatively. He perched down on a bar stool next to the center block. "Maybe I'll have somethin' like this when I'm published and rich and famous."

"Sure." Gail moved around to the other side. "Sure you will, Erik."

The huge kitchen was a magazine showcase. Edged with six wooden barstools, a large center block was angled across the middle of the room. Above, sparkling copper pots and pans hung from a wire rack. All the appliances blended in perfectly, their fronts subtly matched with the same wood as the cupboards and pantry. Caster didn't even see the fridge at first, but the tall, custom-made wine cabinet in the far corner caught his eye. It was an ornate piece made from solid mahogany.

"How many bottles?"

Gail turned to see what he was looking at. "Around a hundred."

He looked impressed. "Climate-controlled?"

She nodded, surprised he even knew what it was, let alone be astute enough to ask something like that. Caster and 'astute': two words Gail never imagined would have shared the same sentence.

"What's the rest of the house like?"

"None of your business."

"What about your room?"

"Don't push your luck, Caster."

"Testy, testy." He swung around on the stool. "Just think of all the nice things I've done for you."

He wasn't smiling – his eyes coldly intense. Bitter. Gail sensed his seething anger: she couldn't risk pushing him too far. And she didn't even know how *far* was. Not yet. There was too much to lose.

"You're right. After all, we're partners." The thought brought bile to the back of her throat.

Caster grinned wickedly. "Well, yes. Yes we are." *He-he.* Erik seemed to be toying with the idea; rolling it around and tasting it the way a child plays with a new swear word.

"We're both a little tense. Perhaps we should celebrate with a drink." Gail stabbed her knife into the cutting board with a ferocity that made him recoil. The hilt quivered. "Finish the lime."

She turned and walked over to the pantry, feeling his hungry eyes leering her ass. Caster grinned and yanked out the knife. "You're my type of woman, Gail." He shook his head. "My type of woman."

Meredith leaned over a little too long, and left her legs a little too far apart, her dress rising up over her thighs as she pulled a bottle of rum from the bottom shelf. "Next time it'll be champagne," she said. "But this should do for now." She poured them each a double as Caster sliced the lime.

"Ice?"

He nodded, slowly looking her up and down. Gail felt her skin crawl. "I heard about Danielson on the news again this afternoon," she said quietly, not bothering to turn away from the fridge. There was a little bottle beside the ice maker.

Caster snorted. "You had to be there to really get it." He started spinning again, mentally replaying the horrible scene once more. He'd re-lived it a hundred times already, but he'd never get tired of going over it again and again. Each time brought more grisly details and memories, more blood, more screams, more splattered pieces of flesh. His cock started to unfurl: he'd already found out it was a great way to come.

"You should have seen his face. God, it was something to see."

She dropped a couple of ice cubes in each glass and a wedge of lime. Caster had completely mangled the pieces.

"So everything went fine?"

"Fine? Ha! Like clockwork, baby. Like absolute fucking clockwork."

Gail spoke through clenched teeth. "I've warned you, Caster. Don't try to get too close. I'm not your *baby*."

His eyes widened with a sudden rush of hatred, but his venomous smile quickly returned. "Sure, Gail. Sure. We're partners though, right?" He held up his glass. So did Gail. "To partners."

Caster downed his drink in one long gulp, then reached for the bottle. Gail watched him coldly.

"Yeah, you should'a seen the fucker's face. You can't imagine the blood."

Gail smiled vindictively. "It looks like you didn't come away unscathed either."

His anger exploded. "What the fuck you looking at?"

"Nothing."

"Fuck me *nothin'*!" He instinctively did up another shirt button so that more of the hated birthmark was covered. *The curse.*

Gail's implicit understanding was immediate. "All I meant was that you've got blood on your shirt." *My God*, she thought. *Unbelievable. He murders someone and not only keeps the evidence, but wears it around like a badge.*

"Leave it, *Gail*. Understand?"

"Of course I do. I wasn't staring. I just meant your eye is pretty swollen." Leaning forward, she smiled empathically, squeezing her breasts together with her arms.

So it wasn't the birthmark, Caster thought. She was fucking lucky. Sneering, he self-consciously touched the side of his face. His eye was bruised a mottled orange and black, and a jagged cut zigzagged across his forehead and down toward his ear.

"He put up a fight, that's for sure," Caster admitted with a touch of admiration. Even with that stuff you gave me, that – suchhie – succoco – that paralyzing shit –"

"Succinylcholine."

"Yeah, that stuff."

"Did you give him all of it?"

"Naa. Half. Figured that's all I needed."

You stupid piece of useless shit!

"It didn't keep him down and out for long, but long enough. He fought back pretty hard. Until I stuffed his mouth with paper and sewed his lips up."

Gail shivered. "You got in through the back door?"

"Sure did." *Same way I'm gonna' get into you, Gail.*

"And no-one else was there?"

"Like you said, I had the whole place to myself."

"I told you. He was expecting a private meeting – just not with you."

Caster winced as he downed another double. Gail pulled her own glass away.

"Slow down," she cautioned. "We've got business to discuss."

"Yeah, my book," Caster smiled, pausing. *Inside.* He poured himself another shot anyway. "But don't you worry about me, partner. I know when enough's enough." He grinned spitefully. "So did Danielson."

"What do you mean?"

"Well shit. Like I said. For an old guy he struggled like a son of a bitch."

Gail muttered over her glass. "He was fighting for his life."

"Aren't we all?"

"But there weren't any problems?"

Caster feigned hurt. "What? Me? Of course not. I told you, everything went like –"

"Clockwork. Yes, I know."

Caster frowned. He didn't like her tone. "He never saw me until it was too late." Caster spun around on the stool, refusing to let Meredith look away. "I hit him once, just to stun him, like a farmer does to a cow. I caught him on the side of the jaw and his head snapped back. I hit him pretty quick – maybe four or five good ones to the face. Shit the man could bleed."

Caster lingered over the next swallow but kept staring at Gail over the rim of his glass. He leaned across the counter on folded arms and grinned maliciously. "But he stopped quickly, too."

Gail nodded at his wound again. "How'd he hit you?"

"The prick swung around with a fucking paperweight or something. Tried to scratch my eye out."

Gail gulped down the fear. She wanted to ask, but she didn't really want to hear the answer. "So you killed him, and then –"

Caster guffawed. He didn't speak until the echo died. "Fuck no. Not after that. When I shoved the old geezer's arms into that shredder he was still kicking and screaming. The blood was flying everywhere. All you could hear – "

"Stop!" Gail was surprised at the strength of her own voice. Startled, Caster sat back and finished his drink.

"You did your job Caster. *Erik*. But I really don't want to know all the details."

He smiled with mock sincerity. "Sure, Gail. It's just that – " He struggled with the words.

"What?"

"Well, it's just that you should have seen him when I rammed that needle through his lips."

"Fuck you, you shit!"

Caster grinned. "And what does that make you, Gail darling?"

Meredith tossed back the rest of her drink and poured them both another. She could see it in Caster's eyes: the GBH she added to his drink with the ice was taking effect. All she could think about was Danielson's arms being pulled down deeper and deeper into the shredder. Was he really still alive when Caster started sewing . . . No, she couldn't think about it. Focus, she thought. Caster's here, I'm here, she told herself. *Wait until it's all over.*

"I really thought you had the stomach for this kind of stuff."

"You thought wrong."

"So you do have a sweet side after all. Maybe that's a good thing."

Gail watched him drink. "Another toast," she said, raising her glass. "To the success of *Inside*." She took a sip. "Here's to a writer's dream - - TBL."

Caster frowned.

"The bestseller's list."

He grinned broadly, his eyes filled with the promise of glory. Glory, recognition, respect. *And no more fucking rejection letters.* But above all, money. Money money money.

"I've got your contract, just like I promised," Gail told him. "Do you want to sign it now?"

"Sure as fucking shit," he whispered. Caster banged his glass down and ogled the front of Gail's blouse. She felt him squirm as she walked past. He stared at her tits, his balance off.

"It's on the credenza in the hall," she called back over her shoulder.

"Don't be long."

Caster had poured himself another shot when Gail walked back into the kitchen cradling a thick wad of papers.

"What the fuck is that? *A book?"*

"It might as well be. You, as the *writer,* and me, as the *publisher*, have to protect ourselves. The lawyers are always swimming around like hungry sharks looking for the scent of blood. A copyright infringement, plagiarism, anything like that."

"Plagar – what?"

"Plagiarism. If you use someone else's work." *You stupid fucking moron.*

"Oh yeah, right."

"We have to make sure we're completely covered."

"For libel and shit like that? So we can't be sued?"

"We can be sued, Erik. But we don't want to *lose*." She tossed the stack of papers on the counter, her eyes on Caster's face. "I swear the thing gets bigger every time I sell a book. Like their fees."

"Fucking lawyers," Caster agreed. His speech was getting slurred. But he liked the idea: you have to protect the writer. And *I'm* the writer. He turned the documents towards him and started scanning the first few pages. Smiling as he sipped his drink, he didn't look up until he heard a sudden, unmistakable, metallic *click.*

He looked into Gail's eyes, then down at the gun. It was pointed directly at his heart.

She grinned when she saw him wince. "It was in the credenza with the papers," she explained. "But you were so intent on getting your grubby little fingers on that contract you didn't even notice me reach behind my back."

Caster grimaced and tightened his grip around his glass. *Could he break it?* He'd been in situations like this before – it wasn't time to panic. *Yet.* He kept staring at Meredith, but he was quickly running through his options and the things within his grasp. *The pots above his head? The cutting board? The rum bottle?* The knife block was on the other side of the counter – just out of reach. The bottle would have to be the weapon of choice. He'd have to lunge for the knives. But if she wasn't afraid to shoot, she'd nail him as soon as he started moving. What else could he get his hands on? If he smashed the bottle . . .

"I can't believe you're doing this."

"Believe it."

"I fucking killed Danielson for you."

Meredith flexed her finger around the trigger. "And I'm glad and extremely thankful you did."

Caster gulped. "You promised to help me."

"And you promised to kill me if you ever got the chance."

"That was before. We're partners now, remember?"

"Don't be absurd, you obtuse little shit," Gail scoffed. "That means 'stupid.' Partners? I don't think so. You served a purpose and removed quite a vexatious threat to my livelihood. You expunged a deleterious obstacle in my path, nothing more. Perhaps you can understand it this way: you burst a pimple on my ass. You were a stooge. But that's all you'll ever be, Caster. Surely deep down, you must realize that."

He stared back coldly. *If he faked a move to his right and then tried to grab a knife before she realized what he was doing, maybe . . .*

"Don't move a muscle," she warned, reading his eyes. They were clouding over nicely and his balance was off.

"You need me."

Gail laughed. "The fuck I do."

"You don't have to do this. Danielson's dead and you're in the clear. Doing me doesn't help."

"Sure it does. I don't have to worry about you sneaking up behind me one day and skewering me with a blade." She smiled grimly. "Or stuffing me head first into a shredder."

"I wouldn't do that."

"That's sweet. You're almost pleading."

"I wouldn't. We've got a contract, and that's enough for me. About all that promotion shit –"

"A contract!" Gail chortled indignantly. "With you? Don't be ridiculous." She smiled when Caster looked down at the stack of papers. "Tell me you never really thought I was actually going to go through with it and publish that useless piece of self-serving trash some four year old helped you write?"

Caster gulped, his body rigid. Gail felt the burning hatred in his eyes. *Careful.*

"It was absolute garbage, Erik. You don't mind me calling you Erik, do you? Now we're so close?" Gail's smile turned into a bitter leer. Caster's hands were shaking, his muscles spasming. It wouldn't be long before the drugs kicked in completely.

Caster's jaw slackened. "You're dead."

"No Erik. You are."

Gail raised the gun a little higher so the barrel was pointed at the center of his chest. Two body shots, the guy told her. Safe and sure.

"Listen," he began slowly, raising his hands in surrender. It was the pause he needed.

He moved the instant the gun wavered. He deked to the side and then twisted away in one fluid, life-saving motion. He hurled the glass at Merediths' head as he tried to duck down behind the counter, but she squeezed off a round before he was out of sight. The bullet caught him in the shoulder and spun him back around against the counter. The reverberation seemed to echo through the kitchen for hours. Blood splattered against the cupboards. Caster reached for one of the blades just as the second shot rang out. The bullet bored into his chest, shattering the middle of his rib cage and sending shards of bone spiraling into his right lung. Gasping for air, he lifted the knife with a quivering arm and tried to aim through the veil of darkness descending over his senses. But as he brought the blade back his knees gave out and he collapsed to the floor. The knife clattered into the sink.

Wheezing, Caster heard Gail inch slowly around the block. He tried to speak, but the only thing he stammered was choked off by the warm blood bubbling over his lips. He convulsed on the floor as his eyes blinked open and closed. Gail stepped around the counter, the gun aimed at his stomach. Caster held up a hand in feeble protest. He saw the muzzle flash in slow motion, heard the deafening explosion, and felt his insides burst into the air. The impact jerked him up from the floor. He stayed there for a second, suspended from some invisible string, then collapsed back down in a distorted heap. Blood seeped out in a widening circle across the floor. His eyes were open and he stared up at the ceiling.

Gail waited until the ringing in her ears subsided before she gave Caster's body a prodding kick. Another one, right into his stomach. Nothing. She smiled and gathered up the papers strewn across the counter. Ten seconds and they'd all be shredded: almost all of the pages were blank, like Danielson's face. She grinned hatefully.

Her senses exploded with a rush of adrenaline. Steadying herself, she tore off the top sheet of their "pact" and picked the knife up from the sink. She was careful not to touch anything except the blade.

She gave Caster's body another kick, hard, right into his blood-soaked chest. Not even a groan. She scooped up the papers and hurried down the hall to her study. She started feeding the pages into the shredder, but stopped. All she could think of was Danielson's arms and the blood splattering back into his face as Caster pushed him in deeper. Gail shuddered, then crammed a few more pages of the "contract" into the shredder.

She scurried down the hall to the back door, stepped outside, and smashed a hole through the window with her elbow. Her heartbeat was almost back to normal when she walked into the kitchen. She took a deep breath and pulled one of the other blades from the rack. She counted to three, took another slow inhalation, and then slashed the blade across her forearm. Her eyes teared and she choked on a gasp of pain. Not waiting, she drew the blade over her arm again, then made a quick slice across her palm. She wiped the blade on her shirt and tossed the knife onto the counter top.

Blood droplets dripped across the floor as she staggered to the sink. She let the blood trickle down onto the knife before she rammed it under Caster's body. Then she stumbled back towards the pantry to the phone.

That's when Caster's hand shot out, his bloody fingers grabbing her ankle. She never saw him move. Gail screamed. She spun around and stomped on his arm with her other foot, making him groan. She brought her heel down again, stabbing him, then kicked him viciously in the head. Again. But he was trying to roll up onto his side, his hand squeezing her ankle even harder as he desperately tried to pull her down to the floor.

She felt herself starting to fall. She'd cut herself too soon, and she'd lost more blood than she thought. Pulling at her leg, Caster was trying to drag her captured foot underneath him, praying he could roll over and use his weight to break the bone.

But a second later another shot rang out, the gun closer this time, the bullet blowing his head apart. Blood and tissue and ripped arteries and pieces of bone blasted backwards, sticking to the cupboards in quivering splotches. Chunks of his skin slithered down the wooden panels into stained pools. Even as he spit up blood and choked on his last breath, he still tried to hold on. Meredith leaned down, drove the gun barrel into Caster's wrist, and wrenched her ankle free. A last gasp, then silence. The stink of cordite permeated the kitchen. If only he could have written as well as he died.

Gail staggered backwards to the wall. The cuts on her arm had widened. Her hand was completely covered in blood, and more trailed down her arm in widening rivulets. She grabbed the land line on the wall, dialed 911, and let the receiver fall. It bounced up and down on the cord like a bungee as she slowly slumped to the floor. Her head at an awkward angle, Gail stared at the blood seeping across the floor. She couldn't feel her forearm and her hand throbbed with a searing pain she knew she'd never forget.

But then again, it was a small price to pay for freedom.

Chapter Forty Nine

Dr. Tantor's ensemble for the evening was all faded denim from the sixties – bell-bottom jeans, a long sleeved blouse, a short jean jacket and blue running shoes. When she heard a car pull to a stop under the portico, she hustled down the hall to meet Kincaid at the door.

"Good timing – I'm glad I caught you before I had to leave. The station's been trying to reach you for hours. Were you and Stephanie . . .?"

Her entire demeanor changed as she looked up inquisitively into her friend's eyes. "You look terrible. Did something happen when you had the CT scan?"

The CT scan? He couldn't even remember it now. It seemed like weeks ago. And what did it matter? He sighed dismissively.

"What is it, Kincaid?"

He was trembling.

"K –."

"Not now, Cecelia," he barked, surprised at the strength of his own voice. "Please." He reached over and took her hand. "Sorry."

Her body tightened instinctively. The world collapsed. She felt just like she had when the two plain clothes officers knocked at her door the morning her husband was shot. "Tell me, my friend. What –?"

He couldn't speak. He looked into her eyes, fighting the tears, the pain.

"Not Ryan?"

He nodded dully. Even the sound of the child's name was a cold, heartless dagger that stabbed him through the chest. He collapsed forward into Cecelia's open arms. Seconds later, all the pent-up feelings and emotions cracked through the veil of his consciousness and he was sobbing against her neck. Gently, ever so gently, she led him along the hallway and eased him down onto a settee across from the credenza. It was several minutes before he'd shed enough tears he could finally speak. Between choked backed sobs, bitter accusations and angry, frustrated laments, Kincaid told his companion everything that had happened at the hospital. Cecelia listened sadly as she stroked his hands.

"Where have you been?"

The question perplexed him. Where *had* he been? "I'm not sure. Driving around. Thinking. I didn't want to go home. I parked somewhere and took a walk. I drove by Carolyn's house a couple of times, but didn't go in. I couldn't." He frowned uneasily. "I don't remember . . ."

His voice trailed off into a mournful silence. He looked around uneasily, seeing bits and pieces of the crime scene, but not really *seeing* it. *Did it matter?* Wasn't it all just more death? The endless cycle of finality?

Cecelia wrapped her arms around his shoulders and hugged him close. "I'm so sorry, K." She felt him shudder. "Why don't you let me take you home? I'll get Davis to send Amy and some Blues. I'm sure he can find someone to back her up."

Kincaid shook his head. *Home* was where he and Ryan watched Berger play on the small flat screen he'd bought so they could catch some games by the old woodstove. At *home* they guzzled sodas and ate fistfuls of popcorn until Ryan thought he'd explode. *Home* was the place they roasted marshmallows in the backyard fire pit, giggling at who could make the gooiest one that could still be eaten. The nurse he'd hired set up a hospital bed at *home*, and Kincaid rented all of the equipment Ryan would need on the occasional nights he'd been able to have a sleepover. *God, how long ago was that?* At *home*, the boy had fallen asleep in seconds with almost no pain. *Before.*

Whispered words. "I have to keep moving. Stay focused. Or I'll lose everything."

Cecelia sighed empathetically. "If you need to talk –."

"I will. Thanks."

They rose slowly together, and Cecelia took him back into the kitchen. Kincaid took a deep breath, dried his eyes, and started doing what he'd come to do. He glanced quickly around. "Meredith?"

"EMT picked her up about an hour and a half ago. A couple of uniforms I didn't recognize were already here, taking statements and all that. A CSU team was here, too."

"Did you see her?"

"Yes. Two lacerations on her forearm, one on her palm. She lost a fair amount of blood – two cuts were relatively deep, and barely missed an artery. She was coherent and helpful, actually."

"She didn't seem terrified?"

"No."

"Still in shock?"

Cecelia thought for a moment. "No, not really. Not like the 'shock' I normally see. More like a controlled adrenaline rush."

"She didn't seem upset when I saw her after the attack in the parking garage, either."

"You told me yourself she's a tough woman. I've seen similar reactions before. It doesn't mean she won't break down and manifest symptoms later."

He shrugged and wiped his eyes with the back of his hand. "Do me a favor?"

"Of course."

"Double check everything."

Cecelia frowned. "What am I looking for?"

"I'm not sure. Anything that doesn't feel right. Watch her emotionally, too."

"Done. I'll take a good look at her when I get back. There was one thing I thought a little odd."

"Go on."

"Her right ankle and foot were covered in blood."

Kincaid frowned. *Why just one leg? And just the ankle and foot?*

"Do you want to know what we're looking at so far?" she asked gently.

"Please."

"Outside?"

"No, I'll stay here."

Cecelia gestured toward the rear of the kitchen that led out into the hall. "Forced entry at the back door. One of the window panes was smashed. The lab boys who took the initial pictures and set up the scene said no obvious prints or blood. The CSU team checked the entranceway, the porch landing, and the front rooms."

"Was the glass inside?"

"You don't trust her much, do you? Yes. The window was broken from the outside."

That didn't really mean anything. "Security cameras?"

"Apparently malfunctioned. Stuck in a loop or something."

"Timely. What else?"

"Caster took four shots. One to the chest, one in the shoulder, and one to the stomach. And oddly enough, the *coup de grace* was a close one right to the front of his head. That's the brains you see slithering down the cupboards. He died in minutes."

"Blood?"

Cecelia pointed to the center block. "Patterns around him are what you'd expect. It looks like he was leaning over the counter, then slumped down to the floor after he was shot. There's a definite splatter pattern to the one around his head. Like an aura. The blood seeped out from the back and side of his head."

"He didn't move around?"

"Not much."

"What about Meredith?"

Cecelia stepped back and gestured to a spot in the middle of the floor. "From what I can tell so far, she was cut about there – Cecelia drew an imaginary trail over to the phone with her finger – and then stumbled over to the pantry. There are a couple of bloodstained prints on the wall by the phone."

Kincaid seemed puzzled. "Apart from the knife marks, did she have any other noticeable wounds?"

"No obvious ones. But I only gave her a cursory look. She didn't mention anything else to the paramedics when they checked her over."

Kincaid paced slowly around the kitchen, stopping, as usual, at various intervals and studying everything from a new perspective. Caster's body was still behind the kitchen's huge center block, his feet sticking out obscenely from the end of a thick yellow sheet. Blood seeped out from the edges. Kincaid leaned down and lifted the corner of the plastic. Caster was on his side. The last shot had torn his head apart, but he was still recognizable. He studied what was left of the man's face, then lifted the cover higher so he could see the other entrance wounds. His chest was soaked with blood.

"You're right. She must have been fairly close."

"My guess would be not more than a couple of feet."

"I assume the gun was registered?"

"Still checking."

Troubled, Kincaid shook his head. "The cuts on her arm?"

"What about them?"

"When you first saw them, did they look like defensive wounds?"

"Again, I'd have to have another look to make sure. EMS took her away fairly quickly – they didn't want her to bleed out. Why?"

"I'd like to know if he sliced her before he was shot, or whether she managed to squeeze off two rounds first."

"To know if he cut her first and she tried to protect herself?"

Kincaid let the sheet fall back over Caster's chest and face. Perfect shots, he thought. Cecelia was right – death was likely instantaneous. Then why the other shots? The overkill? Few police officers he knew would be that accurate under duress and pressure. *Strange.*

"Did the on-scene officers take the gun?"

"Yes."

"Tell me what you saw when you first came in."

Cecelia thought back for a moment. "The body was there, half-hidden by the center block. The knife was where it's marked."

Kincaid gestured to the little numbered plastic flag on the floor. It was about a foot away from Caster's shoulder. "There?"

"Exactly."

"And Meredith?"

"Over there." Cecelia pointed to another little flag at the edge of the pantry. "Slouched down on the floor. The phone receiver was stretched out from the wall outlet beside her."

Kincaid walked over and stood next to the pantry. "Here?"

Cecelia nodded.

"What about all this broken glass?"

"It appears as though Caster threw one at her. My guess would be that he missed and it smashed against the wall, because I didn't see any glass fragments on her at all."

Kincaid squatted down. He inhaled deeply and ran his palms over the tiled floor.

"What are you doing?"

"Smelling."

"I don't understand."

Kincaid wiped his hands together. "The glass wasn't empty. There's a trace of rum on the floor."

"So?"

"So maybe she was having a drink with Caster." Kincaid stood up and peeled off his latex gloves. "Which would change everything."

"Not necessarily," Cecelia replied. "Maybe she saw him before he lunged out at her and she threw her own glass."

"But then the fragments should be over there as well." He pointed toward Caster's body, then walked over to the sink and gestured down with a nod. "And if that's the case, then whose glass is this?"

Cecelia checked the sink. A few small blood splatters marred the chrome. "Maybe it was left over from earlier." She noticed the green peels. "Or she might have nicked herself cutting the lime."

"It's possible." His frown suggested he didn't believe it. "Take another look at those knife wounds, okay?"

"Of course."

"And Cecelia? Thanks." He reached over and took her hand. "Thanks for everything. I –"

The cry of Kincaid's cell phone echoed through the kitchen. He walked out to the hallway. When he returned a few moments later, his face was as white as fresh snow, his eyes heavy lidded and dull. His arms hung down rigidly at his sides, and his hands were trembling.

Cecelia frowned and put a hand lightly on his arm. "Kincaid?"

Had he heard her? "K? What's wrong?"

He closed his eyes and massaged his fingertips over his temples, willing the pain away. He looked down at Cecelia but he was really looking past her, *through* her almost, at some other place or some other time.

"I have to go," he mumbled. "Can you call the station? Tell Davis to send someone out with Amy – she'll need help with protocol and wrapping things up here when CSU finishes. Just the basics. I can go over it with her later."

"Yes, of course. But what's wrong? Tell me."

He stared into her eyes with a volatile mixture of fear and uncertainty. "Carolyn needs me."

Chapter Fifty

Kincaid was tired. Tired, and afraid. Ryan's – he still had trouble even mouthing the word – *death* –had scarred him deeply. He'd experienced others – lots of others that never stopped bleeding through his mind – but this was a wound that would never heal. He missed the boy, missed him with an ache that made his chest tighten and his heart race every time he thought about him, and he thought about him with every pulse of blood that seeped through his heart. He hadn't left Carolyn's house until morning dawned and the sun started burning the dew from the grass. He promised her he'd be back. He'd always remember how she looked at the door when he left: the fear in her eyes, the jaundiced tone of her skin, the loneliness that was beginning to show in the lines of her face, the haunting weariness as she seemed to shrink down farther into herself. Would she ever come back?

He cried unapologetically when he picked up Stephanie. She held him in her arms and listened quietly to his anguished questions, tormented whispers, promises and denials and abject laments that rose and fell beneath tear-stained prayers. Finally, he stopped. There'd be time to grieve later. Forever. God, it was all so much like *before, years* that were only *yesterdays*, when their unborn child was lost to eternity, and Stephanie's wounds crushed the spirit from his heart, and he'd taken his first steps on the long, long road to loneliness to save her from a life of fear. He hugged her tightly to his chest and told her he'd never let her go. Not this time. Not again. *Not ever.*

*

"What?" Gail Meredith called impatiently.

Pushing past Darla and two private guards who'd followed him angrily down the hall, Kincaid stopped, turned, and stared the men down. They issued standard warnings that were almost a threat, but didn't try to stop him from walking into the office.

"What the hell –"

She started to get up but slowly sat down when she saw who it was. And the look in his eyes. A plainclothes guard stood statue-still next to the window. A holster bulged under his arm.

"Kincaid. I should have known. You have a penchant for showing up at the wrong time. I'm too busy for this."

"Are you?"

"Extremely. Especially after the evening I had."

"Then I won't take up too much of your time. It must have been some night."

"The police weren't any help."

Kincaid eyed the guard, but neither man spoke.

"It's alright, McNamara. Unfortunately, I know the Detective. You can go. But stay by the door."

She dismissed him with a curt nod. He walked past Kincaid, close, their shoulders almost touching. "I'll be right outside, Ms. Meredith."

"I'm surprised you're in today."

"Life goes on. So does business."

"You're a good shot."

Meredith keyed in something and didn't bother looking up.

"How's your arm?" Poking out from the edge of her sleeve, the bandage was thick and smelled of blood. No jangling bracelets today.

"Better," she mumbled. Then, a little louder, "thanks."

"Pretty sore?"

"It is." She turned back to her computer, but stopped. "Detective, what –"

"You must feel better knowing the extra security isn't needed downstairs."

An acquiescing nod. Gail leaned forward across the desk, and carefully folded her hands together. "Kincaid –"

"It must be nice not having to worry about Caster any longer, either."

Her lips curled into an acrid grin. "As a matter of fact, it is."

"Although there's still the other threats, of course."

She tensed noticeably. "What do you mean?"

"Well, Caster wasn't the only person who sent you hate mail or threatened your personal safety, was he?"

"Oh." She relaxed. "No, I see what you mean." She shrugged noncommittally. "One lunatic can always incite another. I don't feel like taking chances right now. You never know who's out there. But as I've already told you, that's the nature of the beast.

Hate mail's an occupational hazard. That's why I moved the security staff a little – closer."

"It's a tough way to live. Some of your colleagues haven't been as fortunate, have they?"

Silence.

"But this time, you were doubly blessed, weren't you?"

"I don't understand."

"Caster's out of the way for good."

"And?"

"So's Danielson."

"What do you mean?"

"The take-over bid. From what I understand, with Danielson removed from the picture, his sons won't be pursuing their father's interest in *Meredith House*. They'll have too much in-fighting to do solidifying their ownership of *Excalibur Books* without that added stress."

Kincaid's anger was simmering. He looked out the window and watched a seagull swoop down from the clouds. Ryan had always liked watching the gulls.

"The proverbial two birds with one stone," Kincaid went on quietly. "Neither Caster nor Danielson are a threat."

"This is getting boring." Gail tapped a key. "I'm genuinely sorry about Danielson. Sure, we weren't on the best of terms. But business is business. Today's enemies are often tomorrow's partners. You can't possibly believe I have any remorse about Caster, do you? The man was a maniacal murderer. Danielson, Turner, and McCabe. He hated being rejected and he wanted to settle the score with people in the publishing world, it's as simple as that. But he's dead now. I'm not just relieved, I'm overjoyed." She turned back to the pages strewn across her desk. "Now, if you'll excuse me, there's a great deal –"

"Why did Caster kill Danielson?"

"You're the Detective."

"Humor me."

She shrugged. "He must have rejected Caster's book before or after we did."

Kincaid shook his head thoughtfully. "That's what we first thought. But Sergeant MacKenzie and I checked through all their files. Danielson certainly kept better submissions records than you do, but it still took us awhile. We confirmed Caster never submitted his manuscript to *Excalibur Books*."

"So?" Gail replied angrily.

"So, what reason did Caster have for killing Danielson?"

"He was a publisher. Caster hated publishers and agents. He hated everyone in the field. The rejections were too much for him, and he started killing anyone he could reach."

"Possible," Kincaid admitted behind a half-smile. Gail shifted uncomfortably. "Turner and McCabe I could see. They worked on his manuscript. But Danielson? There are lots of publishers and agents in Toronto. So why him?" He paused and stared. "Or why not you, Ms. Meredith? No, there had to be another reason Caster wanted him dead."

"Well, I haven't any idea," Gail said indifferently. "Perhaps he was intimidated with my extra security. Especially after what happened downstairs. Now, if you'll excuse me, I'm extremely busy."

Kincaid noticed the tremor in her hands and ignored the dismissal. "Yes, the assault. You were fortunate to escape with your life."

Suddenly, Gail looked weak and almost defenseless. "Yes, Kincaid, I was. But like I said – "

"I couldn't stop wondering why Caster – a *maniacal murderer* – didn't simply snap your neck when he had the chance. Anyone can hold someone's jaw for just a few seconds and bruise the tissue without putting any pressure on it at all. Someone like me, for example – or certainly Caster – could have crushed your hyoid bone with his thumb without even squeezing."

"Look, Kincaid – "

"And the other thing I couldn't figure out was why there were two cigars – I'm sorry, *triangulos* – by your car, but only one had your DNA on it."

Meredith's patience exploded. The defenselessness was gone. "I don't know where the fuck you think you're going with this –."

"So if Danielson wasn't directly related to Turner or McCabe, there had to be another reason Caster needed him dead."

Meredith was still – too still.

"Isn't it true Danielson's death has greatly helped your company?"

She looked up, shocked and disbelieving. "What the fuck are you suggesting –?"

"That without Danielson, *Meredith House* is in the clear again. No takeover bids. No worries."

Gail stared back at Kincaid with an intensity he hadn't seen in a long time. She was grinding her teeth so hard he could hear it from across her desk.

"Now, if Danielson had to be removed, who better to do it than Caster? After all, he'd already killed two other people in the industry, hadn't he?"

She clasped her hands together so tightly her fingers were red.

"You needed Danielson out of the way, and you had Caster do it for you."

"You're insane," she seethed. "When my lawyers get through with you –"

"Save your lawyers for when you'll really need them." The icy edge to his voice silenced her rebuttal.

"You must have offered him something important," Kincaid continued. "The first thing that struck me was a publishing contract. After all, it's why he threatened you in the first place."

"You're so far off base it's ridiculous."

Kincaid ignored the pain in his spine. "You made a couple of mistakes, Gail. Do you mind if I call you Gail?"

"Your career's over, you arrogant –."

"Remember being attacked in your underground?"

"Don't be absurd. Of course I bloody well remember. You just –."

"You called James Lamberton and told him you were on Bloor and traffic was horrific. You said you needed about twenty minutes to get back."

"So?"

"You've had problems in your underground before, haven't you?"

"A couple of robberies."

"And an attempted rape about six months ago. Your CCTV system was installed last fall."

Fuck. Meredith knew the cameras couldn't see her parking space. She'd had them designed like that so "private conversations and meetings" would stay that way.

"I checked the tapes. They don't show your parking spot, which I found quite odd. But they did show the time you actually drove into the garage. And do you know what? You had already been downstairs for almost fifteen minutes *before* you called Mr. Lamberton. You phoned him from your car."

Meredith watched Kincaid's eyes. She didn't flinch. *Yet.*

"The other thing I found disconcerting was your story about killing Caster."

"It happened exactly the way I said," Meredith whispered coldly. She touched the bandages covering her forearm.

"Oh, I have no doubt you shot him."

"So?"

"The knife troubled me."

"It was found right beside him. And his fingerprints were all over it."

"Yes," Kincaid said thoughtfully. "Yes, they were. So were yours."

"It's my fucking kitchen knife, Kincaid. I *have* used it before."

"Naturally. But that wasn't the problem. The problem is the cuts you sustained when you were valiantly trying to fight off Caster."

Gail self-consciously covered the bandages with her other hand.

"There were a number of knives in that block, Gail. Each one is unique and designed for a specific purpose."

"Oh, you're a fucking knife expert, too," she said bitterly.

"Your blood was on the knife beside Caster. But you put it there, Gail. You probably wiped it on something you managed to hide. But Caster's knife didn't cut you."

Meredith's lips parted but she didn't say anything.

"The knife on the floor was serrated. The coroner double-checked when you were taken to the hospital. The knife that cut your arm was smooth edged." Kincaid stared back. "You slashed yourself to make it look like Caster attacked you."

The office was deathly still. Gail Meredith tried to hide her fear. And her hate.

"There's something else," Kincaid finally said. "I know you're busy, so I'll try to be brief."

"Fuck you, Kincaid."

"And here I thought we were getting along famously." Kincaid smiled. "I forgot to tell you. I also have a witness."

The color drained from her face.

"Someone went to see you that night. They needed to talk to you about everything that's happened. They realized it had all gone horribly wrong and out of control. Death and murder had never been part of the plan. Money, yes. But not killing for it. So he wanted to confess – *needed* to confess – and tell you it was all over."

"What are you talking about?"

"I'm talking about Ian."

"Ian? Who the shit –"

"Your writer. *That* Ian. Nuraki."

"What?" she stammered incredulously. "You're nuts, Kincaid. I've never even met him. Everything went through Turner, you know that. His biggest and most closely guarded secret. The contracts, the cheques – everything. I never met Nuraki."

"I know," Kincaid admitted. "But Ian Nuraki came to me when Danielson was murdered, right after Brent Jacobs finally succumbed to all the pressure and self-recrimination and hate, and took his own life. Ian had his own breaking point, too, and knew it was all because of what he'd done. He'd tried to do what he thought was right in the very beginning, but it quickly snowballed out of control, and he became something he wasn't, or never wanted to be. Something he couldn't live with anymore. In fact, it might have eventually cost him his own life."

Kincaid kept staring. "Nuraki felt guilty – well, far more than guilty – about his part in the scheme. Yes, he rewrote the books. And the movie scripts. And yes, he pocketed the money. But I don't think he ever really stopped to consider the pain he'd put people through. You see, he needed the money for a very special reason. He kept hardly anything for himself. He was being blackmailed, just like Turner."

"I don't understand."

"I didn't think you would. But finally, Ian did. He helped Turner a long time ago, and they worked together ever since. Ian has a special flare, a unique style that draws people in, whatever he writes. What he couldn't do was create story lines. But give him a plot and some characters and his innate talent turns a mediocre book into the perfect novel, regardless of the genre. A true artist. Turner would get the manuscript ideas from the submissions and queries people sent to him, as well as partial scripts or even complete books. Ian would turn those ideas into novels, writing them in his personal, didactic, characteristic style, and transform someone else's idea into a bestseller in months. He looked after the film scripts as well, and that just enhanced the mystery around Mr. Nuraki. Devlin brought his work to you to publish, and everyone was happy. Ian was hidden quietly away, Turner was the toast of the literary world, and you and everyone else became hedonistically wealthy. Well, except for the writers who'd poured their lives into their work and never even saw their name on a book jacket."

The veins in Gail's temples throbbed with pulsing blood.

"But Ian realized how far things had gotten out of hand when McCabe was murdered. At first he figured it was just an unfortunate incident, a random slaying. Then, it was Turner. Ian knew it wasn't a coincidence. Especially when he heard about what happened to several people who worked in the industry over the last few months. There's no jurisdictional problems on the web, Gail. When Ian read the stories, it wasn't difficult to piece things together. Social media was abuzz with what was happening in the publishing world. A young editor, Roland Steinberg, was murdered in Seattle. Shirley O'Donovan, a literary agent from Chicago, is missing. And Chamille Nasson was mutilated in New York. The police managed to find parts of what was left of Ms. Nasson just in time, and made a positive identification with her dental records. Three more murders in the publishing industry. Ian panicked. Would he be next? Had someone found out who he was and who he was involved with? He went to your home to admit who he was and explain everything. That he was the mystery. He wanted to tell you face to face that it was all over, no matter what happened to him. He wasn't going to write anything else. He was going to deal with the blackmailer through me."

Kincaid's head was pounding. The blood was rushing through his veins, and his vision was starting to get a little blurry. He remembered what happened in the parking lot. *Not now*, he thought. *Please, not now.*

"He came to see you, but no-one answered the bell. He was about to leave, but realized the door was unlocked, so he crept inside. He heard you and Caster arguing in the kitchen, and he was able to sneak in a little closer. He was actually hiding behind the staircase when you went out to get the "contract" from the credenza. Ian heard everything you told Caster, and he heard you shoot him. He ran before you had the chance to know he was there."

Gail slumped back into her chair, her face ashen, her eyes dull and devoid of any life.

"He knows he has a price to pay for what he's done, Gail, and he's willing to pay it. He's given a statement about what happened last night, too."

"I don't believe this," Meredith muttered down into her hands. "I don't fucking believe this."

"I think Jacobs's death gave him the final little push over the edge and into the abyss."

"Jacobs?"

"It's too late to pretend anything, Gail. You and Turner stole Jacob's book and had Ian rewrite it. What's it on, the fourth printing already? And the movie made millions. Ian's world fell apart when he learned Jacobs committed suicide. His sense of responsibility was numbing and overwhelming, so that's when he came to me. Regardless of the consequences."

Kincaid walked over to the door. He poked his head around the corner and nodded. Gail Meredith strained forward and looked up. She almost choked on a laugh when Stephanie walked into the office.

"What the fuck? You're insane, Kincaid. She's your Goddamn friend, for shit's sake. Don't think I don't know about you two." She shook her head and her eyes started sparkling once more. "If you think she'll be able to pretend –"

Stephanie had listened long enough. Still looking at Meredith, she spoke in a clear, light voice. "Sergeant MacKenzie? Could you bring Ian in now, please?

Chapter Fifty One

Bagelicious.

The little sign was flipped around to face the street. **Closed –
Making more bagel holes.**

Three people perched on counter stools each picked up a
large styrofoam cup and quietly walked out of the little restaurant.
A couple, three booths away, declined a refill and followed them
into the street, heads down. A scruffy young man pretending to be
homeless stuffed the last half of his cheese bagel into his mouth,
grabbed a *'please help'* sign, and left like a shadow.

Andy's large gold-toothed smile turned to an uneasy frown as
he walked Kincaid and his guest to the rear of the shop and into
"his" private booth.

"I'll close the shutters, dim the lights, and let the music take a
rest after I bring you some coffee. I'll be cleaning up in the back.
Yell if you need anything – I won't be coming out." He leaned
down closer. "And don't be leaving me any reds, K. Do what
you're doing. The place is yours."

"Thanks. But you're losing business."

"That's the least of my worries." He looked closely at his
friend. "We're okay?"

"Just fine, Andy. Thanks."

"No *reds*?" his guest asked.

"Fifties," Kincaid explained quietly.

*

The confession had been intense and unsettling. No, more
than that. They'd talked for almost two hours before Kincaid
suggested coming to Andy's shop, to take a break and have a
change of scenery and at least a small respite from the frustration,
the emotional upheaval, and the tears. Ian had held on for so long,
but the stress and strain had become unbearable. People were
dying. *Dying.* And the guilt, the suffocating guilt, had become an
oppressive weight that couldn't be carried any longer. Ian needed
to let everything out, to confess to the lies and deceit. Turner.
McCabe. Danielson. And Jacobs. Their blood was on his hands,
and it had become physically and emotionally insufferable. He'd

lost everything to try and save everyone. Deep in his soul, Ian knew a priest wouldn't help. The harder he scrubbed the more the blood stained his skin.

Kincaid blew the steam from his coffee. Ian couldn't stop now.

"Go on. Finish your story."

Chapter Fifty Two

Gail's mouth fell open when Amy led Leeanne Davidivitch into the room. A laugh froze in her throat.

"You can't be serious, Kincaid. Leeanne? A first reader? She's never had her name on anything. This is bull shit."

Leeanne was immaculately dressed in a charcoal-gray pin-striped jacket and skirt and plum scarf. Four quick strides brought her to the desk. Patiently reaching into her purse, she withdrew a small cassette and USB stick. She placed them down on the papers layered in front of Meredith.

"It's true, Ms. Meredith. I wrote the books. All the ones Devlin Turner wanted re-written. The film scripts as well."

"What are these?" Gail asked, not touching them.

"The cassette's an old-fashioned audio recording tape," Kincaid explained, stepping up beside Leeanne. "I found it when we swept Caster's apartment. He recorded your meeting in the underground, Gail. He might not have been technically astute, but he wasn't a complete dolt, either. He'd read the papers and knew about Jacobs' court case, so he was going to send Jacob's a copy of your "meeting" before he went to your home because he wasn't sure whether he could trust you. But he didn't have Jacob's address. Imagine. *Caster* couldn't trust *you*." Kincaid looked sadly at Ms. Davidivitch. "And you know what? He was right."

Leeanne's hands were folded in front of her, and they were shaking. "I've done a great number of things I'm not proud of Ms. Meredith. But this – she gestured to the tape with a nod – was something I knew I could never live with. Jacobs certainly didn't deserve to be treated the way he was, or to die the way he did." She took a deep breath. "Neither were all the others. I never really stopped to consider the ramifications and the damage I've done."

It was too much to take in, and Meredith was obviously still in shock. "So you've been *Ian Nuraki* – all along?"

Leeanne nodded like a chastised school girl and wiped a tear from the corner of her eye.

Meredith glared spitefully. "Then don't get so high and fucking mighty on me, Leeanne. If it's true – *if it's true* – and you really did write the books, you played the game for a long time and made a fortune ruining other people's lives. It didn't bother you before."

"You're right." She looked at Kincaid. "But now I've seen what happens to the other people involved. The story in the *Gazette* took away whatever sense of self Jacobs had left. He took his own life because of me. That's why I went to your house that night – the night you shot Erik Caster. I wanted to tell you it was me right from the beginning, but that it was all over, too."

"And the stick?" Meredith flipped it way with her fingertip.

"My complete confession to Detective Kincaid."

*

My complete confession.

Kincaid's thoughts drifted back to the final disconcerting hour they'd talked at *Bagelicious* earlier that morning. Andy was a ghost. He kept the coffee coming and discreetly left a box of tissues on the table.

"Go on, Leeanne. You have to get it all out. Tell me."

She didn't need much prompting. Her deep sigh seemed to draw the air from the room.

"So Kincaid, as I was trying to explain, it wasn't long before I realized I had a rather unique ability. On the one hand, I had an enormous difficulty *creating* stories. Thinking about the plot and storyline and then inventing the characters and writing the narrative. I couldn't write, or even draft for that matter, a story from start to finish. I simply couldn't put the whole thing together, the book I tried to imagine into being. Dialogue, characters, plots and themes – they just wouldn't come, no matter how hard I tried. I had ideas, naturally, but I could never put them all together into a cohesive, meaningful whole that made a novel everything it was supposed to be."

"But –"

"But I could take pretty well anything that had already been written and make it better. Stronger, deeper, clearer, thematically intense and character driven. And not the way an editor or publisher does, either. It's something more. I can make practically any story better than it was when it was sent in. Arrogant? Supercilious? Of course, but that's not how I felt. I loved the 'writing'."

"So it all began when Turner saw you were much more that a first reader."

- 440 -

"After I started at Meredith House, yes. When I forwarded some scripts to him I thought had some merit, he gave them back to see if I could do any editing as well. My 'editing' was actually a full re-write. The stories were intriguing, or even just 'good', but when I re-wrote scenes and then chapters, Turner realized I possessed that special knack, that intuitive skill, for making each part of the novel better. That I had an elegant writing style rarely seen today. Something beyond commercial, obviously, but something that's even more poetic and engaging than most literary fiction as well."

"So Turner realized your potential right away."

"Yes." She took a quick sip of her coffee. "He knew I could write – and write extremely well. I just needed –"

"Inspiration."

Leeanne tried to smile. It sounded a lot nicer that way. A lot cleaner than plagiarism.

"Turner immediately saw that I could take an over-the-counter mainstream piece of fiction and transform it into what it was meant to be – a commercial or literary masterpiece, whatever he wanted."

"You could take another writers' mediocre attempt at a novel – "

"And make it into a literary dream."

Kincaid watched Leeanne's eyes, felt the sadness, the loneliness. "It's really what Turner was known for, wasn't it? Searching through the slush pile and finding that one query, that one book that had potential –"

"And mining that nugget into gold. You're right. I could write in any genre, or to whatever level of audience was needed. That's kind of where we 'fused.'"

Kincaid frowned.

"Devlin Turner could see the potential of something that everyone else had missed –"

"And you polished that little nugget into the perfect diamond."

Kincaid handed Leeanne the box of tissues. "And the screenplays?"

"Were the same, Detective. "They had the plot, characters, the theme – everything I needed to make that non-descript, run-of-the-mill play into the next movie blockbuster. It was the same as writing another bestseller. I could take the latent potential of some other writer's script, and transform it into whatever Turner, and eventually Gail Meredith needed. It was actually easier for me to write a screenplay than a novel. You've seen the prosaic books that continuously line the bestseller shelves."

More tears. Andy tip-toed to the table and topped up their coffees without a word. Leeanne wrapped her hands around the cup. She looked older now, weary and distraught. Non-caring and unforgiving.

"Naturally, I couldn't let anyone else know who I was. Who I pretended to be. Once I started being 'rewarded' for working my 'magic,' I started sending as much money as I could to my relatives back home and to the ones I knew had emigrated, if I knew where they were. And the day that money started was the day I realized it couldn't stop. That's why I kept writing. So they'd have a chance at a good, safe life."

"The nom de plume?" Kincaid asked. He knew the answer.

Leeanne smiled for the first time since they'd sat down. "Yes. My heritage, an acronym, nothing more, nothing less.   I'm obviously not Japanese."

They finished their coffee in silence, sharing a stare that gradually grew stronger. A beautiful woman, Kincaid thought. Inside, and out. Intelligent, thoughtful, and one of the greatest writers he'd ever read or come to know. Yes, she was a fraud and a thief who'd helped Turner and Meredith make a fortune. But all of her money was gone. The unexpressed question hung between them like a slowly closing curtain. Did the end ever justify the means?

And what would happen to her family now?

He took her hand and led her away from the table. *Would she have said the silence in the little restaurant was deafening?* He leaned back and laid three beige hundreds under her cup and saucer. The little bell tinkled as they stepped back out into the street.

*

Gail's sarcastic burst of laughter brought Kincaid back from his reminisces.

"Oh, I'm sorry about your family. I know you must have done everything out of the truest sense of altruism possible." She sneered. "Your crocodile tears may have fooled Kincaid, but I can see right through them."

"You're in for fraud," Gail seethed. "Theft, tax evasion, plagiarism, whatever."

"I realize that. And I'll pay for my sins. But it was never important enough to kill for."

"You see, Gail," Kincaid said softly, "your motives are vastly different. Your sole reason to go in with Turner and be a party to the whole scheme was simply to make money. Lots of it, no matter who it hurt."

"And hers?"

"Ms. Davidivitch was being blackmailed. She needed the constant cash flow to pay her owners. The Russians. Once the money started they were never going to let it stop. It was the only way she could protect what was left of her family. Her aunts and uncles and cousins still back in the Ukraine would be allowed to stay alive, to have jobs, apartments, simple privileges. Everything we take for granted. So would her relatives who'd emigrated to other countries.

"I was there, Gail, during the Maidan uprising, when the Russians faked the humanitarian convoys. All of her relatives could be brought back at any time if the money stopped flowing. The Russians have their boot on Ukraine's head and could push it into the mud of despair any time they like. They've burned their books, decimated their schools, and forced them to adopt Russian as their language. Putin would crush out their rights in a heartbeat. Or their lives."

Kincaid stared back at Gail. "But now that we're involved, the game's changed. CSIS has already been contacted, along with the FBI and Border Control. With the recent Russian breach in the Ukraine, Putin doesn't need the publicity. Here or at home. And that's all on the stick as well."

Leeanne reached out and touched Kincaid's arm. She squeezed it lightly.

"Do you need anything from your office?"

She sighed deeply. "Only what tatters are left of my dignity."

"Stephanie, you'll walk Ms. Davidivitch down the hall. Sergeant MacKenzie, you'll escort Ms. Meredith." Kincaid asked Gail to stand.

Hatred burned in her eyes. "If you think —"

"Don't make this any more difficult than it has to be. Believe me. It won't be worth it."

He waved her away from behind her desk. She didn't move. Amy stepped closer.

"Think about it, Gail. You've got to walk down that corridor, past all those offices and cubicles. Do you really want to take that last walk with your hands cuffed? I'm giving you the opportunity to go placidly with my Sergeant. To save whatever you feel you have left."

Gail Meredith chewed on her bottom lip for just a second, then stood up slowly with a heavy, worn-out sigh. She flipped her hair back from her forehead, adjusted her skirt, smoothed the wrinkles from her jacket sleeves, and stood beside Amy. She whispered to Kincaid as she passed him.

"Leave the door open, all right? Closing it would make everything seem – more final."

He paused, then nodded. It wasn't too much to ask. Picking up the cassette and stick, he took one last look around the office, and left the door ajar.

Chapter Fifty Three

Straddling the edge of Yorkvilles' trendy shopping district and Harold Town Park, the multi-leveled Resource Centre was an important artery in the city's heart. Aesthetically undistinguished and architecturally banal, it nevertheless housed a great number of hard-to-find books on just about any subject imaginable. After identifying himself and showing two librarians the photograph, Kincaid was directed to the third floor. Blending in behind the counter on the same level, Amy had already taken up a position behind the reference desk. She was in charge of the uniformed officers manning the exits and protecting the civilians.

Kincaid pointed to a small table tucked into the corner, half-hidden behind the sagging leaves of a tall, artificial silver Bismarck palm. Stephanie followed his gaze and quickly recognized Richard Barclay. With his feet tucked underneath and his body bent over the table, he looked like a thin question mark. His goatee was gone and he'd cut his hair. Several books were scattered across the table. Apparently deep in thought, he was supporting his head on an upraised hand.

Unaware of Kincaid's approach, Barclay jumped when he suddenly heard his name called. He jerked back and looked wildly around, then squinted angrily.

"Goddamn it, Kincaid. Why do you have to sneak up on me like that?"

Kincaid introduced Stephanie while he stared at Barclay. The man's startled expression disintegrated into an appreciative smile as he looked at Stephanie and nodded hello. Stephanie didn't offer her hand, but acknowledged him with a rather non-descript half-bow. Kincaid brought him back from whatever thoughts had painted the hungry expression on his face.

"Do you mind if we sit down?" he asked, pulling out a chair for Stephanie. Barclay quickly gathered up the books and notes he'd been working on and piled them to one side. He spoke to Kincaid, but couldn't stop staring at Stephanie.

"I don't have much time today. I'm working on my book." Stephanie wasn't as impressed as he'd hoped. "What do you need now?"

"Some help."

"Can't it wait? I've got to —"

"No."

Barclay leaned back and waited. His distress deepened with Kincaid's silence. The Detective finally told Barclay about Danielson's murder, scrutinizing the man's reaction. He went on to explain what had happened at Gail Meredith's house, how she'd shot and killed Erik Caster. Barclay listened without interrupting. He felt Stephanie watching him. It made him feel even more restless and uncomfortable.

When Kincaid was finished, Barclay's forehead was etched with a confused frown. "I don't understand." He twirled a pen between his fingers. "Meredith killed Caster, after Caster killed Danielson, Turner and McCabe. I got bail for originally assaulting McCabe. So why are you here?"

Kincaid kept staring, desperately trying to force Ryan from his thoughts. "There's still a couple of things that bother me about the whole thing, Richard."

"Ahh, the nefarious 'loose ends?'"

Kincaid mulled over the phrase. "'Nefarious loose ends.' I like that. But yes, that's exactly what I've got. A puzzle with a few pieces that just don't fit when you take an objective look at everything."

Barclay appeared disinterested. The pen twirled like helicopter blades. "Like?"

"Like the fact we found footprints at Danielson's house. In the blood, at the back door. There were even a few imprints on the driveway. Two sizes smaller than the ones we found at Turner's house."

"So why is that a problem?"

Kincaid smiled condescendingly. "That doesn't pique the interest of a mystery writer like you? When Devlin Turner was murdered, his attacker wore gloves."

"So –"

"He also had something over his shoes. Plastic bags stuffed with paper, perhaps. That way, he was fairly certain he wouldn't contaminate the crime scene. And his prints would seem a different size."

"So everything was planned carefully."

"That's what I thought. McCabe's death, however, was different. There didn't seem to be any planning or forethought at all. I think it was actually an impromptu act, a spur of the moment decision. I don't believe the killer set out that evening to take Mr. McCabe's life."

"I didn't, and you know that. So what's that got to do –?"

"Patience, Mr. Barclay, patience. Then, there's Danielson's murder. What troubled me was why the killer would wear gloves and something on his feet to protect himself when he went to Turner's, then only wear gloves when he attacked Danielson? It doesn't make sense. With the amount of blood at the scene, it would have been impossible to leave without stepping in some splatter and leaving a print, however doctored, behind. After all, the poor man's arms had been stuffed down into the shredder right up to his shoulders. Well, almost to his head, actually."

Barclay didn't say anything. He looked away nervously, his face flushed, the whirling pen slowing down.

"No, it just didn't make sense," Kincaid repeated thoughtfully. "We knew the killer wore gloves when McCabe was killed. It would have been virtually impossible to obtain a definable set of footprints in that alley, so he probably wasn't worried about them. But why did our killer choose *not* to wear them when he murdered Danielson?"

The question hung in the air. Barclay couldn't help fidgeting. Stephanie folded her hands together and leaned a little closer across the table. Barclay moved back.

"My guess," Kincaid continued, "is that whoever killed Danielson wasn't responsible for Turner's murder. What do you think, Richard?"

"I don't know," he whispered.

"You'd think if someone was careful enough to cover their hands and feet at one crime scene, they'd be smart enough to do it at the second one, wouldn't you?"

Barclay was sweating. He shrugged and glanced anxiously around. "Maybe he just forgot. Or maybe you're right and it wasn't something he'd planned ahead. It was a spur of the moment thing, and the timeline was off."

Kincaid smiled again. "His timeline? No, he remembered all right."

"But you said . . . "

"Yes, you're right. Whoever murdered Danielson *did* wear something on his feet."

Barclay's gaze wandered back and forth between Stephanie and Kincaid.

"But Erik Caster wasn't quite as bright and conniving as the other killer, Richard. The person who killed Turner knew enough to wear oversized shoes stuffed with newspaper, and plastic wrap under the bags. Caster wasn't as neat, or as cautious. He simply tied regular grocery bags over his running shoes. The partial prints we found tracked through the blood in Danielson's study aren't perfectly clear, but they're enough to rule you out, Richard."

"So rule me out."

Kincaid kept staring. "Anyway, that was just one thing." He let the silence lengthen again.

"What was the other one?"

"The other thing? Ahh yes. The other thing I found disconcerting was the fact that after checking Caster's records at his house and then reviewing those at Michael Cormier's agency, it seemed pretty obvious that Caster never knew Mr. McCabe."

Barclay tensed forward, sighing dispiritedly. "So?"

Kincaid leaned back and watched Barclay's eyes. "But Brian McCabe *did* send you a letter about *your* book, didn't he, Richard? Caster didn't know him, but you certainly did."

There was a noticeable tremor in Barclay's hands, so he shoved them under the table into his lap. Sweat beaded on his forehead.

The man was wound up and Kincaid knew it. "Let me tell you what I think happened in the alley, Mr. Barclay. I think everything occurred very much the way you initially described it. I'm sure you followed McCabe to the bar that evening, and that you waited for him to come out so you could confront him about your manuscript."

Kincaid paused and looked deeper into Barclay's eyes.

"I think things got out of control and you panicked. You struggled with McCabe, and when he wouldn't stop, you grabbed a piece of pipe and struck him with it."

"I admitted that, Kincaid. We've already gone through all this. I told you I was in the alley, that we fought. I even told you about hitting him and pushing him against the wall. But that's all I did. Like you said before, someone else came later and – and finished him off."

"Someone else with gloves."

"Right. Someone with gloves."

"But we have a witness who puts you in the subway, covered in blood, around midnight."

Barclay looked confused. "So?"

"So, if McCabe was attacked at around ten-thirty, what could you have possibly been doing during all that time before you went to the subway?"

Barclay was flustered. "I don't know," he stammered, trying to control his breath. "I can't remember, I was scared. But I sure as shit didn't hide any body or anything like that. I think I just walked around for a while."

"In the alley?"

"No. I must have walked – I don't know. I must have walked somewhere else. God, I thought I just killed the guy. I wasn't thinking straight."

"That's not quite true, Richard. You were stained in blood, but I believe you were thinking pretty clearly."

Barclay frowned. He held the pen tightly under the table.

"You went back when you knew the alley was clear again. You put on a pair of surgical gloves, picked up the same piece of pipe you'd hit McCabe with when you fought earlier, and hit him again. He was unconscious, and you figured that would be the best time – well, the best time for some symbolic revenge. For sewing his lips together."

"You're insane!"

"But you didn't have time. You heard someone coming." Kincaid glanced at Stephanie. "The two punks who wanted to bash poor Mr. Toller. The ones who followed him from the bar on Church Street. Mr. Toller found the pipe under the edge of the dumpster where you were hiding. He tried to defend himself with it."

Stephanie frowned. "With McCabe's body just a few feet away?"

"Tucked in behind the dumpster, probably." Kincaid turned back to Barclay. "After they were gone, you stuffed McCabe's mouth with pages ripped from a book. The only saving grace I can see is that at least poor Mr. McCabe was unconscious when you pierced him with the needle. Turner was alive and kicking when you did it to him. It must have been horrible. But then again, you hated Turner a lot more than McCabe."

"No way, Kincaid. No way. You knew my prints were on that pipe from the beginning. Why would I have used gloves?"

"To make me think that two different people were involved. And you know what, Richard? You had me going for a while."

Sweat lined the creases in Barclays' forehead. He shook his head in a vigorous denial and started mumbling to himself.

"And I couldn't help wondering about Danielson. The motive wasn't there."

"Sure it was," Barclay replied angrily. "Caster hated everyone in the publishing world. McCabe, because he criticized his work. Turner, because he led him on, milked him for the editing, then made fun of his book."

"And Danielson?"

"He must have rejected his work as well. He wanted to kill a publisher, and he did."

"But if that was the case, don't you think he would have wanted to kill Gail? It was her company who sent him the rejection letter, not *Excalibur Books.*"

Kincaid sighed. "Turner and McCabe weren't random, Mr. Barclay. Danielson was a publisher, yes. But he wasn't related to McCabe in any way at all. The only way he was connected to Turner was being involved in the potential takeover bid. No. The motive for having Danielson murdered was very different. It was Gail Meredith who wanted Danielson out of the way. Permanently."

"Gail Meredith? I don't understand."

Kincaid offered a quick synopsis of the relationship between *Meredith House* and *Excalibur Books.* Barclay was aggressively still, his face pinched. His breaths came in short, shallow bursts.

"If you put all those things together, Richard, you can see why I was so confused. But it was something else that really bothered me."

Barclay looked down and absently shuffled his books and notes into new piles.

"It was the stitches."

"What?" he asked numbly.

"The stitches. The autopsy showed a small puncture mark on Mr. McCabe's upper lip. You started to work with your needle, Richard, but you gave up when you realized there wouldn't be time."

Barclay's breathing rapidly increased. He was almost gulping for air. His hands were shaking and he had a wild, glazed look in his eyes. Under the table, he held the pen like a knife.

"You started stitching his upper lip, but stopped. The act was symbolic, Richard. It meant you were silencing your critics, and literally making them eat their words. You did the same thing to Devlin Turner. But with Turner, you did it before he died."

Kincaid sighed. "Mr. Danielson's lips were sewn together and his mouth was stuffed with paper. And, just like Turner, he was alive when it was done."

Kincaid shook his head. He still had trouble imagining the pain and horror. "But there was one major difference."

He waited, but Barclay didn't say anything.

"Caster's left handed, Richard."

Barclay frowned.

"The stitches on Devlin Turner's mouth went from the right to the left. The puncture mark on McCabe's lip was on the right hand side as well. But Danielson's stitches went from left to right. Just what you'd expect if the man was left handed."

Barclay moved with a desperate suddenness that momentarily caught Kincaid off guard. He leapt up from the table, knocking over his chair and sending it crashing against the wall. He swept his arm across the table, hurling the stack of books at Kincaid's chest. Grabbing the gnarled trunk of the plant with one hand, he hurdled over the fallen chair and swerved around the corner of the table. Scurrying away, he managed to take two frenzied strides before Stephanie grabbed his arm and spun him around.

Barclay's feet seemed to keep going while his body was jerked back against the wall. His shoulder took the brunt of his weight and he groaned with a spasm of numbing pain. He glared at Stephanie, reached into his back pocket, and pulled out a knife. He flicked it open, then beckoned her closer with the gleaming blade.

The library exploded with a burst of activity. Startled by the noise, people hunched over the nearby tables jumped up from behind stacks of books and started running and crawling away. Watching the scene unfold from the 'reserve' counter, Amy called for backup and unholstered her gun. Motioning the people to get down and keep out of sight, she kept them moving towards the back of the library as she slipped behind the nearest bookcase. Whispering, she berated the ones who stopped and tried to take phone pictures, jeopardizing the others, and warned them to keep moving.

Kneeling down, their guns drawn, the other officers covered the civilians and quickly hustled them past the elevators and to the stairs. Staying close to the floor, Amy darted around the labyrinth of shelves toward Kincaid.

Stephanie inched closer, studying Barclay's knife hand and the position of his body. Barclay waved her nearer, his lips in a sneering grimace.

"Come on, little girl. Come on."

Stephanie circled to the man's right. Barclay's steps followed hers. Stephanie stopped when Barclay moved out aggressively from the wall. She feinted towards him, watching how he slashed out. She weaved out of the way as the knife cut the air in front of her. Another feint, this time to the other side. Barclay swept his arm at her face, missing by inches as Stephanie ducked out of the way. Barclay's eyes narrowed with hate. Hate, and frustration. He circled the knife toward her, daring her to move again, to come closer.

When she did, Stephanie sprung so fast that for a fraction of a second she seemed to be in two places at the same time. Barclay lunged out with the knife, but all he stabbed was air. Stephanie faked to the right, pivoted around on her left foot, and sent a vicious roundhouse kick deep into Barclay's chest. The blow sent him flying, slamming him against the wall. But as he ricocheted back, the knife lashed out in a circular sweep.

Timing it perfectly, Stephanie waited for the blade to *swoosh* by. As soon as Barclay's arm passed, she stepped in close and unleashed a series of straight leg kicks and punches that came in a blur. Barclay's head snapped back. Blood fountained from his mouth and a deep cut above his eye. A vicious spleen kick doubled him over, and a brutal elbow that came up from her hip caught him in the jaw and straightened him up again. Face, chest, stomach, then face once more. Three or four seconds and it was over, seconds that would always seem like a lifetime to Richard Barclay. The knife clattered harmlessly to the floor as he slipped unconsciously down the wall, his legs splayed and his head slumped awkwardly to the side.

Blood seeped down Barclay's chest and pooled on his legs. Satisfied he wasn't going to move, Stephanie relaxed her aggressive stance, slipped her feet back together, took a deep breath, and carefully readjusted her suit jacket. She looked over at Kincaid and Amy, and smiled.

Chapter Fifty Four

Kincaid had a disturbed sleep, but still felt more relaxed than he had in months. He hadn't stopped dreaming about Ryan, but it was wonderful waking up and having Stephanie beside him. He loved the scent of her body on his skin. Anxious over what loomed ahead, they'd talked long into the night with a numbing sense of immediacy that was both exhilarating and disturbing at the same time. They'd shared everything they could, but it still hadn't been enough. They traded whispered hopes and aspirations until Stephanie, curled and molded into Kincaid's body, finally drifted off into her own dreams.

He glanced out his bedroom window. A bright orange sun shimmered through the upper branches of the trees, and the sky was already a delicate, pacific blue. A hummingbird hovered by the feeder, its tiny wings a greenish blur. He could almost hear its little vibrating *hum* as it flitted over the geraniums. A pair of translucent dragonflies courted over nearby wildflowers. It was going to be a beautiful day. He looked at Stephanie as she slept and wondered how it could possibly be otherwise. Ryan's image crept back into his thoughts. So did Amy's. No matter what shadows followed you, each day was still precious, *wasn't it?*

Kincaid woke Stephanie slowly and gently, softly stroking her long, silky hair and trailing warm kisses down her neck and shoulders, her spine, the smooth, strong lines of her back. She stirred, inching back and forth like a cat in the sun, but kept her eyes closed and pretended to sleep. Yet the longer she felt the warmth of his lips against her skin, the more the senses deep inside her reawakened. She couldn't take it any longer. She surrendered and snuggled closer, burrowing beneath him and wrapping her legs around his hips, quietly, gently, urging and luring him ever nearer. With the blankets peaked above them and the burgeoning morning light slowly warming the window, their lovemaking was deliciously soothing and comforting, until that last moment when their bodies trembled together and they shared a breathless, loving moan.

Stephanie hadn't realized she'd fallen back to sleep until the enticing scent of fresh coffee and croissants curled around her senses like a siren's song, calling her from the last tendrils of her dreams. Dreams about Kincaid. Padding out into the kitchen on bare feet, she joined him at the small table. There was no need for words. Kincaid could tell by the serenity in her eyes that the years in the city had slowly drawn a veil over her thoughts, and that Stephanie had forgotten how delicately invigorating and reassuring a morning in the country could be.

They'd eaten in silence, shared a restorative shower, then languidly dressed together in front of the dying embers of last night's fire. Before they left, Kincaid took the time to show Stephanie some of the things she'd missed with the darkness: the new rose bush that crept up a trellis on the far side of his house; a robin's nest tucked beneath the edge of the roof where it hung over the back deck; the thin band of arched earth that ran along the side of the yard like a snake where tenacious little moles were digging underground; and the shaded patterns the sun had beaten against the old wood that framed the ancient shed.

Knowing where they had to go, but anxious and uncertain about where the journey was really going to take them, they walked around the yard arm in arm, constantly finding more treasures to share. The sun gradually burned the morning mist away. Neither of them wanted to leave, but Kincaid knew the time had come. Dr. Chadpur was waiting.

Kincaid drove. Pensively still, time lost its meaning while Stephanie quietly watched the gently sloping hills of the countryside roll by. Bands of purple loosestrife stood stoically still in the grassy meridian. When the openness of the moraine, the last vestiges of the Ice Age's receding glaciers, finally started to thin out and the undulating land flattened, Kincaid turned onto the highway that led into the cities' core. Stephanie's body tensed instinctively. It wasn't long before the trees and bushes were completely gone, eerily replaced with office towers and sprawling shopping malls and condominiums surging higher and higher. The highway quickly thickened with merging cars and idling trucks that crept forward with belches of black smoke. Kincaid and Stephanie rarely spoke, but every time they turned and exchanged a smile or a glance, they knew they were thinking about each other.

Kincaid pulled into a small lot behind the medical centre. There was a little parkette across from the building, a tiny oasis of green in a sea of concrete, steel and glass. A narrow walkway meandered past fledgling trees and well-tended gardens. The flowers were in full bloom and the grass had recently been cut. The edges of the gardens were sharp and neat, the mounds of earth black with fresh topsoil.

They sat together, side by side, on a wooden bench half-shaded by a lilac tree. Soft petals of purple and white were sprinkled over the grass and filled the air with a sweet scent of calming freshness. Two little chickadees safely hidden in a nearby maple called each other with trilling songs. Kincaid watched a small red squirrel scamper up and over a concrete flower box several feet away.

What could he say? He thought about Ryan and how brave the child had been. He remembered Carolyn at the front door of her house before he left the other night, leaning against the frame and desperately trying to stop shaking as she released another anguished sigh, her thin body wracked with loss. The funeral would be hard, but Ryan would want him to be strong for his mother. The fear of death had the power to bring out the worst in people, he thought. And the very, very best.

He exhaled heavily. "If I had to do it all over again, I wouldn't have done it any differently."

Kincaid paused, and felt all the turmoil, all the pain and loneliness, once again. "Nothing's changed, Stephanie. I made the only choice I could make back then. No matter what it cost."

He reached over and took her hand. "But if" – he seemed to falter – "if I have the chance to change what I can now – from this moment on –I will."

He stared into the beguiling darkness of her eyes.

"I don't want to lose you again. I've loved you all the time we've been apart, and I know deep down I always will."

His words drifted off into silence. He knew he was losing Amy. Not as a friend or a confidante or a special person he'd always have in his life, but as the thing only Stephanie could become. His one true love. "If everything turns out all right, I hope you'll stay with me."

Stephanie smiled through tears. "Of course I will," she said softly, running a hand through Kincaid's hair. "I never want you to leave again."

"I'm sorry about not seeing everything clearer before. About not being able to –"

"Shhh." She touched a finger to his lips. "Shhh. There's no need for that now. We're together, and that's all that matters. Life is far too wonderful to spend whatever time we have thinking about what might have been. It's more important to think about what we are, and what we have. And especially what we could become, my love."

My love. Kincaid's eyes glistened as he took Stephanie into his arms. She buried her face in his neck and hugged him like she'd never let him go.

"It's time," he finally whispered. He looked up at the medical centre, squinting from the late-morning light reflecting off the polished glass.

"Do you want me to come with you?"

Kincaid shook his head.

"I want to share everything with you."

He smiled gently. "I know. But this is something I have to do on my own."

He brought her hands up to his lips and kissed her fingers. He squeezed her gently, then let her go. He turned, took a deep breath, and walked toward the front doors of the building. He glanced up at the sky and felt the warmth of the sun on his face, the soft breeze in his hair. Simple things. Important things, things not to be forgotten, and never, ever taken for granted.

A car wheeled into the parking lot, spitting up loose pieces of asphalt, and jolted to a stop right in front of Kincaid.

Amy.

He walked around to the driver's side.

"I had to see you," she said, frowning and flustered. She glanced over at Stephanie. A friendly wave. But something else, too. *Oh, if only . . .*

She slipped from the car and hugged him as hard as she could. Tears trickled down her cheeks. "I couldn't let you go in without . . . without . . ."

Kincaid smiled, leaned down closer, and kissed her delicately, thankfully, on her lips. He watched her eyes, then kissed her again. How could two women, so different yet so very deeply alike, make him feel so incomplete yet so fulfilled at the same time?

"I didn't want to interfere . . ." She glanced back once more at the lilac tree.

"How could you possibly interfere?"

"I just wanted . . ."

"I love you, too, Amy."

This is where the "*if only we'd met somewhere else, at some other time,*" confession surfaced. But neither of them wanted to say it out loud. Then again, it wasn't really a confession.

Silence.

Feeling it was hard enough. They just wanted their moment together. Needed it. Cherished it. They'd always be more than "partners" for as long as they breathed.

Amy wiped the tears from her eyes. "Do you think Stephanie ...?"

"I know she'd want you to stay with her."

"Then I'll be here when you come out."

"You don't have to –"

"Oh, yes. Yes I do."

He squeezed her hand, kissed her palms, then walked towards the glinting front doors. With two people like these praying for him, how could anything possibly go wrong? He thought about Ryan.

Three people praying.

*

Waiting anxiously on the bench, Stephanie felt frustrated and tense at how slowly the time passed. She got up several times to pace back and forth, and kept staring up at the windows, hoping for some clue, some omen, about what was going on behind the glass in one of those rooms. What could be taking so long? She didn't want to think about it, because that made it more real, more possible. Amy reached out and took her hand as she passed the bench once more, and guided Stephanie down beside her. They spoke in muted whispers, calm one minute and agitated the next.

What would . . .

What if . . .

Why . . .

*

It was almost three hours before Kincaid came back out, the heavy glass doors winching closed behind him. Stephanie felt his presence before he'd even stepped outside. So had Amy. He was walking slowly and thoughtfully, his head up, his movements fluid. Kincaid saw them both and offered a thankful smile and the tiniest of waves to the two most important women that defined his existence: a woman he loved, and the love of his life.

Amy swung around, staring over the bench, a lilac branch swaying in the breeze above her head. Her chest throbbed – her entire body was shaking. She waited for a moment, her eyes tearing, sad and happy and jealous and longing, as she watched Stephanie hurtle the bench and rush to meet him, her long black hair flying in a whirlwind behind her as she ran across the parkette. As Stephanie's steps drew her closer, Kincaid opened his arms. She fell into his embrace, sobbing and shaking, shuddering when his arms folded around her. He kissed the top of her head, her eyelids, her cheeks, and hugged her as warmly as he could, their hearts pounding to the same beat. Amy was moments behind her, her eyes hurriedly scanning Kincaid's face, his eyes, his lips. A little smile, just for her, but enough. He stretched his arms open even wider, calling her in against him, pulling her as close as he could against his side. Amy felt Stephanie's arm around her shoulders, her waist, and then Kincaid's lips brushed the tears from her cheeks.

They stood there together, warm, safe, uncertain of the world, but sure that everything that could be was in place. They breathed as one, hugged as one, prayed as one.

Epilogue

Six rows back from the little parkette, the Honda with the New York plates was tucked away between two large SUVs. Hidden in the shadows of the larger vehicles, the windows were open. Crouching on the back seat, Dieter Vollger leveled the Glock on the headrest to steady his aim. Long and sleek, the silencer had been custom-made and fit the barrel perfectly. Expensive, with a Vortex Venom, but death was always worth it. At this range, there'd be no need for anything except a small calculation for the breeze. Held snugly like a lover, the weapon wouldn't move so much as the width of a hair when he eased back the trigger. There was a hand-made hollow point in the chamber and nine more in the magazine, all of them weighted with metal filings that would make a head explode into nothingness.

The marks huddled together outside the front doors of the hospital. Dieter stared down the sight and made a small adjustment. Smiled. Hidden by the branches of the lilac tree, the purple petals twisting in the wind, he let the silencer drift between his targets – Stephanie, Amy, Kincaid. Amy, Kincaid, Stephanie. Tightening his grip, Vollger watched the crosshairs fall on each face in turn. These were the people who'd stopped his 'comrade in arms' before they'd ever had the chance to meet.

He thought about Barclay and Caster and all of the other writers who'd been rejected. *Atonement*. This time, *he'd* send the ultimate rejection back. Stephanie, Amy, Kincaid. He focused on each of their heads, aiming for the crease right between their eyes. He squeezed off a couple of imaginary rounds, mentally watching faces explode, skin shred, eyes tear apart, arched rainbows of blood spewing into the air, flesh splattering against the people beside them. He felt, and half-heard, that glorious second of deafening silence that came after the world was fractured into panic and chaos and lives changed forever.

Back and forth.
This face or that one.
Back and forth . . .
Back . . .

Donald Crowe holds an Hons B.A. and B.Ed from the University of Toronto. He enjoys an eclectic range of literature and has a special affinity for Shakespeare, Dickens and the great writers of the late 1800's. He also admires the nuances of Spanish and European authors.

Please feel free to visit him at www.donaldowencrowe.com